I0676595

FALLEN

THE AFTER SERIES
BOOK 1

TRACI L. SLATTON

parvati
press

If you purchased this book without a cover you should be aware that this book is stolen property. It was reported as "unsold and destroyed" to the publisher and neither the author nor the publisher has received any payment for this "stripped book."

This book is a work of fiction. Names, characters, places and incidents are either the product of the author's imagination or are used fictitiously. Any resemblance to actual persons, living or dead, or to actual events or locales is entirely coincidental.

Fallen

Copyright © 2011 by Traci L. Slatton. All rights reserved, including the right to reproduce this book, or portions thereof, in any form. No part of this text may be reproduced, transmitted, downloaded, decompiled, reverse engineered, or stored in or introduced into any information storage and retrieval system, in any form or by any means, whether electronic or mechanical without the express written permission of the author. The scanning, uploading, and distribution of this book via the Internet or via any other means without the permission of the publisher is illegal and punishable by law. Please purchase only authorized electronic editions and do not participate in or encourage electronic piracy of copyrighted materials.

The publisher does not have any control over and does not assume any responsibility for author or third-party websites or their content.

Cover designed by Gwyn Kennedy Snider
http://www.gkscreative.com

Cover art: Copyright © iStock 19190174, Paris through the haze; iStock 158620, squiggle4b; iStock 19409679, tropical butterflies

Published by Parvati Press
http://www.parvatipress.com

6Visit the author website:
http://www.tracilslatton.com
6ISBN 978-0-9890232-9-0 (Paperback)
ISBN 978-1-935670-88-9 (eBook)

BOOKS BY TRACI L. SLATTON

IMMORTAL

THE BOTTICELLI AFFAIR

FALLEN

COLD LIGHT

FAR SHORE

DANCING IN THE TABERNACLE
(poetry)

PIERCING TIME & SPACE

THE ART OF LIFE
con Sabin Howard

THE LOVE OF MY (OTHER) LIFE

PRAISE FOR *FALLEN* AND *COLD LIGHT*
BOOKS 1 AND 2 OF THE AFTER SERIES

 This series continues to haunt me. I fell in love with the characters in the first installment, **Fallen**. Within this story [**Cold Light**], the characters have changed for the better. The tension was high throughout the story. As the reader joins in the adventure, they continue to wonder if Emma will be in time to save her daughter, if she will give into the overwhelming love and desire between her and Arthur and if the mist will catch them. The surprises were thrilling and sprinkled within the story adding fun to an already compelling plot. The ending is left open allowing for the possibility of third installment. For which this reader, hopes is more than a possibility. I have loved both books in this series.

HC Harju, *Night Owl Reviews*

 Slatton displays exceptional storytelling abilities in **Cold Light** by weaving fragments together at the end in a way that was delightfully unforeseen. And her poetic prose spirit the reader away into complete submersion. She also leaves a few mysteries behind to make you ache for the third book.

Rebecca Skane, *Seacoast Online*

 It [**Fallen**] is well-written, and I love the sci-fi aspects of it, the paranormal activities. It makes for a great read. . . . This book is incredible. It puts life into perspective for me. . . . It's not for the faint of heart. It is for women who want to hear their voice

and are as comfortable chopping wood, as wearing make-up. As the world changes, I like to read about women who make their own decisions, have opinions, and possess inner courage and strength. We older women worked long and hard to fight against antifeminist media and men. We want all of us to have choices; our sons and daughters, grandsons and granddaughters.

I love the main character, Emma Strong; knows her own mind, down-to-earth, smart, talented, powerful, not unlike the author! I highly recommend it!

Jennifer Jilks, *Country Cottage Reflections*

 **Cold Light** picks up over a year after **Fallen** left off. Emma has made it back to the Safe Zone in Edmonton, Alberta with Haywood and the girls, and quickly brings the reader up to date on how it happened. Even though my heart broke at the end of **Fallen** when she left Arthur, I understood her reasons . . . an excellent story that I wouldn't hesitate to re-read in the future. New characters are introduced early, and many of them are easy to like and amazingly relatable considering the circumstances of. My favorite early on was Gaff but edged over to Kangee by the end. Emma is still the survivor, Arthur is still the leader, Gaff is the resourceful kid, Kangee is the enigmatic mystery; the rest have their own unique attributes as well. Ms. Slatton did an excellent job creating believable characters and situations based in a hard to imagine post-apocalyptic world.

Daysieanne, *My Book Addiction Reviews*

 I read **Fallen**, loved it. I read **Cold Light**, loved it. Now I must wait for what will seem like an eternity for the last of this amazing trilogy? . . . **Cold Light** leaves us with another heart-wrenching, cliffhanger ending. I cannot WAIT for the last book. I must know what happens. I NEED to know. Grrrr.

If you haven't started reading **Fallen** yet, do it *NOW*. Then read **Cold Light**. I believe you will be as spellbound as I am by these marvelous reads.

Julie, *Books Complete Me*

 I have long awaited this second book, **Cold Light**, after the way **Fallen** ended. I was NOT disappointed! Emma's daughter has been kidnapped by a rogue group and she goes on a suicide mission to get her back. I was very excited to be reunited with a few of the cast from **Fallen** and am still in anxious need of book three now to see how this all wraps up.

Emma is one strong and determined woman but Arthur is just as determined. I am torn on which way I want Emma to go because with the one man her husband she has the strong history and children but she shares something with Arthur that I don't think she and her husband ever really had or ever will.

I can't say much more without a spoiler comment but I will say I didn't really like the way **Cold Light** ended. I would not want to be in Emma's shoes and have to make the choices she is being forced to but it's time . . . there can be only one victor in this war.

Jennifer, *Gimme The Scoop Reviews*

 There are a lot of twists and turns . . . . **Cold Light** is a book of survival, fighting all the odds and trying to rebuild what has been lost. It is a love story between Emma and Arthur, only will Emma make the right choice? Does she live with a man she doesn't love for her children's sake while living in misery without the man she loves? This is a situation that many people have faced throughout history.

The book is a cliffhanger, as was book one, and I am one of those people who hate that and almost always give a poor rating because of it. The reason I didn't in this case is because the story is just too absorbing, the characters are amazing and the author's description of post-apocalyptic Earth is fascinating. I read at least a book a day. Often times when an author leaves you hanging at the end, by the time the next book comes out, you don't remember all the details of the book you just read. That is not the case with Ms. Slatton she brings the reader up to date on what happened prior so I know I will not be floundering about wondering what happened before. I can't wait for the next book in the series.

Linda Tonis, *The Paranormal Romance Guild*

 This book [**Cold Light**] in one sentence: A haunting, heart-wrenching, action-packed emotional roller coaster of a read that will leave an impression on you long after your finish the book.

To say that I love this book or this series would be an understatement. Traci Slatton has done an impeccable job with what I thought would be an impossible hurdle for her two main characters to overcome after the ending of **Fallen**. Not only did she do the impossible, but she made me love the characters and the new additions to the book even more.

Evelyn Amaro, *Paromantasy Blog*

 The After trilogy is a post-apocalyptic romance story that is as heart-breaking as it is realistic. Earlier this year, I dove into Slatton's **Fallen,** quickly immersing myself in a world that sucks you in and characters that keep you enthralled in their very existence. As I began reading **Cold Light**, I immediately felt like I was home again. The way of life for the survivors of the mists really keeps you cheering the characters on. I couldn't imagine living in the After world. It's disturbing on so many levels. I have to admit that some of the survivors really do make the best of their situation, revealing a spark of hope amongst the darkness. . . .

Slatton once again has created a brilliant post-apocalyptic world that will have you on the edge of your seat. I couldn't read it fast enough. The *After* trilogy is, by far, one of the most exciting reads I've read all month. I'm dying to find out how Slatton will end the trilogy. The worst thing about **Cold Light** is that it ended leaving me wanting more of the After.

Jennifer, *Fictitious Musings*

 Slatton's ability to weave a tale that is filled with adventure, loss and love is unmatched. Her writing makes it so easy for you to fall in love with the characters so much so that you find yourself riding a roller-coaster of emotions. One minute you are mad, then your lips curl into a smile, and sometimes you cannot help but reach for a tissue.

The Mists are changing, and our favorite Russian cut-throat is back in **Cold Light**. But don't get me started on the ending. I only hope that the final installment comes out quickly, and things work out the way I want them to. (I am totally on team Arthur!!)

An exceptional series that will keep you reading and ignoring your family. So grab **Fallen** and **Cold Light**, grab a bottle of wine, head to your favorite reading spot and be ready to spend the next four to eight or so hours falling in love with this series.

A MUST have series!

Annette Marie Guerriero Nishimoto,
Gothic Mom's Book Reviews

Emma's courage is only matched by her determination to find her daughter. But her heart is torn between the man whom she married and the man to whom she has fallen in love.

. . . Arthur's relentless pursuit of Emma is both heartbreaking and remarkable given the circumstances of the day. Finding a woman like Emma is a once in a lifetime occurrence, but his love has forced many of his friends into life-threatening situations. But like family, they argue and fight, and in the end, the survival of one means the survival of them all.

Cold Light is an amazing look at one person's passion to find someone they love- Arthur's pursuit of Emma and Emma's hunt for Beth. The storyline is slow to evolve as Traci takes the reader on a cold, dark and deadly trek across the snow covered fields of Alberta, but once Emma reaches a survival Outpost, the interaction of the characters quickly uncovers a series of plot twists and anxiety ridden re-introductions to the colorful characters from the series first book. Arthur's reunion with Emma is heart-wrenching and painful knowing he has travelled thousands of mile and 18 months to find the only woman he will ever love.

The character development continues as each of Arthur's family members seeks to find a place to where they belong. And survival 101 after an apocalyptic nightmare can also mean finding someone to love for all of the right and wrong reasons.

Sandy, ***The Reading Café***

 Traci Slatton nails it with her follow up to **Fallen**. In **Cold Light** Emma is faced with hard decision after hard decision—and we're not talking about decisions on simply where to live or who to be with. We're talking life and death decisions in a place that is just simply not pretty.

The end of **Fallen** leaves of with the reuniting of Emma with her family. She leaves behind someone she's grown attached to and does what is right and honorable. But now her life in Europe has followed her to Canada—in more ways than one.

What I appreciate about the After trilogy is how the world can be so bleak, but yet there is so much hope in the story. There's love, and thoughtfulness, and honor in a place where those just don't seem like they'd exist anymore. And what I love even more is how honest Traci's writing is. She doesn't hesitate to do what needs to be done to move the story forward. When writing a story like **Cold Light** (or it's previous book), there are hard things which need to be done to give the story credibility. You cannot write about bad people and have them not do bad things. This is not a young adult dystopian or post-apocalyptic story—this is hardcore, knuckle-whitening stuff and it kept me riveted from page one.

Lydia, *The Lost Entwife*

 **Fallen** is another captivating story about the end of civilization as we know it. . . . Knee-gripping suspense and a host of great characters bring the post-apocalyptic world to horrifying life in **Fallen**. . . . I eagerly anticipate the next installment.

Margaret Marr, **Nights and Weekends Reviews**

Slatton is a fantastic storyteller. . . . **Fallen** awakens emotion and captivates with the turn of each page. . . . From every angle, **Fallen** is a captivating adventure with just enough romance to keep you enthralled and begging for more."

Jennifer, *Fictitious Musings*

Fallen is an exhilarating post apocalyptic thriller that contains superb twists and spins, which keep the reader wondering what next. The fast-paced story line grips the reader early on with the vivid description of a world gone mad and never slows down. . . . An exciting end of the world thriller.

Amazon Hall of Fame Reviewer Harriet Klausner
for *Alternative Worlds Reviews*

Excellent book [**Fallen**], I mean Unbelievable! So I tracked down the author because I was dying to know when the next one came out. . . .

Taking Time for Mommy Blogspot

The reader is forced to consider previously stable definitions of time, obedience, psychic powers, science, and most importantly, love. Powers exist, perhaps, that enhance long-ignored mental skills but is the power of memory too strong to allow for new ways of relating and the freedom to explore same without guilt and ignoring the instinctive inclinations of the heart?

Many, many questions arise as one reads this story [**Fallen**] that defies what can be falsely read as a simplistic story/plot. Traci L. Slatton is a writer to watch closely, including in whatever sequels follow this unique, well-written sci-fi novel!

Viviane, *Crystal Book Reviews*

 This is so not a world I want to live in—a mysterious mist that kills, rogue bands of survivors who round up women and children for far more nefarious purposes than you could imagine, dwindling food supplies . . .

I like Emma. She's strong, she's resolute, and she's fearless in standing up for those who can't help themselves—almost to the point of getting herself killed . . .

The plot is simple (survive), the story is moving. I enjoyed reading **Fallen**, and the realization at the end makes me antsy to find out what happens in the sequel to this first-in-a-trilogy.

Drey, *Drey's Library*

By the end of the book [**Fallen**], I wanted to know more about everyone. What will they do? How long can they survive? Will they find happiness? The book ends with a very emotional cliffhanger. This is the first of a trilogy, and I can't wait to find out what happens."

As I Turn the Pages Blogspot

 Slatton's natural storytelling ability takes over and the reader finds themselves engrossed in another well envisioned story world. . . . Slatton has once again allowed her ability with words to develop a post apocalyptic world that draws the reader in, and allows them to work towards the struggle of survival right along side the characters. The characters are compelling and real. . . . They have weaknesses, and compulsions that are both horrifying and ennobling. Slatton has developed characters that have the courage to face a failing world, while at the same time demonstrating not only everything that is right about mankind, but everything that is wrong, as well. . . . I look forward to the future installments of this trilogy.

Lisa, *The Book Worm's Library*

 In the post apocalyptic world of **Fallen**, survivors are tormented by a mysterious mist that can disintegrates animate and inanimate objects alike. Many have also developed psychic powers, like Emma's ability to heal. Emma was in Europe with her young daughter when the mists descended and the apocalypse began. As they travel to find a safe haven, more children joined their group and Emma protects them from both the mists and the roving bands of marauders. When they come across Arthur and his men searching for provisions in a dead town, Emma strikes up a deal. . . . Slowly, they fall in love, but Emma is torn between her new feelings and the husband she left behind overseas. When Arthur's devastating secret is revealed to her, she doubts the strength of her feelings for him.

Fallen has a very vivid world populated with interesting characters.

Laura Lehman, *Bella Online, The Voice of Women*

 What would you do if your daughter was stolen by Raiders? This is a story [**Cold Light**] that will stir every parental emotion in you and then take you for a ride. Emma's daughter was taken by raiders and there is nothing she will not do to get her back. The books plot and pace was stunning with its action packed story line and the dangers lurking around every corner. But she is not alone, she has loyal companions along the way. The world building is set in a post apocalyptic world. The characters were creatively built and I love how much they were relatable. Over all a great addition to the 1st book in this series.

Melissa, *Were Vamps Romance*

The second exciting "After" post-apocalyptic thriller moves forward on two fronts: Emma's relationships and the anticipated suicidal Armageddon Mists war as Traci L. Slatton deftly blends both subplots into a superb dystopian tale through her quality cast. The triangle participants fear the repercussions on the young at a time when nightmares are prevalent yet none of them can leave. Readers will wonder who will quote Dickens' A Tale of Two Cities: "It is a far, far better thing that I do, than I have ever done; it is a far, far better rest that I go to, than I have ever known."

Amazon Hall of Fame Reviewer Harriet Klausner
for *Alternative Worlds Reviews*

I haven't read the first book in the *After* Trilogy, but after reading **Cold Light** I have already ordered it on my kindle and will be reading it within the next few days. The way Traci L. Slatton has created the After world is amazingly real to a reader. I can picture it easily in my mind without even trying too hard. The characters in the book are very easy to relate to as well. The way people have to live now really hits home and makes me wonder if I would even be able to do that. Life without phones and computers and even tvs… kinda scary. As I previously stated I haven't read the first book but the way the author fills us in at different places in the book tells some of what I missed in the book. I didn't feel lost at all.

Jen's Corner Spot

 **Cold Light** is absolutely thrilling, even better than **Fallen,** but a bit shorter. I burned through the book in a couple of days and it left me longing for the conclusion to the story.

Once again, I love the characters in Slatton's story, as well as the intense and horrifying storyline. This is post-apocalyptic storytelling at its best. I'm a sucker for disaster movies and stories of post apocalyptic survival and I can visualize Slatton's stories as if they are a movie in my head. That's what great storytelling is all about. Highly recommended.

Game Vortex

 I've fallen for Fallen . . . Let me just throw this out there: I love dystopian books. . . .

A few other things you might want to know about me is 1) I love science fiction, 2) I love the conflict of man against nature gone wrong, and 3) I love a hearty romance thrown in there for good measure. Fallen had all of these ingredients, and more.

Full of action, adventure and a very intelligent read, I absolutely loved this story. . . . **Fallen** ends in a place where you know there will be a sequel, and this was fine by me, because I wasn't ready to let go of this world Traci L. Slatton had created so beautifully.

L. V. Lewis

 If you'd read **Fallen,** there is no way you can forgo **Cold Light.** I read this immediately after reading **Fallen,** but am just now getting to review. However, don't let that lead you to believe that this book isn't as stellar as the first. In fact, this book is more action-packed and the stakes have gone even higher than Emma and her family just avoiding the mists that can consume them. This is a do-or-die, life-and-death story that leaves you guessing at every turn—How is Emma going to get out of these newest pickles? Read **Cold Light** and find out.

This is a dystopian romance for the mature set, (Hunger Games and/or Divergent on steroids). Don't ignore this wonderful series.

I give **Cold Light** Five out of Five Stars!

L. V. Lewis

 From page one I was riveted to this bleak world where hope and honor can still exist. Yes, there was evil, greed, fear, bad people taking advantage of others, but love, strength and the will to live still existed, too. The author told an amazing story, brutally well. **Cold Light** is Book 2 in the *After* Series, following the book **Fallen**.

Tome Tender

Fallen is well written with twists that keep you reading. Traci L. Slatton does a good job describing the scenes, you feel like you're there with them. The characters were well-rounded, having good and bad sides, which helped make them feel real.

This is a solid, enjoyable story for fans of the post-apocalyptic and/or dystopian genres."

To Read Perchance to Dream Reviews

 **Fallen** definitely had my attention from page one. It is an intense post-apocalyptic action/romance that's so well written you feel like the mists exist; (and you will probably avoid fog after reading). Being a fan of the survival-horror genre, I didn't know how a "survival-romance" would mesh, but Traci Slatton made it work. Her writing style is really descriptive and has a great flow to it; one minute your heart is racing, and the next minute you can't help but smile. The characters, Emma especially, had an authentic quality to them. They weren't just cookie-cutter characters, but 3-dimensional, and the dialogue fit them perfectly. As for the plot, it was very well developed, fast-paced, twisty, unique, and you won't see the ending coming. I personally can't wait for the next book in the trilogy!

Allizabeth Collins, ***The Paperback Pursuer Blogspot***

 I was pulled into **Fallen** from the first few pages. Traci L. Slatton's apocalyptic world seems eerily possible. . . . **Fallen** is billed as the first of a trilogy. . . . This is not a girly romance. Slatton has written an apocalyptic novel with a romance built in— like most good stories should have. **Fallen** is excellent. I'll have to watch for the sequel.

Jandy's Reading Room

To the inner circle:

Gerda Swearengen

and

Stuart F. Gartner

FALLEN

1 THE WORLD HAD ENDED, AND MY HEART WAS shattering. Almost everything and everyone was gone, and now I was about to lose my five-year-old daughter.

I was flattened against a brick wall, watching in terror as she struggled not to inhale the killing mist that pulsed a few centimeters from her face. If she breathed it in, it would kill her. If she moved into it, or if it moved to engulf her, it would kill her. Dissolve her from within, filling her mind with madness before blistering her cells with heat until she ruptured into steam and water droplets. All that would be left of her would be a splatter of water on the ground and a fine beige powder sifting down from the air.

"Don't breathe, Mandy! Don't move," I called. Mandy didn't move, didn't even blink to acknowledge she'd heard me. Had to be hard for her, with the nightmares roiling through her brain, deluding her. But we'd drilled for this, Mandy and I and the seven other children I'd come to care for, survivors I'd picked up along the way who now thought of me as their mother. They were lined up and pressed back against the wall. Bright yellow sunlight fell down upon us from directly overhead, the sky was cerulean, and in every other way, except for the deadly pearlescent mist, the May day was lush and perfect early summer.

"Don't breathe! Be still, Mandy!" the kids shrieked. Genevra and Marco were crying. I crawled my hand out along the brick to grip Genevra's bony shoulder, to calm her. She leaned her wet cheek against my knuckles.

We were in this together. We were all we had left.

The first mists came out of the ground ten months ago, out of caves and clefts in cliffs. White miasmas, smelling of both sulfur and lilacs, that floated and randomly scorched anything in their paths: objects, structures, pedestrians, animals, insects. Not plant life, though. Anything that contained chlorophyll was left untouched. At first, the mists burned without killing. People suffered third- or fourth-degree burns and their minds were filled with images that haunted them, but they survived. Buildings were strangely weathered and bleached. Cities took on odd pale hues, after the mists went through them. People did not know what to think. Scientists scrambled to explain the inexplicable. It was one of those years with special numerical significance, and as such, it called forth the crazies. From Bangkok to Boise, they preached sin and the end of the world. Our time had come. Who would have thought they were right?

But was it really about sin, about laying waste to the Sodom and Gomorrah that the world had become?

Mandy stood still, frozen, a skinny sculpture of a big-eyed little girl. The thick white mist moved closer to her face. We'd found a village with several dwellings still standing amid tall groves of sweet chestnut trees. We were looking for potable water, for a well or a cache of bottles, when the mists moved in. She was chasing a butterfly among the rock roses, and was caught out in the open. The mists ringed around her, a wreath of white that slowly squeezed in like a lasso. Sometimes they seemed to act deliberately, with awareness.

"Don't breathe!" I called again. My voice caught in my throat and trembled.

"Just pray," whispered Newt, who seldom spoke. Marco recited his catechism in Italian, Shoshana murmured in Hebrew, rocking slightly from side to side. I was afraid to pray. Maybe too angry. In the beginning, when the mists first broiled people and buildings and vehicles and anything else they rolled across, I prayed. I sent out pleas to the Presence I'd always sensed in my heart. But then the mists rose up out of the oceans. They were powerfully reborn. They'd morphed into weapons of awesome power. They didn't just burn things; they fully dissolved them. Turned them into a splash of water and a scattering of sand, destroyed them utterly. The destruction accelerated and reached a crescendo of unimaginable dimensions. The entire world was vanishing inside them.

That was why I could no longer pray. I'd watched too many people die.

The mist shifted again, closer, almost touching the tip of Mandy's nose. A lock of her auburn hair sizzled and splashed out as water. I pulled the gun from my waistband and raised it. The kids and I had discussed this. We agreed that a bullet was better than the mists. The mists killed slowly, agonizingly. Sometimes it took hours. There'd been a day, five months ago, when the entire earth rang with screams. That was the Day that divided everything into Before and After.

I steadied the gun. I'd found it and taught myself to use it when it became clear that some survivors had gone mad. They were so unhinged with grief and shock that they would commit brutal crimes. Two of the children had joined me after I'd shot the men who were beating them. It was a shame to kill the men; they'd survived when billions hadn't. But they'd forfeited their lives when they had hurt children, and I did what needed to be done. I did it without shedding a tear.

So here I was, about to put a bullet in my own sweet little daughter's head. I looked at her through the white mists, which seemed to press memories into my head: Mandy dressed as Christopher Columbus at her preschool play, running offstage into the audience to hug her big sister Beth. Mandy as a toddler, drawing on the wall with lipstick. Mandy as a nursing infant. We'd shared a blissful bond. I'd spent hours holding her, sniffing her cotton-candy-sweet hair. Her life meant more to me than my own.

It was starting to feel as if the mists were reaching into my brain and rearranging its electrons. All my will was required to stay present, focused, sane. There was so much I couldn't let myself dwell on. Mandy's tender connection with me was just the latest distracting thought. It was enough to know I could touch my past inside myself. More than that would be self-indulgence. Especially now, when I had to be strong and ensure that she did not suffer. Her suffering would be unbearable. I could not allow it. I pushed away the memories, of her, of her father and her sister Beth, both of whom I loved and missed. There were things I could not allow to linger in my mind. Memory was a debility. I aimed for the white spot between her eyes: instant peace.

In the distance, hooves pounded, fast. The earth reverberated. The white mist obscured the view but galloping horses were approaching—many of them. Sometimes that kind of resonant thrumming influenced the mists. Percussive sound was the only thing that ever seemed to alter the mists' movement. I paused, listening. The memories relinquished their grip on my mind.

And just like that, the mist receded. It rose like a smoke ring, a soft donut of poisonous white vapor, wafting up and collapsing in on itself until it became a cloud. But it was no fluffy benign cumulus thing. It was lethal. It would dissolve anything it encountered, wires or birds or planes or satellites—though at this point, no planes flew overhead. The satellites were probably mostly gone. Birds had adapted.

But I wasn't thinking of those things. I was hugging Mandy. So were the other children, all nine of us huddled together, laughing and whooping with joy and relief. It was so intense to wrap my arms around her that I forgot about the horses until they'd come up around us, whinnying and chuffing and stamping. Forty or so horses with riders, all men.

"You almost lost her," a man said. "The mists would have consumed her for the iron and zinc in her body." I looked up into brooding gray eyes, a huge thicket of black beard, and the roan muzzle of a big friendly horse. The man's eyes lingered on my mouth but did not threaten me. I'd learned to trust my instincts about threats.

"The galloping sound drove it away," I said. "Thank you!"

"It came out of the limestone cliffs a few kilometers away, seemed headed somewhere, so we chased it," he said. He sounded American, like me, but a faint Brit tonality hung over some of his words, as if he'd spent a lot of time in England.

The man dismounted. His eyes effervesced as they touched mine again. He looked over the kids, and then he strode off through what was left of the town: a dozen homes and several standing stone or brick walls, some piles of debris, a few rusty bicycles and cars packed with belongings the vanished owners had thought they'd drive away with, before realizing there was no escape. One car was split down the middle, with each half flopped over, as if unzipped; a mist had cut through it like a laser.

The other men dismounted after he did. They looked at us briefly, but mostly watched him. He turned back to make a few gestures, and the men fanned out. They were scouting for food and supplies. He was the leader. I watched the men for a moment. A red-haired guy about my age, early thirties, touched his hand to his freckled forehead and grinned at me and the kids. Others nodded but didn't try for familiarity. They were mannerly. They were a mixed group, in terms of races and nationalities, and they went about their business with quiet discipline.

"They have a camp," Newt said, clutching my arm.

"Nearby?"

"A safe camp, with a well," she said, and her lips made a quirky lift, which was as close as she ever got to a smile.

"Safe?" I asked, for clarification. She nodded. A safe camp. *Safety.*

Just like that, in a moment of total intentionality, I made a decision. I did not realize how far-reaching the consequences would be.

"Caris, take the kids," I said. Caris, at fourteen years, was the oldest of my little tribe. She was the one who helped me care for the others. I trusted her completely. She carried a gun, too, in case I was the one trapped by the mists.

"Everything okay, Emma?" she asked. I nodded, and trotted off after the bearded leader. He'd disappeared into the remains of a house, one of those quaint stone residences with slate roofs typical of this region of southern France. I thought we were near the Lot river. I wasn't sure, because we'd wandered for so long and the familiar landmarks had vanished, but it was my best guess. I wasn't French and didn't really know the country, or what was left of it. Mandy and I had been in Paris on business the day the world ended.

I went into the house after the man. I knew where he'd go because it was where I always went first, when I found an intact structure: into the kitchen. To look for food. Cans, bags, bottles, containers, anything edible. Anything that could be boiled into being edible. Then knives, can openers, and matches: useful items. Then I hit the closets to look for shoes and clothes. And bathrooms to look for tubes of ointment or bottles of medicine.

He must have heard the door open and close because he was waiting for me, leaning back against the sink. He was tall and broad-shouldered and that giant dark beard obscured his features. His head was tilted, and his gray eyes were bright and very intense. I sensed, without knowing why, that he was glad I'd followed him.

"I never heard it said that way, that the mists consume

people for the iron and zinc in their bodies. I remember that being said on the news, Before. Just that y were attracted to metal."

He looked away. "Iron, cobalt, nickel, copper, z. palladium, platinum, and silver—but not gold."

"And they're attracted to flesh. It didn't occur to me at it was because of the metals in our bodies. But I guess t, explains the pattern of destruction. Why they don't eat bu terflies, for example."

"Butterflies have the right ratio of sulfur, phosphorus, and potassium to balance off the mists." He looked back at me. He was direct and intense. "You're not here to talk about the elemental composition of things."

"You have a camp, and we need protection," I said, coming to the point. "There are roving bands of survivors and most of them aren't friendly."

"You're doing well for yourselves," he said. He moved against the sink as if restless and I had the sudden tingly sense of his body responding to me. It came in a stupefying flash: he saw me as a woman. Of course I was, but it had been a long time since I'd thought of myself that way, as female, as desirable. Since December I'd been a survivor, a warrior, a scavenger, a nurse, and a caretaker of eight precious children, only one of whom I'd known Before. Sometimes I'd been an executioner, when someone tried to hurt one of my kids. I'd even been a dispenser of euthanasia. There'd been a couple of adults with me, Germans who had called themselves Bavarians. They'd come along for a few days. But they'd gotten trapped. They'd held their breath for as long as possible, but when I saw them gasp in the mist, I did the necessary thing— the kind thing.

"We need a safe group to live with," I said. I stepped closer to him. My cheeks were warm, but that wasn't going to deter me.

"We're a nomadic band of men...."

"...ve a camp."

"...e's no place for women and children with us," he der...ed.

...ake a place," I said. His breath picked up and his pupils d...ed.

"I'm not... not a good bet," he said, hoarsely. He reached ...t reluctantly and pulled a strand of my fair hair off my face, rubbed it gently between his thumb and forefinger. The yellow strands contrasted with his deeply tanned hands. "I've done things."

"Haven't we all?" I stepped in so close that the toes of our shoes touched. He smelled of salt and cedar, sweat and leather and horses. He wasn't rank, but he wasn't clean. I didn't know if I'd wash regularly either, if I wasn't trying to civilize a group of children. This wasn't a time for judging. We'd all been judged too harshly already, according to an arbitrary code that none of us understood.

He shook his head but didn't release my hair. "There's a women's camp in the forests."

"That's a rumor."

"It's real. I know the woman who runs it, Tara."

"I don't know where it is, and we'll be picked up by one of the bands. You know what they're doing to women and children."

"I can't guarantee your safety with my men."

"Yes, you can," I said. I lifted to my tiptoes and put my arms around him. His body was warm and strong and vibrant with life. "Your men are devoted to you. We'll be safe at your camp. And I'm here, now, so what do you have to lose?" I nuzzled him a little so he'd be clear on what I was offering. His breath accelerated and rasped in his chest. It smelled of meat and something tangy, like a citrus fruit or a radish. He was eating pretty well, I thought. It made me even more determined. If there was a way for me to ensure a steady food supply for the children, I was going to take it. Safety and food: those were my purpose.

"This is not a good idea," he said, his voice gravelly.

I said, "I'll contribute to your camp."

He moved quickly, and I was glad I was wearing a sundress. He undid his pants and lifted the dress up around my waist. Then he picked me up and set me on the edge of the kitchen table, a plain wooden thing with big black knots, could have been made last year or anytime in the last few centuries. A thick sueding of dust rubbed off onto my bottom. It didn't take long. He handed me a rag that was stiff and dirty with disuse.

"Your contribution," he started, then paused. I nodded as I cleaned myself. He said, shrugging, "No expectations, no demands, no commitments."

"That works two ways," I answered, which seemed to surprise him, because it brought a crinkle of amusement to his gray eyes.

"I would like a lot of contribution."

"You betcha."

"No backchat and no attitude," he finished. He lowered his head and stared directly into my eyes, willing me to understand. I did.

"Agreed," I said. "Lots of contribution, no attitude, and we get food, shelter, and safety." I held out my hand to shake his. He hesitated and then shook my hand. His eyes glimmered. Then he turned away and opened the cupboard doors. Glasses, dishes. He kept opening cupboards until he found the pantry. He took out two glass jars of *marrons glacees*. He opened a box of crackers and saw the mealworms, closed it and replaced it.

"My men will give me shit for taking on a woman and a bunch of kids," he said. His tone was conversational. Perhaps this was his way of being warm and cuddly.

"Probably so."

"How'd you know I have a camp?" He set out a few jars of asparagus and a can of *choucroute garnie*.

"Lucky guess," I murmured. What was I going to say, that a child in my care was psychic? A child whom I'd named "Newt" because she had no recollection of anything from Before? No memory, not of her name or her parents or her age or where she was from. It wasn't unique; lots of survivors were like that, flayed of their old identity. When they weren't crazy. Our girl spoke English with a broad British twang and her stringy hair reminded me of a child named Newt in an old sci-fi movie, so that's what I called her. And now she didn't speak except to voice prophecies.

The man gave me a sidelong glance but didn't pursue it. I wondered if he'd discovered what I had, that the mists had not only killed most of the people on the planet, but had also changed the survivors. Even I had been changed.

"Someone's been through this place," he noted.

"We ate here last night." I touched the can of *choucroute*. "This one's dented, see? Possible botulism. May not be safe to eat."

He turned abruptly and went out. I followed with the jars of *marrons glacees*. He paused in the doorway, watching his men and my band of children. I followed his gaze. Six men had remained on horseback and were posted like sentries on different street corners. My kids clustered around Caris, though Mandy, always the inquisitive one, had walked out a few paces to stroke the dappled chest of a horse.

He took a jar of *marrons* from me, opened it, and ate handfuls of the sweet nuts. He wasn't rationing. It boded well for the kids and me.

"They're watching for mists," I noted, of his sentries. "We were lucky you spotted that one and came to check it out."

"They're watching for rogue bands. The crazy ones are

more dangerous than the mists. The mists dissipate skyward
at the sound of galloping horses."

"Usually," I said. I remembered the early days, when there
was still television and radio and Internet and newspapers,
when scientists had discovered that the "global eco-disaster"
frequently responded to rhythmic sounds. Not that it had
helped us.

"The particular drumming of horses' hooves sends them
away. We've had good luck with that. Half the men joined us
that way, when we rescued them with hoofbeats."

"That's why you ride toward the mists, instead of away,"
I said.

His eyes took on a faraway look. "There's got to be a way
to drive them away for good, using percussive sound. They're
susceptible to it."

"All the mists?" I asked. I was skeptical, but intrigued. We
didn't know how or why they'd come to be. We didn't know
what they were made of, or why they did what they did. How
could we get rid of them?

His tone was determined. "I want to see this planet free
of the mists. It's the only way we'll live safely. The only way
we'll rebuild."

"I just want to get to Canada," I said softly. Western Canada was a pocket of civilization. There were a few areas that
hadn't experienced the mists, and had never been swarmed:
the South Island of New Zealand, the islands off the coast
of Washington State, a broad swath of Uruguay, part of
Iran, a strip of Eastern India. That was what I'd heard in the
days Before. The first few days After, some cell phones still
worked, and survivors reported that those places remained
untouched. Europe had been devastated. It was scoured clean.
There couldn't be more than a hundred thousand people
left, if that many. Besides the mists, there'd been gas explo-
sions, building collapses, murderous hysteria, airplanes and

satellites falling out of the sky, a frigid winter with diminish-ing food supplies, and medical issues like infection that would have been routinely resolved Before, but that now meant cer-tain death.

"Everyone wants to get to Canada," he said. "Everyone who's still alive."

"Everyone who's still sane."

"There's an ocean between here and Canada, and the mists destroy boats and airplanes."

"Because they have the wrong ratio of sulfur, potassium, and phosphorus to metal," I said.

"It's all in the balance." He gave me a sidelong glance. "Canada might as well be a million miles away."

"There are planes left, and pilots who are brave enough to try. Private pilots."

"That's some dream you've got," he noted. "Your fantasy private pilot would have to be more than brave. He'd have to be suicidal. I haven't seen an airplane in the sky in months. It's way too dangerous to fly."

"I didn't say it would be easy. But a woman's grasp should exceed her reach, or what's a heaven for?"

He grinned with one side of his mouth. "Gather your children. I'll tell my men. We move out as soon as we've picked through the town." He strode off. I watched him for a moment, a tall man with a tangle of black hair and a resolute demeanor, even from the back. What had I got myself into? I watched him speak to a wiry white-haired man who was somewhere in his seventies. The older man shrugged, looked across the empty town and caught my eye briefly. Maybe he was asking himself the same question: what has that blonde woman gone and done?

The kids waited in a tight cluster in the center of what had once been a cobblestone street. The red-haired man had given them chocolate *Baci* from a tattered box at his belt. Mandy had pulled him down so she could tuck a cornflower behind his ear. He was grinning and wriggling like a puppy dog, and the kids were laughing, even quiet Newt and reserved Caris. My heart lightened a bit.

He saw me and straightened, stuck out his hand. "I'm Robert."

"Emma," I said, shaking his hand.

"Tasty group of wee ones you've got here," he said, with an Irish lilt.

"Glad you think so, because we're coming with you," I said. He beamed.

"About fucking time we had a juicy betty and some snappers," he said. "There's a coupla gangs be scooping you birds up."

"I'm trying to avoid that," I said.

"We're going with them?" asked Caris, anxiously. Caris was a beautiful teenager, half African and half Danish, who looked older than her fourteen years. She'd had a rough time of it before we found her, imprisoned by two men. We burned their corpses in a bonfire south of Paris, near Orleans. It took her weeks to speak to us. I didn't think she understood English or my high school Spanish. When she was finally coherent, it turned out that she was fluent in English, French, and German, along with her native Danish and Hausa. She worked hard and mostly kept her cool. She'd been a great help.

"Don't worry. They're good people," I reassured her. I stroked her forearm gently.

"You never know what they'll become," Caris said. She shifted her weight from foot to foot, her dark eyes tangling up inside themselves, looking as if she was about to have one of her keening episodes. I hugged her, hoping to calm her. Her episodes went on at length, and the bearded man, my new partner, wanted to leave right away. Genevra who was seven, Shoshana, who was ten, and Mandy circled Caris with their arms. Marco and Felix stepped closer. Even little Dragomir, who claimed to be four but who I thought was only three, sidled up beside her and stroked her hip. Newt stood off to the side with luminous observant eyes, as always.

"You know that I take care of you," I said. "I'd never do this if I wasn't sure we'd be safe. But we can't go on forever the way we have been. The gangs are getting bigger and more dangerous, and food is harder to find. I don't know what we'll do when winter comes again. I need help."

"You don't have to worry, girly, there's not a wanker among us," Robert said. "We're too busy being soldiers for the big Mister." His tone was blithe, but his expression had saddened and aged, furrowing like a wax mask softening over a flame.

"But when the mists come, people die and change, they become something else," Caris cried. Her pretty face was twisted with anguish.

"Caris, they have a good camp," Newt said. It resolved the tension immediately. We'd all learned to listen to Newt. Caris' shoulders relaxed and she stopped swaying. The kids all hugged her some more because that's what we did, our group; we held each other. I touched in briefly to the past that held and supported me: my husband Haywood, my older daughter Beth, and Mandy, who was with me. They were my innermost heart. Reluctantly, I relegated Haywood and Beth to a closed compartment. They were not here, and I could not let my thoughts dwell on them. The kids put on their backpacks and lined up. Around us, men finished their sweep of the town and mounted their horses.

The big Mister himself rode up alongside us on his big roan horse. He carried the lead rope of a leggy brown horse with a tiny weathered saddle. "You ride," he said. His voice held a command, not a question. Frisky and ready to run, the horse gamboled alongside us.

"Not that horse, if you want me around to contribute to the camp," I said. "I know you're interested in my contributions." I was teasing, but he frowned. Was he humorless? It didn't bode well for our arrangement. I sighed.

"I ride," Shoshana offered. She smiled a little. She was a sturdy-looking Israeli girl who'd joined Mandy and me in Paris on the Day, when we'd all been streaming out of the city on foot. A ball of mist the size of a skyscraper had rolled down the Cours de Vincennes like a giant tumbleweed. It had decimated the fleeing hordes. Shoshana's whole family—parents, grandparents, and three brothers—had vanished into the white clouds. Their screaming joined that of the others who'd been engulfed. Mandy and I were walking alongside, and I grabbed Shoshana's hand and we kept walking. I did not know why we three were spared. Random coincidence.

"You ride well?" asked Mister.

"I took the blue ribbons," she said shyly. He tossed down the lead rope to her and she immediately went to fix the stirrups and check the girth. He grinned, or at least I thought that's what it was; it was hard to tell because of the unruly beard. When she was satisfied, she vaulted atop the horse. The men who were watching applauded. Shoshana's cheeks turned pink. Devilish Marco called out something in Italian that elicited some laughs from the men who understood. I did not.

Mister sent the other kids to different riders, who fastened the backpacks onto their horses' saddlebags and then scooped up the kids to ride in front. Robert invited Caris onto his horse, and she twisted her fingers but agreed. I was the last one standing.

Mister's gray eyes crinkled. He was staring at me with both amusement and wry concern. At least, that's what I deduced, more from his vibe than from his expression. Finally he said, "You're with me."

"I know," I said. Maybe he wasn't so humorless after all.

2 THAT FIRST DAY, WE RODE SOUTH AND east for six hard hours, trotting over rolling green hills that looked pristine and unexplored, as though people hadn't lived here continuously for thousands of years. It amazed me how fast nature had overgrown man's depredations. Gaps in the trees, flat lots by bare dirt roads, and heaps of flotsam indicated where structures had been. The mists had had their way with this area; no complete buildings of any type remained. I supposed that my bearded partner was right, that the mists were attracted to steel—although I'd never heard it articulated that way before—and steel rebar must have been an appetizer to the main course of human flesh. Even the pavement was gone. Over one passage of grassland interspersed with juniper and pine, we disturbed a vast exaltation of butterflies, thousands upon thousands of them. They rose and fluttered in the soft warm air like confetti. Maybe they were the unwitting inheritors, and they would remain when we were gone.

My eyes still didn't quite know what to make of the seemingly endless kilometers of uninhabited terrain. I was used to the crowded bustle of modern civilization. The kids would grow up differently, imprinted on unarticulated space. Of course there would be small groups of squatters hiding near where we passed, hoping we wouldn't see them, fearing that we were one of the bands that had become harsh, enslaving gangs.

We took a single break, during which I led my group off to pee behind some bushes, and then gave them water. None of the kids complained. Little Dragomir had vomited a few times, but his rider waved it off and used the break to pour water over the horse's shoulders. What was a little puke when the world had been erased? When I came back out, Mister was looking off into the distance.

"Anything?" I asked, by which I meant: *Any mists?*

"Just regret," he said, but it was a murmur to himself that did not include me. I wanted to shake him out of his lonely reverie but the white-haired man ambled over.

"I'm Vasily," he introduced himself. He had piercing blue eyes over a sharp, jutting nose, and he scanned me thoroughly. I shook his hand. He asked, "You sure this is what you want?" His tones were cultured and neutral, very upper-crust British but with an underlying sibilance that bespoke other origins. I nodded. He shrugged. His brilliant eyes took in the kids, who were trying to get more candy out of Robert.

"Are any of them mad?" he asked.

"Caris, the oldest one, has fits. Newt and Felix don't remember anything. Genevra is seven but she's reverted, mentally, to about four."

"Brilliant," he said. He went back to his horse, shuffling a bit, his left hand at his hip as if it hurt him. I caught him before he climbed back onto his horse.

"Hold still," I said. I laid my hands on his hip, felt them grow warm, heavy, tingly. Vasily's eyes widened. Newt had become psychic, Marco could interpret dreams, and I had found myself with healing power in my hands. Still didn't know what to make of them, these paranormal gifts that had come in the wake of the mists. Were they some sort of cosmic joke? Were they supposed to be compensation for all we'd lost, people and culture and civilization?

But there were no answers, and the tingly burning in my hands didn't need any. The heat ran from my hands into

Vasily's hip like a current of bubbling water. It filled up his pelvic block and he sighed, then relaxed. After a moment the tingles receded, and I removed my hands. He stretched a little and then smiled, his pain gone. He bobbed his head and swung himself more easily up into his saddle.

We slept that night rolled up in blankets under the stars. It was the best night's sleep I'd had since Before. Other adults kept watch through the night. I didn't even need to bolster myself with the certainty of the loved ones living within my core, even if I didn't let myself muse on them; I just fell asleep. We rode all the next day with a few breaks to eat and relieve ourselves. I was sore in new ways, but what did that matter? It was just pain.

We arrived at the camp at dusk. Camp consisted of a sprawling, thickly-walled rectangle with rounded corners, set atop a lush expanse of land. The walls were chest-high, and made of rocks, tree limbs, earth, and the varied detritus of imploded buildings. Inside the walls was a flat square of land covered with neat lines of tents. The two long walls and one of the short ones had gateways with wide dirt paths running to the opposite and perpendicular gates, so that, together, the paths formed a T. From horseback on the plateau north of camp, I could see that a big table stood at the center, at the T-junction. The camp had been carefully organized.

Outside the walls, green lavender ran wild. The whole area was bordered on one side by a tall hill. Outside another edge of the camp was a scree field littered with gorse and detritus from whatever development had been here. The far lip of the basin tumbled down into a green meadow criss-crossed by streams and covered with lavender; a horse corral stood there, with big open tents and crudely-constructed stalls. Near the stable was a well with a wooden platform around it. It was a fine place for a camp, defensible and easily sentried. There were no obvious places out of which the mists would come, although of course that really meant nothing.

The mists were strongest out of the ocean, and less strong but still deadly out of rock clefts; but they could also seep out of mines and underground shafts and be almost as lethal. With the mists, there were probabilities, not certainties, and there were guesses, not answers. We could still all die, either by breathing in the mists when they approached, or by being subsumed into a mist that crept over us.

But not here, because Newt had said this camp was safe. *"I want to see this planet free of the mists. It's the only way we'll live safely,"* he had said. It made me shiver to contemplate. Hope was a cruel joke.

"Who knew the south of France was so beautiful without people?" I said, as Mister reined in the horse. I shifted forward. I'd been pressed against him, his arms encircling me to hold the reins. Riding double this way forced me to meld myself into him and during the last hour he'd been thinking about my contribution, if the bulge against my bottom was any indication.

"We're near where Valensole once stood," he said. "It was beautiful even with people. We'll make it beautiful with people again."

The other riders drew up behind us at the edge of the camp. Other men came out of the tents and helped riders dismount, holding onto bridles and offering a hand or shoulder for balance. Silence fell down like a curtain closing as the new men noticed the kids and me. The kids, stiff from the hours of riding, clustered around me in a tight knot. I pressed them into me and we stood looking out at the men, who watched us warily.

"I'll talk to them," Mister said. He pointed to a largish white canvas tent abutting the short back wall, the wall that didn't have a gate. The tent was the kind that used to evoke weddings and graduations. "That holds supplies. Empty it; the children can stay there. My tent's that one." He swung his finger toward the T-junction to indicate a pine-green nylon camping tent with a pole and pennant posted outside it. "You'll bunk with me." He strode off, waving his arms to gather his men together, before I could argue that the children needed me at night. But they would adapt. We'd all become good at that.

As I hustled the kids off toward the canvas tent, a tall blond man with a close-cropped beard passed me. He was lean and rangy and carried himself with a military bearing. He peered at me in appraisal and calculation. The man gave me an oily smile but not before he'd checked out my chest and the tear in my skirt. I looked back over my shoulder and saw Mister waiting for his men to line up in formation. I wondered whether he trusted the blond guy.

We wound past a few rows of tents to the white canvas tent at the back of the camp. I lifted open the door and peered in. It was full of neatly-organized stacks of supplies: cases of canned and jarred goods, including bottles of water, juice, and soda; packages of foodstuffs like pasta and crackers from Before, when there was manufacturing; fire extinguishers, canisters of natural gas, and boxes of bullets; piles of clothing and shoes; crates of medical goods; bundles of silverware and belts and reams of paper. There were wooden crates filled with scrap metal. These people had collected all sorts of odds and ends that could be useful. It was almost as if they'd been prepared for the mists. I tied back the flap. "Mister didn't say where to put this stuff, so we'll just pile it outside."

I gave the kids juice, and then we set to work clearing out the tent. A slim man with a receding hairline and prematurely gray hair bustled up and touched my arm gently, took a box of hardware out of my arms. "I'm James, the camp doctor. I hear you folks are staying with us. Do any of the children need medical attention?"

"They're pretty healthy, considering," I said.

"All right, how about we wait until tomorrow, and then we'll get each of them in for a thorough exam." He smiled a little as his eyes went over each of the kids.

The box rattled and clanked as he set it next to the other boxes that we'd shoved up against the back wall. "How about you?" He scanned me intently, top to bottom. His gaze was warm as a laser and just as impersonally penetrating.

"I'm fine."

"We'll see you tomorrow, too," he said, in an authoritative medical-doctor voice that brooked no disagreement. Then he smiled, and his face softened. "I'm glad to see a woman and some children here. This camp's been awfully dry."

"Some of the kids don't like to be touched," I warned.

"The other kids will go ahead of them. You can be with them." His face was transfigured, momentarily, with sadness and disgust. He knew what I meant. Then his smile returned. "I'll get some guys to do this for you. You folks must be hungry. Have you met Cook?" He gestured to the kids. They looked at me and I nodded, so they followed after him. Mandy took one of his hands. Tilting her head like a curious bird, Newt took the other. That put the kids at ease, and when he told them Cook was serving venison, Marco whooped.

I darted back into the supply tent and grabbed a pair of trousers I thought would fit me. They were men's but they were small. Besides, there was a whole stack of belts. I slipped on the pants under my dress and found a t-shirt, folded my dress, and tucked it into my backpack as I ran to rejoin the kids.

The mess tent was a red-and-white-striped special-event canopy, the kind people used to rent out for large parties. I found myself wondering what we were celebrating: just being alive? It was bittersweet, and far more bitter than sweet, but I'd long since come to the conclusion that life is always right. Even if it followed watching millions of people die. Card tables, picnic tables, and dinner tables were set up around the space, and in back, buffet tables were set up for cafeteria-style self-service.

"Wow, fancy," I said. It came out sounding sardonic, but I meant it. I hadn't expected to eat this way ever again. I came up behind Mandy and kissed the top of her auburn head. Shoshana looked a little forlorn, so I kissed her too. Then the other kids all wanted kisses except for Caris, who squeezed my arm.

James glanced back with a small smile. His face was much younger than his gray hair would suggest. "Cook was a chef at a three-star restaurant in Provence. Meals are tasty, even though feeding troops probably wasn't his great ambition in life." A shadow passed over his face and we shared a meaningful look.

Cook was a small, shaggy, fortyish man with an enormous girth and an unlit cigarette tucked into the corner of his mouth. James introduced us, and he nodded curtly. He was doling out food onto mismatched plates; some were delicate Limoges wonders and some were chipped earthenware pieces, no two alike. The silverware was the same, some of it actual silver and some of it half-melted plastic.

After the kids had been served and seated at a table with James, I went back to Cook. He expected that I was getting a plate for myself, and he slopped peppery venison stew onto a Portmeirion plate with yellow flowers on it.

"Oh, no—I'm getting a plate for the Big Mister," I said. It struck me as a bit odd that I didn't know what else to call him. I figured Cook knew who I meant.

"*Oui*, eez good for him," Cook said, shrugging. I set down the plate and reached over the table, grabbed Cook by his stained collar. I thrust my face so close to his that I could see the goo oozing out of his pores.

"Listen, you stinking frog, you go back into your kitchen and get me the real stuff, the good stuff you keep for yourself and your cronies," I said. "Whatever it is that's making you fat, I want that for him!"

"I cook what I have, *c'est vrai*," he said.

"Bullshit," I said. "Get me the good stuff." I shook him a little to show him I meant it. The soft flesh of his neck wobbled around my fingers, so I added a hard pinch.

"Bloody sheet, you beetch," he said. He wriggled free and went back behind the tent, into a separate enclosed tent where the cooking was done. I caught a glimpse of a couple of grills, the outdoor kind that use natural gas. He came back a few minutes later with a plate which was heaped with food. It was of far better quality.

"There's a nice chef." I favored him with a smile. He said nasty things in French that didn't need translating. I said, "This is what I expect from now on. I'll be getting his food, and I expect the best." He called me a few more names—can anyone curse like the French?—but I was off. I passed the table where the kids sat. They weren't eating; they were waiting for me, all of them quiet and orderly. Nothing like an apocalypse to teach children to mind their manners.

"Eat; I'll be back," I called. I kept going, walking through the tents and out, back to the clearing where we'd entered the camp. The horses were gone, but Mister stood there with a group of men, including Vasily and the blond man. A conversation was underway, and it looked intense. I came up quietly behind him. He was saying something about a marauding band riding down from the north and the men he'd sent to watch for them, but he paused to swivel around and look at me.

"Dinner." I handed the plate to him and turned on my heel to leave. He followed.

"Wow, what's this?" he said, his mouth full of some kind of sausage.

"Food? Formerly considered such," I said. He lifted one corner of his mouth.

"Attitude," he said.

"You don't mind. You won't turn us out now that we're here." I surveyed him carefully to be sure I was right. This camp was as close as I would get to safety and security for my little tribe. I was determined to make it work here.

"Cheeky, and intelligent." His eyes glowed as he surveyed me back.

"Enjoy." I was set to keep going, but he grabbed the waist of my trousers.

"What's this?"

"You've never seen pants before? I'm pretty sure you're wearing a pair."

"Backchat."

"That isn't backchat," I informed him, a bit archly. "Backchat will be obvious."

"How am I supposed to...?" He was chewing as he asked, but the look of hunger on his face encompassed more than the plate of food.

"I should only wear dresses?"

"Works for me," he said. He winked and went back to the circle of men. I went to the supply tent that was now home for my children and changed back into my sundress. A deal was a deal.

AFTER THE MOST civilized dinner we'd had in months, with the light fading into purple and the sky lit up with more platinum stars than I had known existed Before, I took the kids to the well with their toothbrushes. It might sound silly, but when the whole world crumbles, it's the little things that keep you moored to sanity. Every morning and every night, you brush your teeth, wash your face, and comb your hair. Every day, you scavenge for food and edify yourself a little bit. The kids and I carried around books in our backpacks, each of us with one work of literature and one text on something educational—even wee Dragomir, who spoke a bastardized patois of tongues. I thought his first language was something Slavic. I spoke English to all the kids because my Spanish was bad, and Dragomir spoke some crude French. He must have been absorbing it from the pretty French woman who had shot herself right after she came across me and the other kids in the vast, intact, and completely empty Cathedral St. Etienne of Bourges. She smiled and gave Dragomir a push toward us, then swallowed the muzzle of her pistol. A lot of survivors committed suicide. Shoshana said a prayer over her, and then I dragged her body outside and set fire to it. I kept her pistol and the bullets I found in her purse. And Dragomir was one of us.

By the corral, Mister's men had built a platform and raised torches around the well and the crude system of pipes that led out of it. Some of the pipes had holes to let out streams of water for washing. Trenches had been dug for the runoff. We stood to one side and rinsed faces, heads, and necks and then brushed our teeth. I collected tubes of toothpaste whenever we found them, and now I gave the kids each a dab. Some of the guys stood around watching, visible only as dark breathing forms where the edges of the flickering yellow light met the rich, plummy dark. On the other side of the well, horses were being led in to drink from troughs. They stamped and whinnied and slurped, good solid sounds. I felt Mister's arrival before I saw it, because the men stirred and stepped back respectfully. I wondered who he had been Before, that he commanded so naturally now.

"What are you doing?" he asked, from behind me.

"This small brush holds a cleansing paste which is applied to the teeth for purposes of oral hygiene...."

"Cheeky," he grumbled. He touched my waist. "Nice dress. When are you done?"

"Soon," I assured him. He moved away. I grabbed my backpack and chased after him. "Here." I held out a spare toothbrush. I collected those, too.

"A toothbrush?" he asked, incredulous.

"Put toothpaste on the bristles and apply vigorously to your teeth." I dug out one of my precious tubes of Crest and gave that to him as well. "Been a while for you; you might have forgotten how."

He flushed, or I presume he did, because the vibe changed. Hard to tell, between the dark and the huge thatch of black beard. "Lady, there's been an apocalypse. I've had other things on my mind than dental perfection."

"Mister, I'm not judging. But since we've got an arrangement and all, you might as well try to make it pleasant for me. Me, Emma." I was testing him, and he'd asked for no attitude, but how much reverence did he think he deserved when his breath smelled like the gutters of a charnel house?

"Arthur," he muttered, scowling at the toothbrush. "That's my name."

"I don't have to call you Big Mister, because of our arrangement? Love the perk." I left him there with my gifts, and I couldn't help smiling as I returned to the well. I felt like I'd scored a point, and I didn't mind one bit.

When I finally had the kids tucked into bed in their new home, I went to his tent. Arthur scored a few points off me.

3 FROM THE MOMENT I AWOKE ON THE first morning, I was determined to make myself and my kids useful around the camp. It wouldn't be difficult because, despite the neat appearance of the camp's rectangular walls and even rows of tents, the men lived crudely. They slept on the floors of their tents under blankets and rode out on "missions" with Arthur. They ate in the mess tent. It looked like they didn't bother to clean anything except the dishes, which Cook oversaw. Even Arthur's tent was smelly, filled with soiled and torn clothing.

Dawn had awakened me while he still slept, so I slipped on my clothes and went to get his breakfast. When I came back, he was sitting up, blinking.

"Morning, Sunshine," I said. "Hungry?" I passed him the plate, while staying out of reach, just in case he had notions about a morning contribution from me. The man had a strapping constitution. I had no qualms about that, just as I had no qualms about our arrangement. We were both getting something we wanted, and we'd defined the terms: *no expectations, no demands, no commitments.* It worked for me. But I didn't think he needed anything other than breakfast right now.

"I thought I dreamt you," he said.

"The mists don't bring good dreams."

"Did I say it was a good dream?"

"Not with words, last night," I said, a little dryly. "More with moans."

"I wasn't the only one moaning," he teased back, scratching his head. Probably had lice. I'd noticed several of his men scratching. I'd been using olive oil to drown the bugs on the kids' heads and mine.

"You have a broom around here?"

"Somewhere," he said. He dug into his food with gusto, but his eyes were fixed on me. "This is good."

"I'm going to check on the kids." I scooted out of the tent, and he scrambled to follow. He was slowed down by not being dressed, which gave me time to get away.

Everyone was awake, and less tentative than might be expected. Shoshana brushed Genevra's hair; Genevra sang a silly rhyming French baby song which made Dragomir laugh. Mandy threw herself into my arms, and Caris looked up with a smile from where she was removing a splinter from Newt's toe. Marco and Felix were looking over an old Asterix comic book. One of the guys must have given it to them. I'd have to track him down and thank him.

After breakfast, I found a broom and organized the kids into two groups. James wanted to examine the kids, so I sent Shoshana, Newt, Marco, and Felix with him to the modular camouflage-green tent that he called his "hospital." I took the others, along with the broom, a bottle of dish soap that I purloined from Cook, and a bucket of water with rags. We went to Vasily's tent, which wasn't far from Arthur's. Vasily stood outside his door with his arms folded across his chest. I figured we'd start with him, since he was a sort of second-in-command. I hoped that would convince the other men to cooperate.

"Tent cleaning service," I said brightly. His grizzled eyebrows rose, but he stepped aside. I lifted the door and quailed at the odor, but I managed to tie the flap back. We set to work. Dragomir just smeared the grime around in circles on the canvas walls, but otherwise, we made some progress.

The morning wasn't far gone when shouts went up from

somewhere at the edge of camp. There was a particular piercing quality to the shouts that made the hair stand up on the back of my neck. I told the kids to keep working, and I went to see what was up.

A group of men had arrived on horseback. They'd come to a halt outside the walls of camp, by the corral. One man was draped over another's horse, blood dripping down onto the horse's withers. Two other men sat slumped in their saddles, bleeding. James came at a run as the three wounded men were pulled down.

"Pyotr, Pyotr!" cried a short, stocky man with a ruddy face. He had been carrying the draped man on his horse, and he tumbled down, weeping. Pyotr was laid out on a bench that two men had hastily carried over. Blood gushed from his chest. James bent over him, then straightened, looking sad. He went to examine another man.

"No, no, you must save him!" the stocky man wept. "Please, save my brother!" He knelt at Pyotr's side, clutching Pyotr's limp hand.

"I can't, I can't suture him with that kind of blood flow," James said. His voice was anguished, but he was fully intent on his next patient, who wasn't as badly wounded.

I stepped up to Pyotr. I didn't know if I could help him, but my hands felt as large and feathery as eagle wings. They tingled as though with a thousand cresting, burning fireflies. Everything else faded away, all the sounds dwindling to a tiny distant buzz, all the commotion disappearing into a high, sweet stillness. In all the world, there was only me and Pyotr.

I held my hands a few inches over the jagged tear in his chest. The crimson geyser stopped; his chest froze. Had I killed him? Then Pyotr took a deep, sighing breath, as if he were asleep. His chest rose and fell, rose and fell. His pale face relaxed.

"Doc, she stop blood, he live!" the stocky man screamed, a faraway shrill. I could feel James looking but I didn't dare disrupt my concentration. The next moment, James knelt beside us. He merged in, became part of our dyad, part of the silence.

"Heart is still beating.... Can you keep this up?" James asked, tightly. I nodded. "What the hell, it's a different world," he murmured. He went to work, giving Pyotr a shot, and then reaching into the man's chest to sew him up.

Some span of time elapsed before James squatted back on his heels and wiped his forehead. "Best I can do," he muttered. "Alcohol!" Someone poured a bottle of rubbing alcohol on his hands to rinse them. He rose and went back to the other injured man.

My hands still felt swollen with healing power, so I laid them directly on Pyotr's arm and let the tingles run out into him. His breathing continued to be regular. Some color washed back into his face. After a while, my hands finally felt empty. Sounds approached: people talking, horses stamping, Mandy laughing somewhere nearby. Motion sped up around me. Colors and forms whirled, dizzying in their intensity. I stepped back, shocked to find that I was covered in blood. I had backed into Arthur, and his arms steadied me.

"You all right?" he asked, staring at me.

"It's not my blood," I said. I slipped free and looked around for Mandy. She and the other kids sat in a clearing, a little ways off. I went toward them.

The short stocky man, Pyotr's brother, grabbed and embraced me. "I am Theo. I am your brother now, you save Pyotr." He was babbling thanks and weeping into my neck. I patted him, and was glad when someone peeled him off me. Arthur again.

He said, "I sent the kids to get lunch. You can wash up while they're eating."

He was right: my dress was frightful, drenched in Pyotr's blood. And I was trembling, more unnerved than I'd expected. I wasn't tired, but I was sweaty and warm and exhilarated.

I'd never used the healing gift in this way before. I had only recently realized I had it; when I grabbed the kids' boo-boos, the way mothers always do, the kids felt better and their wounds healed faster than could be expected. Stopping blood entirely, though, was new. I smiled thanks at Arthur, veered off, and went to change. Head tilted, he watched me go.

I had only one other dress. I made a mental note to check the camp's supplies, just in case a dress had somehow made its way here. There were supply tents interspersed all through the camp; Arthur and his men were incredible packrats. I could ask Arthur to have his men collect kids' clothes, too.

When I came out of Arthur's tent, the blond man who gave me the creeps was waiting for me.

"Nice work, saving Pyotr," he said. "Arthur will approve. It will secure your position in the camp."

"James saved him," I said. I headed off toward the kids.

"Theo says you saved him. Theo's a good man to have as an ally."

"I'm just trying to help."

"Everyone needs allies, especially now. The world is at war."

I paused to look at him. "The world is under attack, not at war."

He smirked a little, as if he knew something I didn't. "I'm Xavier."

"Emma," I said.

"Everyone knows you," he said, in a voice that was way too familiar. I didn't look at him. He squeezed my arm, so I tore away from him.

Later that afternoon, James approached me. The kids and I were sitting outside camp by a stream, soaking our feet. It was a breezy, sunny day, perfect for outdoor lounging. A year ago, this area had been full of the wealthy and the celebrated from all over the world, enjoying vacations and festivals and time away from crowded concrete cities. Now the cities and the crowds and the concrete were all gone, and this place was an empty rural region traversed by savage gangs and refugees seeking shelter from the gangs. And then there was this strangely well-provisioned camp. I ruminated on another contrast. All of us, gangs and refugees alike, were desperate to avoid the mists. Only Arthur and his men seemed less afraid.

"The rabbit drives the truck," Mandy said aloud, slowly. The kids were reading. It was lesson time. I was sewing a button onto a pair of Arthur's pants I'd dug from a pile in his tent. Pretending to sew, actually; I was really daydreaming, relaxing a little for the first time in months. James sat down next to me.

"What you did earlier, stopping Pyotr's bleeding...."

"I can't explain it."

"It's from After?"

I nodded. Marco and Felix were blowing spitballs at each other. "Guys, if you tear those books again, you'll be in trouble!" They giggled and went back to reading. I thought about reminding them that it would be a long while before new books were made again, but why upset the children? There was little enough to giggle about.

"Mommy, can I be done?" Mandy called. "I want to walk around and feel where people used to live."

"This is reading time," I said, firmly. I eyed her, wondering what she meant about feeling where people used to live. But James was touching my elbow.

"There are some men I can't help," James said. "Take a look-see?" So I laid down the mending, and followed him inside the camp walls to the hospital tent.

Once inside, I saw that the hospital consisted of a series of modular tents joined to each other. In one of the canvas "rooms" were Pyotr and three wounded men, lying on cots. In another room were two more men, but they were sick rather than injured. One of them, a dark-haired man with a

moon face, was terribly wasted. He seemed to be asleep but
he frequently writhed, as if in pain.

"Parasites," I said. I stood beside him and took his hand. It
was clammy and cool.

"You sure?" James asked, unhappily.

"No, but it popped into my head, so I'll go with it." I leaned
over the man, whose lids fluttered. He tried to smile at me.

"I heard there was a woman," he whispered. "I didn't
believe it. Arthur was afraid to have women here. You're real
pretty, too."

"Arthur doesn't strike me as the kind to be afraid of anything," I observed.

"He fears what the mists could do to the men's minds,"
the man said, and groaned. His pain was palpable. My hands
filled up with that feathery feeling, so I laid them on his belly,
let the warm tingles flow down into him. After a few minutes, he sighed. His face uncrumpled, and his head rolled to
one side. Then he was snoring.

"His first peaceful sleep in weeks," James murmured. I'd
forgotten he was there, and I started. My movement didn't
disturb the sick man, he slept so deeply. After a while, my
hands were empty and I stepped back.

"What's his name?"

"William. He's a close friend of Arthur's—used to work
with him, I think," James said. He ran a hand over his thinning pate. "I have nothing to treat him with."

"A good herbalist could work wonders," I said.

"I'll send away on the Internet for one," James said. It
made me smile.

The other man was curled up in a fetal position. He was
a very dark-skinned African wearing wire-framed glasses.
I opened my mouth. "Cancer" was the word that emerged.
James sagged. He sat down on a low tripod stool in the corner, curled forward with his elbows on his thighs, and rested
his face in his palms.

"I was afraid of that."

I seated myself on the floor beside him, hugging my knees into my chest. "What kind of doctor are you?"

"Now? Every kind of doctor. A surgeon, an internist, a podiatrist, and, since you came, a pediatrician." He lifted his head and smiled slightly. "Before, I was a dermatologist."

"I think I'm getting a wrinkle on my forehead. Can you fix it, before the mists get me?"

He smiled crookedly. "When I did my surgery rotation, I considered it as a specialty. But then I wanted to go into private practice and do facelifts and charge rich people a lot of money, fix cleft palates in India a couple of weeks each year to soothe my conscience. After all the years of med school and internship and residency and specialization, my life was about to start. I was going to have a golf membership and a six-bedroom house and a Jaguar, and a blonde wife who was very pretty and very, very useless."

"All fine ambitions. You could still have a Jaguar. There are a few cars around."

"I'll tell the guys to drive one back here next time they go raiding. They can use my American Express platinum card to buy gas." He paused, and slapped his forehead in mock dismay. "Dang it all, I haven't seen a standing gas station in months."

"Arthur will get the guys to set up a golf course. There's that big pasture...."

"There must be golf clubs to be found somewhere. If the metal ones have all been eaten by the mists, we can carve them out of wood." James shook his head. "What kind of cancer?"

I didn't know, and didn't have time to answer anyway because right then Arthur came in. He was so tall that there were only a few inches of space in the tent over his head. His eyes narrowed a little as he looked at us. "What's going on?"

I rose. "I'll see if I can help this man, too. Can't hurt him."

"Charles Nwokocha," Arthur noted. "One of the greatest

linguists in the world. Wrote a brilliant study of linguistics and haplogroups. I want him to live so he can document the languages we've lost. There should be a record for when the world rebuilds. We're not reverting to Neolithic times."

"You think we'll rebuild?" I asked.

"Of course we will."

"You're more optimistic than I am," I said. Arthur wrinkled his nose and squinted, but didn't engage. My hands were filling up, and I laid them on Nwokocha. He groaned, but I had an instinct about him feeling cheerful.

A FEW DAYS LATER, Arthur went out with some twenty men. I was overseeing the kids' nightly toothbrushing adventure. We had our usual circle of onlookers, who were becoming more comfortable with us and had taken to teasing us in various languages. Blissfully, I didn't understand any of them. Some of the men had requested toothbrushes of me.

Arthur came up behind me and laid his hands on my hips. He leaned up close to the back of my head.

"I'll wake you when I get back," he said into my ear, in a low voice.

I looked back, and all I could see was that giant black beard. "Okay, Fidel."

"Fidel?"

"Fidel Castro was Cuba's—"

"I get it!" He released me and tromped off. I followed.

"I just meant...."

"I know what you meant." He took my hand and pulled me up to walk alongside. "We're going on a mission to look for antiparasitics."

"Mission or raid?" I wondered.

"Not taking from people, so it's a mission. James has given me a list of what might help Will. There's a group of structures about thirty kilometers south, and one of the men thinks there's a clinic among them. Might have medicine."

"If one of the other bands hasn't gotten to it."

Arthur lifted the gun I didn't know he was carrying. He cocked it with an easy, practiced gesture. "I'm very persuasive when it comes to getting what's necessary."

"You betcha," I said. "Why are you going so late?"

"Cover of darkness—avoid the bands." He shrugged. "Persuasion is good; discretion is better." We'd approached the corral and the staging area where men and horses were finding each other. Robert held out the lead to the big roan Arthur rode. Arthur took it and turned to me. "About the beard."

"Might have lice. I think your camp is infested," I said. He gave me a look of frank disbelief. I shrugged.

"Lice. Tooth brushes. You're a pain in the ass, woman." He leaned toward me and kissed me on the mouth for the first time. He swung himself up onto his horse.

"Safe journey," I called. He pretended not to hear as he trotted off. Probably too sentimental for him.

THEY WEREN'T BACK for several days. During that time, James examined all the kids, and me. We were all healthy, a little underweight, remarkably strong for what we'd been through. Caris had post-traumatic stress disorder, he thought.

"We all do," I replied, in a neutral tone that included him. He shrugged.

One afternoon, James came to get me. I was with the kids at the stream, ostensibly washing blankets. We were more focused on singing a French round that Caris had taught us. James tried to join in, failed miserably, and was laughing at the kids' mockery when he grabbed my hand.

"They're back?" I asked.

He shook his head. "That's not why I came to get you." He led me away from the stream to a copse of cypress trees where we had a little privacy. I waited expectantly. Slowly, with a flourish, he took a book out of a bag at his side. I couldn't help but smile. I leaned back against a tree trunk and covered my face with my hands.

"Oh, no."

"Oh, yes," he said. *"Alice's Adventures in Wonderland."* He opened the book to the first illustration. There it was, a whimsical picture of a blonde girl peeping into a hole. But this girl didn't look vapid, as so many Alices did. She looked inquisitive and ready to explore, brimming with intelligence and life-force energy. I'd taken her expression right off Mandy's sweet face. Mandy was born wanting adventure and plotting ways to get it. It was my task to see that that quality stayed alive, even when the world died. Most days I didn't know how I'd succeed.

James pointed, in the corner of the page, to my name: the very tiny block letters I'd loved to use spelled Emma Stella, my first and middle names. That was how I signed all my work. "That's you," he said.

"How did you know?" I breathed. I took the book from him and cradled it against my chest. It was almost like a baby, this sumptuous leather-bound volume with its vellum pages, so precious, a memento of a time when I wasn't always afraid, wasn't always desperate. The time Before. The time when I was a sought-after artist and illustrator living in an apartment in Manhattan's West Village with my beloved family. A time when I was chosen to do a set of paintings for a high-end edition of *Alice's Adventures in Wonderland.* I missed that time so much that I couldn't bear to think about it.

"We were on holiday in Paris and saw you at that bookstore talking about it," he said. "I kept wondering where I'd seen you. It clicked in just a few minutes ago. I've kept the book with me all this time. I liked what you said, about taking inspiration from the world around you, about looking into the faces of those you love for inspiration."

"We?" I asked softly.

"My brother and I." His face took on that gauzy, blank look

whose meaning I'd come to know too well: his brother hadn't made it. He mumbled, "You can't imagine what we've been through together, me and this book. Oh, maybe you can." He put his hands over mine and pulled the book down from where I was hugging it, then leaned over to riffle through the pages. "This is my favorite." It was Alice talking to the mouse, who looked horrified and ready to jump out of the book, caftan and all. I'd taken the mouse's expression from my neighbor when she'd seen a rodent in her kitchen, and I had always enjoyed the irony. I'd taken such glee in my neighbor's fear, back in the days when fear was funny.

But I didn't have time to tell James the story. Nearby, a loud click rang out. We both knew the sound of a gun made ready. We turned around slowly at the same time.

"What are you two doing?" Arthur pointed a gun at James' head. James went pale, the crow's feet around his eyes looking like dark stripes on a primed canvas.

"Arthur, what the hell?" I stepped in between Arthur and James so that the gun was aimed at me. Arthur's eyes narrowed. His beard obscured most of his face, but the cool fury in his eyes was obvious. It took him a few beats, but he lowered the gun. I passed the book back to James. "Thanks for showing me. I'm sorry about your brother." I marched off, not looking in Arthur's direction. Arthur took hold of my arm as I passed.

"I won't share you."

"No one asked you to," I said. I shook him off and went back to the stream and the kids. What was his problem?

Later, when we were alone in his tent with a candle flickering in the middle, Arthur lay on his side and smoothed the hair off my face. He ran his thumb along my nose and over my cheekbone. "I love your face. It's delicate but strong, like you."

"I'm sure you have a nice face under the bearskin."

"Funny." His lips quirked into a grin.

"Not cheeky?"

"That too. I should send you off to fend for yourself, but you're right, I won't."

"What would make you send me off?" I teased. But I wanted to know. I ran my hand along his stomach, which was taut and carved with the lines of his abdominal muscles.

"It's more likely that you'll take off on a whim, and I don't want that."

"You might be glad to get rid of me, because of all my cheekiness." I smiled.

"No," Arthur said, emphatically. He pulled my hand up to his mouth and kissed my palm.

I felt uncomfortable with his intensity. "Anyway, I'm not someone who acts according to whim. Not anymore. I can't afford to."

"You're someone who acts according to her own mind." His gray eyes narrowed at me. "Why didn't you tell me you were a famous artist?"

"You never asked." I pulled his blanket up under my arms. "It isn't relevant now."

"Anything about you is relevant."

"We have a deal, remember? No expectations, no demands, no commitments?"

"Hmm," he rumbled. He rolled over on top of me. Words were extraneous.

4 ARTHUR AND HIS MEN HADN'T FOUND any antiparasitics. They weren't saying much about the mission and their faces wore tight, gloomy expressions, so I figured it hadn't gone well. I was surprised when Arthur beckoned to me the next day as I made my way to see Will and Nwokocha in the hospital tent. I thought he'd be out searching for the meds.

Instead, he looked determined, and he walked with a jaunty step. "Come with me," he said. He drew me to the corral, where his roan was saddled and ready. Robert, who seemed to be the head groom, helped me mount the horse.

"Where are we going?" I asked.

"It's a surprise," Arthur said. He buckled two bottles of water into a saddlebag along with a coil of rope, and swung up behind me.

"I don't like surprises."

"You'll like this one. We're going to do some good."

"How do you know I like to do good?" I asked. "I'm just trying to survive, and keep some kids alive."

He looked at me quizzically. "Of course you do. You're like me that way. Come on."

"What about the children?" I objected.

"I'll watch the wee ones," Robert said. "I've a guitar. We'll learn some tunes. Don't fret, I won't be too bold with what I teach them." He waved and grinned, and we set out at a trot.

WE RODE OUT for over an hour, neither of us talking. The land was rugged, green, rocky, rolling, and hot. Thyme and lavender scented the air. We passed abandoned vineyards and desolate olive groves and a shimmering blue lake. The earth's beauty here was wild and poignant and ancient, and the erasure of humanity seemed fitting. We could have been Adam and Eve jaunting through Eden. Distant hills approached, and suddenly the illusion of paradise was shattered: a pearly white mist moved through the hills. It looked tiny from this distance, but it must be huge in order to be visible at all.

"Stop, stop!" I cried. I grabbed his arms and jerked on his wrists to rein in the horse. The horse reared to a halt. "Don't you see the mists?" I was pushed back against Arthur's chest as far as I could go. "Arthur, we've got to turn around!"

"We're looking for them," he said. "Ya!" He kicked the horse, and it broke into a gallop. Cold sweat ran all over my body. What was Arthur doing? We had only one horse, and that wasn't enough to drive away the mists!

Another hour, and the hills had resolved into deep cliffs cut by a gurgling turquoise river. It would have been a feast for the senses, with the riot of Provençal fragrances and the imposing beauty of sheer limestone walls, but we were chasing a vast, menacing bank of mists, the largest I'd ever seen. It was even larger than any of the tumbleweed wheels that had rolled down the streets of Paris, killing everyone in their paths and shattering huge buildings. I was paralyzed with terror. Arthur pressed on.

We followed the bank of mists into the heart of the cliffs, and through a gap caused by a contraction in the mists, I saw people huddled against a sheer limestone wall.

"Arthur!" I pointed. The mists expanded again, and hung between them and us.

We kept riding, halting just a few meters away from the mists. The sickly sweet odor of lilacs and sulfur clogged my nostrils and I gasped and coughed.

"That's what I was looking for," he said.

"So we can die with them?" I asked bitterly. My bowels went queasy. Was Arthur mad? Along with the unholy odor, feelings accompanied the mists, tumultuous, wordless feelings that stirred up terror and eclipsed reason. Had Arthur succumbed? Butterflies floated up the stone above the mists, graylings and heaths, their wings fluttering slowly.

"We're not going to die."

"I have a daughter and seven other kids who depend on me!" My throat was dry, which made my voice husky.

Arthur dismounted and held out his hand. "We'll ride back to them," he promised. He took my hand firmly and pulled me down from the horse.

I stood quivering, staring at the puffy white apparition that floated between us and the people on the other side. The mists were thick enough to obscure the people, and I could only discern dark shapes: one, two, perhaps five people, huddled together. They were oddly quiet. Were they praying? Were they already dead? Had they killed themselves to avoid the mists?

"The Verdon Gorge," Arthur said, his voice musical. "I used to climb it."

"I'd rather climb it and fall than be eaten by the mists," I said, my voice bitter. "Falling is quick. Splat. The mists, you've seen that. Hours of agony. I carry a gun so the kids won't have to endure that kind of suffering if they get taken. Caris has a bullet for me. You have your gun, don't you? Put me down, if the mists come for us. One through the heart."

"This area was first formed during the Triassic period, when the sea subsided and left layers of limestone deposit. Then, during the Jurassic period, a warm sea here allowed the growth of various corals."

He really was mad. I said, "Now is not the time for a history lesson!"

He shook his head. "You're so impatient. Have some faith."

"What's there to have faith in anymore?" I cried. "God? Happy endings? Those don't exist. We can't help those people! They're dead, and we will be, too!"

"Have faith in me," Arthur murmured. His eyes half closed and he held one hand out into space. I waited. After a few minutes, I fidgeted. I was frightened, I was hungry, I had to pee. I wanted to climb back atop the horse and ride back to camp as fast as the horse could gallop. Arthur had it all wrong about me: I didn't want to do good, I was just trying to stay alive. His breathing evened out and slowed down, as if he were meditating.

Then I saw it. Another mist was threading out of a crack high up on our left. It arrowed toward the huge bank of mists, as if magnetically attracted. I cried out.

"Wait," he said. The mist came out faster, spinning out of the cleft in the rock, and streamed toward the huge bank of mists, which seemed to open and embrace the new mist. All over the gorge, as far as the eye could see, mists stitched themselves out of fissures and arced toward the pulsing white mass. The sky overhead resembled a sparkly spider web that was weaving itself into a gigantic ball, taller than a skyscraper. The scent of agonizing death enveloped us. My knees softened to something the consistency of pudding.

The mists pulled away from the cliff and the people on the other side. Maybe they had a chance—but now the mists were moving toward us! The vast bank hovered only a few feet from our faces. I had a flash of Mandy's sweet, loving face. I was not ready to leave her.

"Watch!" Arthur commanded. He made a circle with both hands, thumbs and forefingers pressing together. The mists became a giant donut, with a diameter of hundreds of meters far up into the air. I gasped. He put his wrists together and fanned out his fingers. The mists mimicked the shape. He made two fists and held them next to each other. The mists halved themselves, and the two giant gleaming white balls hung side by side in the air.

Abruptly, Arthur flung out his hands. The mists dispersed. They were gone.

"Holy shit!" I exclaimed. His smile carved an arc in his black beard. "You can control the mists!" Before he could answer, the people from the cliff face raced toward us. There were seven of them, silent, white-faced, sprinting. They did not slow down as they approached. They meant to run past us. Arthur reached for one of the men. I grabbed a woman's nylon shirt sleeve.

"Wait!" I said. "We can help you! We have a safe camp!" I could hear Arthur calling the same words.

"There is no safety! We run from death to death," she said. Her large, dark eyes were glazed and red-rimmed, did not meet mine. She shook herself free and loped off after the others. I turned toward Arthur, who was stroking his beard and watching the fleeing people.

"We could have brought them to our camp," I said. I grabbed his hand. "You can control the mists!"

"They're not ready for our camp. They have to be ready to accept safety." He chewed his lip. "It's not controlling the mists, exactly. It's a sense thing. I can sense them. I can, I don't know how to explain...make a rapport with them."

"You dissolved them!"

He sighed. "Sometimes I can do that. Sometimes I can only drive them away. I can't explain that, either."

"You need to try to figure it out!" I said, with excitement. For the first time since last Christmas, I felt a flash of something wonderful: hope. "Is that why the camp is safe, because you can drive them away, dissolve them?"

"The mists will leave the camp alone," he said, with great certainty.

"They didn't before. There was a town there."

"They won't return. I sense the safe zones." He draped an arm around me and hugged me to him, kissed my forehead. "Controlling the mists isn't a hundred percent for me. I have to be in a certain state. Calm."

"You risked my life on a hit-or-miss phenomenon?" I asked. Anger spiked up, sharp and hot, now that I knew I wasn't about to die.

"I knew I could do it today." He stroked my hair back off my face, perused me intently. "Your eyes are variegated, like a cat's. Amber and brown and green and gold. They change so fast and express so much. Mercurial. Never seen anything like them."

I stepped back. "When did you realize you could do that, control the mists?"

He didn't answer, but glanced up at the sky. His gray eyes were wide and dreamy. "We've all been changed by what's happened. The mists have parapsychological effects. Some people don't know who they were. Some try too hard to forget. Some have gifts. Did you know that James can see inside bodies?"

He'd never told me. I shook my head. I felt a little hurt. I had thought James and I were friends. Of course, I'd never told him about Newt's psychic gifts, either. I murmured, "He asked me about Will and Nwokocha. Why would he do that if he can see inside bodies?"

"His clairvoyance is intermittent, and he probably wanted confirmation." Arthur took my hand and held it to his chest. "Your hands have the power to heal. Mine can summon and dismiss the mists."

"That's why you think it's possible to get rid of them entirely," I said. He shrugged. I asked, "Why didn't you just tell me you could do this? You didn't have to drag me here and terrify me!"

"This makes more of an impression. I'm sorry you were so frightened. I wanted to share it with you." He was entirely fixed on me. His eyes grew serious and sharp, as if they wanted to penetrate my mind. I wondered what he was thinking, but I didn't want to ask. He was feeling things that I wanted no part of. I enjoyed what we shared in his tent, and I appreciated the security of his camp, but that was the extent of it. For me, it was a fair and limited exchange. What was left in me that could feel was wrapped up in Mandy and the other seven children who had become my reason for being. I wanted to reach Canada with them, somehow. I wanted to give them safety and what was left of civilization. I wanted them to grow up happy, with all the benefits of humanity's passage through time, and none of the perils that now beset us.

"Let's go back," I suggested, before Arthur could kiss me. He kissed me anyway.

"Have you ever climbed a rock wall?"

"No, and I don't want to."

"Come on, I'll show you how. It's fun."

"Fun?!"

"Yes, fun. It refers to enjoyable experiences that human beings are hardwired to have. And not just in bed."

"That's not fun, that's duty. I made a deal and I'm keeping my end of it," I muttered. Arthur laughed heartily.

"That's what you're telling yourself, Emma?"

"That's the truth."

"Liar. Come on. We're safe here. Those mists are gone forever. This gorge is now a safe zone. Let's enjoy it. Just for a little while. Be here, now, with me."

"Rock climbing? As the world ends?"

"The ending is finished. We're at the beginning. And we have this moment, you and I, with no past and no future, no regrets and no worries, just to be together, alone in this beautiful place, enjoying the day."

"I always have a past and worries."

"I don't." He went to the horse and reached into the saddlebag, pulled out a strappy thing. "Put this on."

"How nice for you, having no past and no worries. As for me, I have to get back to the children."

"You have a self without them, don't you? Who are you without them?" he asked, a little tartly. "Can't you be her, the woman you are within yourself, for a little while right now, with me?" He laid the strappy thing in my hand. "I've been so lonely."

"Well, you know, darling, it's been a lonely apocalypse," I snapped.

"Put your harness on."

"You've got to be kidding! I have to get back to the kids!"

"Why, are you on a schedule? You have to rush back to brush everyone's teeth? Your eight darlings are happy in a safe zone, well-fed, and if I know Robert, laughing at some inappropriate song!"

I couldn't argue with his rationale. Maybe I didn't want to. I let my hand relax, and the strappy thing unfurled into a harness. "Then we'll go home?"

"Yes. And I will make it worth your while at the top." His tone was playful.

"This looks complicated."

"Let me show you." He held open the belt so that the thigh loops hung down. I stepped into it. "Do you know how to belay?" I shook my head. He said, "I'll free-climb up, then belay you from the ledge. It's an easy climb, practically a scramble. Five-five, five-six. Maybe five-seven at the crux."

"You expect me to climb up this cliff and stand on a ledge without falling off?"

"I'll clip you in." He shucked off his shirt and kicked off his shoes, indicated that I should take off my shoes, too. He pulled on his harness. He ran the coil of rope through his hands very fast, expertly checking it and recoiling it. He draped it over his bare arm.

"Arthur, I don't have a self anymore, apart from the children."

He gave me a sharp glance. "Yes, you do. You can't let yourself be defined by the mists, what the mists have done. None of us can. It's self-indulgence. If I allowed myself to do that, I'd have no choice but to commit suicide."

His words were quiet, but unexpectedly biting. I was taken aback. "Suicide, Arthur? As drastic as that?"

He didn't answer. He tied one end of the rope onto my harness and then leapt onto the rock face, clinging to it as elegantly as a spider. "Climbing! Keep your weight centered over your feet. Emphasize footholds, not handholds. Hips close to the rock."

He was fluid and graceful as he moved up, far more so than his tall, muscular form would suggest. Above him the sky stretched up into infinity, endless, fathomless. I got dizzy looking up, and I swayed. I put my hands out to keep from falling, and I shuddered as my palms met limestone. The cliffs here were safe now. They hadn't been before. How many glistening white mists had come forth out of fissures in rock faces just like this, to kill how many billions of men, women, and children? How did Arthur expect me to forget all that for even a few moments?

"Emma, climb up! You are on belay!" Arthur called. I hopped up and clung to the rock. The limestone felt cool and rough to my fingers and toes.

"Stand up straight, stay in balance, keep your weight over your feet!" he called. There was nothing else to do so I ascended. It took me a lot longer than it took him, and I was helped by the tension in the rope, which ran through bolts in the stone. Hopeful sprouts of green grew out of small cracks. The limestone held the sweat left by my hands and grew slippery, so I couldn't place a hand back where it had been. Once I changed position, there was no return. I had to solve the puzzle of the next hand position.

Arthur was right: it was kind of fun, once I slipped into the rhythm of it. There were delicate, fingery moves and strenuous, thrusting motions when my feet climbed almost to the height of my waist to find the next foothold. I was aware of the ground fading beneath me. Then I was only aware of my own body and my movement on the rock face; nothing else mattered. Time slowed down and fell away. It was just me and the gray rock and the blue sky. My breath joined up with my heart, for the first time in months. I was alive again.

Finally, Arthur was pulling me up to stand next to him.

"I did it!" I yelled. I slapped his hand in exultation.

"You weren't half bad," he laughed. "You're a better climber than rider, that's for sure." He clipped me to another bolt with several loops of rope. Then he stood next to me. "So you enjoyed it? Taking a little break from the usual routine of trying to avoid death, starvation, and attack?"

"I enjoyed not falling to my death."

"Liar! You enjoyed climbing. It puts you in touch with yourself. My question is, what did you find?" He was doing it again, staring at me with blazing, intent eyes, trying to see inside me.

"I found my children at my core."

"Liar again." He picked me up and pushed me gently into the cliff face. "Ready to do your duty?"

"No, let's go home," I said, but my breath had picked up.

"You're full of lies today. I always wanted to make love on a ledge," he murmured, and then proceeded to do just that. It wasn't easy with the harnesses on but he was inventive, and he was determined. It was well worth it.

WE RETURNED TO camp in the evening. I had dinner with the kids, tried to charm Cook but ended up harassing him about better food for Arthur, and then left the kids to read while I tended to Will and Nwokocha. When I'd finished letting the healing energy pour into them, I looked up. James was watching me from the corner of the hospital tent.

"I didn't hear you come in," I said.

He nodded. "I didn't want to bother you." He lifted the tent flap for me and then followed me out. "You were pale when you returned. You okay?"

"Arthur can call the mists, and send them away," I said.

"Sometimes I think that Before, Arthur had a lot to do with—" James started. Then he stopped. He shivered and gazed up into the sky. Evening was settling in, violet and gold and soft as a silk blanket. The kids were laughing and singing with Robert. A few men had joined them in a song that had them all in giggles. It was good to hear their levity. A month ago, I would not have believed that we'd find this semblance of peace and normalcy.

"You can see inside bodies. Were you looking inside mine, just now?"

"He told you…." James compressed his lips and looked away. "We're all different now. I never know if that means we're crazy. If I'm insane."

"You're not."

"It happens, you know. I've seen it. People start off with extrasensory abilities and then…." His voice lapsed.

"You won't go mad."

"You can't promise that," he said. He took a few breaths. "Arthur dragged you to the cliffs to show you what he can do? He could have just told you." Scorn laced his words.

"It wasn't exactly like that. Somehow he knew that the mists were chasing some people. He was able to dissolve the mists and free them."

"He could have told you instead of scaring you," James repeated, stubbornly.

But I realized that some of the greater peace in me came from the visceral knowledge of Arthur's power, and from the few moments of diversion on the rock wall. "I'm glad I know. I feel safer here."

"He should have avoided scaring you. You've been through enough. We all have." James shook his head. "Will is feeling better, but he needs medication. They're going to do another run in a couple of days, look elsewhere."

"They didn't look too happy after the last run," I observed. We walked together toward the children.

"That was a cluster fuck," he said. "They rode up on a small group, three women and six children. The women saw them, shot the kids, and committed suicide."

I closed my eyes and let the wave of sadness rise up and roll over me, and ebb out toward the sea of suffering we'd all endured since the mists first scorched their way across the earth. Nine more innocents dead. What were nine, after all the billions? But life couldn't be quantified that way, and there was no one of whom to ask that question. Not even a cruel Deity would condone the wanton destruction the earth had sustained. I could have gone far down the rabbit hole of despair, but the faces of my daughters and husband rose up inside me, to keep me from falling in. I said, "They must have thought Arthur's men were one of the rogue bands. Some of them are brutal."

James nodded. "Before she died, the last woman said they'd escaped and had vowed not to return." I looked out across the camp and saw Arthur standing with a semi-circle of men around him. Was he telling them about the mists at the cliffs? Or was he planning and strategizing, according to his own goals? I wondered suddenly how ambitious he was: "*I want to see this planet free of the mists. It's the only way we'll live safely.*"

He might even be capable of it. But did he understand that I had my own ambitions? That I did not share his?

5 ARTHUR TOOK A GROUP OUT FOR ANOTHER mission. They returned some mornings later with supplies and kids' clothes, and even dresses for me, but none of the medicine Will needed. I took two plastic bags full of clothes to the kids' tent and then went to tell them. They were playing soccer in the pasture area. Robert had left to care for the horses, which were haggard and dirty after the mission. So were Arthur and the men who'd returned. He'd given me a sardonic look but assented without comment when I'd suggested that they wash themselves.

Newt was not playing with the others, but stood to the side, twisting her fingers in Caris' gesture of anxiety. Damp from rinsing his head, Xavier stood watching her. I set the bags down and approached him. "What are you doing, Xavier?"

"There's something wrong with your girl," he said.

"I'll handle it."

"You're handling a lot here at the camp now."

"Trying to fit in, trying to help. And she is my responsibility."

"Arthur finds you a big help." His voice was thick and sleazy with implication. I gave him a sharp look. He leaned close to me. "You two are thick as thieves. But how close are you really? I mean, what do you know about him?"

"Everything I need to know," I said firmly. "Go on your

way. I'll take care of Newt."

Xavier pretended to saunter past me, but brushed up
against me. He leaned too close and put his mouth practically
on my ear. "Ask him what he did Before," he whispered. "Ask
for specifics." He pulled away and winked at me, then trotted
off. I wanted to pursue him, but Newt was making soft mewl-
ing noises. I knelt in front of her and clasped her shoulders.

"Newt, what's wrong?"

"They're scared," she said. "Scared. They're dying. You
have to help them!" Her face was taut and urgent, and her
tear-filled eyes pleaded with me.

"They, who?" I asked. I peered carefully into her eyes. Was
she devolving into madness?

She leaned her head close and whispered into my ear. "The
hidden family. They're starving and thirsty. They're hurt.
They're hidden in trees. They're dying, Emma!"

"It's okay, it's okay. I'll help them," I reassured her. "I'll
get James—"

"No! They'll be scared of him! They'll go away if they see
a man. They'll do something to themselves. It has to be you!
You, Emma!" She grabbed my shoulders. It was unlike her, all
these words and this intensity. "Go now! Don't wait! Now!"

I stood and considered. "Where are they?" She pointed at
the scree field. "It's a long way through the field to get to any
trees," I said, doubtfully. "How far out are they?"

"They're there," she insisted. "You'll find them."

"Okay. I'll go. If I'm not back by tonight, send someone
after me." I squeezed her hand gently.

"You'll come back safe if you go now!"

I sighed. "I'll get a bag of supplies together."

Newt held up a canvas backpack. "Here, Emma!" Her tears
had magically dried, and a big grin stretched across her face.

"Newt, are you playing me?" I asked, putting my arms on
my hips.

"Mandy says you're an old softie for tears." She swung her head forward to hide her eyes behind her fringe of hair. I could see the uplift in her cheeks. She was grinning, pleased with herself.

"You and I and Mandy are going to have a serious discussion when I get back. You should not manipulate me," I scolded. "Now, please, Newt, tell Robert I've gone. In case something happens to me."

She nodded, then seized me by my shoulders and kissed my cheek. I scruffled her hair and clucked my tongue a bunch of times, which made her giggle. She ran off. I peeked into the backpack and saw water, candy bars, bandages, and a precious tube of antibiotic ointment. There was even a bottle of aspirin.

I walked out into the scree, twelve or thirteen kilometers. The land changed, gradually rising and thickening with trees, most of which were shrubby bushes. Lavender was everywhere. It was another gorgeous summer day, and the walk was pleasant. I remembered Newt's prediction that I'd be back safely, and I relaxed. It was actually sweet to be alone. What had Arthur asked me: who I was within myself, without the children? I seldom considered that question now, because I seldom had any solitude now.

I enjoyed being alone, Before. Those hours were the creative time when I painted and drew. There was space for my thoughts and my essence then that I never had now. I hadn't realized that it was still possible to enjoy time alone. I feared what my mind would disgorge for me to contemplate, like images of Haywood and Beth. I wanted them to remain a secret, unexamined bulwark within, from which I could draw strength. Arthur, I mused, wanted something else, and he would not be pleased with the source of my strength. He wanted me to rely on him.

After a while, I wasn't alone anymore: someone was following me from just inside the bushes. I sat down on the ground and unscrewed a water bottle. I took a sip.

"There's plenty to share," I said loudly. I held out the water bottle. A little girl seized it from my hand.

She was Japanese, about Mandy's size, and covered with caked-on dirt and blood. Her denim jumper was torn and her braids were ragged. She took a long swig, shuddering as she did. She didn't finish it all, but clutched it to her chest.

"There's more," I said. She stared. I took a candy bar out of my bag and held it out. She grabbed it and tore into it, wolfing down nearly half before holding it to her chest with the water. "Sweetie, take me to your family." She blinked and looked down at the water and candy bar, then skipped off ahead of me, at a tangent.

We were walking next to each other when she grabbed my hand and yanked, hard.

"What? What are you doing?" I said. She butted me in my stomach with her head. I thought she was crazy, and I grabbed her shoulders to calm her. Then I heard voices. The girl's eyes widened, and she dragged me into the bushes. We knelt down, hiding ourselves deeper in the brush despite sharp, stabbing thorns.

Two men walked by. They were not two of ours. They wore layers of muddy, ragged clothing under vivid red capes. They came to a halt in front of the bushes in which we hid. I could not see anything above their waists, but I could see the butts of the rifles they carried. At their belts they had handguns, knives, and binoculars. They were speaking in low voices in a language I did not understand. I took a deep breath, and the Japanese girl covered my mouth with her hand. She was willing me to silence.

One man asked the other a question. The other didn't respond, and they walked in a circle around the area where we had just walked. The girl burrowed herself into my side. Neither of us breathed. One of the men came closer, within a few feet. He unsheathed his knife and held it in his fist, as if he sensed us. He turned, and I saw a package hanging by his side. It was a chunk of smoked meat wrapped in waxed paper. I wondered what animal they'd killed that had such a femur-shaped body part, because that hunk of meat looked like a flayed figure maquette I'd done in a sculpture class—specifically, a human thigh, from the head of the femur to just above the kneecap.

The men walked a few more circles. Their voices held questions, and then finally dismissal. Their feet set off in a different line than the one we'd been traveling. The girl sagged against me, inhaling in gasps. We waited a long, long while before we climbed out from the bushes. Our hands interwove tightly as we set out once again.

Her family was ensconced in a thicket of trees: two women, two more children, two men, and a very elderly man. The stench of vomit and human waste rose up, only partially dispersed by the breeze. They were badly dehydrated, the men covered in blood, and they could barely move. One of the women was lying on her side on a pile of leaves. She lifted slightly and her black hair shifted, revealing an infant nursing beside her. She whispered, *"Aidez nous, s'il vous plaît."*

"I speak English," I answered, and knelt beside her. I gave her water, and she drank. My hands tingled so I laid them on her. The healing current ran into her, and some of the pallor left her face.

She took a deep breath. "We ate some berries that were not good." Her words were heavily accented. "My throat hurt. I did not eat many."

The little girl took her bottle immediately to her grandfather; at least I figured he was her grandfather, because Newt had called them a family. He lay back against a tree and couldn't sit up, so I removed my hands from the woman and came around to bolster him while the girl drizzled water into his open mouth. He blinked after a few gulps, which I took to mean "enough." The girl and I went to the children next, an older boy of about twelve and a toddler girl. The boy's arm was broken, with bone sticking through the skin. His eyes were open but glassy, and he couldn't talk. Probably shock.

"He fell," the woman said. She tried to smile. "Your hands are good. Can you help him?"

"I'll do what I can," I said.

But there were too many of them, and they were too weak and injured, for my healing skills to save them all. I had to go for help—immediately. It was the only way. The little girl took a bottle of water to the other woman, and I went to give bottles to the men, who were trying to stir.

The men were very bloody, and one was gory with knife wounds, big patches of skin laid open to show the pink and pearlescent fascia beneath. The other man was able to muster some energy. He ate a candy bar ravenously. "I am Shinji. That's my wife, Hikaru. My father Masashi. My brother Michio, his wife Kimiko. My nephew Kei." His English was excellent.

"My name Hoshi," the little girl said. She gave me a tentative smile. Her front left tooth was broken, but it didn't dim the sweetness of her smile.

"I'm Emma," I said. "I'm from the camp a few miles from here."

"We have seen your camp," Shinji said. "Very smart camp, like Roman legionaries made." He tried to smile, but a wave of pain washed over his body and he grimaced. "We didn't know if it would be safe for us. We fought out of a bad gang." That explained the knife wounds on the three men.

"You were lucky to get out." I wondered if the two men in the bushes had been searching for them. I gave Shinji all the food and water in my bag, along with the bandages and ointment. "I'll walk back and get help. It'll take a few hours."

"We may not have a few hours," Shinji said, looking at his wife, and then at Kei. Hoshi put her arms around him, and he clasped her in return. "Michio has lost a lot of blood. My father, too. They are dying."

"No other option. I came on foot. We'll ride back on horses." I stood.

"Take Hoshi and the baby. And Kimi," Shinji indicated the toddler girl. The little girl stood and swayed.

"I don't know if I can carry two children," I said. It wouldn't do for me to drop one, or to get exhausted half way back and not be able to return to camp. That wouldn't help anyone. I steeled myself to the decision and looked from the toddler to the infant. Which had the best chance of survival? I didn't want to take the weaker and risk both dying before I brought help.

"I have baby carrier," Hikaru said. She pointed. Lying near her, on a pile of jackets and empty Fanta bottles, was a baby carrier with criss-crossing straps. I thought for a moment, put Kimi in the carrier on one hip, and carried the infant in my arms on the other. Both were very light. I set out without saying anything, hoping the adults and Kei would survive until we returned. Hoshi walked alongside me.

But we hadn't gone more than a kilometer before a leggy roan horse flew up alongside us. Arthur leapt off. Three other horses behind him raced toward us.

"Why did you leave camp?" he demanded. His cheeks above his beard were flushed to high scarlet. "Don't you realize how dangerous it is? We killed two watchers from the rogue band just a few kilometers back! They could have taken you!"

"They didn't," I said, softly. It didn't seem wise to tell Arthur how close I'd come to that.

"This far out, anything could happen to you! The mists, an accident!"

"There's a family back there, and they're hurt." I pointed.

"Doesn't matter, you don't risk yourself!" he roared. "I told you I didn't want you leaving on a whim!"

But I'd been through too much to take his nonsense. I

stepped in close and spoke in a low voice. "Arthur, I am not a child to be spoken to that way. Stop it."

"You acted like a child when you left camp without letting me or anyone else know where you were going or why."

"I didn't know I had to. Am I a prisoner?"

"No, but you're mine, and you owe me an explanation when you leave!"

"I am a free agent," I hissed back.

"Don't be a bloody fool," he said. "That page has turned."

We stood like that, both of us furious and unyielding, as Robert, Vasily, and Theo dismounted nearby. Their horses bore the weapons I'd seen on the rogue watchers. The red capes were rolled around the weapons.

"I knew we find her," Theo sang out.

"So herself found some more chisellers," Robert said, as merrily as if we were dancing instead of arguing. "They sprout like weeds around you, is that right?" He came up and took the infant from my arms, held her and rocked her and cooed at her as if he'd been born doing that. He looked up. "This bird needs a new nappy."

That broke the tension. Arthur and I looked away from each other. I stepped away from him and unstrapped Kimi.

"Are we to surmise that these children have a family?" Vasily asked. "Is that what inspired you to wander off and risk yourself?"

"Back that way," I said. "If one of you will take the babies, I'll show you where the parents are." I pulled the baby carrier off my chest, disentangled the tiny girl. Theo came over to take the carrier.

"You return to camp," Arthur said.

"No, the children are going to camp. I am taking you to their family," I said, between gritted teeth. Arthur wheeled on me so fast that I flinched. Kimi wailed. I stroked her back until she quieted. Theo hurried to fit the baby carrier on his barrel chest. It looked ridiculous, but he was finally ready, and I seated the toddler in it, showed him how to loosen and tighten the straps. Then I turned to Arthur. His eyes looked funny, hard and soft at the same time. The beard looked as it always did, thick and black and unruly.

"What about the infant?" Arthur said.

"I can tie him on," Robert said. "Won't be the first time. Hold him for a moment, will you, Em?"

"Him?" I asked, as Robert passed the infant to me.

"Didn't you peek under his skirt? First thing I do with a babby." Robert winked. He took a blanket from his saddlebag and a knife from his belt, and cut the blanket into strips. "Once upon a time I had eight brothers and two sisters. I was third from the top and got to help with the younger ones, and all the nieces and nephews."

Arthur stood beside me, simmering, not speaking. Robert secured the infant to his chest with the blanket strips, put Hoshi up on his horse, and mounted behind her. He and Theo rode off.

Vasily mounted. Arthur made a gesture with his head, and I climbed up on his horse. He swung up behind me without a word.

Miraculously, we got the whole family back to camp alive.

Vasily and Arthur had to make the trip back on foot, as their horses were fully occupied. Back at camp, I let Mandy hug me and cling to me for a few private words of love and assurance. Then I ran to help James tend to Kei. A young Frenchman named Claude had ridden back with the men on one of their last missions; he was a Parisian fireman with paramedical training, so he hydrated the women and cleaned the men's knife wounds. After working on Kei, James stitched Michio for several hours. I put my hands first on Kei, then on Michio; they both seemed calmed by the warmth that eased into them. It was well after dark when I was emptied of healing juice. I left the hospital tent to get Arthur his dinner.

"*Ma petite choucroute*, she eez here *encore*," Cook said, with a laugh. He was chewing on a toothpick, and he moved it from one side of his mouth to the other. "Do not threaten me today. It eez you who are in deep sheet."

I stood in front of him, as I did every day. "He's already eaten?"

"*Oui*, and he eez not so happy with you!"

"He'll get happy," I said, tartly. Cook was amused and handed me a plate of the regular slop. I ate it standing there while Cook snickered. Then I set the plate on the table for dirty dishes and hurried to check on the children.

It was a cloudy night with few stars and no moon, and at first I couldn't identify the dark form that cut me off.

"The kids are fine. Robert gave them dinner and got them to bed, including the new girl," Arthur said. "Come. We need to talk."

"I'm sleeping with the kids." I stepped out so I could pass around him.

"Try it, and I'll pick you up and bring you back to *our* tent," he said. He moved to block my path.

"It's not *"our"* tent, it's *your* tent, and I have the right to sleep wherever I choose," I said. "Get out of my way!" I pushed his shoulder. "Move it!"

He didn't say anything. He grabbed me up like a sack of potatoes and slung me over his shoulder. I tried to kick him and punch him. He pinned my knees against his chest with his arm.

"Put me down now, damn it, Arthur!" I pummeled his kidneys with my fists.

"Stop yelling. You're making a scene! You'll wake the children," he said. So I bit him, hard, right under the shoulder blade. I clamped down with all my strength, felt the meat of his flesh tear and the wet of his blood on my mouth. He grunted, but didn't stop until we were inside his tent. He tossed me onto the floor and knelt beside me. "How are we going to play this?"

"You arrogant ass," I swore. I scrambled to my feet and he encircled me with his arms, brought me down again onto my back. I punched and scratched, but he was a lot bigger and stronger. He held me while I fought. I tore up the flesh of his neck and his shoulders and his face by his eyes with my nails. When I was finally worn out, he pushed my dress up around my waist. He tore off my panties and kissed my navel. Then he kissed in a line all the way down. His mouth was warm and insistent, and his beard tickled my thighs. I clamped my legs together, but his tongue had access where it mattered. Then he was inside me, and I was screaming and bucking up against him.

"Glad to know there's some fire under all that ice," he said finally, lifting up off me and onto his elbows. His scent of pine needles and leather, cedar and horses, consumed us both. I thought of a hundred sharp ripostes, but opted for none. Better not to engage. Besides, I was sweaty and loose in every bone, sinew, and ligament. My brain was fuzzy with exhaustion and pleasure. Every square inch of my body felt as if it had been released. I could not remember ever feeling like this; it was as if I'd died and come back to life. I looked away.

"Don't leave camp without telling me," he said. "It's too dangerous."

I thought about how close the rogue watchers had come to finding me, but held that in reserve. There was nothing to be gained by telling Arthur now. I said, "What about 'no commitments, no demands, no expectations'?"

"That's been superceded."

"I belong to myself." I wanted to snap at him, but it came out soft, like a kitten's purr. I sort of hated myself for that.

Arthur cupped my chin with one hand and turned my face toward his. "Mandy freaked out when she couldn't find you. Caris realized that Newt knew something, but we had a hell of a time getting her to talk. Mostly she spoke in circles and kept telling me not to give up on you, after the battle. What battle? Why would giving up on you ever be an option? We're together now. It made no sense."

It made sense in some future that only Newt could see, but I didn't say that to Arthur. I felt a pang at the thought that my daughter had been worried. I'd barely seen her since I had returned. Mandy, who was everything to me, who'd seen more and lived through more already than any kid should ever have to. Mandy, who was part of all that was still good and right with the world. "I'll leave word next time."

"Not good enough," Arthur said. "Tell me. And don't leave camp. If those watchers had found you—I don't want to think about it. You're the one person that makes this camp worthwhile. If you're not here, what does it all matter?" For just a moment, he looked tired, and terribly sad. "I can't lose you," he said. Then he kissed me, and rocked into me. Whatever I had felt before, it was nothing like the searing bliss I felt now.

6 NONE OF THE MEN IN CAMP COULD QUITE meet my eyes the next day. Arthur, with his scratched-up neck and brow, went around whistling, the very image of a man enormously pleased with himself. In fact, if I'd painted an illustration of such a thing, I'd have used him as a model, his expression was so exquisite. It made the men quail when they looked at me—everyone except for Xavier, who smirked at me in an oily way. By lunch, I couldn't take the men's embarrassment anymore. It was time to tackle it head-on. I left the kids in Caris' care, and went to the mess tent to eat with a group of a dozen men which included Vasily, Robert, Shinji, and Theo.

Theo scooted over on a bench to make room for me. "Pyotr doing well," he said, in a low voice. He sent a shy glance in my direction but didn't meet my eyes. "He sit up now."

"I know you all heard us last night," I said, loudly. Everyone at the table froze. Then they all began to speak at once. Then they all fell silent at the same time

"Shinji is a physicist," Vasily said, attempting to relaunch a neutral conversation.

"Really? I am mechanical engineer," Theo said. "Brother Pyotr is engineer."

"Will has something to do with that field, physics or engineering, used to work for an army group Before," commented Claude, the fireman. He was genial in crowds, but when he sat alone and thought no one was looking, he held his face and shook.

"Really? Physics and engineering? That's the best you guys can do to change the subject?" I said.

"The closeness between a man and a woman is a beautiful thing," Robert said. He gave me a speculative look, his freckled face scrunching in concentration. "My question is, does he know you're married?"

"Nope," I said.

"Bloody hell." Vasily threw down his fork, a piece of sterling with a boar's head on it. "You're *married*? How do you know your husband is even alive?"

"He was in Canada the day it happened," Robert said. "Mandy said he was visiting her grandmother. He and her older sister."

"Bloody hell," Vasily said again. He pushed his plate away. "This is not going to go well. Married! Arthur will not be happy."

Some things didn't need to be discussed. What was the point? *We're together now*, Arthur had said. A confrontation awaited, but I was in no hurry to undergo it. The very thought of it brought on a cold sweat.

"Good topics, physics and engineering," I said brightly. "I don't know anything about them. Nothing. *Nada*."

"Force equal mass multiply by acceleration?" Theo asked. "Newton? Faraday? Einstein law?"

"Nope. Sorry. Hated that stuff. Equations, theorems— ick," I shuddered.

"You not stupid," Theo said, but it was sort of a question, and he raised an eyebrow at me.

"No, I'm an artist. I think in form, light, and color, not in numbers. But I did once illustrate a young-adult biography about Nikola Tesla. He was a brilliant but crazy Serb inventor."

"I have studied Tesla," Shinji said. "The American

government hid his work when he died."

Vasily interjected, "I've known Arthur twenty years. He's never been this way about a woman. I didn't know he had it in him. He was too busy with his work. He was consumed with it. With his research, to make the world a better place. Ending war once and for all. Now he's crazy for a woman who's married."

"Wasn't he in the army? And he was trying to end war? What was Arthur's work, anyway?" I asked, remembering Xavier's suggestion. Vasily looked away.

"Tesla is big hero in my country," Theo said. "Great inventor. Genius. Pyotr read his patents. We build Tesla coil in garage."

"I built a Tesla coil in college," Shinji said, his face lighting up.

"I drew a Tesla coil once," I offered.

"Arthur will have a bloody shit fit," Vasily said, still not looking at me. "A million women chase him, and the one he decides on, he can't have."

Was it my stupid idea to clear the air about last night? What a mistake. I did not want to talk about feelings. I did not want to hear about feelings. I had locked all mine away in a drawer marked "Survival for My Children." It was the lock that had kept me alive all this time, and kept me sane. I owed it everything. What were we talking about? Tesla? I tried to remember what I had read. Long-idle synapses sputtered as the rusty brain engine tried to turn over. Tentatively, I asked, "Didn't Tesla figure out how to use the earth's energy as power? Too bad we can't do that. We could really use a power source."

"Mists eat generators, windmills, wires, solar panels and car batteries, first. Then buildings and people," Theo said. "So: no power."

"What does it mean, the mists target metal, people, and buildings?" Claude wondered. "It sounds almost strategic."

"It's tactical," Vasily said softly.

"God is tactical," Robert said, with great assurance. "He has a grand plan."

"There is no God," I muttered. "No God would allow this to happen. All this destruction, all this death."

"God sent a flood last time; this time He sent mists," Robert argued. "He has a plan for us. We just have to follow it, and look for the rainbow."

"Tesla is rainbow," Theo said.

"Tesla, interesting," Shinji mused. "Tesla made use of ambient energy. He claimed to transmit electrical energy through the upper air strata to almost any distance."

"He was a dreamer," I said, remembering the book. I had enjoyed the project. Beth was little, and I was pregnant with Mandy. The world seemed safe and full of limitless promise. How innocent I had been.

"Yes, dreamer," Theo said. "Weather control. Free energy and light. Communication with Mars."

"You must be talking about Nikola Tesla, the Croatian inventor who lived from 1856 to 1943, and who turned down the Nobel Prize in 1915 because he didn't want to share it with Edison," said a voice directly behind me. I swiveled around to look at Arthur. Was there anything he didn't know? He rested a hand on my shoulder.

"Join us, Perfessor Smarty-pants?" I teased.

Arthur grinned with half his mouth. "Will is obsessed with Tesla. When he gets better, he can try to recreate Tesla's experiments. It would be a great improvement around here to have light at night, if nothing else."

"I know Tesla's work," Shinji said. "I talk to Will. The ball lightning, perhaps we can make that."

"We talk to Pyotr, he have good memory," Theo said. He and Shinji were staring at each other, hard. I guessed that they didn't want to talk about feelings, either.

"I've been hoping to use solar power and eventually rebuild

windmills. We've got a supply of portable solar harvesting blankets, which we were going to adapt. But Tesla is a better option, if we can recreate it," Arthur mused.

"Will, Shinji, Pyotr, me, we do it!" Theo banged his fist on his chest. Shinji laughed at his bravado.

"Bloody hell," Vasily grumbled. "Bloody hell." He glared at me. Was it my fault that I got married nine years ago and that I had two young daughters? Did it even matter, with an ocean and insurmountable dangers between me and my husband and oldest girl?

I had gotten one phone call through to them After, just before all mass communications ceased. My husband and daughter were safe. It was a miracle, more than I had a right to hope for. It was *the* miracle, and it had become my touchstone. I missed them every day but I lived here, now. Living here, now, meant being with Arthur. But I didn't belong to him. We'd have to have that out, sooner or later. But not this minute.

I left, and went back to the children. Vasily meandered off in the opposite direction.

Arthur watched us go.

WILL'S PRECARIOUS CONDITION worsened. His pain increased. He was sweating and writhing continuously. The healing powers in my hands eased his distress, but not enough. He fell asleep but remained pale and drawn, moaning.

"We have to do something," I told James, some days later.

"I'm open to suggestions," he snapped. He wiped his hand across his face. It was warmer, probably July now, and we were both sweaty. He said, "Sorry. You're trying to help. I can see Will's organs failing, and it's just killing me." His shoulders slumped.

"The women's camp!" I said, seized by an inspiration like the one that had brought me and the children to Arthur's camp. Not exactly an inspiration—a knowing, a certainty from my core that couldn't be gainsaid. Was it a spark of madness from the mists? I hoped not, because I felt compelled to heed it. "They'll have an herbalist there."

"Big maybe." James' voice was bitter. "Most of the world is dead. We'd have to be pretty damn lucky if a herbalist survived, joined the women's camp, knows something that will cure Will, has it on her, *and* will come here to help him."

"Where there are women, there is always someone who knows about plants," I said. "It's a woman thing." All of us were stripped down to basics now, and that kind of knowledge was something that some women seemed to have in their DNA. My mother had been one such. When I was pregnant, she gave me a list of herbs to take and others to avoid. Red raspberry leaf tea for toning the muscles of the pelvic region, ginger root tea for morning sickness, nettle infusion for easing leg cramps. My two pregnancies were easy and the deliveries went smoothly, probably because I was young, but Mama's herbs must have helped as well. It was worth asking at the women's camp whether they had an herbalist.

I went looking for Newt. Maybe she would get one of her intuitions about the camp, about an herbalist, about me surviving the journey.

The kids were outside the camp walls, playing soccer with some of the men. Hoshi and Kei, his arm secured between two thick sticks, were also playing. A jumble of languages floated up off the field, but the babble didn't seem to matter. The game went on as if they all knew what to do and could communicate perfectly. I stood next to Hikaru, who sat on a stool nursing her baby. Hikaru gave me a shy smile.

Marco made a goal and danced around with glee. His team cheered. Mandy was on the other team, and she and her mates bumped fists, encouraging each other. Mandy looked over and saw me, ran over and threw her arms around my waist.

"We're winning, Mommy, four to three!"

"Better get back in there, lovey. Your team needs you," I said. I ruffled her hair.

Mandy nodded. "It's so fun, Mommy. I love playing soccer here. They used to play here, too, in this same field. I can see them like shadows running past me."

"Who are 'they'?" I wondered aloud. "Who do you see?"

"The people from Before," Mandy explained. "The men and boys from the village. I see them. Like shadow puppets on a wall, but they aren't puppets, and there's no wall." She hugged me again and then ran back. Her teammates were hollering for her. I was left surprised, puzzled, and concerned. What did Mandy see? Was she experiencing one of the mists' parapsychological effects, as Arthur had termed it? Or was she slipping into the madness from which there was no return?

"She not crazy," Hikaru said, as if she could read my mind. "Mandy is good girl. Sweet. Everyone see things now."

I bit my lip. "I don't see Newt."

"One girl went." Hikaru shifted the baby's head so she could point toward camp.

Newt sat alone in the children's tent, drawing and coloring on a torn piece of brown wrapping paper with a pristine package of 108 crayons. It was always strange, what we discovered and where, in the sea of flotsam that lay over the land, the artifacts from Before. Fragile items of great value sat intact next to durable goods that were shattered into dust, and all of it was jumbled up together, the rare and the ordinary, the hand-made and the manufactured, antiques and objects minted the very last day Before. In one garbage heap I'd seen an emerald and diamond necklace tangled up with a bracelet made by a child out of noodles. What was really valuable now wasn't the gems, but the metal in the chain. Metal that was both useful for practical purposes, and a hazardous summons to the mists.

All of it, metal and gems and noodles, was now the residue of a time that would never again return, despite Arthur's intention to rebuild. I considered his goals idealistic, but impractical. Ridding the earth of the mists, rebuilding, Tesla technology. Could the mists really be vanquished? Even if they could, whatever came next, after this passage, would be different.

Newt was hard at work, completely absorbed in what she was doing.

"Newt, what's that? What are you making?" I asked.

"A card for Dragomir's mother," she said. She didn't even lift her head to look at me, but kept working.

"Dragomir's mother?" Wasn't she dead? I had assumed so. Was Newt now making things for the dead? Was she slipping into madness? It was always there, waiting for us: insanity.

"She's coming back with you," Newt mumbled. She kept coloring, coloring. I stepped closer. She wasn't a good draughtswoman, but her figures were obvious: Dragomir and the other children together, including Hoshi and Kei. I stood to the side of the group of children, a narrow female with long, shaggy blonde hair and a gun in her hand. Newt's picture was spatially well organized, and the figures had big heads, which indicates self-esteem in a child. She was sane, then, even without her memory. Maybe she was sane *because* her memory was gone, gone with all the people and animals and buildings and metal things that had vanished from her life, consumed by sulfurous, lilac-scented clouds.

I waited for Newt to say something else, but she wasn't talking. I was coming back, she had said. That was good enough for me.

ARTHUR STOOD AT a big table with Vasily, Xavier, and a few other men. They peered at a map that was spread out on the table. Arthur drew me in with one arm, slipped me to stand in front of him, my back grazing his chest, his chin resting on my head. I could feel the steady strong drumming of his heart and his life, like a vast, pulsing river that drew me in and swept me away. He said, "Those watchers we killed, they're from that rogue band to the west. They've come down from the north. I think they're planning to attack." His finger swept the map to indicate relevant locations. "We'll strengthen fortifications, take a page out of the Roman army's playbook."

"That's what you've done with the camp," I said, remembering Shinji's words. "Built it as the Roman legionaries built their camps!"

"Most advanced army of their time, in terms of weapons, equipment, mobility, training, and strategy. Can't do better than to emulate them," Arthur said. "Maybe we should make a pre-emptive strike. Liberate the people in that band who don't want to be there. Our scouts say the rogue soldiers are mean, crazy bastards."

"Liberate, as in add more people to our camp?" Vasily asked. "I guess we've got room along the Via Decumanus, near the children's tent. Need to build shanties. We're running out of tents, even with our extra supplies."

"That band will hold off," Xavier said. "They're parked there for the same reason we're here: potable water, abundant fruit, wildlife. Plus, the mists are fewer here. Is it our business who's with them?"

"Only if we still care about human misery," Vasily said. His tone was silky, but dry enough to indicate that he felt the same way toward Xavier that I did. He brushed his hand through his white hair.

Xavier made a moue of distaste. "That's a luxury now, to care about misery when the survival of the race is at stake, don't you think?" he asked, bristling a little. "Should we risk ourselves for people who might be crazy?"

"We're going to do more than survive," Arthur said, with utter confidence. "We will thrive. We will reconquer the earth. Make a better civilization. We've been given an opportunity to grow and change. We will take it."

"Long-term, sure," Xavier said. "Short-term, let's save our own skins!"

"We've done that. Now we have to save others," Vasily said.

"Where's the women's camp?" I asked, both to change the subject and because I wanted to know.

"Last we heard, in this area." Arthur pointed south and a little east of our camp's location. "They're using the forests outside Cotignac for cover. There's a lot of greenery, and the developments that were there are gone now. Nothing to attract the mists."

"Nothing except people," Vasily said.

"How long will it take me to ride there?" I asked.

Arthur stiffened. His pectoral muscles tensed along my shoulder blades, and I felt it when his breath seemed to stop. He said, hoarsely, "You're not leaving this camp. The children are safe here. You don't want to risk taking them that distance, and the women's camp won't be safer or better provisioned than here."

"Just me, and I'm coming back," I said. "They might have an herbalist who can help Will. I've had a feeling about it for a while. I have to go and get her."

"No," Arthur said, flatly. Vasily raked me with a fiery glance. I thought he was angry, but his words were cheery.

"Has to be her," Vasily said. "They won't let a man get close. They'll kill us on our horses as we ride up." His voice darkened. "Will is in a bad way."

"We'll find the medicine he needs. No need to send Emma off on a dangerous wild goose chase," Arthur declared. His hands clamped down on my shoulders. He was leaning close, and his thick beard was tickling the back of my arm.

"We looked everywhere," said Claude, the Parisian fireman. Just last night, he'd spoken to me for over an hour about a *pain d'epices* recipe that was passed down through his mother's family, which was from Dijon. He was anguished that he

could not remember it. His English was excellent, since he'd
spent a year in his teens as an exchange student in Cleveland
and, miraculously, had retained his fluency. Claude threw up
his hands in a very Gallic expression of frustration. "There
are no more places. We have searched every building that
stands."

"You're not going to find it in time," I said. "Will's organs
are failing. He'll die."

"Tara won't send someone out of her camp," Arthur said.

"She'll let them go if they want to leave," I said. "The
women's camp won't be based on hierarchy and discipline,
the way a men's camp is. A women's camp will be based on
connections and relationships. Isn't that why the women have
separated out?"

"I hypothesized that the women banded together because
so many men have gone mad with the mists, and they brutal-
ize the women and children," Vasily said. "They're safer as a
group without men."

"They're not having as much fun, though," Xavier said,
winking at me. I looked away.

"The journey isn't safe," Arthur said.

Theo said, "She not go alone."

"I've got to deal with that band gathering on our western
flank," Arthur objected. "They're pressing, or we wouldn't
have found their two scouts. Our sentries have seen others.
I'm not as optimistic as Xavier. They're a problem."

"They'll leave us alone," Xavier said. "Why would they
spend their resources attacking us?"

"For our resources," Arthur said. "Weapons, food, horses,
supplies, women, tents, clothing."

"A small group is fast and maneuverable. I'll take Robert
and Theo. The four of us will ride with dispatch," Vasily said,
as if Xavier hadn't spoken. "It's, what, eighty-some kilometers? Two days there, a day to rest, two for the return trip.
Five days and we're back, and Will gets to live."

"If you don't get killed or enslaved by a rogue gang, shot by Tara's defenders, or swallowed by the mists," Arthur said. "I won't be there to head off the mists."

"We're coming back," I said. Newt was making a card for a woman I was bringing back with me. I trusted that. Couldn't explain it to Arthur, though. "We're coming back. We'll bring an herbalist. It will be fine. I know it."

"You know it?" Arthur retorted. "Really?"

"Yes. I know it, from inside, as the woman I am within myself," I answered, sharply.

Abruptly Arthur let go of my shoulders. He stalked away from the table and kicked a rock which exploded off into the air. "Tara will want something in return. The woman is ruthless at trading."

"We have items she'll want," Vasily said.

Arthur shook his head. "Emma's a terrible rider. I should have given her lessons. She'll fall off a bloody horse at a canter."

I knew then that I was going, and I grabbed Vasily's sleeve in jubilation. He smiled, leaned over, and whispered into my ear.

"Theo's the meanest son of a bitch you've ever seen with a knife and pistol, and he says you're his sister since you saved his brother. We couldn't have a better man with us." Vasily drew back with a wide grin.

"Where Robert?" Theo asked, his broad face creasing with a smile. "I tell him to saddle horses."

"Playing soccer with the kids, where else?" I said.

AN HOUR LATER, I'd changed into a pair of boy's sweatpants and a U2 t-shirt. I sat astride a small chestnut mare which had been carefully chosen by Arthur. He held her bridle, and I tried to find my balance in the small saddle. "Heels down!" he barked. "Hands quiet, heels down, and you're not sitting in a goddamn rocking chair. Keep your back straight."

"Relax. I'll be fine," I said. "Have some faith in me."

I touched my heels to the horse's sides and walked her in a circle around him. All eight kids, plus Hoshi and Kei, stood by the fence and cheered me on. Mandy was giggling at my indifferent incompetence. It was good to see her at ease this way. It felt almost normal, almost ordinary—whatever that meant in these end times.

"You're not walking in circles for two days," Arthur said. "You're riding hard and fast. Your legs should be directly under you. Sit firmly."

"You're relaxed and in charge, so she's calm," Shoshana called. "Watch her ears. They're perfect now, alert and ready. If she lays them back flat, that's bad—she's feeling scared and aggressive." Shoshana climbed up to sit on the top rail of the fence. "Remember, you're always communicating with your horse!"

"Horses are complicated critters," I commented. "They have lots of feelings. Who knew?"

Arthur shook his head, not taking his eyes from me. "You like this."

"This what?" I said. I steered the horse to walk circles in the opposite direction.

"Getting ready to go. Leaving on an adventure."

"Having a little break from the usual routine of trying to avoid death, starvation, and attack?" I asked in a low voice, so the kids wouldn't hear. "I thought you wanted me to have fun. Isn't that what you said at the gorge?"

"Have fun with me. You're at risk of death out there, alone," Arthur responded grimly. "This isn't like in the gorge, where I could keep you safe. Carry your gun. Be prepared to use it."

"I carry my gun. I'm always prepared to use it," I said. "I'm a good shot. I once shot a Belgian man right between the eyes from, well, as far away as the yellow supply tent. The mists had gotten him, and he was sobbing with pain. Screaming, too. Blood was coming out of his mouth and nose."

Arthur looked deep into my eyes. "Cut that memory loose. Don't carry it."

I shrugged. "We need the herbalist. For more than just Will. There's a runaway infestation of lice in the camp. Genevra has a fungal infection." I paused, pushing away a sudden pang of worry about myself: birth control. Arthur and I weren't using any. I didn't want any more children. This was not a world to bring children into, and it was obviously no time to be pregnant. I was hoping an herbalist could also help me. "Other issues, too. We're running out of manufactured medicines. We've got to learn how to use what's on hand to heal illness and injury."

"Can you post to a trot?" Arthur asked. I vaguely remembered how, from when I was ten and took riding lessons at summer camp. I lifted my rear end slightly, sat down, and lifted again; the mare picked up the pace. A second later I lay on the ground, staring up into the endless blue sky. My bottom hurt, but I could remember only a split second of weightlessness as I flew through the air.

"One of the Japanese women can go," Arthur said, helping me up.

"I can do this," I said. I limped back to the horse, took myself around to her left side, and mounted again.

"Shite, herself'll learn as she goes," Robert called. He and Vasily and Theo sat on their horses just outside the corral. "Come along then, Emmy. We ride at night and rest during the day, stay out of the crosshairs of any buggers who might be looking."

"Christ, you're not ready for this," Arthur muttered. He crossed his arms over his chest. "When you get back, I'll school you properly."

"Isn't that what you do every night?" I asked, wryly.

That made Arthur laugh. "There's some schooling going on, but I won't let you lay it all on me, Emma. You give as good as you take." His gaze was warm.

"Remember that." I waved to the kids and blew them kisses. I'd already hugged and kissed them all, promised to return, and made them promise to look after each other and listen to Caris. The Japanese women, who seemed to be feeling better, had promised to look after them, too.

"Just in case anything happens to me, you'll keep them safe, right?" I said to Arthur, in a low voice.

"Nothing's going to happen to you. You're coming back, you'll bring an herbalist, and it will be fine. I trust your inner knowing," he added, to himself more than to me. Then he gave me his sardonic half-smile. "Safe journey." I guided the horse around him and walked her over to meet the others.

"Vasily, you've got that bag of weapons for Tara?" Arthur called from behind me.

Vasily held up a bulky nylon sack, an old laundry bag. "Two Glocks and four boxes of ammo."

"Oughta rent us a plant lady and her tricks for a few weeks," Robert said.

"One would hope." Vasily turned his gaze to me. "Try not to get yourself killed, Emma. That would be of great benefit to us all." His tone was, as usual, quiet and full of irony and precision.

"If anything happens to her, I'll hold you three responsible and execute you myself," Arthur called, as if he'd heard. But Vasily's low voice couldn't have reached him; Arthur was sitting all the way back on the fence, between Mandy and Felix. He was scratching his beard and staring out after us.

Then Shoshana led a horse out of the tents that were used as a stable, and his attention turned to the children. It looked like a riding lesson was about to begin. We turned our horses, and set off.

"Brilliant," Vasily said. He made a slight quiver with his calf, and his horse sped up. In a few minutes, we cleared the camp, and we were trotting out to the south.

THE FIRST NIGHT was a long passage of muscle pain; the horses were conditioned to ride hard for hours at a time but I was not. Vasily and Robert coached me through my initial attempts at posting, and pretty soon my thighs and derriere were sore. I rediscovered my psoas and iliopsoas muscles, which I knew only from my Anatomy for Artists class in art school. Who knew they could ache this way? I liked them better when they were pictures in a textbook, not throbbing inside me.

We stopped for a brief meal before dawn. I couldn't help but moan as I seated myself on the ground. Robert handed me a can of cassoulet that he'd opened. Theo and Vasily were already eating out of cans, so I figured the whole can was for me. It was fragrant and delicious, white beans and sausage and duck confit. It had been made by Reflets de France. I wondered if any of their plants still stood, anywhere.

"What are we going to do when we run out of cans?" I asked.

"Smoke meat," Theo said. He grinned. "Cure it, dry it. Hunt it, roast it, and eat fresh. Wild boar very, very good!"

"Arthur's got a plan," Vasily said. "He's got a schematic for an orderly transition away from manufactured items we find to what we can grow or make ourselves. Of late he's talked about using Tesla technology for power, so we can build mills and eventually factories. He is on fire with the notion of rec- reating Tesla's work."

"He say me and Pyotr and Shinji and Will to do Tesla's experiments, when Will better," Theo said. "Make power source, turn camp into city."

"Arthur and his plans," I said. "What's his story, anyway? What'd he do Before?"

"You never asked him?" Robert said. "You and the Big Mis- ter spend a lot of time alone in his tent."

"We're not exactly talking," I said. Though, on reflection,

that wasn't entirely true. Arthur and I spoke more and more. It was no longer purely physical. Conversation had become a part of it. Whatever "it" was. About which I didn't want to inquire too closely, because it was obvious that Arthur and I had different notions about "it," and I had no desire to upset the status quo. There were children who depended on me, children who were thriving at Arthur's camp in a way I'd never expected.

"Arthur was a polymath, Before." Vasily smiled. "*Homo universalis*. Extraordinary man, really."

"What's a polymath?" I asked.

"Jack of all trades," Robert said. He winked at me. "Like Leonardo da Vinci."

"Or Albert Schweitzer or Andre Malraux." Vasily was nodding. "He was my student at Cambridge fifteen years ago; that's how I met him. A voracious mind. Remembers everything. Also an athlete; he medaled in two sports, rowing and equestrian. Wrote books and papers, set up a research foundation for some cutting-edge stuff. He was ROTC as a student at Harvard, and got involved in some sort of classified military research project, a defense collaboration between the US and the UK. A natural leader with limitless energy. Everything he tries, he does well."

"Impressive," I said. "Never married?"

"He availed himself of the women chasing him," Vasily said. He sighed a little and gave me a sour look, still mad that I was married. "He told me he was waiting for the right one, and he'd know her when he met her."

I shook my head. "Someone like Arthur, a Renaissance man, he'll pair up with a really spectacular woman. Before, it would have been an actress or singer. A celebrity, politician's daughter. Pickings are slim now, but I don't believe that woman is me."

"Neither do I." Vasily looked disgruntled. "There's no accounting for taste."

"Thanks," I said. "Let's just agree that I was in the right place at the wrong time."

"I think you special," Theo said. He lifted his can of food in a toast to me.

"You're a beautiful bird, love," Robert said. He ran his hands through his red hair so that it stood straight up. "I'd scuttle you, wouldn't even have to be polluted to like it!"

Robert was a sweetie. "Thanks, Robert—I'd scuttle you, too." I patted his shoulder. We exchanged a grin.

"Ha, ha. Don't speak this way around Arthur," Vasily said. "James says Arthur nearly shot him when he showed you a book." I shrugged. We all knew Arthur was jealous.

We got back on our horses and rode for a few more hours, skirting the Verdon gorge. Then we hid ourselves and the horses as best we could in a copse of trees.

I thought of Mandy, wondered how she was doing back at camp. If she got upset, Caris and the others would comfort her. She would be wondering about me, would ask me a thousand questions about this trip after I returned. I looked around so I could describe to her the place I'd slept. There were runnels along the ground, filled in with pine needles and leaves and beetles and the dun-colored dust the mists left behind. I fell asleep wondering what had stood here a year ago, and whether Mandy would be able to see it if she were here. I dreamt of the earth floating in space, a variegated phthalo green and cerulean marble in an indigo sea. Arthur was holding it in his palm. Then it cracked into pieces and fell away.

THICK AND FRAGRANT, night was pushing up into the pre-dawn of the second day when an arrow smacked into the earth near Robert's horse. His horse reared, but he kept it under control. A hundred meters in front of us stood a dense forest.

"That's my cue," I said. I slid off the chestnut mare, tried

not to shudder with pain mixed with the relief of no longer
having to hold my carriage in the saddle.

"Shite, I don't like this, you going in alone," Robert
muttered.

"They won't hurt me," I said. "I'm their kind."

"Crazy bunch of betties." Robert scowled.

"Take the bag," Vasily said, passing it down to me. I cradled it to my chest. Theo said nothing. Another arrow landed
between Vasily and Theo. They drew back a few yards, then
watched as I walked across the grassy clearing and into the
forest.

7 I WASN'T MORE THAN A FEW PACES INTO
the oak and pine trees when I was surrounded by
women. Literally surrounded. Dozens of women
of all ages and colors, most of them carrying flashlights or fire-tipped torches. There were black women, white
women, Asian women, women of all colors and nationalities;
women in salwar jameez, in pants, in dresses, in leggings and
tunics. They were all lean and angular. There was no need
for diets now. They carried weapons, guns and knives, clubs,
sharpened sticks, bows and arrows. The bows appeared to be
both manufactured and handmade, as were the arrows.

"I'm not here to join you," I said. "I came to speak with
Tara." A burst of voices in many languages erupted, and I was
grabbed by both hands. The women pressed in around me
and hustled me forward. With the handheld lights dappling
the trees, we wound our way through an increasingly thick
forest. As we went deeper, I heard sounds of children nearby.
I couldn't see much in the gloom, but I could hear small
feet running and young voices laughing. Occasionally there
were thuds when a small body dropped out of a tree. They
sounded—felt—healthy and sane. I had a moment's wistfulness, wondering if staying with Arthur was the best thing for
my troop. But then I remembered that, even if they were safe
from the roving bands, the women and children here were
still at risk. The mists seeped into forests.

We stepped into a clearing. "You ask for me," said a blonde

woman with a slight, crisp accent. Dutch or Frisian, maybe. She was younger than I expected, of middling stature and broad-shouldered, radiant with life and intelligence. Her blue eyes took me in fast and then swept around, checking her women.

"I'm from Arthur's camp," I said. "My name is Emma."

She smiled. "How is Arthur?"

It was the knowingness of her smile that told me that she'd slept with him. I felt a twinge of unease. "Healthy."

She made a slight gesture with her head. "You don't have to stay there, Emma."

"He's good to me."

"Very good, I'm sure," she said, raising a blonde eyebrow. The women around us caught the entendre and laughed. I smiled with them. She asked, "Why are you here?"

I tossed her the nylon bag. She seemed surprised at the weight, then opened the bag. She pulled out one of the guns with a smile. "Very nice," she approved. She passed the bag to a tall Asian woman standing beside her, then checked the gun and loaded it. She weighed it with her hands, taking the measure of it. Then she raised the gun and pointed it directly at my chest. "What do you want?" she asked.

"To borrow an herbalist."

"What makes you think we have one?"

I glanced around the circle of women. "My mother was an herbalist. She said women were born with the interconnection of life in our hearts. Where there's a group of women, there's someone who knows about plants and their power and who's willing to share the knowledge."

"Smart woman. You didn't learn from her?" Tara dropped the Glock to her side. "Not a very good daughter."

"A better mother," I said. I felt relieved that the gun wasn't pointed at me.

"How many children?"

"Eight, since last winter."

Tara nodded. "Let's eat. The sun is rising; we'll have breakfast." She gestured and we all moved deeper into the forest. Tara walked beside me. "Interconnection of all life? It's poetic. But accurate?"

"Sounds good," I said. "And aren't you living it, here in the woods?"

"We're living, and for now, that's enough. We weren't prepared, as Arthur was."

We came to another clearing as the woody darkness lightened to gray murk, and then to green and pink shadows. This clearing was a hollowed-out bowl in the forest, with some trees hacked away and some burned down. It was about a hundred meters in diameter and was filled with all kinds of resourcefully rescued stuff, some of it used as intended, some of it used in ways its creators could not have imagined. There were tents and makeshift shanties laid out in concentric rings around an empty center of packed earth. The innermost circle consisted of tables and chairs, and even a few sofas. In the trees around the periphery, draperies, blankets, and even what looked like yoga mats were strung as hammocks. Women and children dozed in them. Several trees were decorated, Christmas-tree fashion, with objects that had been tied on with twine or nylon stockings: cell phones and scissors, lamps and clocks and coffeemakers, paintings and canvas bags and computer keyboards, purses and toasters, cameras.

"Memory trees," Tara said, following my gaze. I was ushered to a table where people were already eating. I sat down, and a plate of food appeared before me: porridge with berries and honey. It was warm and delicious. Some kind of fragrant yellow tea came alongside it. Tara seated herself a few chairs away, fell to eating with gusto. A petite dark-haired woman sat beside me.

Tara began to quiz me on what I'd been through, the children I'd taken on, how we'd arrived at Arthur's camp.

"I didn't think he took in women and children," she said.

"We came to an understanding."

"Uh-huh. Arthur can be very understanding."

I gave her a sidelong look. "You knew him Before?"

She nodded, but her face shuttered over. "He has a doctor in his group?"

"How did you know him?"

"He consulted with me sometimes, on his special research project."

"Why? What did you do?"

"I was a research psychologist," Tara said. Her eyes took on a hooded, predatory look and she made a flat motion with one hand, cutting off this line of questioning. "Why do you need an herbalist if you have a doctor?"

"We're running out of medicine."

Tara nodded. "We all will. It's a problem. Our antibiotics are nearly gone. We have no analgesics left."

"Who is sick?" asked the dark-haired woman beside me. Her accent was very French, very self-assured. Her hair was short and chic. Even in the woods, in torn jeans and a t-shirt, she looked well put together, as though she were accoutered head to toe in Prada. I was a little envious. I suddenly felt frumpy in my sweatpants, with my unruly mass of hair.

"There's a man with parasites; he's wasting. He'll be dead soon. He's why I came. We've also got rashes, fungal infections, and skin rots; there are two guys with coughing fits. One man with cancer. Occasional diarrhea. Sunburns, broken bones. Head and body lice." I tried to remember what else.

She pursed her lips. "Yes, the lice is a big problem."

"What are you doing for birth control?" Tara asked, with a small grin.

"I need something for that."

"I will go," the chic woman stated, very firmly.

"You're an herbalist?" I asked, surprised. "You don't look like one!"

"I should wear a mustache and a muumuu to prove I know plants?" the woman asked, her tone arch and incredulous.

"Birkenstocks, for credibility," I said. "The mustache only if you're going the extra mile."

"Look at you with eyebrows like caterpillars," she said. "That mop on your head. You're a blonde gorilla."

"You say that like it's a bad thing. At least I survived."

"Americans dress so poorly," she said, and snapped her fingers in disgust. She looked at Tara and said again, "I will go."

"This is a matter for the council," Tara demurred.

"This is a matter for me to decide, where I go," the dark-haired woman said firmly. "The council advises, it does not determine. We choose for ourselves."

Tara looked like she was about to argue, but at that moment, a commotion broke out. A group of women bustled to our table. The women were clamoring in what sounded like French, Italian, Spanish, Portuguese, and Russian. Tara shushed them and then looked at one woman, a tall black woman with high cheekbones and a sculpted face. She wore a snub-nosed rifle slung by a strap across her chest, criss-crossed by a belt of ammo. A knife was stuck through the belt loops of her trousers. Something in her eyes said she was adept at using it. I'd want her at my back in a fight.

"Jeannie?" Tara asked.

"We found *him* following her!" said the black woman. She had a broad Liverpool accent and sounded indignant. Robert was thrust forward, stumbling. Jeannie kicked him in the flexion fold of his knee, and he thudded down onto all fours.

"You birds got some fry for an aul' fella?" Robert said, with his usual insouciance. A few of the women smiled.

"Robert," I said, sighing. He winked at me.

"How'd he get in?" Tara wondered. "Who wasn't watching?"

"I couldn't let herself face danger alone. Besides, an Irish-man's hard to keep out of anywhere, we have the gift," Robert said. He was really pushing his lilt, didn't usually have such musicality to his voice. He must have thought it charming. He looked around. "Sweet place you've got here. Fixed it up real attractive."

Tara frowned. "This isn't a place for men."

"I'm only one man, darlin'," Robert replied. "But I've got the vigor of ten!"

"*Mignon*," a woman called.

"*Beau*," called another.

"*Porcino*," crooned a third voice, eliciting laughter. Robert craned around to smirk at the crowd.

"I'll give you birds a grand time!" he offered, with a small hip motion to make his meaning clear, as if it wasn't already.

Tara motioned with one hand, and the black woman hit him in the head with the butt of her gun. Robert fell over, unconscious. Tara stared at him, her lovely square face puckered in thought. She seemed to be analyzing something from a few angles. I decided never to play chess with her. Of course, there probably wasn't an intact chess set anywhere in Europe. Then I glanced at the memory trees and wondered if I wasn't being hasty. Tara's group had tied all sorts of things into those trees.

"We trade," Tara said. "Laurette goes with you. We keep Robert. When Laurette returns, we give him back."

"*On a besoin*, I need at least two weeks, probably three." Laurette pushed out from beside me. "I need a few hours to collect my medicinals."

"And a manicure kit?" I muttered. Tara grinned.

"I warn you, Laurette likes things just so," she said, in a low voice.

Laurette snapped her fingers again and threw a glance back over her shoulder. "The two boys come with us. This is no place for them. They'll find a home at the other camp."

"They're thirteen, hormonal," Tara said. She shrugged. "This works out well for us, a relationship with Arthur's camp. At a certain age, boys must move on from here."

"There's something else," I said. "I'm looking for someone. A woman. The mother of one of my kids."

"Surely she is dead," Tara said.

I shook my head. "One of my girls is, well, psychic." I was nervous about saying it aloud. It wasn't the kind of thing I believed in, Before. When I was a teenager, I didn't participate when my girlfriends played with a Ouija board and paid to have their palms read. The mystical realm, apart from the magic of painters like Hieronymous Bosch and Odilon Redon and Chagall, did not interest me. Everything that could be seen was a play of light, I believed. And light could be massaged to reshape visual form, so spirits and the like were all illusions.

Like everything else I had ever believed, though, that had changed.

Tara was nodding. "We have one of those. Why do you think you aren't dead? We were expecting you." Tara grinned a little, looking away, and her grin drooped into sorrow. It made me think that she'd been keeping people out lately. But madness was rampant, and she probably felt her first obligation was to keep safe the women and children who were already ensconced here.

"My girl says I'm bringing back Dragomir's mother."

Tara made a face. "I will ask someone to look for her." She was done eating, and she rose and gestured for me to come with her. A few other women tagged along with us as she gave me a tour of their camp. She held a terse conversation in Dutch with an elderly woman whose left bifocal was cracked. I heard "Dragomir" mentioned.

Out from the main camp radiated a labyrinth of paths through the trees, and we followed one to a smaller, burnt-out area where foodstuffs and supplies were kept and cooked. They'd built a crude wooden smokehouse for preserving meats. As at Arthur's camp, they had gas grills. They'd also dug a pit for roasting, and they had a fire within a circle of stones with a huge cast-iron pot sitting atop it. Stacked around the perimeter were cans, cartons, bottles, and jars of foodstuffs.

"How do you find the supplies?" I asked. Tara gave me a long, thoughtful look, as though she hadn't expected such a question—as though it implied that I didn't know something I ought to know. It left me feeling confused.

"We make excursions at night," Tara answered, finally. She studied a distant tree. "Supplies are dwindling. We're making trips further out. We got lucky the full moon before the last; I was with a group who found part of a Champion *supermarché* standing. The store was mostly rubble, but the basement was full. We took everything."

"You go out on horseback?"

"We have a corral. I will take you there next."

"You're well set up, but what about the mists?" I asked. "Aren't you sitting ducks, if you all stay here?"

"We have a system." Tara drew me around a beech tree and showed me a covered barrel tied to the trunk with a bungee cord.

"Barrels?"

"I am not tied into the mists the way Arthur is, but this works for us." She slapped the cover of the barrel as if it were a drum—which, of course, it was. She struck the makeshift drumhead several times. Nearby, someone picked up the beat, joining her. The cadence was specific and rhythmic. Then two more drummers joined in, and then dozens more. Within a few minutes, the entire forest throbbed with resonance.

"Percussion!" I cried. "Of course! Arthur uses the hoof beats of horses running."

Tara stopped drumming and plucked a whistle from a string at her neck. She blew a long, shrill blast. The drumbeats ceased. The silence that followed was intense, richly saturated. Tara and I both savored it. Then she smiled, a little grimly. "The drums, the rhythm, were Arthur's idea. That is what makes it possible for us to have a home here."

"You've created a safe zone!"

"We've lost women on excursions." Tara gave me a side-long glance. "For a few days. Then we find them again. Who-ever took them pays."

You betcha, I thought. But then a young woman with Dragomir's soft-featured face came running toward me and grabbed my arms. "Dragomir?" she cried. I nodded, and she wept and babbled in the same Slavic language of which I'd heard Dragomir use a few words. The elderly woman came to translate.

Score another point for Newt.

Laurette and I took our leave of Tara. We stood just inside the tree line. Looking out into the distance, I could see four horses, two with riders. Dragomir's mother Bojana and the two thirteen-year-old boys stood with us. Tara had declined to send horses with us, insisting that we could double up. I understood her compulsion to save what she had. Impulsively, I hugged Tara. "Go easy on Robert."

She squeezed me and grinned. "He will be popular here, I think."

"We won't be able to live with him when he gets back."

"Not my problem," Tara said. Then her face dropped into serious lines. "I like you, Emma. I know Arthur does, too. There are things he should tell you."

"Why don't you tell me?" I asked, peering into her face.

She shook her head. "If your men come here without you, they wear yellow. Yellow visible on each man. Then we know who it is and we don't kill them."

"*Vraiment*, you will stand here all day gossiping like two old men drinking *café*?" Laurette called. "I have work to do. *Vite,* please." She waved a brisk *adieu* and marched out toward Vasily and Theo. Over one shoulder she carried a large gray duffel bag filled with her medicinals; over the other was a satchel-purse, ivory, quilted, Chanel, pristine, stuffed with personal items. I had an extra pair of panties in the pocket of my sweats and a toothbrush in a saddlebag tied to my horse. Camp was about to be a lot more interesting, with Laurette in it.

8 IT WAS MID-MORNING A FEW DAYS LATER when we rode back into Arthur's camp, where the walls seemed thicker and taller than before. I didn't wait, but slid off my horse right at the entrance. Bojana was riding behind me, and she clambered down, too. I pointed her to the children's tent and then led the horse toward the corral. She ran toward the tent as fast as she could, legs flying out behind her; it would be a sweet reunion. After I got the horse settled, I'd see for myself.

At the fence post grew purple thistles, around which spiraled several brown-and-white butterflies with red underwings. Nearby, watching, stood a couple of men, Claude and a new guy. He was very tall and muscular, with close-cropped black hair. His face was a study in the gorgeousness of precisely aligned planes and angles. A smattering of fine red rash ran along his cheeks and chin, but all of us survivors had been roughened by this life; there was no mistaking the symmetrical perfection of the forms of his face, like an Apollo of the new world. I didn't quite meet his eyes as I walked past, and I didn't let my gaze linger because jealous Arthur was sure to be nearby.

Arthur.

I swiveled on my feet, dropping the horse's lead. I gaped. He threw his head back and literally roared with laughter. Vasily had joined him and was smiling, watching Arthur's amusement. Men nearby turned to look, and to smile.

Arthur came over and took my face in his hands. He kissed me on the lips. Then he said, with keen delight, "You didn't recognize me!"

"Holy shit, you're gorgeous!"

That made him laugh some more. "Just don't call me Fidel anymore."

"You betcha," I said, and my breath caught a little in my chest. I couldn't stop ogling him. This put a whole new spin on our arrangement. It shouldn't have; looks were less important than ever, in this harsh world After. But I had been a painter, and the beauty that I could see still mattered to me. And Arthur was very, very beautiful.

"When Laurette goes back to the women's camp, Robert will be returned to us?"

"Not, I think, with his virtue intact," I said. Arthur chuckled. He wrapped his arms around me and snuggled me into his chest.

"Two new kids?"

"Not kids," I said. "Boys turning into men."

"They wouldn't fit into Tara's camp," he said, musing. "I'll assign some guys to mentor them. They'll learn to be soldiers."

"As long as they brush their teeth."

"You'll make them soft with all that hygiene," he teased. "They've got to be fighters, warriors."

"Speaking of fighters, did you ride out against the band in the west while we were gone?" I asked. What I really wondered was whether they'd encountered more watchers, but I was reluctant to broach that topic. I'd never told Arthur that two watchers had almost gotten me.

"Not yet. We dug trenches and built ramparts. I want Vasily and Theo around if there's any real action." He kissed my forehead, stepped back. "You probably have to eat and do a dozen other things."

"Probably."

"Seen the kids yet?"

"Need to."

"'Til later?"

"You betcha!" I said, breathlessly. Arthur laughed again. He stepped away and took the horse's lead rope. I went out of the corral and gave Vasily a look of disbelief as I passed him. He shrugged, palms up: what did you expect?

Not this.

Then I remembered what Tara had said about things that Arthur should tell me, and I wondered what else I wasn't expecting. I didn't have long to ruminate, though, because right then Xavier found me.

"You were successful," he said, squeezing my elbow.

I jerked my arm away from him. "What do you want?"

"I heard you want to get to Canada," he said, looking around as if to make sure no one could hear him.

"Everyone wants to go to Canada. There's a civilized zone there."

"I'm from Alberta," he said. "Edmonton is my home town."

"The center of the safe zone."

"That's not an accident," he whispered, putting his mouth too close to my ear. "I know people there. When we make contact, I can get them to come for us...."

"What do you mean, not an accident?" I exclaimed loudly. Xavier hopped backward, his lean face panicked, his hands making shushing motions.

"I've said too much," he muttered. "I'm just saying: choose your alliances carefully. There's more going on here than you know." He stumbled backward and then ran off, leaving me bewildered and even more uneasy than before.

I FOUND THE kids down by the stream at the same time Bojana did. She ran past me, shrieking Dragomir's name. He stood up with a wet shirt in his arms, looking puzzled. Then his little face was transfigured. He dropped the laundry and ran toward Bojana, was caught up in her arms and squeezed tightly. He wrapped himself around her. They were both crying, shouting. It left the other children with wet eyes. Not me; I no longer cried. Mandy threw herself at Bojana and Dragomir, hugging them, and the others leapt to follow suit. I joined in. After a few moments, Newt stepped away.

"I made a welcome card!" she said, in her piquant way. That made us laugh, and the kids and I backed away from mother and son. Bojana looked at me with a question in her eyes. She did not relax her fierce grip on Dragomir.

"Newt, go ahead," I said. So Newt proudly held up the brown paper picture and ceremoniously presented it to Bojana. Bojana settled Dragomir on one hip and took the paper with her other hand. She smiled and murmured something in her language that none of us spoke, and then she held the paper to her chest and bowed a little. Marco slapped Newt's back and called out his compliments, and all the kids praised her handiwork. Mandy hugged me.

"I missed you, Mommy," she whispered into my ear.

"I missed you, too, Mandy, love," I whispered back. I stroked her auburn hair and felt how lucky I was to have her. We were just us two; Haywood and Beth were not with us, but we had each other, and that made us lucky. We shared our private smile, just for a second, not long enough to make the other children feel excluded. Both of us were sensitive to the feelings of our comrades, who had lost so much.

"You know how I made myself feel good?" she said.

"You tied Marco's shoes together? No, let's see. You put a bug in Felix's bedroll?" I placed my arms akimbo and pretended to think. "You took Caris' pants out of her backpack and put Marco's in, to make Caris think she got confused?"

"No, silly! I only do that when you're around, because it makes you laugh even though you try not to!" She giggled. "I could see your shadow in the places you go a lot. Especially at the rock by the creek. You like to sit there and think. I could see you doing it. At night your shadow was like bright wings, telling us to brush our teeth."

Mandy was seeing shadows again. But she was right, I did like to sit on that rock. "Yes, I go there," I acknowledged.

"What do you think about, when you sit there?" she asked, burrowing her head into my tummy.

I stoked her auburn hair some more. "About you and the other children, how we're a family."

"Now we are eight," she whispered.

"It's different now, now that we're at Arthur's camp."

"There'll always be something special with us, because we were together first," she said. "Me and you and Shoshana and Marco and Ginny and Caris and Newt and Felix. Even Dragomir, he's still one of us, even though he has his mom now."

"Yes, we've shared some hard times, and it's made us close."

"It's made us love each other. And once you love, the love is always there. You can't ever run away from love," she said. She gave me her bright five-year-old smile, and my heart expanded with something bittersweet, filling my chest and leaving me breathless with ache. Her words had the ring of prophecy, and I both feared and treasured them.

LAURETTE HAD MADE her way to the hospital tent and was bent over Will on his cot, palpating his stomach. From the door, I could see that she was alone with her patient. "Where's James?" I asked.

"The doctor? They say a man split his foot with an ax, and the doctor went to see him. Stupid man," Laurette said. She opened Will's eyelids and observed the sclera of each eye, then stuck her fingers into his mouth and examined his gums. He groaned. She made a small moue that expressed a lack of sympathy better than any number of words could. She picked up his hands and inspected his fingernails.

"Yes, okay, I can help him," she said in her French-accented English, her lips pouting as she spoke.

"There's an herbal cure?" I felt hopeful.

"Combination of herbs. Powerful—it will be ugly for him. He should be isolated, because he will pass the parasites through his anus." She stepped back, squatted, and opened her duffel bag. "Last winter, just before the Day, an English-woman gave me the best elecampane. I never saw her again."

"I'll see where we can move Will to," I said.

"Move who where?" asked James, coming into the hospital tent. He saw Laurette and nearly fell over.

"You are the doctor," Laurette noted, unimpressed.

"James," he said, breathlessly. He stuck out his hand, and she lifted her perfectly arched eyebrows at him. He blushed to the roots of his thinning gray hair and dropped his hand.

"I am Laurette. I am the herbalist," she said. "You will do as I say. I will make a tincture for him. We start with a weak dose and give it to him every four hours, round the clock. By tomorrow he takes stronger doses." She heaved her duffel bag onto her shoulder and brushed past James on her way out.

"How long will we be doing this?" James asked, meekly. I slapped his shoulder with the back of my hand, gave him an incredulous look. "Right, right, I'm the doctor," he said. He darted out after her. I turned to Will and smoothed his hair off his face.

"How are you doing?"

"I like her," Will wheezed. "Think she'll give me a go, when I'm better?" He tried to wink, but he was so feeble that he lapsed back into semi-consciousness. I went to the other side of the tent and checked on Nwokocha. He was sleeping peacefully. I went out after Laurette and James. They were engrossed in conversation. More accurately, Laurette was speaking, and James was carrying her duffel bag and hanging onto her every word like a puppy dog.

I went to find an extra tent in which to house Will through his convalescence.

CLAUDE SET UP the tent outside the camp walls. The tent was new in its package, a bright red camping affair just big enough to hold a cot.

The paramedic's lean face was shuttered, and his dark eyes were ravaged. He was completely closed to conversation. After the tent was ready, I took him aside anyway, and quietly asked him what was wrong. He tried to move away, but I held his arm.

"James told me the date: July tenth. My brother's son's birthday is today," Claude said. "My nephew. He would be ten."

I felt sick. "I'm sorry."

"My brother had a wife and two young sons." Claude's hazel eyes were dull. "I have twenty-seven years. I liked women, many women. The smell of women, the feel of them, skin and hair. I always wanted some day a wife, a family. A pretty daughter with long curls, to buy her dresses and bonbons. Sometimes when I took people to the hospital, I would see a pretty face and think, maybe her. She is the one. But now I am so glad I never married. I don't know if I will ever marry."

I wanted to say something that would soothe Claude. So that I could feel I was helping him. But it would have been dishonest. There was no helping Claude. It simply existed, his suffering. That it was shared by all survivors could not solace him. I laid my hand on Claude's shoulder. "Tomorrow will come," I said. "It will be July 11."

"Yes. I didn't know it was so late in the summer," Claude said.

"Me neither. I've barely noticed the passage of time."

"Time is not important as long as you keep living every day," Claude noted. His shoulders sagged. "It just rolls away, like drops drying in the sun."

"It passes differently now," I agreed. I would have said more, but Laurette swept up to us. She said something to

Claude in French that sent him scrambling back to the tent to
lengthen the collapsible poles.

"Where are these children of yours?" she asked. "We can
put them to work. I can show them which plants to gather for
use, now and in the future. I can teach them how to dry herbs
and prepare tinctures. They should be every day collecting
sunflower seeds. Why should the birds get them all?"

"This way," I said. I led her toward the stream. "Where's
James?"

"I set him to make the infusion. He is a doctor; he can follow simple directions for boiling a few herbs in water, I hope."
Laurette narrowed her eyes at me. "This thing you do with
your hands...."

"I can't explain it."

"Attention, Emma: you must try. It is important for you
to take an orderly approach. James says you are the reason
Will has lived this long. It is too important a gift for you to
squander."

"I didn't think I was squandering it," I said, with asperity.
But we had joined the children at the stream. They dropped
their laundry and came to hug me and meet Laurette. Laurette
greeted them all very properly. She spoke to Marco in Italian,
and he drew himself up straight and sucked in his gut like a
young soldier.

Then her canny eyes took in Genevra's blank, infantile
expression, and she barked out something in French. Just
like that, Genevra's eyes snapped clear. She stopped seeming
four and returned to her real age, seven. I couldn't help feeling both amused and exasperated. All my cooing tenderness
toward Ginny, and what she had really needed all along was a
dose of sharp-tongued French instruction.

ARTHUR CAME TO watch the first dosing of Will in his
new tent, which had finally met with Laurette's approval
after Claude had rebuilt it several times. James, Claude, and

I stood in a semicircle around Will's cot as Laurette spooned a cup of her infusion between Will's cracked lips. Will was in and out of consciousness, moaning and half-choking on the fluid. Laurette had to pause and stroke his throat to get him to swallow.

"That's my oldest friend in the world. Be good to him," Arthur said.

"He is very sick," Laurette said. "I think it will not be until tomorrow that he starts to pass the parasites."

"How will it go?" Arthur asked. He stood in the doorway with a concerned expression on his handsome face, and I had to force myself not to stare.

I was not used to his new appearance. I was unsettled by it. It was hard to believe that this stranger of godlike beauty was the same man whose bed I had been sharing for the last span of time. In fact, if it weren't for the old wild thicket of beard, I never would have had the courage to approach him that very first day. He was far out of my league.

"He will pass them through his anus," Laurette declared.

"Do we have bedpans?" Arthur asked.

"Oh, I should have thought of that," James said. He started to wring his hands; I elbowed him to get him to stop. He cleared his throat. "No bedpans. No. And it's going to smell in here."

Arthur's gray eyes swept the entire tent carefully. "Cut a hole in the roof for ventilation. Off to the side, not over him, in case it rains. And dig a pit."

"A pit?" Claude said. He knew he was the one who'd be digging it. He sent an anxious look in Laurette's direction.

"*Oui*, yes, very good." Laurette was nodding. She cradled Will's head in her lap as she spooned in the infusion. "A pit underneath him. And we put him in a chair with his bottom sitting through."

They didn't need me, so I went out. Arthur followed.

"You're exhausted, Emma," he said.

"I'm fine," I said. "It's almost dinnertime. A few more hours and I can rest."

"You're not resting tonight; you have to do your duty," Arthur teased. He touched my hair gently and grinned when I rolled my eyes at him.

"You slept with Tara," I said.

His dark eyebrows rose. "Well, you know, darling—it's been a lonely apocalypse." He leaned into me, nuzzled my cheek.

"Not so lonely for you," I muttered.

"Jealous?"

"No!" I said indignantly, my cheeks warming. "But you could have told me before I went to the women's camp and looked like an idiot because I didn't know."

"Liar. You're jealous," he said. A satisfied expression scrolled over his face and he went off whistling.

I thought about calling him back, to ask him about what Tara had meant about things he should tell me. Was he hiding something from me?

But Caris waved me over. The moment passed.

LAURETTE WAS RELENTLESSLY energetic. After she'd settled Will into a chair and hassock, she informed us that she was now checking for lice. She grabbed Claude by his ears, twisting the cartilage to get him to drop his head so she could examine it. She promptly pronounced it infested. Vasily and Theo were nearby; their heads failed her inspection as well. Shinji stood with them, but he was louse-free.

The children were eating dinner, and when she ordered me to get them immediately, I refused. She muttered a few pithy French things whose meaning I probably could have guessed if I'd tried. I skipped off to join the kids before she could lay her talons on my head. But her attention was already on her duffel bag, and she was murmuring about a concoction for treating the problem.

"I will need olive oil, lots of it!" she called to me.

"I'll introduce you to Cook. He'll show you the stores," I called back.

"*Très gentil*, I met him already," she said gaily. I wondered if we were talking about the same person.

After dinner, Laurette instructed me, in a voice that would have boiled battery acid, to line up the children. I complied. Only Felix was free of lice. She directed me to kneel in front of her. She picked through my hair, draping it over my face as she looked.

"Emma, there is a lot of lice here."

"Really? I thought the mists made my scalp itch."

"No, the mists make your brain different. Lice make your scalp itch." She said it as if correcting an imbecile. I was about to ask her if she understood the concept of irony. She said, "You will have to cut your hair before the treatment."

"I love Emma's hair. I don't want it cut." Arthur's deep voice rolled out, surprising me with its proximity. I freed my face so I could see him. He stood beside Laurette. For a tall man, he always moved lightly on his feet. I had not heard him arrive.

"Look at it, this long mop, there is too much," Laurette said. She waved her hand in dismissal. "If we do not cut, some of them will hide and return and re-infest the camp."

"There's got to be an alternative," Arthur said.

"You want to comb the nits out of her hair?" Laurette laughed. "It will take you hours! Even I do not have that kind of patience." I didn't think she had any kind of patience, but I held my tongue so as not to offend her. She had her hands in my hair, and I didn't want any bald patches.

Arthur was nodding. "Yes. I'll comb out her hair."

"Really? You will comb out all that mess?" Laurette was skeptical.

"Arthur, it's okay to cut my hair," I said, awkwardly. In truth, I liked my yellow mane. I'd always had it, ever since I was a girl. Now it kept me connected to the woman I'd been Before, and all her hopes and dreams that were still precious, even though now they had no chance of ripening. It was only hair, after all, so frivolous a matter in the face of everything that had been lost. Still, I felt a little forlorn at the thought of cutting it. It was like throwing away the only concrete piece of myself from Before that I'd managed to save.

"I will comb it," Arthur said.

"I will get one of the women to do this. Bojana, or the *Japonaise*."

"I will do it," he said.

"Look at you, with your big hands," Laurette said. She lifted one of Arthur's tanned hands. "You think you can do a perfect job? Because it must be perfect. You must get every last nit. Not one can remain. Every hair must be combed."

"Laurette."

"It will take hours," Laurette argued. "Much easier to cut the hair."

"Laurette, get me a nit comb," Arthur said, in a low but terrifying voice, like a drill sergeant.

Laurette's eyes bulged, and she almost jumped out of her skin. She moved quickly to get a small fine-toothed comb out of her duffel bag. She gave Arthur a jar of olive oil and a rag, and demonstrated the process with a small skein of my hair. Muttering something about a bonfire of hair, she flounced off to get shears from Cook for the others.

"You can't kneel here all night," Arthur said. "Let's find a place for you to sit comfortably." We ended up by the stream, with me sitting on my rock, the rock on which Mandy had seen my shadow.

Arthur worked adeptly, methodically, pouring olive oil onto my head and combing it through tiny sections of my hair. His hands felt firm and gentle as they worked around my head, and I found myself relaxing deeply. The sun, yellow with lavender undertones, slanted down in the west.

Insects buzzed and birds sang and the camp hummed with
life, sounds of laughter and argument floating up like butterflies on a summer haze.

Arthur and I were quiet at first. His presence was comfortable. His strength and tenderness were palpable, and they
held me in a way I'd never before experienced, not even with
my husband. After a while, my relaxation turned to a near
doze. I'd not slept since we returned from the women's camp.
I decided that conversation would keep my head from nodding onto my chest and undoing Arthur's work.

"Did you ever think you'd be doing this?" I said. "Back
when you were setting up a foundation and writing books and
winning Olympic medals! And what else? Working on some
sort of classified, multinational army research project? Who
are you, anyway?" I tried to keep my tone light and playful,
like I was just trying out a new way to tease him.

"You've been talking to Vasily," Arthur said. I could tell
by his voice that he was smiling. "I'm not the man I was. That
guy doesn't matter. That's a long time ago, now."

"Everything seems like a long time ago. Whatever time
even means, now."

"Time doesn't mean anything now. I don't have a past. It
doesn't exist for me anymore."

I thought of Haywood and Beth, our apartment in New
York City, my agent who'd gotten me illustration gigs, friends
I used to like to meet for dinner in the West Village. "The
past can't be obliterated that easily, like buildings or people
when a mist eats them."

"Not obliterated."

"Then what?" I wondered.

"I'm sorry about what's happened," he said, his voice somber. He laid another segment of my hair over. "All the people
who've died. Who've suffered. What's been lost. I'd give anything to have prevented it. My life, anything. To have never
even been born, if that's what would have averted this."

I could hear something unspoken in his voice. "But?"

"But I can't torture myself about it. The past doesn't matter to me. It can't." His hands paused. "The past is gone. I know that this is what I was born for. Now. This challenge."

"Rebuilding, After."

"Yes. Driving away the mists. Making a new world. You."

"I'm the least of it."

"You're the most of it. I'd do a lot more for you than comb out your hair, Emma."

My heart took in the sweetness of his words, but I couldn't respond. I simply didn't know how. It was on my lips to reciprocate, and I wish I had. There'd be less to regret.

9 WILL PASSED THE PARASITES, AND MOST of the camp was shorn nearly to buzz cuts. Shoshana and Ginny opted for short bobs of which Laurette vociferously approved. Caris, Mandy, and Newt clamored to keep their long locks, so I picked them out, as Arthur had done for me. Laurette bustled about, mixing concoctions for everyone and instructing Genevra in the herbal arts. Laurette then discovered that Caris was both sweet-natured and competent, so she drew Caris into her orbit as well. Laurette had a way of making them feel special, which gave them both a new luster. I was happy to see some shine in my girls, and I tried not to resent Laurette for co-opting them—even though she took every opportunity to scold me about something or other.

Arthur decided to ride out and surveil the rogue band still gathering to the west of camp. I went to say good-bye to him at the corral, where he was tacking up his horse. The corral was full of men saddling horses; Hikaru and Kimiko were there seeing Shinji and Michio off. Michio had finally recuperated enough to ride with the other men, and, though still scored with stitched-up red knife slashes, he looked eager to do so.

"Coupla days," Arthur said, tightening the girth. "Day to ride out, day for recon, day to ride back. You're in charge."

"Me? What about Vasily?" I was startled and dismayed. What did I know about running a camp?

"He's riding." Arthur looked at me over his horse's roan withers. "I need every able-bodied soldier with me. This could be the decisive confrontation. I know one's coming. Those red-caped rogue soldiers aren't camped out there for fun."

"I can't be in charge!"

"You'll be fine. Just keep everything going the way it is. Don't let anyone in. Masashi will be here for support. The old man's smart, and good with a gun, too."

"He doesn't speak English."

"Hikaru or the little girl will translate. I've left six men as sentries; they'll rotate watches. Just try not to bedevil Cook, eh? I want the food to be edible when I return."

"Without you here, the mists...."

"Will not be back," Arthur said, firmly. "I sense whether or not they'll return to a place. They won't come here. I'm more concerned about attack from a gang we didn't see coming. Carry your gun."

"Always. Are you taking James with you?"

"Will you miss watching him moon over Laurette?"

"You should definitely bring her along. That gang to the west needs a good herbalist!"

Arthur laughed. "It was your idea to bring her in."

"Will seems to be mending. Do we need her anymore?"

"If we don't return her to Tara, we won't get Robert back."

"I'm sure he's having so much fun, he doesn't want to come back," I muttered. Arthur laughed again. Vasily, Claude, and Xavier approached, guns clanking and knives rattling at their belts, so I backed away. My elbow banged into someone, and I turned to find Newt standing there, rubbing her clavicle. I put my hand on the red mark and let some of the healing tingles flow into her. She sighed.

"I like his hair cut," Newt said, in her piquant way. She was looking at Arthur.

"Me, too." I put my arm around her and squeezed. Her shoulders were sturdier now that we ate regularly, and her face had filled out. Xavier walked toward us, halted a few feet away with his hands on his hips.

"So how we gonna do out there?" His eyes blazed at Newt. She wriggled and looked away, her cheeks turning a dull pink.

"Go away, Xavier," I said.

"You can always tell, you know. The ones that have been marked by the mists."

"We've all been marked by the mists."

"But I know how," Xavier said smugly.

"Really, Einstein? Why don't you enlighten me, then?" I snapped.

Xavier brightened and preened. "People who have succumbed to the mists get heightened neural activity in regions of the brain that are only dimly understood," he said smugly. "Because humans have a perceptual system that most of what used to be Western Science never wanted to acknowledge."

"You sound like a science textbook. I hate science," I said. I looked at him scornfully, so that he'd know I lumped him in with science.

"Let me put it in terms that even an artist can understand," Xavier said, his condescension almost palpable. He leaned into me but continued to stare at Newt, who crumpled her head into my armpit to hide her face from him. He said, "Their minds come apart!"

What a jerk, I thought. We didn't need a textbook to tell us that—or Xavier to tell us, for that matter—and he certainly didn't need to say it around Newt. "You're upsetting her, Xavier. Get lost." I wrapped my arms around Newt.

Xavier strode around us in a tight circle, speaking in a superior singsong like a grad student tutoring a freshman. "We all have a biomind equipped with indwelling faculties for transcending space and time. Every one of us, because the biomind is carried in our gene pool. Those faculties have never been locked into the known laws of physics. The mists attack the biomind. There are effects."

"I hate physics. We know what the mists do. We don't need a lecture."

"Arthur's the one who should be giving you the lecture." Xavier reached over and tapped the back of Newt's head. I swatted at him, furious, but he just laughed. He said, "You aren't gonna tell me what's coming, little girl? Too bad. I'll just have to find out for myself." He smirked at me. "Remember what I said about alliances, Emma. Choose your friends carefully." He wheeled around and sauntered toward the other men.

"He's gone," I said.

"He knows too much. He's dangerous," Newt said. She peeled herself away from me. I smoothed back her hair.

"Don't take on what he says. Throw it away. He's troubled."

"I wonder who will win, him or him," she said, pointing at Arthur.

"What do you mean?" I asked. Something about the way she said it made my breath catch.

"Xavier's going to surprise Arthur," Newt said. She shrugged and tilted her head, her hazel eyes going nebulous.

"Surprise Arthur how?"

"There's a lot of blood."

"That doesn't sound good!" I cried. Where would we be without Arthur? The kids, me, the camp? *How would we handle the mists?* We were safe now because Arthur knew where the mists were, where they'd be. He could send them away. His well-being was crucial. Not just to us; perhaps to the world. I thought he was probably the only person still alive with a vision bigger than living through the next day.

Newt's large eyes softened as they perused mine, and her voice went wistful. "But you don't have to worry, do you, Emma?"

I hesitated. I wanted to press her about the blood. I wanted to shake her and get a full report: *whose blood?* But I'd learned that she couldn't be interrogated; she would only say what she was directed to say by the mysterious inner knowing that prompted her words. I pushed down my fear for Arthur's safety and asked, "Why don't I have to worry?"

"'Cause you'll go to be with Mandy's father." She smiled tremulously, her young face vulnerable, resonant with everything she'd lost: her family, her home, her memory, her identity. I wondered if she spoke from precognition or from insecurity. I was what she had now. Losing me was probably terrifying for her. It made my heart ache for her. I wanted to soothe her. I also wanted to protect Arthur.

I wondered if I should warn him about Xavier. But he was laughing with Xavier, had his hand on Xavier's shoulder. Even with my privileged relationship to him, Arthur wouldn't believe me.

I turned back to Newt, who was still staring up at me, soulful and open.

"I can't imagine leaving you, Newt." I brushed her stringy hair off her face and kissed her forehead.

"You won't, Emma." Her voice was desolate. She pressed herself into me, sweetly but briefly. I clasped her back fiercely. She stepped away with one of her sad smiles; I realized that, even with her memory mercifully taken from her, some part of her knew that she'd lost everyone.

Theo walked by on his way to his horse, a rifle over his shoulder. He patted Newt's head as he passed. I squeezed Newt again and hurried after him.

"Theo, Theo!"

"Emmy, we ride today. Next time, Pyotr come. I tie him on horse, he come today!" He looked jovial and flashed some funny hand gestures at Claude, wresting a grin from the serious Frenchman.

"Theo, did you mean it when you said I was your sister?" I gripped his sleeve and willed him to take me seriously.

His broad, ruddy face went stark. "You save Pyotr. I owe you!"

"That's not how it works." I shook my head. Arthur called for me, so I leaned close to Theo's ear to whisper. "I need a favor."

"Anything!"

"Stay close to Arthur. Don't let Xavier near him. Please!" I drew back as Arthur marched over to us.

"Xavier?" Theo murmured, stunned. "He with Arthur so long." I nodded.

"What are you two whispering about?" Arthur asked, slitting his eyes at Theo.

Theo took a beat, then said, "Just us girls tell secrets." He winked at us both. Arthur jerked his chin in response, then took me by the arm and led me away.

"Do you have to be so flirtatious?" Arthur sounded irritated. "Try not to hit on Masashi while I'm away."

"Arthur, please. You're being ridiculous." I let him kiss me, tried to look past his shoulder to see if Theo had understood my request.

"You're not present," Arthur grumbled. He ran his hand through my hair, which was still soft and a little gummy from the olive oil he'd combed through it a week ago. His gray eyes searched mine.

"Arthur. Your jealousy is silly. It's unseemly."

He laughed, a short bark with no humor. He stepped away and swung himself up onto his horse. "The world is destroyed every day by mists that dissolve metal, shatter buildings, alter our consciousness, and kill people. I give a fuck about seemly?" Everything in him smoldered: eyes, mouth, affect. I could not fix that for him. But maybe I could keep him alive.

I looked past him. Theo gave me a thumb's up: he understood. I was so relieved that I almost sagged where I stood. If anyone could protect Arthur from Xavier's bloody surprise, it was Theo.

I wondered if Newt had seen that, too, or if she would now see something different. Had I tipped the scales for

Arthur's benefit? Or had my intervention always been part of her vision? Had we altered time, or secured fate? There were no answers—there never were anymore—and Arthur, on his horse, was chafing against delay. I smiled up at him.

"Safe journey, Fidel," I called, in a light voice. "I'll be waiting for you."

"Cheeky," he said. But his handsome face eased. Vasily rode up alongside him and saluted me the way Robert would have, were he here. Then about eighty men—most of the camp—rode out to see what was happening on our western flank.

I WAS FORCED to make a decision. I was in the hospital tent, seated on a wooden tripod stool beside Nwokocha, hands on his chest. Laurette stood at my shoulder, arms crossed over her abdomen. It had been a few days since the men had left.

"Tapping your foot won't make him heal faster, Laurette," I said. "If he gets better at all. I don't know if this will help him, in the end."

"You should think about what you are doing and try to improve it so it does help him," she said. "Does it feel the same as when you put your hands on Will, or the children? What does it feel like?"

"I don't know. I don't think about it, I just do it!" I was exasperated.

"Precisely," she sang, with an air of triumph. "But since it can help people, you have a responsibility to analyze."

I shot her a jaundiced look. "This is a mystical thing. It can't be analyzed."

"Bullshit," she said. "It has a physical component and a mental component, so it can be analyzed for greater understanding. He looks better and moves better since you started working on him twice a day."

"I do have more energy," Nwokocha said softly. "Not so weak all the time. Something underneath is knitting together." He added something in French, at which Laurette nodded sagely.

"We do not know what is coming in the future, how we will help sick or injured people," Laurette said. "This thing you do, it is effective."

"Not always," I said.

"Often enough that we must consider if it can be taught to others, and if so, how," Laurette said. "We have a responsibility to those who are left. You think Hoffman-LaRoche will present new cancer drugs that help sixty percent of the people and give the other forty percent strokes? We should be so fortunate. We are on our own now."

"I own their stock," Nwokocha said. It took me a beat to realize that he was joking. Laurette was already laughing uproariously. I was about to respond, but Mandy and Newt came in. Mandy had a resolute look on her face; Newt's eyes were red-rimmed. Hoshi trailed after them.

"Girls, Emma is busy," Laurette said.

"I'm done." My hands had emptied of the fluttery feeling—whether because Nwokocha was filled with it or because Laurette had irritated me, I couldn't say. Laurette would probably want me to figure that out, too, damn her. I stood and stretched. "What's up?"

"Why is Newt crying?" Laurette asked.

"Newt is worried. You have to listen to her," Mandy said. Her chin was raised in determination, but her tone was pleading.

"No manipulation, just out with it," I said, crisply.

"Emma, you have a heart of ice," Laurette reproved. "Come, girls, I will listen to Newt. Speak."

"I listen to Newt," I said, with both irritation and trepidation. The girls must be onto something big, something they knew I wouldn't like, for them to act this way.

"Let him in!" Newt cried. Mandy put her arms around Newt in consolation. Laurette put her arms around both of

them. I thought about smacking her. Then I decided that
Laurette could probably take me in a fight. She was skinny
but ferocious, that one.

"Who, my darlings? Who must we let in?" Laurette
crooned. I rolled my eyes despite my worry.

"Newt says a man is coming. She doesn't want the guys
with guns to shoot him, because he's good." Mandy enunciated with great care. It was hard to believe she was only five,
and I had to smother a smile, she was so cute.

"Where's he coming from?" I asked. Newt pointed: north.
"I don't know. There might be other men coming who aren't
so good. Do we take the chance?"

"Of course we do!" Laurette snapped.

I shrugged. "Ah, what does he look like, so we know he's
the one?"

"He has a big brown bag," Newt said.

"It's not just him," Mandy said.

"People are coming," Hoshi chimed in. She pointed east.

"People?" Now I was acutely uncomfortable. Arthur had
told me not to let anyone into the camp. So this was why the
children were acting this way. They'd been told, many times,
to alert the adults if they spied anyone approaching camp.
Usually the sentries functioned as snipers and shot anyone
within a certain radius, a warning shot or two, and then an
accurate one. It was the only way to protect the people here.
There were malevolent watchers in the woods. There were
also survivors infected with madness. Sometimes I thought
madness was a refuge, and almost envied the crazy ones. To
live here, now, was to live in near-unendurable insecurity and
loss. Only the images in my deepest heart, and the needs of
the children in my care, kept me from coming apart.

But Mandy took my hand gently, and my heart stuttered
with love. This was, after all, the better way.

"They need help," Newt said softly. She wrung her hands
the way Caris did.

"Stop it." I reached out and gripped Newt's hands to hold them still. "We'll think about this."

"What is to think about?" demanded Laurette. "If they are hurt, we help them."

"Arthur said not to let people in."

Laurette shrugged the way only the French can. "Arthur's not here."

"Let's see what Masashi has to say," I said. I wasn't eager to gainsay Arthur's orders without support.

Masashi sat at a table in the mess tent, with a pot of tea and a pile of guns. Cook sat across from him, watching as Masashi stripped and cleaned the guns with a rag and a sooty bottle of linseed oil.

Cook threw a dirty look over his shoulder when we came in. "*Merde*, you beetch. I find some poison *champignons* for your dinner." He rose and lumbered back to the cooking area. Something savory was cooking, but I doubted I'd get a heaping plate of it.

"Nice to see you, too, Cook. Masashi, I need some advice," I said. The old man flicked a glance at Hoshi, who translated. I explained the dilemma: people were coming, they needed help, Arthur had told me not to let anyone in. Hoshi translated rapidly. Masashi listened as he cleaned a Kahr pistol methodically, slowly. Hoshi finished, and we waited for him to say something.

He spoke a single sentence. We all looked expectantly at Hoshi.

"Grandfather said the guns will be good for the men on their next mission, but they need to find more bullets," Hoshi said.

"What?" I put my hands on my hips and glared at Masashi. He wore the tiniest smile as he cleaned the gun and otherwise ignored me. But there was no point in being angry, just as there was no point in tears or regret or anything else now, After. What mattered was looking ahead to the next hour, the next patch of ground to place my foot so the steps would be safe for my children. What was I going to do?

"Please, Emma," Newt whispered. There was no way to gainsay her luminous, pleading eyes. Arthur would have to live with my decision. He left me in charge, after all. Laurette was watching my face and she nodded, slowly, and squeezed my shoulder. She knew what I would do. Neither of us knew how the world, what was left of it, would change. Maybe Newt knew, though she wouldn't be here to see the results.

"I'll talk to the sentries," I said, with a sigh. "Let's keep the kids inside the camp walls, in case some of the people are mad."

The men weren't happy about it, but they agreed to do as I asked. Arthur had told them I was in charge. They were to look for a single man riding in from the North, and to let him through the perimeter and into camp if he carried a big brown bag. From the East, wounded people were coming. They were to be let in. The camp would grow again.

THE MAN WITH the big brown bag arrived later the same day. He walked right up to our Praetorian gate and hollered, "Ya, hello?" His booming voice couldn't be ignored, and it drew me out of the mess tent.

I trotted to the gate and saw a very tall, very lean man with shaggy blond hair. He looked as if he'd once been stocky, and there was a large brown leather bag slung over his shoulder.

"I am Torsten. I am here," he said, with a giant grin that showed an immense number of perfect white teeth. He stayed respectfully outside the gate, holding a bicycle by its handlebars.

"I thought he'd be riding a horse," I said *sotto voce* to Laurette, who stood at my elbow.

"Newt, she does not always explain her prophecies," Laurette said.

"You've been talking to Newt?"

"Of course, haven't you?" Laurette said. She narrowed her eyes as she scanned Torsten from head to foot. Bojana, with Dragomir on her hip, sashayed up beside us and cut her eyes at Torsten. He straightened, raising his eyebrows back at her.

"He doesn't look crazy," I said. Bojana said something.

"She says he looks just fine," Laurette said, with a sultry smile.

"I didn't know you spoke her language."

"I don't." Laurette smiled more widely. "Don't you have eyes? Or you can only see Arthur? It's all that time you spend in his tent. *Vraiment*, Emma, he has you pussy-whipped. You should get some self-respect."

"That term refers to men, and no, he doesn't!" I sputtered, furiously. "I have plenty of self-respect!"

"So, here I am waiting outside all day, and something smells delicious from inside your walls," Torsten called, in a lilting baritone. "I have not eaten in two days."

"I am Emma. Come in," I said. Mandy and Newt and the other kids crowded around me, waving at him. Torsten walked his bicycle in and leaned it against the wall.

"Lucky I am that your fellows with the rifles did not shoot me," Torsten said. "I could feel their sights on my forehead. I like my forehead as it is, uninjured, ya?"

"You betcha," I said. "Why don't you get some food, and then grab a rifle yourself. We've got other folks coming. But we've got to keep the crazies out."

A FEW HOURS later, the first refugees arrived. They were two Turkish women and a Swiss boy, the three of them emaciated and scared. One of the women hobbled on an infected foot that she'd swathed with torn strips of cloth. We fed them in the mess tent, at the next table over from Masashi, who cast not a single glance our way.

Laurette knelt on the ground to tend to the bad foot, gesticulating and muttering in rapid French as Ginny and

Caris observed. I sat and listened, trying to piece together the refugees' story. The boy spoke decent English and one of the women spoke German to him, although my polyglot girl Caris explained that they spoke different dialects.

Their story was one I would hear with many variations over the coming days. The two women had each separately survived the massive incursion of mists that day in December. They started walking—where to, neither knew. It was just to stay on the move, to try to avoid the mists, which sometimes still rose up with lethal intent. The cold was brutal. They found each other in Austria and traveled together, mostly by night. They were near the Dolomites in Italy when a rogue band wearing red capes passed them. The women hid. Children were roped together at the rear, and the two women took advantage of a moonless night and a lazy rear guard to release the last two kids, via quick swipes of a knife through ropes. The girl, twelve years old, died a few weeks later; they thought it was appendicitis. The boy was hardy. The three of them kept traveling by foot, scrounging, eating anything edible. They'd run into a small group of women who told them about a camp in a mist-free safe zone, a camp with women and children. They'd spent weeks looking for us.

"Emma, let us speak," Laurette said. She waved for me to follow her outside the mess tent. "It's very bad, her foot. I can try to help her, but she really needs amputation."

"James isn't here," I said. I looked around. The camp was without its usual hubbub and felt empty. It was just the kids and us, with Bojana and the Japanese women, the six sentries, Cook and Masashi, and the new guy, Torsten. Will and Nwokocha slept inside the hospital tent, both feeling better, neither strong enough to move about freely.

"I don't know how long we can wait. She is feverish, did you feel her? Burning up like a flame. How she walks at all, I don't know. Just the forefoot, I think, from here," Laurette knelt and swiped her hand across the top of her foot. "That ought to keep the gangrene from spreading. It should save her life."

"Laurette, we are not performing an amputation!"

"You want her to die? Now? After everything she has endured?" Laurette placed her arms akimbo and scowled at me.

"Do your best to take care of her for now," I said. "James will be back soon."

"Maybe not. And her foot gets worse every minute. You want this woman's death on your head?" Laurette flounced off toward the mess tent, muttering in French. I had a feeling she wouldn't leave well enough alone. I was going to follow Laurette and have it out with her, but I was cut off by Mandy, who attached herself to my elbow.

"Mommy, we better get clothes for the new boy," she said.

"Oh, right, the Swiss boy's rags are falling off him." I sighed and veered off toward the supply tent. We went inside.

"Mommy, I keep seeing a giant stone."

"What stone? The one by the creek?" I bent over a pile of spare kids' clothes.

"A shadow stone. A giant white stone that covers the Earth," she said.

"The mists are white."

"It was a stone. A giant stone."

I held up a pair of trousers. "These will fit him if he rolls up the cuffs."

"He's awful skinny," Mandy said doubtfully. "Better find him a belt, too."

"Those are over there." I pointed. "You're seeing shadows again? Shadows from what used to be here?"

"I think so. I don't know. While I was at the creek washing clothes, it was like I floated up and saw everything from way up high," Mandy said. I paused to stare at her. She was picking through the belts, unconcerned. But I was concerned. Her visions were changing. Again I asked myself: was she slipping into madness? She said, "But not shadows of people. Of a giant white stone covered over with lines and lines of writing. I can't read the writing. And Arthur came and used a knife to scratch out all the lines, all except a few letters."

"Arthur? He was here? Before now?"

"I don't know. It was like he was and he wasn't. He was watching everything next to me, before he went down to the giant stone."

"So it was different from other times you've seen shadows," I murmured.

"Yep. But I had the same soft feelings inside."

"And Arthur was watching?"

"Uh-huh." She held up a plain brown leather belt. "The new boy can use this."

I took it, wondering why Arthur was in her visions. But Mandy was done with what she needed to say. She kissed me and skipped out of the tent, laughing about a bocce ball game.

I went down to the creek and looked around curiously, but I did not have Mandy's gift. I did not see shadows and visions. The mists had made of me a conduit for a current that healed people. All I could see was the orderly rows of empty tents.

THE NEXT AFTERNOON, I spied Laurette sneaking into the hospital with an axe. She disappeared inside. I bolted after her.

I found her in the back room, which was really a modular tent added in behind the three conjoined tents that served as the main treatment area. The Turkish woman lay on a cot. Caris, whose smooth brown face was pasty, was tying the woman's arms to the headboard with white twine. Laurette was securing her feet and a sturdy box was wedged beneath the end of the cot, under her feet. A bottle of surgical cleanser stood on a tray table between the axe and our last bottle of Percocet. Bandages and tape, surgical needles and suture were laid out on a clean cloth on the other side of the tray table.

"Laurette, what do you think you're doing?" I cried.

"I am saving her life. You may be too frightened, but I will do what needs to be done!" She glared at me. "I will not let anyone else die if I can help it!"

"You'll kill her, chopping her foot off!" I glared back. "James can do it so she survives!"

"We can't wait!" Laurette said. She faced me directly, squaring off against me. I stepped back, turned and touched the woman's forehead. She was boiling. I squatted and looked at the woman's unwrapped foot. It was ghastly: swollen, red, and weeping yellow-green pus out of black and bronze toes. Red lines ran up the woman's ankle into her calf. The woman moaned and writhed on the cot. She murmured brokenly. I didn't need to speak Turkish to know that she was incoherent and talking about the pain.

"Get Caris out of here," I said. Laurette flashed me a grateful look, turned and flicked her fingers at Caris. Caris flew from the room. I checked the Turkish woman's wrists; they were solidly, but not painfully, tight. "Feet are good?" I asked. I closed my eyes for a moment. "Okay, who gets the honors, you or me?"

Laurette giggled nervously. "I would give anything for a cigarette right now."

"Cook has that thing stuck in his mouth, but I can't remember the last time I saw anyone actually smoking," I murmured. I picked up the axe from the tray table, examined the blade. This same instrument had sliced into the foot of one of Arthur's men two weeks ago, when Laurette first arrived.

"My *grand-père* smoked Gauloise, obtained them even after they were banned," Laurette said. "I loved the smell of them, the dark tobacco. I used to follow him around and sniff the thick smoke."

"Gross," I muttered. The blade looked unblemished. I tested it with my thumb. Faint pressure was all it took to yield a fine red line. It was sharp.

"Okay, I'll do it." Laurette held her hands out and gestured with her fingers. I laid the axe in her hands. She looked at the surgical cleanser, which I doused liberally over the blade and her hands. She looked at the woman's foot. I leaned over and squirted the cleanser over the foot. The foul odor coming from the foot made me gag.

"Where are you going to chop? How much of the foot do you need to take?"

"I don't know; I'll have to guess," Laurette said. She gulped. "Give her the Percocet."

"So, the party is in here?" asked a deep voice. Torsten stood in the door with his giant smile, his leather bag, and a rifle resting against his shoulder. His brilliant blue eyes swept over us and the Turkish woman, lingered on the axe in Laurette's hands, dropped to the woman's pus-filled, oozing foot. Cheerfully, he said, "I will join the party, yes?"

"What are you talking about, fool?" Laurette growled.

Torsten set his rifled against the tent wall. "Caris is crying by the gate. Tells me, she does, about a party. I like parties."

"There's no party here, we're performing a medical procedure," I said.

He marched over and swept the items on the tray table over to one side. He picked up the bottle of Percocet and laughed, a rich jolly thing like Santa Claus might emit. "Not going to help her!"

He set down his leather bag and unsnapped it. It folded open, a kit with all kinds of tools held in place by stretchy bands. There were needles and hoses and thermometers, forceps and scoopers and clippers, pads and pumps and tubes, and various scopes, including a stethoscope. Then there were items that looked like blacksmith tools. Torsten cast a glance at the woman's foot and brought out a hooked instrument with a sharp, curved, highly polished blade that was bent down at right angles.

"You are a doctor?" Laurette asked, suspicious.

"Veterinarian," Torsten answered cheerfully. "This is castrating knife for lambs. Nice, ya? Toes maybe we harvest instead of testicles?" He laid it down and picked up a syringe, tested it by squirting a drop out of the top. "It will put down a bull for a whole day. Much better than tooth medicine!"

"A veterinarian?" I repeated.

"I teach in Bologna." His face fell. Just for an instant, the death's-head flashed over him, making an empty skull of his face, remorseless black caves of his lightning-bright eyes. I wondered how crazy he was, and whether we should stand next to him while he held a sharp instrument. He said, "Bologna is no more. I used to teach there."

"Bologna?" Laurette still had the axe poised in her palms, but now it was tilted toward Torsten. Just in case, I thought. She exchanged a glance with me, confirming it.

"Yes, Bologna. Beautiful food and more beautiful women. The world will not be the same without it," he said. His English was rhythmic and accented, as if he were reciting Chaucer. "Rock and roll!" He injected the woman with his syringe. He bent close to her face and watched her; a few seconds later, complete relaxation swept over her, unfurling her body completely. He grinned. "Always it is nice when the patient does not try to bite me or gore me." He pulled a large pan from the corner of the tent, and gestured with it while he showed us all his white teeth in a giant smile. "Who is catching the meat?"

I WAS HAPPY when Laurette threw up right alongside me, outside the hospital tent, after the procedure. It made her seem more human and vulnerable like me, less like an invincible, eternally chic, herbal-knowledge-wielding Gorgon. Torsten was going to bury what had been culled from the Turkish woman. He'd taken her toes first, then decided that most of her foot had to go, to ensure that no infected tissue remained. He'd sewn her up. Then he had given her a shot of a strong antibiotic. He seemed confident that the woman would be fine when she woke in two or three days, which was how long the anesthetic he'd given her should last.

On his way out, he paused beside us to ask when dinner might be ready. I wiped my mouth with the back of my hand and pointed shakily to the mess tent. Another heave took me, and when I glanced to see where he'd gone, Torsten was swinging his rifle up against his shoulder while balancing in his other hand the pan full of a human appendage.

"What providence, that God sent Torsten to help us," Laurette said. She made a funny face, smacking her lips together as if after a meal.

I spat out a big gob of saliva, trying to clean off my tongue. "God? What God? I stopped believing in fairy tales a long time ago."

"No, you must believe," Laurette said, coughing. "Not in the silly formal God of catechism. If we are lucky, the mists erased that old barbaric notion, and religion with it."

"We've been so lucky, let's count on more good fortune."

"We can count on an excellent dinner right now, and that is good fortune," Laurette said. She picked up her chin with her usual saucy air and traipsed off toward the mess tent, swinging her hips to let me know that she had recovered before I did, and that she considered that a victory.

Laurette and I found Torsten seated at a table with the kids. He was regaling them with a story about delivering a baby racehorse while four generations of an Arabic family watched and cheered. He switched between languages easily, gesticulated, and shouted "Ya!" at random moments in his recitation, provoking laughs and gasps of wonder.

"Do we like him?" Laurette asked, as we stood at Cook's buffet table.

"Yes, but never, ever let him near me with that crooked knife," I said. I couldn't repress a shudder as Laurette and I shared a grin. Cook snarled at me, but disappeared into the

back with Laurette's plate. He waddled out and, with a flourish, presented her with some of the special stuff. Laurette
cooed back at him. I told them to get a room. Then we sat
down at the table with Masashi, who sat with his arms folded
and his eyes half-closed. I wondered what he was thinking.
Was he remembering everything he had lived through in his
ninety years on this planet? Or did he, like me, now live from
this moment to the next, haunted by a past that could never
again be? A past whose artifacts we were using up as they
crumbled around us, with no clue as to what new objects the
future might bring, or whether a viable future even existed?
Did we, the human race, have any time left?

"I would have performed the amputation, but it would
have been ugly." Laurette half-smiled. "It really might have
killed her. You weren't totally wrong."

"Really? You admit that I'm not always wrong?"

"I would not go so far as that." Laurette sniffed. "You are
certainly wrong in your disbelief. There is a God. Not in the
old sense, an angry man with a white beard. But a sense of
purpose that fills everything, everywhere, from an infinite
source. Yes, that exists."

"Once, maybe, I would have agreed with you." I thought
of the mists, and all the deaths I had witnessed. I recalled
the mists sweeping through the Paris *Opéra*, the *Apollo, Poetry
and Music* sculpture heating from verdigris to red, and then
imploding into grit and water. I thought of making my hand
ready to shoot Mandy in the head. "Now, no. I can't believe in
that. In anything, anymore."

"The purpose is bigger than we can comprehend, the
Source deeper," Laurette argued. "It is beyond our intelligence to grasp. Who are we to even try to understand? But
there is some reason why we are all here, now. Still alive.
Together. I feel it."

"I believe in the food in my hands right now," I said. "I
believe in every morning that my children open their eyes, and

every night that they lie back down to rest. I believe that life is random and chaotic. Empty and meaningless. We humans are an evolutionary accident. Now evolution is moving past us, going in a different direction. The mists will eradicate our children, or at best their children, from the whole earth."

"The mists are temporary. Meaning is eternal, it is everywhere and in all things," Laurette insisted. "Humanity is the Source's ultimate vessel for meaning. We will continue."

"Everything's gone. How can you say that?"

"Not everything is gone. The most important thing is left!"

"What is that?" I demanded.

She pointed her fork at me. "The information."

I stared at her. "Information?"

"The invisible information of all people," she explained. I gave her a blank look. "No, that's wrong. Not information. It is information, but it is bigger." She chewed thoughtfully, swallowed, nodded. "The mind. The mind of all people, everywhere. How do you say, collective consciousness. That is what is left."

"Even if there is a collective consciousness, what does that have to do with God?" I shot back.

Laurette smiled. "Everything."

10 MAYBE LAURETTE WAS ONTO SOME-
thing about the collective consciousness.
Over the next week, as we waited for
Arthur and the men to return, refu-
gees streamed into the camp. They came singly and in small
groups. They were wounded and hungry, filthy and terrified,
damaged, traumatized. They carried eclectic assortments of
goods and belongings: food and photos, paintings and books,
jewelry and a teapot that had been passed down from a grandmother's grandmother. One woman and her son brought a
skinny cow and two chickens in a wooden crate. Cook was
happy about the fresh milk since the canned stuff was running out. He informed me that I was no longer the only "*Belle
vache*" in camp. I mooed back at him, which brought laughter
from Newt and Mandy, who stood at my elbow.

The refugees spoke divers languages, but they all said the
same thing: they'd heard there was a safe camp. Some of them
had heard it was a camp with a woman who could heal with
her hands. I wanted to ask them, where did you hear this?

Who could possibly have known about the camp being a
safe zone, and about me? To whom could they have spoken,
when they were afraid of the marauding bands and hid themselves against discovery? Where did they get this information?
Was this what Xavier had meant when he spoke of a biomind,
and was it the same thing that Laurette meant by a collective
consciousness?

The refugees couldn't explain, and didn't want to. They wanted to eat and wash and find a tent to call their own. We used up the last of Arthur's store of tents, then built shanties. We took in forty people, mostly women and children and the elderly, plus a few men whom we sent to speak with Masashi and with Arthur's sentries. Torsten and Laurette tended wounds, with Torsten making endless jokes about hooves and horns.

The three of us were examining the Turkish woman, whom we'd moved to the main hospital area, when the kids came running in.

"They're back!" Mandy sang breathlessly. She flung her arms around me and squeezed. "We can see them riding in." She darted back out.

The men galloped around the camp walls in a thundering and unruly cluster, dust and torn green leaves spewing from the horses' hooves. Arthur was in the lead, but he didn't seek me out with his eyes when he reached the corral, as he always did. He leapt from his big roan, which was foaming at the bit, and pulled a bound man off the horse behind him. He jerked the man upright. I was thirty meters away from the corral, but I could see Arthur shaking with fury.

The bound man was Xavier, and they were both covered in blood.

Theo didn't ride into the corral, but threw himself off his sweaty horse and grabbed my shoulder. "Tell children leave!" he said urgently. His shirt was splashed with blood.

"Theo, are you all right?" I cried. "What's going on?"

"I good," he said. "Please tell children go!" He grabbed the reins of his horse and threw a pleading look over his stocky shoulder as he led his horse into the corral.

"Caris, Shoshana, take the kids back to your tent," I said. I used the voice they all knew meant, *Don't argue with me.* Shoshana looked aghast at the horses' near stampede. She ran off, holding Felix with one hand and Mandy with the other.

Caris herded the other kids into a tight group and ushered them off. Bojana approached with Dragomir to see what the commotion was. I waved for her to stay away. She nodded, and looped back around in the direction from which she'd come.

By the time I'd turned back to watch Arthur, he'd lashed Xavier to one of the posts with a leather strap. Xavier was pleading and babbling, squirming desperately at the post. He'd been shorn, as all the men had, and his close-cropped blond head was spattered with blood, which I traced to an oozing wound on the top of his shoulder.

"Arthur, no, I've been with you from the beginning!" Xavier screamed. "You must understand! What you're doing is too dangerous. You can't outmaneuver the mists! I had our best interests—"

"Enough!" Arthur shouted. "I and I alone know what to do with the mists!"

"Interesting camp, this is," Torsten said, from behind me. "The men ride the horses hard, yes?"

"Not usually, no, they are usually conscientious," Laurette said, her tone thoughtful. "Emma, what is happening?"

"I don't know," I murmured.

"We need a stronger alliance, that's all I was trying to do, if any of us are going to survive! You know that! Please, Arthur, you of all people know...." Xavier begged.

"Stop!" Arthur grabbed Xavier's throat. I walked toward them but Arthur shook his head once, not meeting my eyes. Vasily and Claude hung back, too. James went to join them, gave me a sick look through the crowd of panting horses and somber men. They were all dirty and unshaven, ten day's worth of beard grown in, and their eyes were hollow and dark.

I swallowed and stayed back. The men had barely all dismounted when Arthur called, "This is the penalty for betrayal!"

Arthur leaned forward. Something caught the sun and flashed, a bright silver streak. Then Xavier screamed. His head fell forward onto his chest. I wended my way through the knots of men and horses. Finally I could see: Arthur was holding a knife. He'd slashed a straight line down Xavier's stomach. Arthur punched his hand in through the wound and pulled out a slimy, bloody length of tubing that wriggled like a serpent. Arthur kept pulling out the tubing. Xavier's screams intensified to a pitch and volume I would not have believed possible for a human, and I had heard a lot of screaming when the mists consumed people.

Arthur stood back from Xavier and threw the viscera onto the ground. Xavier screamed and writhed, but he was held to the post by the leather strap. I glanced at Arthur's face. I had never seen such a look of satisfied vengeance on anyone's face, ever. He frightened me.

I was unarmed because I'd been healing the sick and injured. I came up beside Vasily and gestured with my hand. Pale and drawn, Vasily looked me in the eye. He pulled out his gun and laid it in my palm. It was an Ortgies .32, smooth and well-balanced in my hand. It had a grip safety that I pressed off. A number of old Germans carried this weapon, and one elderly man, bragging about his, had shown me how to use it. That was in the first few weeks After, when I was just beginning to understand what life now consisted of. One dark night, the old guy had walked away from our campfire without a word. We'd never seen him again.

I hoped he was right about the gun's efficiency. I stepped up beside Arthur.

"Arthur, you will regret this!" Xavier shrilled.

Arthur said, in a voice so low that only I heard it, "I have more regrets, every day of my life, than you can imagine. This isn't one of them." His mouth kept moving, but I raised the gun and aimed at the center of Xavier's forehead.

The screaming stopped.

Arthur wheeled on me. I didn't back down, though I quailed inside. His chest heaved, and a blue vein pulsed on his forehead. His cheeks were scarlet and his mouth contorted; his gray eyes were purplish-black with rage. I turned away and walked back through the silent crowd of men. I pressed the safety back on and returned the gun to Vasily.

I kept walking, back to the hospital tent and the Turkish woman, whose footless leg was no longer swollen, and who felt well enough to eat.

James and Laurette came for me after I'd taken a plate of food to the woman.

"Em, you have to talk to him," James said. "Talk him down off the ledge. It can't go on like this."

"Fine, thanks, and how are you?" I asked. "Good ten days out in the bush?"

"Friggin' nightmare," James said.

"Laurette and I almost performed an amputation with an axe," I said. "A veterinarian did it for us. Lovely bit of work, that. You oughta try it. Torsten buried her foot out beyond the latrines. Have you met Torsten? Big guy with a funny accent. He brought news of Bologna. It's gone."

"We barely ate or slept," James said. "There's a nasty rogue group out there on our western flank, and they're growing. Turns out they were communicating with Xavier via a walkie-talkie that still works. Xavier was supposed to kill Arthur, and, at that moment, they'd attack, kill us, and take the camp and supplies."

"A walkie-talkie that works?" I rose from the stool. "How did Arthur survive?"

"Theo was watching, shot Xavier as he struck Arthur," James said. He ran his hands over the gray and brown stubble on his face. "Arthur took a glancing blow instead of a killing one. Theo said you told him to watch Xavier and protect Arthur." He gave me a look of total despair, and maybe my biomind was reading James' biomind, but I knew in that instant that Arthur was off his rocker.

"Okay, okay, I got this," I said. "Have you seen to Arthur's wound?"

"You're shitting me, right?" James said. He laughed. "It'd be safer for me to dress a pissed-off tyrannosaurus rex."

"Maybe you could use some of Torsten's magic sleeping potion," Laurette suggested.

"Tempting, but we have to let him wake up sometime," I said. I went to collect bandages and a tube of antibiotic ointment from an old steamer trunk that served as our medicine closet.

"Left collarbone," James said. "Superficial, from what I could see." I paused to look at him and he made a rolling gesture with his hands: could I please speed it up?

At the corral, two men were taking down Xavier's body. Arthur stood nearby, reprimanding some poor young guy who'd put a saddle in the wrong place, or some such nonsense. Arthur's knife hung in its place at his belt, but his hand rested on the hilt.

"Arthur," I said. He kept scolding the beleaguered man, who wasn't much older than Caris, and whose fearful eyes kept darting to the knife Arthur was fondling. I yelled, "Arthur!"

He whipped around so aggressively that I had to fight myself to keep from jumping back. In a softer tone of voice, I said: "Walk with me."

Arthur kind of growled, but he followed. I took his hand and led him out past the sunflowers and purple lavender, along the stream to the rock, my rock, where he'd combed my hair. I pointed, and he shifted his weight on the balls of his feet like a restless boxer; but then he seated himself.

"Take off your shirt," I said. His beautiful, ragged face softened just a fraction. I added, "I never have to say that to you twice!" He grinned reluctantly, with only one side of his mouth, and then he pulled the torn and bloody shirt over his head. I took a rag from my pocket, dipped it in the stream, and mopped the crusted blood off his chest. It took several sops of the rag in the water, and then some scrubbing that Arthur bore without flinching, to lay bear the jagged cut that ran down from his neck, over his collarbone, and along his pectoral. It was superficial, as James had observed, but it was probably painful. It should have been cleaned before now. Didn't Arthur understand the risks of infection? I said, "This has festered for a while."

"How'd you know about Xavier?" he asked, in a gravelly voice.

"Never felt good about him." I didn't want to tell him about Newt's warning. He was not unkind to the children, but I didn't want him to think he could use her gift for his own purposes. He had a harsh streak. I also wasn't sure I wanted to mention Xavier's oblique comments about alliances.

"I'd be dead but for you."

"I don't know." I tried for some levity, gave him a lopsided smile. "You're handy with a gun and a blade."

He shook his head. "Never saw it coming."

The cut was cleanish now, although I wished I'd brought some of the surgical scrub we'd used for the amputation. I squeezed ointment onto his neck and massaged it down over the wound. "Cut that loose. Don't carry it."

"I trusted him. He betrayed me!" Arthur's whole body tensed, the ligaments on his neck and the muscles on his belly standing out in high relief.

"You showed him."

"Not funny!" he roared.

"Easy," I said. "We're all so scared and traumatized that we do surprising things these days. Wild, out-of-character things. Stuff we never would have dreamt of doing nine months ago. Like going up to some strange man and offering to sleep with him in exchange for food and shelter for orphaned kids."

Arthur was quiet for a long while. I kept applying the ointment. His broad chest emanated heat. I stole a glance at his face, which, even shuttered with thought and sueded with a week's growth of black beard, was gorgeous in the extreme. I placed my hands over the cut. The feathery tingles of my unasked-for healing gift swirled into him, thick and juicy and rushing. His heart slowed. Some of the tension in his shoulders eased.

He murmured, "Your hands feel wonderful. Now I see what all the fuss is about."

I shrugged. "I let in a bunch of refugees while you were gone." He nodded. "Somehow they all knew we were here. The camp, me, the kids. A safe zone."

"Word gets out."

"How?" I wondered. "People are afraid to talk to each other, afraid of being captured by the roving gangs, afraid of being killed for their food supplies or weapons."

"Human intelligence, the army called it. Humint. It happens. People connect even when they don't seem to. Information is exchanged, tactical and contextual information about ground forces, strength, vulnerabilities, and intentions. All vital in irregular warfare."

"I don't think of you as an army person."

"I was one." He raised his eyebrows briefly and his face blanked out, as if he wore a mask, the sculpted mask of a god.

"The thing is, people don't connect the way they did Before. We're all terrified of each other because of the destruction and chaos. We're afraid of the madness. It's different now."

"The buildings, the global infrastructure, that's gone. People are the same."

"Are they?" I challenged them. "Xavier said something odd to me. I've been thinking about it. He said the mists attack the "biomind." It was very precise, very scientific, the way he phrased it. That strange word, biomind. Do you know what he was talking about?"

"Xavier." Arthur spat the name. He twisted his head away from me, and his breath came in short, fast bursts. The healing tingles in my hands intensified, responding to his agitation.

"Maybe this biomind thing, which he seemed to think was a trait all human beings have, is what other people call the collective consciousness. So the knowledge of this camp is just out there, floating around, like the mists float," I said. My hands wanted to move, so I let them travel to Arthur's solar plexus, where they rested.

"Telepathic transfer of information," he murmured. "There was a biologist who spoke of the Morphic fields, the field within and around a Morphic unit—"

"Whoa, hold your horses, Perfessor. Explain that in simple terms so that even a dumb artist can understand," I smiled.

"You're anything but dumb, Emma," Arthur said, solemnly. He took a breath. "A Morphic unit...is just a fancy way of saying one unit of form, organization, or arrangement. In this case, a Morphic unit is one individual of a species. The Morphic field is a field of information. It holds and organizes that species' characteristic structure and patterns of activity. So the Morphic field of a horse holds the pattern of manes and tails, and also of grazing. The information is propagated from one unit to another—from one horse to another—via resonance."

"You must have an IQ of a million."

His face lightened a little, then hardened. "I don't think in those terms anymore. What matters is our adaptability, our practical ingenuity. That's what humans need now to rebuild."

"Rebuild—you're optimistic."

"With good reason. The human Morphic field is special. It contains thoughtstuff, language patterns, even visual representations. Images. We have an incredible advantage."

"We'll need every advantage we have. But I don't know

how our advantages will get rid of the mists."

"They will," he swore. "The biomind, the collective consciousness. It's creative. It's evolutionary. It will come up with a solution. We'll tap into it and use it. I'll tap into it and use it!"

"You know a lot about this stuff."

"I was a professor of sorts. I used to know a lot about a lot of stuff. Most of it's useless now." He took my hand off his middle and kissed my palm. "You offered yourself to me for food and shelter? I thought you liked my beard."

"You betcha. I'm a sucker for a bug-infested bearskin."

"Cheeky," he said. He put his hands on my hips. "You smell good."

"I smell clean, which is more than I can say for you." I gave him a small smile. His eyes were gray again, and very intent.

"You and your bloody rules about being clean, brushing teeth, and not having lice," he said. I could feel him get an erection. Not directly, but there was a faster tempo in the current of air between us. My nipples pricked in response, which surprised me.

"Have you eaten yet?"

"I'll eat later." He grasped my arms and pulled me up against him.

"I'm not done," I said, trying to push away.

"Neither am I." He kissed me, deeply. It wasn't brief.

"You can't go on this way, you know," I said, when he released me. I was unsteady on my feet, so I scooted up to sit beside him on the rock.

"Can't go on kissing you?" He slipped his arm around my shoulders and nuzzled my hair out of the way. He nipped my neck playfully, flicked my earlobe with his tongue.

"Being ruthless. Like with Xavier."

"Not your fucking business," he said. His body tensed again and he squeezed me against his side, roughly.

"Yes, it is. Remember about rebuilding?" I pushed his arm

away and drew up my knees and clasped them with my arms. "That you were meant to lead people? Now, After. That's not leading, what you did to him. It's terrorizing."

"I won't tolerate betrayal."

"Why take it so personally? These are hard, confusing times."

"It was personal," Arthur muttered. "Xavier has known me a long time."

"Since the beginning, he said. What did he mean?"

"Xavier worked for me, when I was in charge of special research projects for the army. He had specialized knowledge. He was one of the first people I brought in."

"The old structures are gone," I reminded him. He gave me a stony look. I shrugged. "Make people take an oath of loyalty or something. If they betray it, exile them. They'll take their chances with the mists and the gangs," I said. "But you're like...the father of a new world. Isn't that your ambition? You've got to set an example. In order to build something good, you've got to be like Moses or something. Beyond reproach."

"That's Caesar's wife, and that would be you, darling." He gave me a funny, level look, and his eyes were piercing.

"Caesar's concubine, more like it," I said, lightly.

"We should do something about that," he murmured.

Not now. I looked away. "Have you met Torsten?"

"The Swede? Seems like a decent fellow."

"Everything he says sounds like he's speaking Middle English." I laughed. "I feel like I'm back in high school, reading Chaucer."

Arthur grinned. "His Italian and German sound the same way. Reminds me of an old priest who used to lead tours in Rome, at the Catacombs."

"Rome." My heart clenched inside me: was the Sistine Chapel intact? Michelangelo's sublime *Last Judgment*, and the ceiling with the heart-rending *Creation of Adam*—the pinnacles of human artistic achievement. Did they still exist? Could they?

"I try not to think about it." Arthur was watching me intently. I must have looked bemused, because he explained, "You're wondering about the great art in Rome."

"How do you know?"

"Your face shows everything you think."

"It's the telepathic transfer of information," I teased, leaning into him.

He smiled crookedly. "Don't need it with you. Your beautiful face shouts everything. Never play poker."

"I'm good at poker. I used to win all the time when I played in art school in Philly. Being underestimated is a position of strength."

"You would think about the art in Rome. You're an artist. James showed me the book you illustrated. You have classical training. You're talented. Brilliant. You're the real thing."

"Not anymore." I smiled. "Now I'm a shepherdess for eight kids, and your dutiful bed warmer."

"You're sticking with the story that it's all about duty?"

"Well, you know." I shrugged. "It sounds good. Noble. I aspire to that."

"I wouldn't use the word 'noble' to describe you in my bed," Arthur said. "In fact, that's the last word I'd use."

"That's not very gentlemanly of you."

"I'm fairly certain you don't want me to be a gentleman in bed. It's one of the things I love about you. But I will be one out of bed. I'd like to make our arrangement more formal—"

I didn't like this tack, so I interrupted. "When do we take Laurette back to the women's camp and retrieve Robert? If we can tear him away."

"I suppose that's next on the agenda. Will's feeling better, isn't he?"

In the distance, as if on cue, two men came toward us. Blade-thin and pale even from here, Will leaned heavily on a cane. Nwokocha, beside him, walked with a spring in his step and a swing to his arms. I pointed. Arthur sprang to his feet, delight radiating from him. The anger and vengefulness had evaporated. I was glad to see it.

A FORTNIGHT LATER, Arthur was showing me how to saddle the chestnut mare. Her name, it turned out, was some French version of Rosinante, which I shortened for my own purposes. Rosie was demonstrating how horses resist being saddled by bloating their bellies.

"Don't jerk the girth like that, she won't like it," sang Shoshana, who sat on the fence watching us. Sure enough, the naughty bitch whipped her head around and snapped at me. I leapt back just in time to avoid a black-and-blue spot on my arm.

"Quit!" Arthur commanded, jerking once on the lead rope. He gave me a cool glare. "Emma, are you paying attention? Don't let her crowd you. She's testing you to see who's going to be the boss, you or her."

"I don't care who's the boss. I just want to ride her," I said, crossly. I adjusted the waistband of my leggings under my dress, then climbed up onto the horse.

"You have to care, or you won't be able to ride her," Shoshana called. "They don't think like us, Emma. They're prey. We're predators."

"Not me—I'm a peaceful healer!" I said lightly.

"Liar," Arthur chortled. "I've seen the way you grip a gun. There's a stone-cold killer inside you. I bet you've shot twenty people since the Day."

"You're hurting my feelings!" I faked a pout. My pretend outrage almost cost me my seat on the horse. What the hell— I wasn't pretending completely. I certainly did not think of myself as a killer.

"Squeeze with your thighs. I know you're good at that," Arthur said. "Why would your feelings be hurt? To be human is to be born to kill and consume. But if that's all we do, we're in trouble. In fact, we have to consciously channel aggression away from destruction. We have to purposefully use our intention for building and creating. Isn't that the lesson of the apocalypse?"

"There is no lesson from the apocalypse. It's an impersonal and random tragedy with no meaning," I muttered. "I am squeezing with my thighs!"

"Of course there's a lesson. It's that we have to use our power to build and nurture, not to destroy," Arthur said. "It's that we have to take our powers seriously and be responsible, even for unintended consequences of our actions."

His intensity surprised me. I eyed him. "You've thought about this a lot."

"I've had to," he said raggedly, with far more despair than a horseback-riding lesson warranted. I opened my mouth to question him, but Laurette hailed me.

"Emma, may we speak with you?" called Laurette. She stood with Ginny and Caris at the entrance to the corral.

"Saved by the bell," I sang, relieved. I slid down off Rosie.

"That's 'Belle' to you," Laurette punned, making the French lateral "l" so that the word became "Beauty." She and I exchanged a small smile. I was actually going to miss her. Now that she was going back to the women's camp, who would criticize me all the time? The thought made a lump in my throat.

"Are you ready to go?" I asked her, and I couldn't keep the wistfulness from my voice. She nodded slowly, her mouth drooping. Maybe she would miss me, too. Who at Tara's camp would argue with her all the time?

"We want to talk to you," Caris said, in her soft, husky voice. Something about her sweet voice and the vulnerable expression on her lovely brown face made my heart syncopate. My life was changing again; I could sense it.

"What's going on?" I asked. I stopped in front of the three of them.

"We want to go with Laurette to the women's camp," Caris said. She didn't take her velvety dark eyes off mine. She must have seen my immediate bleakness. She put her hand on my arm. "We love you, Emma. But you know how it is for me. I'll feel better there." Her head turned on its stem like a flower in the wind, and I followed her gaze: Vasily and Theo saddling their horses, Arthur standing with Rosie, men moving about camp, doing their business. Shoshana sat on the fence and Hikaru sat on the grass outside the corral, nursing her infant. There were other women, too, now that we'd begun taking in refugees. But it was still largely a camp full of men. And Caris had been badly damaged by the men who found her After.

"I thought you were happy here," I said. "I thought you felt safe."

"I'll feel happier and safer and freer there," she said, in a soft and solemn tone.

"No mists here. No one's forcing you to do anything," I murmured.

"You know what I mean." She smiled. Her hand squeezed my arm. "It's what I love about you, Emma. You always know what I mean."

"I feel happy with Laurette," Genevra said. Now that she had returned to herself, her French accent was strong and sharp. She'd turned into a mini-adult, a small clone of Laurette. Ginny said, "She is like my aunt. I go with her. Please, Emma."

"I would stay if you needed me, but you don't," Caris said, anxiously. She twisted her hands together in her old nervous gesture. "You've got other women. And Arthur. There's a real group here. It's not just you anymore, taking care of the children. You'll let us go with Laurette, won't you, Emma?"

I wouldn't stop them. They weren't my prisoners. They were beloved companions, entrusted to my care during the worst times, the end times. It had been my privilege to have them at my side. I had to swallow the ache in my throat before I could answer. I reached out and clasped Caris' hands to keep them from knotting together. "Of course. You can go. Are you packed?"

"Yes. We talked about it last night, Ginny and me," Caris said. She held up the backpack that she'd carried all the long months that we wandered through France, looking for food and trying to stay alive. The backpack I'd insisted each of them carry, filled with food and a knife and a book and a bottle of water—the necessities. Caris smiled tremulously. "I packed my toothbrush, Emma. You should be proud of me."

"Me, too," Genevra said, "And our lesson books." She lifted her backpack with a bright smile. "Are you proud of me, too?"

"I'm so proud of you, both of you," I said, hoarsely. Caris set down her backpack and wrapped her arms around me. So did Ginny. The three of us stood entwined. I felt Caris' gentle lithe strength and Ginny's fierce, sweet, seven-year-old friskiness. I tried to absorb them utterly, to engrave the sense impressions of them into my arms and chest, so that I'd never forget what it was like to hold them. Who knew if I'd ever see them again? Then I pushed them away, gently.

"Give me a minute, okay?" I whispered. I walked out of the corral. Arthur called my name. I hollered, "Arthur, is there a horse for them to use?" But I didn't look back at him. I didn't want any of them to see my face. There were no tears, just naked loss. They'd been through too much for me to inflict it on them.

STUMBLING, I FOLLOWED the stream out and up to a ridge, from which I could see the whole rectangle of the camp. Inside the walls, the camp was getting crowded, and the tent lines were less precise, with refugees continuing to arrive. We'd even started building shanties on the outside of the walls for the folks who kept coming. I sat on a rock and huddled into myself. Down at the corral, small figures poured through the gates. The other children were arriving, Newt and Mandy and Felix and Marco, throwing themselves at Caris and Genevra, who stood with Shoshana. Even Dragomir showed up—in Bojana's arms, naturally. She would have to let him walk sometime. He wasn't a baby anymore. But I understood her need to clasp him to her, after losing him, and everything else.

Vasily and Theo had mounted their horses and were wait-ing outside the corral. I didn't see Arthur, and Laurette had mounted Robert's horse. I watched as the children finished hugging each other. I should be down there, I berated myself. I should help the children with this parting. We were losing two of our own; it couldn't be easy for the rest of them. Then Ginny clambered up on Rosie, and Caris got up on the saddle behind her.

A lavender butterfly with brown spots on its undersides fluttered up out of the rock roses. I rose to my feet. What was I going to ride?

"You ride with me," called Arthur. He was trotting his big roan toward me. I should have heard him coming—would have, if I hadn't been so thoroughly absorbed in the distant spectacle of farewell.

"You're coming to the women's camp?" I asked. "You'll have to wear yellow. That's what Tara said."

He rode up alongside me, held out his hand. I let him pull me up into the saddle in front of him. I got settled, and he kissed the back of my head. His arms circled me to hold the reins, and his strong, warm chest cradled my back. The knife's edge of my loss dulled. He said, "You'll manage, Emma. You're strong." Those were the kindest words anyone had ever spoken to me.

THE WOMEN MUST have seen us coming, because Rob-ert suddenly stumbled out of the tree line. There was no mistaking the flagrant red hair. I dismounted and walked Laurette, Caris, and Genevra across a hundred meters of vacant meadow to where Robert waited. I wondered what community had once stood here, at the edges of the forest. If Mandy were here, she could look, and tell me about the shadows that roamed the land.

"This is it. Thanks for the hospitality," Laurette said. She stared at me wide-eyed for a moment, and then threw her arms around me, squeezing me in a big hug. "You don't have to be so tough all the time, Emma. You can be like me, soft and open." She stepped back and patted my face. Caris and Ginny waved; there was no need for hugs, because we'd done that already. They followed Laurette into the leafy shadows.

Robert came up beside me. He looked none the worse for his weeks away, and I threw my arm around him, glad to see him.

"Lose some, did you?" he asked. I nodded. He said softly, "Me, too." He didn't explain and my voice was missing, so I couldn't ask what he meant. Then two women stepped out: Tara and the black woman with the high cheekbones and nifty machine gun. The black woman and Robert clasped hands.

"I wanted to see how you are, Emma," Tara said softly. "To remind you, you can always come here."

"She's happy with me," Arthur called. He trudged up behind me and draped his arm around my shoulders.

Tara looked at him with an inscrutable expression. Something passed between them, something intimate but not sexual. I did not feel excluded, although I was not included. Arthur said, almost defensively, "She's safe. She has everything she needs."

Tara's sandy eyebrows arched up near her hairline. "So you haven't told her?"

Arthur drew back as if bitten by a serpent. I asked, "Told me what?"

"I live in the present," Arthur said, biting off his words.

Tara shrugged. Arthur said brusquely, "Laurette has a map. We're here if you need us."

"And we're here for you," Tara said. Another look full of old information passed between them. She lifted her hand in farewell, ushered the black woman ahead of her into the shade. Arthur, Robert and I crossed back toward where Vasily and Theo waited on their horses.

Halfway out, the black woman hurtled toward us and threw herself at Robert. She and Robert kissed, passionately. She stepped back and gripped his shoulders. Her lovely face was haunted. She nodded once to me, then ran back into the forest.

11 VASILY WAS THE CHEERFUL ONE AS WE trotted back in the direction we'd come. He whistled and sang. Turned out he had a fine tenor voice and his *Libiamo ne' lieti calici* from "La Traviata" was worth listening to.

"That was a good evening at the Volksoper in Vienna," Arthur said. His voice held a rare nostalgia. He smiled in Vasily's direction. "I believe you sang that same piece in the Drei Husaren. Will sang Violetta's part."

"And the maitre d' was none too pleased!" Vasily chortled. "I probably shouldn't have jumped on the table."

"We weren't the first fellows to get drunk and sing at that fine establishment," Arthur said.

"Might have been the last, though," Vasily rejoined. "I like to remember Mackridge and Khan and Hammy that way, full of wine and song."

"I don't like to remember anything," Arthur said softly. "Too much goes along with the memories. Too much regret. Too much loss. Guilt. It's unbearable." His voice was soft and distant. I was stunned to hear him voice these emotions. I turned sharply to question him, but he'd already moved on. He was saying, "We should have music at the camp. There's a guitar in the stores. We have to hold on to culture until we recreate it."

"I was singing with the wee ones," Robert said, with a glum expression. "I'm grand, amn't I. Like to go out on the piss."

"That's not the only way to have music. When Will and Shinji recreate the Tesla technology and make an adapter, we can power up speakers and an audio player." Arthur was talking more to himself than to us.

"That's ambitious," I commented, looking sideways at Arthur. I still wanted to ask him about his guilt. Regret and loss I understood, but why did he feel guilt?

"I'm ambitious for a drop of whiskey," Robert muttered, morosely.

"*Bibamus, moriendum est*," Vasily replied. He launched into another aria, raising one hand passionately into the air. His horse laid its ears back against its head.

"Drop of anything," Robert said. "Mouthwash. Lighter fluid. Ladies' cologne. Something with alcohol, just to get myself bollixed."

"We have a case of something or other that Cook found," Arthur told him. "Ask Emma to get a bottle for you. Cook likes her—he'll give her anything." Arthur was teasing, so I made a face. He said, "Let's go another few kilometers and then find somewhere to conceal ourselves. We'll rest for the day. It's safer to ride at night."

Soon after, to the ongoing strains of Vasily's arias, we found a dirt embankment and a tall pile of stone and wood and glass, scattered paper and broken furniture and computer LCD screen fragments. It had once been a *mairie*, a town hall. A tribe of cats, none wearing collars, had taken up residence there, but they were amenable to sharing. Haphazard aisles snaked through the debris, as if someone had sheltered here before us, months ago. The area around the *mairie* was salted with fine yellow grit, which could once have been people or other municipal buildings or homes—or anything, really—consumed and then excreted by the mists.

Arthur caught me gazing at the sand. "It's safe here now," he said confidently. "At least from the mists."

We led the horses in and found places to hole up. Arthur settled our horses next to each other. He lay down with his back to an upended desk and drew me into his arms, settling me against his chest. Robert, still uncharacteristically mournful, curled up into himself beside us, with Vasily and Theo and their horses in the next aisle over. Arthur pulled his gun out of its holster and held it in the hand that was hanging off my ribcage. "Just in case," he said. He kissed my temple and instantly fell asleep.

It took me longer to doze. It wasn't just the bright sunshine. I couldn't shake the weirdness of the many slit golden irises staring at me. Some of the cats were even purring. We hadn't touched them, so they were responding simply to having people nearby.

Before, I'd had a Labrador mix named Kippie, a playful golden-coated mutt with one black paw. He'd been left with a friend from Mandy's kindergarten class when we all went on vacation last December, Haywood and Beth to Canada to see his mother, and Mandy and me to Paris to meet with the French publisher of a book I'd illustrated. We were all going to meet back in Manhattan on Christmas Eve, go to see the Christmas tree at Rockefeller Center. I wondered what had become of Kippie. Was he thinking of us when the mists rolled through Manhattan, bursting everything in their path? Had he somehow lived, and was he even now jumping over heaps of rubbish, wagging his tail at bereft survivors seeking shelter in the wreckage?

WE ROSE AT dusk and turned the horses out to graze, then ate cold canned food, *soupe au pistou* and *cassoulet au confit porc* and William Saurin brand *gratin dauphinois*. I left a few bits in the bottom and put the can near a scrawny orange tabby kitten, who knocked over the can and lodged his whole head in it, eating. I took a few private moments out behind the rubbish heap to relieve myself, and then squirted bottled water and a dab of toothpaste onto my toothbrush and cleaned my mouth.

"Nothing good," Theo said anxiously, as we saddled and mounted the horses. Arthur gave him a penetrating look, but Theo shook his head and shrugged. He had an uneasy feeling. We should have trusted it and rode back the way we'd come. But all of us were eager to return to camp, and we pressed on, as the sun dropped into the horizon like a plumb weight falling, and the sky dimmed from viscous green-blue to peach and gold, and finally to indigo. Vasily was humming, and Robert was reciting Yeats under his breath, apparently for his horse's enjoyment. Theo swung his head around like a German shepherd, looking for something that hadn't yet appeared.

I drew my horse up alongside Arthur's. "Arthur, what are you keeping from me?"

He looked away. "You mean what Tara said."

"Xavier once told me to ask you what you did Before."

"Xavier," he said, his face twisting like a dishrag wrung out.

"So, what did you do, Before?"

"Classified research for the military."

"What kind of classified research? Did it have to do with the biomind?" I pressed him. He gave me a forbidding look, half-closed lids and a tight mouth. I said, "It can't still be classified. There's no military left."

"I'm left."

"Why did you mention guilt, when you talked about not wanting to remember?" I asked. "Loss, regret, pain, yes. But why guilt?"

"Someone here," Theo barked. I felt it, too: we were being watched. I drew up my horse and yanked my gun from my pocket. Simultaneously, Arthur swung his rifle up to rest against his shoulder, and Vasily's Ortgies was trained out over his horse's ears. Theo gripped his horse with both knees while cocking pistols with both hands. Only Robert seemed bemused, and slow.

But it was already too late. Silent men on horseback encircled us, dark shapes about twenty meters out. They were some forty strong, and even in the dimming light, it was clear that they were well armed. I was glad to see that they weren't wearing red capes, though there were other equally dangerous rogue bands. Arthur motioned, and we drew up beside each other. Our horses felt the fever pitch of tension and huddled together.

A bulky man with very erect carriage rode toward us. A hank of hair flopped down over the right side of his face, and when his horse's gait sent the hair flapping up, a huge, ropey scar was visible across his right cheek and chin. "Lower your weapons," he called. His voice was strongly accented. Russian. Arthur did not lower his rifle. The man ignored him, and instead looked at me appraisingly, tilting his head back to survey me.

"Is that the woman healer?" the man called. None of us answered. The circle of riders shrank in toward us. I could see the sclera of the riders' eyes, pearlescent slicks in the lowering dusk. Arthur's left hand inched toward the little pistol in his belt. Theo was scanning the other men, looking for something, for someone. His gaze settled on a tall man in the shadows at two o'clock. The man's head was cocked and his hands were relaxed, and the other riders flicked glances at him.

"Is that the woman with healing power?" the scarred man repeated. Again, we didn't answer. The man in the shadows kicked his horse and rode into the center, directly in front of Arthur, so that his horse's nose almost touched Arthur's horse's nose.

"Hello, Arthur," the man said. He was tall and blond, with craggy, thick features and shaggy blond brows knitting together over deeply-set eyes. He wore a dark shirt with a vest over it, and an ammunition belt around one shoulder.

"Alexei," Arthur said, in a cold, tight voice.

"Are you enjoying the fruits of your labors?" Alexei asked, in a lazy voice. Arthur's face took on a sick cast. He didn't say anything, and Alexei shrugged. "She is woman healer?" When we still didn't answer, he brought his gun up and aimed it at Arthur. I touched my heels to Rosie's sides, startling her. She leapt out of our tight pack. Arthur exclaimed, but I guided the mare to step around and nose in between Arthur's and Alexei's horses.

"Why do you want to know?" I asked.

"Arthur, you have something I want," Alexei said, not taking his eyes from mine. "I take it from you. It is fair. You take everything else."

"Who's sick?" I asked. Alexei blinked once, and in that infinitesimal pulse, fear showed in his ruthless face.

"Emma, come back here," Arthur said, in a low, controlled voice. But I didn't listen. We could neither bluff nor shoot our way out of this confrontation. Nor could Arthur summon the mists in time to save us. We'd be shot dead long before they arrived. These quiet riders had every advantage.

The circle of horses tightened in around Arthur, Theo, Vasily, and Robert, cutting them off from me. Alexei and I were apart, outside the circle.

"Who's dying?" I asked. Alexei's gaze on me sharpened, and his mouth tightened. His brow dipped toward me. And then I knew. The answer appeared whole and full in my head, perhaps because of Laurette's invisible information or Xavier's biomind, or maybe simply Newt's gift of prophecy: *his son*.

"Emma, *now*," Arthur called.

"I can't help your son if you kill them," I told Alexei, as if he and I were alone. "I'll be useless with grief. He's dying, so decide. I'll come with you, and I'll heal him. But only if they live. They live, and he lives. Your decision."

"Dmitri," Alexei said, lifting his hand.

"No!" I heard Arthur cry.

A dull crack sounded. I craned around, saw Arthur slumping in his saddle and the bulky, scarred man pulling the butt of his rifle back from Arthur's forehead. Alexei's men knocked out Vasily, Theo, and Robert, as well. Alexei called out a few words in Russian and some of his men dismounted and pulled my companions off their horses.

"They live," Alexei said. His English was chewy, nearly swallowed by his Russian accent. He smiled humorlessly. "They do not need horses and guns." He focused on the gun in my hand, and Dmitri rode up with his palm out. I gave him the gun.

"Leave them; we have to go now," I said. "Your son is dying. We may not be in time."

"His time is your time," Alexei said, scowling. "I offer you deal like you offer me. He lives, you live. He dies, you die."

"I'll know if you kill them. I won't be able to help your son," I said, pointing to Arthur and the others on the ground. I wanted to make sure he understood: Arthur and the others must not be killed. Alexei glared. Stubbornly, I said, "Leave them there alive!"

"I hope you are good as you think you are." He kicked his heels into his horse and galloped off. I followed, clinging to the mare, bouncing awkwardly. Alexei must have looked back and noticed my ineptitude. He pulled up abruptly. I barely managed to bring the mare to a halt.

"Da, you cannot ride," he said, with an expression of disgust. He reached across and grabbed me by the back of my dress, half-lifted and half-dragged me onto the saddle behind him. "Hold to me," he said. I wrapped myself around him, and he took off.

Alexei rode hard. I was too terrified to guess the direction. He cantered his horse through the night, his focus unwavering. My bladder filled and the awkward straddle behind him left me in pain. I kept my mouth shut and clung to him.

MOUNTED SENTRIES LET us pass just as dawn broke over the land. We rode through a makeshift camp that was clearly mobile, unlike our camp. It had no walls, just groups of ragged people, pallets piled high with objects, and tents in clusters. Around Alexei's shoulder, I glimpsed haggard people rising from blankets on the ground. A dozen Chinese women were roped together, and had slept in a weave. Even from my brief glimpse, I could see that most of them were spattered with blood.

We stopped outside an olive-green tent like the ones used in our camp. I fell down off the horse. A blonde woman rushed out of the tent, weeping. She threw herself at Alexei.

I hobbled into the tent.

Sobbing people stood around a cot. I shouldered them aside. A slim, delicately-boned boy of about ten years lay on the bed, his lips parted, his dark eyes glassy and empty. His chest wasn't moving. With his fine silver-blond hair, creamy skin, and black lashes, he looked like a porcelain doll. I thought he had just passed, maybe a few seconds ago. My hands were empty of the rushing tingles, but I laid them over his heart anyway. His body was still warm.

Nothing happened. Tearful Russian voices clamored around me, and the Russian leader stormed into the tent. He aimed a gun at my head and pulled back the trigger.

But I could not die today; Mandy and Newt and the others needed me. Someday I would take Mandy to Canada to rejoin her father and sister and live a civilized life, far away from places like this. I had a flash of Arthur, and the warm felt sense of his body against mine.

I had to find a way to help the boy. I remembered back to that day at the camp when Pyotr had been brought in, gushing blood. How had I healed him? It wasn't me, of that I was sure. It was a healing force that had used me to its own ends. But how had I gotten there, into its service?

Fierce concentration, I remembered that. It didn't want to

approach today, so I chased it. I forced my terrified breathing to slow down. I forced my mind away from the Russian whose gun was aimed at my head. I concentrated on the boy. There was a muted twang in the air, like the barometer dropping. Despite everything, my heart grew more peaceful, more even. The tent full of people froze into slow motion, their voices deepening and dwindling as though they were zooming through the air away from me.

Something like a gust of air swirled over my knuckles: something that didn't feel like air, but felt exactly like hands touching mine. I could discern individual fingers and the whorl patterns on the tips. It electrified the matrix of air around me. Whoosh! The tingles flooded through my hands, painfully, as if my hands were waking after being dead numb for hours. The tingles didn't want to run into the boy's body. I had to will them to move against their natural tidal flow. It was an enormous effort, and blazing heat suffused my entire being. Sweat dripped off my face and down my back and between my breasts. My legs shook with the heat and the roar of the tingles.

The room, the noises, the other people continued to recede. I was alone with the boy, whose lungs, I could see through the transparent fascia of his chest, were still respiring. He and I were bound together by a vortex of current that I directed into him. It was like stuffing a whirlpool into a small tube. I had to persist, and to use muscles I could not have imagined existed, until now. There was a moment when his flesh rippled as if he were made of pink jelly; the ripples were visible only to me.

Then he was arching on the cot. His back spasmed upward, making a bow, and he was gagging and gasping in air. He fell back onto the cot and clutched at himself, at his stomach. He was heaving with the need to vomit. I didn't dare move when he rolled over toward me. It landed on my skirt, leggings, and shoes. His dark eyes glinted as other hands helped him roll back into place. He smiled a little and tried to say something. His narrow, pale hand reached out and touched my wrist. Then his face eased, and his head rolled to one side.

I didn't stop when he began to snore. As long as the current was present, I directed it to flow into the sleeping boy. I stood for what must have been hours, pumping that current into his small frame. My bladder was painfully full and my body was sore. I throbbed everywhere with exertion, heat, stress.

Suddenly the healing tingles were gone. My hands emptied as if they'd never been full at all. I took my hands off the boy and stepped back. He was breathing quietly, a serene expression on his face. Ambient noises returned, increased in tempo. Alexei stood beside me. His face was wet with tears. The blonde woman stood on the opposite side of the bed. Her face, too, was damp. They looked so much alike, with their strong features and pronounced brows, that they had to be brother and sister. Other people populated the room, as if they'd just now materialized out of nothing: the scarred Dmitri, a few others. I stepped backward, walked out of the tent. Dmitri followed.

"I need a toilet, water, and food," I said. My voice was hoarse, my throat parched. I was dizzied and exhilarated from the current that had passed through me, and I needed to eat in order to ground myself.

"You saved Mikhail!" Dmitri gripped both my shoulders with big hands. "Thank you! I am the finest surgeon in Petersburg and I could do nothing!"

"Really need that toilet," I said, raggedly. He dragged me toward a young woman, a sloe-eyed Asian woman of extreme beauty and grace. Thai, probably. He spoke a few words in Russian, and she motioned for me to follow her.

A short while later, feeling much more comfortable, I was standing at a tub of murky water and trying to clean the stains from my skirt and leggings. I cupped water in my hands and poured it out onto my clothing, rinsing it off as best I could. The Thai woman waited a few meters away. I stiffened: someone else was watching me. Alexei.

"You brought my son to life."

"He wasn't dead," I said.

He turned his face and lifted his shaggy brows. "I know dead. He was dead."

"There was internal respiration, in his lungs." I stepped away from the big tub of water as some horses were led to it. I was as clean as I was going to get.

"I am Alexei," he said. "Now we are introduce properly."

"Emma."

"Come, I take you to food." He motioned to me and brushed past the Thai woman, who shrank back. I touched her arm as I passed. She gave me a tentative smile. Alexei gestured with his arm and shoulder: come this way. He led me through camp. It was my first good look at the place. It was large—several hundred inhabitants. It had been a long time since I'd seen so many people gathered together. It felt odd and precarious, like an invitation to the mists to come calling.

The ground was littered with refuse: wrappers, pieces of paper, junk, human waste. Men with multiple guns, either on horseback or on foot, policed crowds of filthy, gaunt people dressed in rags. Many were obviously injured, others were barefoot. About one-third seemed to have been beaten with some kind of whip: their shirts were torn open in red stripes along their backs. The majority were roped together in groups, waist to waist and leg to leg.

Other armed men walked alongside men and women who were distributing food. The food distributors were workers who mediated between those who were bound and those who lived in tents; they gave out packaged or chopped items. Anyone who grabbed at the food too eagerly was slapped in the head with the butt of a gun.

I eyed a group of children who were shackled together.

The children ranged in age from about two to fifteen years, and they represented all races and nationalities. The scents of urine and sweat, blood and feces hung everywhere on the air.

"Many are crazy," Alexei said, observing my gaze. "They are animals. We tie them to protect the rest."

"They've been through hell and you treat them like animals—how do you expect them to act?" I asked.

"Mists attack minds. I would give drugs if I had drugs to give, to help them. If there were drugs to cure what the mists do. There are not. Those were not invented." He shrugged.

Four men with rifles stood guard at a large tent, and a heady, succulent smell wafted out. Inside, a group of people were eating the way we did at Arthur's, at a variety of tables. They all rose when Alexei entered. He waved for them to be seated. He walked to a table, and the people there scattered while murmuring solicitously to him. He sat, pointed to the chair next to him.

As soon as I was seated, food arrived. I was light-headed with hunger, and I dug in. It was delicious fare, similar to what we ate at Arthur's camp: canned or reconstituted foods, some wild game, and some produce that had been gathered where found—wild berries and vegetables that had reseeded themselves. This year, no one anywhere on earth had planted gardens.

"We have many sick and wounded men," Alexei said. "You will take care of them. Mikhail first."

"He'll be fine," I assured him.

"What of sickness that kill him?" Alexei challenged.

"That's gone." I hoped it was.

A Filipina woman set a bottle of water at my elbow and then slunk away. I watched her obscure herself in a shadowed corner of the tent with a few other women, all young and comely. A man sitting at another table rose, nodded deferentially to Alexei, then crooked his finger at a red-headed woman standing with the Filipina. She followed him out, her eyes downcast, her mouth sullen. I turned to Alexei, who was watching me watch the scene. "Some place you've got here!"

"We live," he said. "For now. Everyone in my camp has food and water. Clothing. Some have shelter."

"Until the mists get you."

"Fever or gunfire. Arrows or spears. We fight the mists." He nodded when I gave him a quizzical look. "I use drums."

"You took women from Tara?"

"Yes, but I did not need them." He ate with gusto. I sensed a backstory that he wasn't sharing. Then he paused with a spoonful of stew close to his lips. "Mists avoid your camp."

"Where are Tara's people?"

"Have to tie them up outside." He made an expression of disgust. "They do not cooperate."

I thought about asking what he meant, but then I realized that I didn't want to know. "My friends are still alive?"

"Yes, but they are not happy." Alexei seemed amused. He fixed his probing gaze on me. "Do you know Arthur plans for rebuilding?"

"No," I said. He furrowed his brow as if he wanted to inquire further.

I made a show of energetic eating and utter absorption in the meal. There was nothing for me to discuss with this remorseless man, except when he would finally release me. He wasn't yet ready to do that.

12

AFTER I ATE, I WAS DESPERATE FOR sleep. Alexei gestured, and the Thai woman scampered toward us. He spoke to her in Russian and she bobbed her head repeatedly, then timidly gestured for me to follow her.

When we cleared the tent, I stopped and pointed to my chest.

"Emma," I said. "I'm Emma." I slapped my collarbones, hoping she understood.

"Kulap," she said. She smiled. "I speak little English." She bobbed her head. "That was good thing you do, for Mikhail. He is light of camp."

"I need to sleep," I said. She smiled even more incandescently and took my hand, leading me back through the camp toward the tent where Mikhail slept. I saw now that his tent was surrounded by a swath of the best tents in the camp.

She stopped at the tent next to Mikhail's and lifted the flap. One glance at the ammunition belt hanging off a fold-up chair inside told me it was Alexei's tent.

"No," I said, unable to control the urge to draw back.

"He said you stay here," she said. I looked around the camp. Hungry, bedraggled people, horses, trees, bushes, some tents and blankets. Random clumps of stuff, most of it piled on litters, so it could easily be carried: small furniture, books, linens, clothing, shoes, toys. I couldn't see them, but I was sure there were litters piled high with foodstuffs, weapons, and medical supplies. This group was well supplied, almost as well as Arthur's group.

I focused again on the survivors. It was true that many of them had the unhinged look of madness in their eyes. The group of Chinese women was still mostly seated, and they looked peaceful. I walked past the tents to where the women sat together on a shady slope. Past their piles of defecation was a clearing where the grasses were matted down and bent together, as if from long sitting: a prior resting place. The women stared as I lay down and curled up at the base of a tree. I thought of Mandy, my older daughter Beth, my husband Haywood. They were all better off than me, and right now, that was enough. They kept the bulwark within me strong. I was asleep even before my arms had wrapped all the way around my knees.

I woke up with a start. Some sort of intense discomfort coagulated the air around me. I looked around without moving. Alexei stood by my feet, staring down at me. His face was taut with thought. He was flexing and unflexing his sinewy hands. His eyes met mine and gleamed. I wondered if he was going to attack me. I curled up into myself into a tight ball, screwed my eyes shut, and held my breath.

Alexei backed away. He stared as he did so, his gaze scalding me. Finally he turned and went away. I was too exhausted to do anything but feel a quick flash of relief.

I dreamt of a beautiful Rastafarian man sitting in a vast field of white lilies. The contrast struck me: the perfect smooth sheen of his black skin and black dreadlocks against the white lilies. He was smiling and jovial, radiant with wisdom. I thought I'd have to remember how he looked, his face and demeanor, for when I illustrated a book about the Buddha. I approached him and he laughed in welcome. "What took you so long?" he asked. He snapped his fingers in front of his chest. "What took you so long?"

Kulap was shaking me. "Mikhail want you!" I sat up,

disoriented. Where was I? The sun slanted down past its zenith in a cloudless sky. The Chinese women had risen and were moving around in concert, some squatting to relieve themselves, others stretching. Armed men wandered through the shackled people, who were now fidgety and restless, moving about in groups like clumps of flotsam on ocean waves. Alexei's camp.

Kulap gestured toward the tent area. "Mikhail want talk to you. I translate."

Groggy and stiff, I wiped my hands over my face, willing myself to wake up. Where was a Starbucks when a tired woman craved a cup of hot coffee? Ten months ago there was probably one nearby, in whatever village this place had once been. I murmured, "You speak Russian and English?"

"And German and Spanish and Farsi." Her dark eyes met mine. "I work with many men since I was little girl."

"How is that?" I wondered.

"Sex trade. I work in Pattaya."

I didn't know what to say. "I'm sorry," finally emerged. It seemed lame.

Kulap smiled, her face so gorgeous in that instant that she could have graced the cover of every fashion magazine in the world. Not that any would ever again be printed; and was the world better or worse off for that? What had those glossy pages ever given us, other than seductive fantasies of a rich, secure world where celebrity lives mattered, and the color of a dress revealed fashion's stranglehold on our thoughts? I wondered what we would all do when we ran out of clothes to scavenge from the wreckage. Would looms be built by then? Spinning wheels? But Kulap was speaking softly. "It is my karma. I did something in past life. I sin."

"Pretty shitty of karma to hold that against you," I muttered.

"We all sin. So the world end." She fluttered her delicate

brown hands through the air, indicating the camp and the grassy flat plain with the heaps of yellow sand that evoked the village that had once stood over it.

"I don't believe in sin and judgment," I said. "This was a grand and savage accident, this ending, no more deserved than our original evolution out of amoebas." We had reached Mikhail's tent, where the mesh door flap was thrown open. The sound of laughter streamed out. Kulap turned toward it, and for the first time, I saw that there were torn fabric and raised red welts on her slim back. I exclaimed. She gave me a quizzical look.

"Your back! Who beat you?" I cried.

"You did not sleep in tent," she answered, her lashes drooping.

"I didn't mean for this to happen to you." My hands filled with tingles, and I lifted them to place them on her back. She stepped away before I could touch her.

"I do not blame the music for my bad dancing," she said.

"Did you know he would do this? You could have told me!" I let my hands drop.

"Not for me to interfere you." She was smiling again, serenely, it seemed; I could not read a subtext in her. My hands still throbbed with current, but I understood that she did not want to receive it. That was her choice, of course.

"Emma!" called a high, musical voice. I looked in to see Mikhail sitting on the edge of his cot, swinging his legs. His fine, poetic face was lit with pleasure.

"I am Marina, Alexei sister," said the blond woman who looked just like Alexei. She was staring at Mikhail with fierce pride. It was just the two of them, there in the tent.

"Hello, Marina, Mikhail," I called back.

"Emma!" Mikhail would have scrambled off the cot, but his aunt grabbed his shoulder. He babbled at me in Russian as I went inside the tent.

"Nice to meet you," I told them both. I extended my hand, and Mikhail grabbed it and shook it with both hands. "How are you feeling?"

"He feel good, and he thank you," Kulap said. I knelt in front of Mikhail. He laughed with easy joy, and held his hands up. I hesitated, so he grabbed one of my hands and pressed it up against his. He held up his free hand and nodded, so I pressed my other hand against it.

Kulap said, "He says you are friend."

MIKHAIL DIDN'T HAVE to wait long to prove his friendship. I left his tent and went to eat. Kulap had vanished, but the mess tent was easy to find. I sat alone, though the other folks there smiled and stared at me.

I distracted myself by thinking of Mandy sitting at a table in our mess tent, eating Cook's food, laughing as Marco teased her about the shape of her ears or her funny accent when he tried to teach her Italian. I hoped that was exactly what she was doing. I could not imagine what Beth was doing. I was just grateful that she was far from here. I knew that Haywood would guard her tenderly, whatever was happening in Canada. Things were good there. Canada was the promised land.

When I finished eating, I wandered through Alexei's camp, taking it in slowly. For as many people as the camp held, it was far quieter than our smaller camp. There was neither laughter nor boisterous shouts of men and children playing soccer, no friendly bickering or bursts of singing. There was just a subterranean anomie, and a pungent smell of something burning.

I made my way back to the Chinese women, who had moved several meters from their original location. One woman's eye was swollen and blackened, so I went to her first, put my hands on her, and let the tingles run into her battered face.

After a few minutes, she sighed, and rested her face against my palm, and wept.

When the flow of tingles ran dry, I went on to the next woman.

Three of the women were mentally unbalanced, and all of them were hurt. One woman—a girl, really—had a fractured right arm. I could feel the misalignment through her skin. Her eyes were dewy with pain. Her face showed despair and resignation and the vacancy of insanity, but no violence. The other women seemed to call her "Hui Zhong." Neither she nor any of the women in the group spoke English.

I dropped to my knees and checked the ropes around her to see if there was a way to release her. Dmitri claimed to be a surgeon; he could set and bind Hui Zhong's arm.

The knots eluded my fingers and then laughter trilled nearby. It was so unexpected and out of context that I had to look. Mikhail was playing, tossing flowers at Marina. It made everyone smile, even the injured Chinese women. I went back to the knots.

Then a line of fire scorched my back. I jumped up, shrieking. Alexei stood nearby, a leather whip in his trembling hand. I stared at it, and despite the burning on my flesh, all I could think was: this whip weathered the mists when so many people didn't?

"My men first!" Alexei roared. I was shocked, completely at a loss for words. Curious workers, soldiers, and tethered refugees gathered to watch. A few of the lucky ones, the camp aristocrats, wandered over. They were all silent, completely absorbed in the spectacle. Alexei's hand jerked, and the brown strap snaked through the air toward me. Just in time, I threw up my arm to shield my face. My forearm throbbed and leaked blood. Another stripe followed, and more blood. Alexei screamed, "These women, they are nothing. They were product for Los Angeles market! My men need your help!" He pulled his arm back to lash me again.

"*Nyet*, papa!" Mikhail leapt at Alexei's arm, caught it, and swung down on it as if riding a tree limb down to earth. "Papa, papa!" Mikhail began to babble in Russian. Alexei threw down his whip, caught up his son in a huge hug.

Alexei scowled at me over Mikhail's blond head. "My son says leave you be. So I will—this time." Still holding Mikhail, he trudged away.

"Do what you wish," Marina said, in halting English. She made a face of sympathy at my arm and then ran after her brother and nephew.

I let out a shuddering breath I hadn't known I'd been holding. I wanted to cry, but instead I did what I always did, since the first moment After: I closed my eyes and willed the tears away. There was no place in this brutal dying world for tears. There was only duty and survival.

The crowd mumbled to each other, but did not disperse. When I had collected myself, I found the Chinese women gathered around me. The sane ones blotted my blood with their torn clothes.

"I'm fine. I'm good!" I held up my hands in a quieting gesture. Barrel-chested Dmitri, walking with a dancer's erect posture, stepped up to me. He pulled my arm out gently and dumped water from a bottle on the welt. He took white cotton bandaging from a pocket on his shirt and wrapped my arm. He turned me firmly by my shoulders, probably to clean my back, but I resisted.

"Can you help her?" I asked, pointing. I tugged on his sleeve to draw him through the tangle of ropes toward Hui Zhong. She flinched at the man's approach, but allowed him to touch her arm. The other women whispered together like a flock of starlings singing. Hui Zhong spat at Dmitri, who wiped his face without judgment.

"I can help her arm. Not her mind. And it will hurt," Dmitri said.

"Everything hurts now." I looked into Hui Zhong's eyes,

tried to find any speck of sanity, some way to warn her. She didn't scream. Instead, she collapsed. The ropes caught her, and the other women held her for Dmitri.

When he was done, I had him cut the ropes that bound the women together.

"Alexei won't like it," Dmitri said, his worried expression puckering the thick scar on his face.

"Alexei isn't here," I said. "These women should relieve themselves in private. The sane ones will take care of the crazies."

I worked my way through the group of women. Dmitri worked alongside me, cleaning and bandaging as necessary. Kulap came to observe, but she didn't speak Chinese, so I continued to communicate through gestures.

After the women had been tended to, I sat down to rest. Dmitri and Kulap sat with me. It was sunset again, and I was drowsy and hungry and probably dehydrated as well. But I didn't want to go back to the mess tent, to be stared at by the privileged few in this camp of horrors. So I asked, "What did Alexei mean, the women were 'product'?"

"Alexei was a trader," Dmitri said. He took a water bottle from his belt, took a draught, and passed it to me. Gratefully, I took a long swallow. Dmitri continued, "Arms, women, computer data. Drugs, stolen automobiles, technology, software. International. Anything anyone wanted, he could get. For a price. He was the most powerful unknown man in the world." He gestured for me to finish the bottle of water. I didn't have to be asked twice.

Mikhail came running toward us then, and Dmitri and Kulap brightened visibly. I couldn't help feeling better, myself. There was something about Mikhail that illuminated the space around him.

"Emma, Emma," he cried. He threw himself into my lap. He was babbling happily. I looked at Kulap.

"He is sorry his father hurt you," Kulap said softly.

"Not your fault," I said. I placed my hands on either side of Mikhail's head and stared deep into his sparkling eyes. "Tell him I'm going to talk to him like he's grown up." Kulap translated. I continued, "Tell Mikhail that he will be... the father of a new world. He must be a good father, treat everyone well." Kulap cast her eyes down and didn't say anything. Dmitri grunted, then translated. I said, "He can rebuild the world into a better place, a good place. A place of peace and kindness."

Mikhail was nodding. He spoke, and his delicate face registered a fierce grace. He spoke at length. By the end, Kulap and Dmitri were leaning toward him, their faces awestruck. He finished and smiled, the dry smile of a mature soul. Neither Kulap nor Dmitri spoke.

"So?" I prompted. "What did he say?"

Swallowing, Dmitri said, "Mikhail understands."

"And what else?" I demanded.

"He said that peace and kindness are real, and what is real can not be destroyed," Dmitri said, his voice thick. "The power of goodness is always with us, when we're thinking, breathing, and feeling. It's doing all the work and using us as its tool." He rose and walked away.

I looked at Kulap and she smiled at me, a smile with so many shades of meaning that I could not hope to parse it. She did not speak. Mikhail settled into my arms, leaned his head back into my chest as if he'd spent a lifetime doing that. He would enjoy meeting Mandy and Newt and the others. Mandy would tease him, the way she did the others. Newt would stand silently at his elbow. Mikhail would like that about her, if he ever met her. I wondered if he would ever get the chance, or if Arthur would slaughter him with the others, when Arthur came to get me.

IT WAS AS though Alexei had read my mind about Arthur, because we were on the move within the hour. Armed men

rode through camp, shouting commands in various languages. Everyone stood. The workers fell to what were obviously well-rehearsed tasks: striking tents, packing chairs and
tables onto pallets to be carried, organizing the others. The
Chinese women were unbound, but clustered themselves
together in the same order, and at precisely the same distance
from each other, as if they were still tethered together. Even
the mad ones took their places. I must have looked perplexed.
Mikhail clung to my hand. He had a serious look on his face,
murmured something.

"He say, the ropes are in their minds," Kulap translated.

Alexei came by on his horse, leading Arthur's big roan. He
called out to Mikhail, who eagerly scrambled up to sit astride
Arthur's horse. Mikhail waved. Alexei stared through me as
if I weren't there, and the two were gone.

I WALKED WITH Kulap. Other women joined us. We started
out toward the back of the caravan, but soon passed the
slower groups bearing pallets or carrying packed-up tents.
We eased toward the front, behind the riders, alongside a
group of workers with filled backpacks. Dmitri came by on
horseback and gave us bottles of water and shrink-wrapped
madeleines, which weren't too stale, considering. Kulap tore
off the wrapper and ate voraciously, and let the plastic fall to
the ground; but what was litter now, anyway? I thought of
the money I had donated over the years to Greenpeace and
similar charities, and it occurred to me that the Earth had
had the last laugh.

Horse hooves sounded beside me and I looked up with a
smile, expecting Dmitri. It was Alexei, who seemed equally
taken aback by my burst of friendliness. He said, "You know
why we move the camp?"

"You won't escape Arthur." I looked straight ahead.

"He is well tied. Maybe he is not free yet. And he is on
foot, no weapons or food."

"Arthur will come."

"I will be waiting," Alexei said. He grinned. "We are old friends, me and Arthur."

"How is that?" I asked, unsettled.

"If Arthur has not told you, you do not want to know." He waited for me to respond. When I didn't, he said, "You are his woman and you know so little about him."

"I know that you should give me a permanent marker if you have one," I snapped.

"Marker?"

"A good pen. So I can put my name on the throats of your children and women. Maybe then he'll spare them."

Alexei burst into laughter, as if I'd told a rich joke. He said, "You could be Russian, you have good humor." I wasn't joking, though. I had seen what Arthur did to Xavier. Alexei said, "What is Arthur's plan for technology?"

"What? Technology?" I started.

"I know Arthur. He is do-gooder. Wants to be angel. There is only devil on Earth, he should learn that from his life. He will never learn. So he plan to rebuild. Bring back civilization. He has idea for technology. You tell me, what is he going to do?"

"Arthur's no angel," I said, nettled.

"So you are not stupid woman. Good. Then he would tell you his plan, at night, when he lie down beside you and touch your yellow hair. I would do that. I would touch your hair, look into your big eyes and tell you how you are beautiful." He was staring at me raptly, his deep-set eyes fixed on me and hugely dilated. I shivered.

"Tesla. Arthur wants to recreate the technology developed by Nikola Tesla." I hadn't meant to say anything, but Alexei's intensity forced it out of me. Besides, what did it matter? We were all a long way from recreating any kind of technology, with the mists and armed gangs pursuing us.

"I will beat him to it," Alexei said, with total confidence.

"You won't beat Arthur to anything," I said. "Arthur's worth ten of you."

"I have seen it. I will have technology before him. Arthur worth ten of me? You are funny woman. Arthur need me, at end. He come to me and beg. But he come too late. Biggest joke of all!" Alexei kicked his horse and trotted off, the strains of his laughter lacing through the rhythmic thud of hooves on the ground and the stamp and shuffle of many feet.

Alexei could threaten and dismiss Arthur, but I could feel Arthur like a hot wind on my skin. Wherever he was, he was angry that I'd been taken. He was coming for me. The smell of sweaty, dirty bodies, the thudding of feet and hooves against the earth, the menace of men with loaded guns, the threat of lethal mists and deadly rogue bands of survivors—none of it mattered. I was marching in a groaning phalanx with the dispossessed and damaged who remained on this forsaken planet, and I'd never felt safer. Arthur was coming for me.

WE MARCHED THROUGH the night and all the next day. We were headed west. We ate as we walked, ran off to the side of the column of people to relieve ourselves in the gorse, and simply kept going.

In the afternoon, we came to a town with a cluster of blond chateaux still standing. Alexei's man fanned through the streets. A gunshot coughed, and two men bustled out toward the main group, driving three grimy children ahead of them. The sobbing children were tied in with the rest of the small ones. Other men combed through the buildings for items of use. Shouts went up as things were found, and the pallet-bearers trotted over for a few more things to add to their loads.

After almost thirty hours of walking, we finally came to a halt on a gently-sloping grassy plain that appeared to have once been a *mas*, a farmhouse, with cultivated lands. By now, these had largely fallen to weed. Leafy sugar beets grew about us in sporadic clumps.

It was evening again: a purple sky, a yellow quarter moon, and chilly, fresh air. Women came by to distribute food. Dmitri gave me a pop-top can of *petit sale à l'auvergnate aux lentilles*, lentil soup, and a sterling silver spoon. I ate fast, then curled up on the ground with the can and spoon still clasped in my hand.

When I awoke the next morning, Mandy was in my thoughts. It felt as if she had just been sitting with me, rubbing the paint spots on my hands that I always got after a day of work, and telling me bad "knock-knock" jokes I had to laugh at or risk offending her. Of course, I always laughed.

My back was still sore from where Alexei had struck me. I looked around and saw that camp had been pitched overnight. Tents and shanties were set up, and the pallets were organized in neat rows. People sat and moved about, as though the camp had been here for months. I spied the Chinese women digging up sugar beets. Hui Zhong, with her wrapped arm, was hopping about and singing.

I rose, shook the bugs off my head and clothes, scratched the new mosquito bites, and took my toothbrush and small tube of toothpaste from my pocket. I squirted a dab onto the toothbrush, and brushed dry. Kulap rushed over and plucked the toothbrush from my hand in amazement. She zigzagged it through the air with exclamations of delight, finally passed it back to me.

"Come," she said. "You eat and help men." She pulled me along by my arm. This camp didn't believe in digging latrines, so I had to squat behind a few bushes on the way to the mess tent.

Alexei and Mikhail sat at a table with Marina and Dmitri. Mikhail called for me and patted the bench beside him, so I went to sit there.

"This my sister Marina," Alexei said. He sat on Mikhail's

other side and did not look at me. Marina winked, and I didn't mention that she'd already introduced herself. A steaming plate of food was set down. I dug in gratefully.

Before I could even swallow the first bite, Marina reached across the table and gripped my wrist. She spoke a few sentences which didn't need translation; the gratitude on her face transcended language.

"After breakfast, you will help my men who are wounded," Alexei said.

"I need to look in on the children," I demurred. "I'll see your men this afternoon, after the children."

Alexei looked over Mikhail's blond head and raked me with hostile, affronted eyes. His voice dropped in pitch and volume. "You are negotiating with me?"

"Papa," Mikhail interrupted. He spoke a few sentences, gazing at his father with complete adoration. Alexei's face eased.

"Morning for the children; afternoon for my men," Alexei said. His voice was grudging and he gave me a narrow sidelong glance.

"One more thing," I said. Alexei gave me an incredulous look. I took a breath and went on, pushing my luck. "Please have your men dig latrines. We don't have to live like pigs."

"There are latrines you can use," he said. "Girl will show you." He paused. "There is latrine close to my tent." His voice held a note of insinuation.

"Latrines for the general camp. You can give your people some dignity."

"I give them food and protection!" Alexei barked. "Let them shit where they will!"

"In Russia, the domes of churches are covered with gold, so that God notices them more often," Marina said, in slow, tortured English.

"There are no more domes in Russia," Alexei snarled. "Mists love metal. They were program that way."

Marina's face expressed both sorrow and humor. She murmured, "Lexi, hear the girl."

Alexei got up and stomped off. Mikhail, looking pensive,
said something to Marina, who shrugged. She touched my
bandaged arm and made a small moue of compassion.

"Marina, what did he mean, the mists were programmed
to love metal?" I asked.

"Who know what Lexi mean," she answered, shaking her
head.

"There are three men I cannot help," Dmitri interrupted.
He smiled, and the thick red scar on his cheek made the right
side of his mouth loop up differently from the left side. "But
you can help. I know you can. And I will clean your back."

DAYS PASSED WEARILY. I spent my mornings with the children. There were about fifty of them tied together. I cor-
ralled Dmitri to help me, and narrowly avoided another
beating one day when Alexei caught us cutting the children's
ropes. Mikhail had been making shadow puppets to entertain
the children, and he positioned himself between his father
and me.

"Children are tied so not to wander off, get hurt, or hurt
anyone else!" Alexei said. He held up the whip, and the hand
gripping it quivered. "This is not crèche. There are no nan-
nies. We pass through a world of danger and enemies!"

"Those children are like Mikhail. They are someone's sons
and daughters, and you would not want Mikhail bound this
way!" I argued. My knees knocked together, and I was glad I
was wearing a dress so it didn't show.

"Mikhail is different. He is special."

"Yes, Mikhail is special!" I cried. "Very special! Mikhail
is the hope of this camp. But these children must be treated
better."

Alexei tucked the whip's handle into his belt. His face registered conflicting thoughts. "You will get them killed."

"No." I took a deep breath. "There are many women and elderly folk. Untie them and set them to work taking care of the children. It will give them purpose, give the children comfort."

"Purpose and comfort are no longer considerations. I don't know if mists will come in one hour and take half people before drums send them away."

"Purpose is all we've got left," I argued. "Stop tying people up. Put the women and elderly with the kids. You'll make everyone happier. It will make a better camp."

"What do I care for better camp," Alexei said. "My wife is not in camp. I watch her breathe in white mists and weep tears of blood. I put bullet in her heart. Mikhail mother. I should put bullet in you, so Arthur feel like me. So he know what it is to lose everything." He pulled out his gun and aimed it at me. Mikhail put his hand over the end of the gun. Alexei cursed in Russian and holstered the firearm. "What is happiness now? I do not untie them."

I wanted to say that we'd all lost everything, but Alexei already knew that. Alexei was more bitter even than I was; he was unreachable. He shook his head and stalked off, muttering.

I took Dmitri's knife and cut the rest of the children's bonds, and summoned the Chinese women to watch over them. Mad Hui Zhong slapped a boy twice before we restrained her.

Kulap theorized that the boy resembled the soldier who had raped Hui Zhong and broken her arm.

IN THE AFTERNOONS, Dmitri and I tended the sick and wounded soldiers. Most of them were Russian. Of the three men who urgently concerned Dmitri, one had parasites, one had a viral infection, and one was beyond help.

"If I put my hands on him, he will die faster," I told Dmitri.

"How do you know?" Dmitri pressed me. We stood inside

a big beige tent that was this camp's hospital tent. The days were getting cooler, and the air was delightful. Dmitri stood with an uncharacteristic stoop to his shoulders, looking tired.

"I don't know. I just know," I said. "I don't understand anything about this healing touch. It came into me After."

Dmitri nodded. "You should try to understand it. It may be important."

"So I've been told," I said. I smiled, wondering how Laurette was doing back at the women's camp. Were Caris and Genevra happy in the company of women, well-fed, safe from the mists and the bands? I hoped they had not somehow heard that I'd been taken—that the news, which diffused among survivors like invisible airborne microbes, hadn't reached them. They'd worry.

I also hoped Mandy and Newt and the others weren't worrying, back at Arthur's camp. They had to know what I knew, that Arthur would retrieve me. He must have promised them that. No one ever doubted a promise Arthur made.

"Can you help the other two?" Dmitri was asking, cutting into my reverie.

"I think so, although that one has parasites. He needs herbs or medicine for them."

"We see much watery diarrhea, stomach cramps, fever and muscle aches," Dmitri said. He rubbed his scarred cheek absently. "Parasites are a serious hazard. It's good that you got Alexei to dig latrines. We need better hygiene in this camp, even if we are mobile. You must talk to Alexei about it."

"Me?" I yelped. "Are you crazy?"

"He listens to you, because of Mikhail."

"He doesn't listen to me. He beats me with a leather whip!"

"No, no, you have much influence with him," Dmitri said. "He likes you." He fingered his scar, and his eyes dulled.

"If this is how he treats someone he likes, I'd hate to be his enemy," I muttered.

"Alexei has no enemies." Dmitri smiled slightly. "They do

not live long enough for that."

Alexei has one enemy, I thought—an implacable one—in Arthur. But I didn't say it aloud.

A FEW NIGHTS later, I dreamt again about the wise Rastafarian in his field of lilies. "What is time?" he asked me. He laughed. "What *is* time?"

I was about to answer, and I couldn't wait to hear what I was going to say, but I was shaken awake. It was Marina. "Emma, Emma," she said. "Come now. Ludmilla have baby. They have danger, maybe die." She went on in fast, incomprehensible Russian.

Marina bent over me in the midnight gloom and helped me rise. She handed me a warm bottle of Orangina to drink as we went toward the swath of tents where the camp's upper crust slept. The sugar pierced my grogginess, and I could not help but enjoy the sweet, effervescent drink. It reminded me of the first week After, when Mandy, Shoshana, Newt, Felix, and I had found an abandoned cache of Fanta, Orangina, and Nutella hazelnut butter outside Paris, in the remains of an empty, half-destroyed train station. The foodstuffs were piled together in a big pyramid under the *sortie* sign. It looked like something kids would have done, though none were in sight. By then we had our backpacks, so we stuffed them with the food, then walked out into a silent, dead town where the tops of the trees had been shaped into boxes.

Dmitri stood at the flap of one of the tents. His eyes brightened when he saw me. He raised the flap and ushered me in. The tent was full of women. A small but hugely pregnant red-haired woman lay on a cot, writhing and moaning. She was young and very pretty, even swollen with sweat and pain and mottled with the red flowers of burst blood vessels.

"I can't deliver a baby," I said, feeling a little panicked.

"You help, like Mikhail," Marina urged. I shook my head no, but she exclaimed in Russian. I didn't have to speak the language to know that she was exhorting me to do my best.

"Wash your hands," Dmitri commanded sternly. He brandished a bottle of rubbing alcohol. I held out my hands. An older woman with salt-and-pepper hair and a sweet face doused my hands, passing twice over my nails. She repeated the process with Dmitri. A wooden tripod stool was parked next to the cot, and they pushed me to sit on it. I smiled at the pregnant girl, whose face suddenly looked hopeful.

"You Emma, save Mikhail!" she said.

"Ludmilla, how are you?" I asked softly.

"Not good," she said, brokenly. Her eyes were glassy and red-rimmed and sunken. Her lids quivered and she exhaled with a gurgle in her throat. She shifted around the cot. "Emma!" she gasped, as a big contraction shook her. A gush of orange and red fluid came out from between her thighs.

"She is not big enough, not dilated enough. Her water broke, and the baby wants to come," Dmitri said. "I don't know if her pelvis can accommodate the head. It is bad."

"You're a surgeon. Do a cesearean," I urged. He shook his head.

"I lost a mother and infant that way last month. We are not a real hospital. We do not have equipment, monitors, drugs, skilled nurses. I will not do that again." The uninflected clarity of his voice, like a perfectly tuned stringed instrument, told me that he had suffered over those deaths.

"Help me, Emma!" Ludmilla cried, scrabbling against the cot in agony until she had turned onto her hands and knees. So I put my hands on her sacrum, hoping desperately that I would be able to help her.

I had been using the unexpected healing gift so frequently that I was more familiar with it now. I was ready when the tingles burst through. I was also more articulate with the healing current. I had learned to sink my awareness deep into the physical body of the person under my palms. It was like diving down into an ocean of flesh with my mind. As I sank, the unique cadence, or resonance, of the individual person revealed itself, loud and musical and palpable. It was like finding the melody in a symphony. Then the tingles shifted frequency to match and reinforce the cadence.

I wondered how Laurette would analyze this discovery. She would be pleased that it wasn't such a crude tool.

But now there were two melodies beneath my hands, Ludmilla's and the baby's. The latter was weak and thready, fading. Hang on, I told it. Don't give up yet.

"*Da!*" Dmitri shouted. He had moved around the cot to see her from behind. "She is opening!"

"No hurt," Ludmilla gasped. She panted heavily, as if in Lamaze class. She tried to smile at me, screamed instead. But then she repeated, "Not hurt!"

The older woman commanded something in Russian. Then she looked at me. "We squat her," she said. It wasn't easy with Ludmilla moving around, but I kept my hands on her sacrum and made sure the tingles coursed into her, while three women helped her into a crouching position. Ludmilla's panting increased in tempo, grew louder and hoarser. Dmitri knelt and stuck his hand into her crotch, checking her.

"Push!" Ludmilla screamed.

"*Nyet!*" Dmitri yelled. He had his fingers inside her.

"*Puskayu!*" Ludmilla screamed. Feces and blood gushed down onto the bed, drenching Dmitri's arm. The women whisked away the sheet and stripped off Dmitri's shirt. The older woman tossed another bottle of alcohol to another woman, who hurriedly scrubbed Dmitri's hands. Ludmilla kept screaming. She bore down again. There was another whoosh of blood and the contents of her bowels. I felt the baby's pulse flicker out, like a candle flame puffing out in a breeze.

"Dmitri," I said urgently. He looked at me, and I shook my head. He sagged. My heart broke a little more. I could not imagine how I'd have endured it if Beth or Mandy had died during their births. I would not have lived through the mists, would not have been able to do what was necessary to stay alive. Poor Ludmilla.

"Aaah!" Ludmilla cried. Blood rained down, and the baby crowned. Dmitri got his hands there just in time to turn it and ease the shoulders out of Ludmilla.

"Oh, *nyet*," Dmitri said, his voice anguished. Against his broad, furry chest, he cradled the infant, which was silent and unresponsive, blue and orange, a vernix-covered doll. He set it down on a blanket on the floor nearby and began to press its chest. Ludmilla wailed. The women in the tent murmured. Some wept quietly.

"Let me try," I said. I didn't have any real hope, just a longing to comfort Ludmilla. Dmitri laid the baby gently in my arms. He and the older woman turned back to the shrieking mother, who had torn badly.

I stepped outside the tent with the motionless baby in my arms. The night was very calm, the sky so purply-black that the stars' intensity was shocking. I had grown used to brilliant night skies, now that light pollution was gone, but this Milky Way radiated a clear light I'd never seen before. I laid one hand on the tiny child's chest. There were no tingles, there was no cadence, no music. The child was dead.

And was this infant better off not coming into this world of pain and loss and danger? Was the child lucky to be spared the terror of encroaching mists, which came randomly, unpredictably, and razed everything in their path? What about growing up in this camp? Even as the offspring of the elite, this child would be subjected to horror and suffering and cruelty. What was life worth in this dying world? Maybe it was grace that the child wouldn't draw breath here. Who was I to gainsay grace?

Then I saw Mandy. She rose up in front of me, whole like a hologram: skinny and big-eyed, her auburn hair plaited like Pocahontas, a grin of discovery and delight playing on her lively face. And my daughter Beth, the serious one, with thick blonde hair like mine. Beth with her arch comments and husky voice, her love of *The Wizard of Oz* and all things dragon. How I missed her! I could never let myself think of her, because I would ache in a way I couldn't contain. I would shatter. Too many people depended on me for me to submit to my grief and loss.

Someone else came: a man. He stood with his arm around me, as he often did. He was beautiful beyond the dreams of women, beautiful in a way that dazzled me, the artist. He was kind and ruthless, and he laughed at my jokes. His gray eyes sought me out when he rode his roan horse back into camp. At night, he held me. The way he touched me made this world bearable, though to admit that was terrifying.

Arthur was coming for me. I felt it like the sun warming my skin. He was coming *soon*.

Arthur would say that a new and better world was in the making. He would talk about looking to the future. He would agree with Mikhail: *the power of goodness is always with us, doing all the work and using us as its tool.*

The thought of goodness triggered it: suddenly, something came through me. It wasn't a prayer, because I didn't pray. I couldn't; I no longer believed in God. But something, some wordless plea for life, radiated out from my core. It was sweet and stricken and full of surrender. It arrowed out into the clear light falling down like webs of time from the sweet span of stars overhead. What took me so long to get here, I wondered, to arrive at this place of surrender? What took me so long?

The healing tingles responded. Gentler and more sparkling than I'd ever felt them before, they sluiced through me, through my hand and into the baby's chest. The fabric of air and space around me quickened, brightened, as if lightening had struck. There was a kind of intelligence to it, to everything around me. Was this the biomind Xavier had mentioned?

A cry broke the silence. It took me a few beats: the howling came from the baby. It was wriggling in my arms.

I was so stunned that I almost dropped it. Dropped him: how could I have missed the obvious gender?

Dmitri shouted inside the tent, but he did not rush over. Marina and several women did, though. They surrounded me, crying and hugging and rejoicing. My cheek got sloppy-wet with their kisses. Finally Dmitri trotted out and kissed me, before taking the infant. He had a cloth, and he cooed as he held the little guy against his ursine chest and cleaned him.

Dmitri walked back into the tent slowly, surrounded by the women.

I looked up, overcome with gratitude. The stars were beautiful. The healing tingles were miraculous. They weren't my doing; I had just been in the right place at the right time to be used by the healing current. I was a crude instrument of another, higher force.

I was in such an uplifted state that I could understand clearly that time and space were illusions. I knew the answer to the Rastafarian's question: "What is time?" Time is nothing; it did not truly exist. Neither did space. They vanished in the merging.

I looked deep into the radiance of night and sent myself to Arthur. He held me.

A sound fragmented the peace. Someone had coughed. Someone stood in the shadows, watching me. It was Alexei.

"How Arthur make Tesla technology?" he demanded, a question like a blow, and it made me contract.

"I don't know." That guy was really a piece of work. "There are men in our camp who are engineers and physicists, used to be, Before. They know Tesla's work." I was suddenly weary. "Anyway, they haven't done it yet."

"I find physicist and engineer."

"Like you used to find things for people?" I asked.

He smiled with bitter pride. "My reputation precede me. Some day you ask Arthur what he want me to find for him."

"I'm sure he had a good reason to employ your services."

"The best, but he is too late. He fail." Alexei paused. "You are Arthur's woman, but you are married to other man."

"How do you know?" I was startled.

He shrugged, and changed the subject again, in his mercurial way. "We Russians, we love babies." Now there was a defensive edge to his voice.

I was tired, and my brain was addled. It was hard to follow his leaps in thought. I asked, "Alexei, aren't we all just people now, those few of us who are left?"

"I am always Russian."

"What about Mikhail? Does he belong only to Russia, which no longer exists?"

"I heard territory in Siberia is still there," Alexei said, with a sudden, unnerving grin. "The mists do not like cold, maybe. Just bodies and metal."

"The settlement on Ross Island off Antarctica was the first to be destroyed," I reminded him. The whole world had been glued to their televisions, watching.

"So the mists do not like old gulags." His craggy face retreated into the shadows of his private thoughts. "I thought they go there first, like good soldiers."

"I don't think of the mists as soldiers."

"You should." He focused on me again. I could see him having a conversation in his mind, one that did not include me. Aloud, he said only, "Soldiers that mutiny, that turn on their generals in field."

"That would mean they have independent thought, that they're self-aware."

"Not as we think of it. As the mind of bees, which are one hive."

"I've never heard anyone characterize the mists that way," I murmured, with a mixture of curiosity and disbelief.

"'Even if we are spared destruction by war, our lives will have to change if we want to save life from self-destruction.' You know Solzhenitsyn?" Alexei asked. "Very smart Russian. He saw mists. He did not know he saw them, but he did."

"You're saying the mists are a form of self destruction?" I puzzled. "How is that?"

"When angels fall, they destroy world, and God does not warn us."

"That's because there is no God."

Alexei laughed. "So funny you are! Of course there is God. God whispers to us always, and we choose to do something else." He fell silent abruptly, rubbing his chin with his hand. A few moments later, he said, "That was good thing you do. Help Ludmilla baby."

I sighed. It was clear that Alexei knew something about the mists, but it was equally clear that he wouldn't tell me. I was frustrated. "It's time for me to leave. Arthur is coming for me. He'll hurt people to get me back."

"I have good sentries with many bullets," Alexei said. "You are useful. You do not want to go back to Arthur. He has big problem, nasty group on his west. Big group, mean. Crazy. Wear red capes and fire lots of guns. They run terrible camp. Make my camp look like heaven."

"I doubt that," I murmured.

"They are much worse than my camp. You know what they do with people who are sick, hurt, or crazy?" His blue eyes blazed in the dark. "They eat them."

I remembered the day I had gone to find Hoshi and her family. I remembered the rogue watcher with the wrapped chunk of smoked meat hanging from his belt. I had thought at the time that it looked like a human thigh. Alexei was telling the truth.

I shuddered with revulsion.

Alexei was still talking. "They approach me. They want me to be ally against Arthur. But Arthur is smart; Arthur has plans. Maybe he is useful to me. Europe is big enough for both of us. For now. I wait and see who wins, when they strike. Maybe them, maybe Arthur."

"Arthur will win!" I cried.

"Arthur does not always win," Alexei whispered.

"Your sentries are no match for the mists," I said.

"Arthur is do-gooder, so he is weak. He will not send mists against children and women here," Alexei said, a little smugly. I started, shocked that he knew about Arthur's control of the mists. He nodded slowly at me; yes, he knew.

Dmitri came out, bare-chested and full of good humor. "Emma, come in, you must see. This great hungry boy nurses like a professional!" He noticed Alexei and waved. "Alexei, come in, come in, meet the newest member of your camp! He will be a strong fighter for you. This boy is a good Russian already."

Alexei's canny eyes rested on me. "We must celebrate. This is joyful occasion."

"There is vodka somewhere," Dmitri said happily. "We will toast to the new soldier just born, and to Mikhail's recovery!"

"We will toast to Emma staying with us," Alexei said. As we went into the tent, he gripped my shoulder and squeezed too hard. There would be bruises.

"Emma, Emma! Blessing for my son!" Ludmilla called. Her sweaty, beat-up face was incandescent with joy. The other women grabbed my hands and pulled me to the cot.

"Blessing, blessing!" many voices cried. There was no choice. I leaned over and placed my hands on his tiny head, with its fuzz of black hair. He wasn't distracted from what he was doing, ravenously latching on to his mama. I cleared my mind, felt again my love for Mandy and Beth, for Newt and the others. For Arthur. My breath syncopated. I looked up, and Mikhail stood in the doorway, beaming. Proudly, his father drew him in.

"This child will have righteousness in his heart, beauty in his soul, and harmony in his ways," I said softly. I stepped away as the women cheered and applauded. Alexei must have translated for Mikhail, because the boy skipped over and circled me with his arms, hugging me and murmuring Russian endearments. Alexei's eyes burned to see the love and joy radiating from his son.

"See, you are one of us," Alexei whispered to me.

I shook my head no at Alexei. No, I would not stay—not for the camp, not even for Mikhail.

13

FINALLY, THE MISTS CAME. I WAS with Hui Zhong, experimenting with the healing tingles. Would they, could they, restore her to sanity? I'd been pumping the healing current into her all morning, to no avail. She babbled Chinese gobbledygook and had to be restrained twice from clawing my face and neck. Either I wasn't a good enough healer, or the current was not useful this way.

"Try again another day," Dmitri suggested. He held Hui Zhong's arms behind her back gently, so as not to put pressure on the broken one. She jerked and made animal noises, then craned her head around and spat on Dmitri. Dmitri grimaced.

"There's got to be a way to help the crazy ones," I said. "Too many survivors are incapacitated this way!"

"Drums," Kulap said suddenly. As I worked, she'd been lying on her back with her black hair fanning out around her, chewing a weed and gazing at the sky. Now she scrambled to her feet. A moment later, we heard what her keen ears had picked up: the faint sound of drums beating. The rhythm was picked up by one drum after another.

Dmitri secured Hui Zhong with a length of rope with a few quick jerks, then leapt to his feet, too. The three of us looked around, our gaze sweeping the rolling hills.

"There!" Dmitri pointed into the western foothills. It was like a giant white cloud in the shape of a caterpillar, shimmying forward slowly, inexorably. It was far distant, but it must have been thirty meters high. It scintillated in the sun, and the front of the mist bank swung around like a head, turning from side to side, searching.

"It's looking for us," Kulap said, nervously.

"Another!" Dmitri pointed again. An undulant sphere rolled toward us from the southeast. It too crawled slowly, as if it were sniffing, seeking.

"And there!" Kulap gestured. "So many coming. I never saw this!" Along the southern border pulsed a diffuse rhomboid cloud bank.

And another in the north. And one from the northwest.

We couldn't yet smell them, but soon, with all of them converging, we wouldn't be able to avoid the sickly scent of terrible death. Ahead of the mists, birds cawed and shrieked their distress as they winged up into the air, and swarms of iridescent blue butterflies swirled skyward in great spirals.

"Arthur," I said.

I bolted into the camp to find Alexei. He stood by the mess tent, surrounded by a group of drumming men. He strode through the central tent area, inspecting drums and drummers.

"Alexei," I shouted, to be heard over the drumming. He didn't hear, and I ran to him, grabbed his shirt sleeve. "You must let me leave!"

Alexei froze.

Then he grabbed me around the neck, and squeezed. I gripped his wrists, trying to pull him off. My oxygen was cut. I felt myself go woozy. Black spots wavered in front of my eyes, like the air above a hot tarmac on a summer day. My knees dissolved.

Abruptly, he dropped his arms. I clasped my throat and rubbed, drew in raspy, shuddering breaths of sweet, nurturing air. He shouted, "Arthur control improves! But he will not send mists into camp while you are here!"

"He'll direct the mists not to touch me!" I shouted back. I didn't know if this was true or not. I wanted it to be true. I was probably bluffing, but my uncertainty didn't show on my face. And Arthur had said I couldn't play poker?

Alexei's face was terrible with anger. "Again he play God. Again he take from me what I want. I will answer this! I will hurt him as he hurt me!"

"Let me go," I pleaded. "Give me Arthur's horse, let me ride out. I'll get him to stop. Please, Alexei! Everyone will die, you and the children and women and the horses. And Mikhail!"

"You ride, the mists destroy us anyway!"

"Papa, papa!" Mikhail's screaming pierced the drumming. Alexei and I swung around to face him. Mikhail spoke urgently. He stopped, and the two of them stared at me.

"Arthur will send the mists away for me. I promise."

"That horse will kill you. You cannot ride." Alexei shook his head.

"Tie me to him, because you don't want to keep Arthur's horse!"

Alexei stepped close, gripped me by my upper arms. He said in a low voice, "I want to keep his horse and his woman, should have drag you to my tent first night I have you." I didn't respond because an unholy gleam lit his eyes, and it was probably some shade of madness. That was now within the normal spectrum of consciousness.

But Mikhail put his hand on his father's arm. Eyes black with anger, Alexei released me.

In the end, they saddled Rosie for me and gave me the lead rope for Arthur's horse. I asked for Vasily and Theo's horses, too, which made Alexei laugh riotously. At least, his face indicated loud laughter, the fruit of the robust, labyrinthine, and almost unsmiling Russian sense of humor which I had yet to fully grasp despite my weeks in this camp. It was impossible to hear for sure because of the drumming, which had grown

louder and more insistent as it became clear that the mists
would not consent to be driven away.

I walked through the camp, leading the two horses. Kulap
and Dmitri marched on either side of me. Everyone who
wasn't drumming lined up on either side of our path. The
Chinese women, the children, the groups who were roped,
the crazy ones, the workers, the camp aristocrats, all the soldiers who weren't drumming desperately, every single one
of the camp's hundreds of inhabitants. They didn't speak;
they just watched and inclined their heads as I passed. Many
of them bowed to me, which left me feeling awkward, and
humbled.

Near the edge of the camp were Ludmilla and her baby,
the women from her tent, and Marina, with Mikhail standing
beside her. Marina kissed me and murmured something in
Russian that I could neither hear nor understand, but which I
felt to be a blessing. Mikhail kissed me with great formality,
and such was his gravity that, even at his tender age, it wasn't
silly in the least.

"You are the hope of this camp," I whispered in his ear,
knowing he couldn't understand. He nodded anyway.

Finally, at the end of the long receiving line, Kulap kissed
me good-bye, also formally, on both cheeks. She wore her
inscrutable smile. She had never looked more gorgeous than
in that moment. Before, back in Manhattan, she would have
stopped traffic and fended off millionaire hedge fund types;
now, After, she was a translator in a refugee camp of many
tongues and many more brutalities.

Dmitri, with studied ceremony, gave me back my gun,
then helped me mount Rosie and situate stirrups and reins.
With his fine military bearing, he saluted me. The drumbeats
grew even louder, even more resonant. My breastbone pulsed
with the sound.

"Emma, you will come back!" I heard Alexei shout. I
turned in the saddle to see him standing, arms akimbo, in

the center of the two lines, a tall blond man of fierce and remorseless passions. He was angry and desolate, as we all were. But he refused to let go of the past and embrace what remained. We were all defended against the terrible immediacy of the present; we all knew too much about destruction and loss not to protect ourselves. But Alexei didn't seem to realize that our defenses kept rewounding us.

He shouted again. "You will be back! I have gift, too. Mists are in my brain and make me to see things. I see it, you will be back here. Without Arthur!"

IT WAS A pleasant ride away from Alexei's camp, although I felt the percussive vibrations the whole time. The drumming sound lessened but never disappeared. They were desperate, and the drummers were determined. But this time I felt no fear of the mists.

I dropped the lead to Arthur's horse and let him choose the way. The big roan whinnied and threw his head up as if scenting the air, then set out at a fast canter. I swore in English, and then I remembered the wicked-sounding French curses Laurette had taught me, and I threw those in for good measure. I was still cursing as Rosie bolted after the roan. It was all I could do not to fall off.

The leggy roan was much faster than good-hearted Rosie, and he pulled ahead of us. After a while we lost him completely. Rosie settled into a smooth trot that gave me much better odds for survival.

And then, in the distance, I spied a small figure: a horse with a man on it. As it came closer, I saw that it was a great piebald beast, racing my way at a flat-out gallop. The horse and rider were a paradigm of lightness, harmony, and flowing movement; they could have been flying together. The image formed a stark contrast to the destruction and desolation that had become the world's lot. My heart leapt. I kicked Rosie's sides in a way I'd never done before, and she flew forward.

I leaned forward in the saddle and, terrified though I was, willed her to go faster.

"Look at you, cantering!" Arthur called, laughing. He rode his horse toward us at full speed, almost running into Rosie, and she reared up and whinnied. I was hard-pressed to keep my balance, and I gripped my thighs around her in a vise-lock. Arthur grabbed her reins and pulled her to order in his quick, expert way. His left leg was brushed up against my right leg as our horses stood beside each other, facing in opposite directions. His horse was foaming and heaving.

Arthur leaned over and grabbed my head, kissed my mouth.

It was the fiercest, sweetest kiss. Everything—the drumbeats, the rolling grassy farmland, the sky and sun, the mists that threatened Alexei's camp, all the people I had met there, indeed, everyone I had ever known, even the apocalypse that terrorized my thoughts—everything fell away. There was only the single instant of Arthur's closeness to me. I wasn't sure where he ended and I began. That kiss made us one being, one whole. In that wholeness, everything dissolved. Only love remained.

What had taken me so long to know this? Only my own resistance.

The constant pain in my heart eased.

Arthur pulled back and looked me over. His large hand remained on my cheek, and I clasped his wrist and kissed the very center of his palm. His handsome face, with its symphony of planes and angles and its breathtaking symmetry, looked gaunt, as if he hadn't been eating, and his gray eyes were piercing and almost black as they scanned me.

"Arthur, send the mists away," I said. "I'm here. I'm fine."

"He took you away from me," Arthur said. His mouth hardened.

"No one can take me away from you."

A pleased expression came over Arthur's face. He sat a

little straighter in his saddle, if such a thing were possible, since he always rode with the perfect carriage and equilibrium of the Olympic equestrian he had been, Before. He gave an imperceptible signal to his horse and rode all the way around Rosie and me, inspecting me. I was glad Kulap had found me a clean dress. The welt on my back wasn't visible. That welt could have cost everyone in Alexei's camp their lives.

Arthur asked, "What happened to your arm?"

"Nothing tragic," I assured him. He rode up alongside me, on my other side.

"Did he sleep with you?"

"Nope."

"Try to?"

"Nope."

"Liar," he said. He reached across and stroked my lower lip.

"Okay, Alexei tried, but not really, and he didn't pursue it," I allowed. "He's mourning his wife." That satisfied Arthur. He guided his horse and Rosie into a walk. I felt relieved that he was controlling my horse.

"I'll hold the mists around the camp until we're far away, discourage them from following."

"That's some control you've developed," I noted. "How did that happen?"

"Practice," he said shortly.

"Huh. If only the rest of us could practice that way!"

"If only."

"Alexei called them soldiers. They're your soldiers, for sure," I said. I said it with a grin, but Arthur gave me a bleak look. I guessed that he was still mad about Alexei taking me to the other camp. I spoke in a cajoling tone. "Tell your minions to stand down. Alexei won't follow us. There are women and children. I don't want them frightened."

"If Alexei didn't want his women and children frightened, he shouldn't have kidnapped you at gunpoint." A pained sneer scrolled over Arthur's face. "The mists are not my minions!"

I reached over and laid my hand on his shoulder. "Send the mists away, Arthur. You have me." I smiled at him in the soft way I usually did only at night, in private, in our tent. His eyes kindled.

"My army's close, else we could take a few minutes to greet each other properly," he said, in a growl.

"That kiss was a right proper greeting."

"I can do better," he said. He gave me a warm and level gaze. "I will do better."

"Ravish me in the bushes?" I giggled.

"Don't tempt me. Cheeky." He smiled and looked off into the distance, where several dozen horses rode toward us in formation. "I will kill him, you know. Not today. But I will."

"You got your horse back," I said. "And me."

"So I won't make him suffer first," Arthur said, his tone contemptuous.

"If I had a son like Mikhail, I'd kidnap a healer, too," I said. "He's special."

"Every child is special, now more than ever."

"True, but for a parent…."

"Being a parent doesn't give him the right to take you."

I looked sidelong at Arthur. "Ever had children?"

"Not yet. Hoping to." He raised an eyebrow at me.

"A baby was born at Alexei's camp. It made me realize…. They are the goodness of the world. The goodness that is always with us, when we're thinking, breathing, and feeling—that goodness is doing all the work and using us as its tool. That's what our children are. Even when they're being awful. And all children are awful from time to time."

"Beautiful thought," Arthur murmured. His jaw was set. "Alexei has it coming to him, trust me."

"You have a history with him."

"I don't have a history with anyone now. No one does. We have only the present and the future. The future that we are responsible for creating. That's our only responsibility. The past is gone."

All the more reason not to hold a grudge, I thought. "Alexei said you asked him to get something, but you were too late...."

"Irrelevant." He smiled. "You came to me, two nights ago." He paused, eyed me quizzically. I nodded. He said, "I felt you. In my arms. It was delicate, almost imperceptible, like a butterfly's wings grazing my skin. But it was you, no question. Your essence. I've never felt anything like it before."

"You held me."

"I liked it."

"Me, too." I smiled at him.

"So what took you so long?" he asked, and his voice was full of an ache that evoked an answering ache in me.

"The weight of what I carry," I told him.

"I know what you mean," Arthur said somberly. "I feel that I carry a huge stone, a giant white stone and I've cast its shadow over the world."

But he couldn't explain further, because the riders from our camp were galloping toward us in a tight wedge formation. Theo was in the lead, then Robert and Vasily, with Shinji and Pyotr and Michio close behind, and more men following them, all of them armed to the teeth. And not just men: Jeannie from the women's camp rode with ammunition belts criss-crossed over her chest, like a commando. Then I saw that James and Nwokocha were riding with them, too! Over the thunder of hooves, I yelled, "Everyone?"

"Just about," Arthur called back. "Don't worry; enough people remained behind to protect the kids."

And that was all he had time to say, because now we were surrounded. Theo slid down from his horse, and pulled me off Rosie to hug me. Then everyone else tumbled down, and there was a lot of yelling and whooping, much of it by me. James and Robert got a little misty-eyed, but we all pretended not to notice. It made me glow inside, though.

A few minutes after we'd set off for camp, I rode up beside Arthur and gave him a look. He knew what I wanted. He stopped his horse and motioned for the others to keep riding. When the whole group had passed us, with playful comments about what we were up to, Arthur gave me an ironic smile. He wheeled his horse around to face the direction from which we'd come.

"You sure?" he asked. I nodded.

Arthur raised his hands. His eyes closed halfway, and his face smoothed out, even to the crow's feet beside his gray eyes. He opened his palms to the sky.

After about a minute, in the far distance, I saw five giant spherical mists float straight up. They kept rising until they were high above the land.

Then Arthur closed his palms, like a conductor silencing the orchestra. The mists vanished.

"Terrifying and marvelous, at the same time," I said. I almost could not breathe.

"Someday I'll do it for the whole world. I'll send them all away for good," he vowed. "The ones we see, and the ones we don't see." He leaned over and kissed me. "I will do it for you, Emma. The time will come."

IT WAS A few days' ride back to camp. We set a hard pace and kept to it. The first day, we stopped only to eat. The men wanted to know what Alexei's camp was like, and whether I'd been hurt. I told them I hadn't, and didn't feel that I was lying because the scabs on my back and arm were healing, and it could have been so much worse.

"Alexei says that band gathering on our western border is worse than his group," I said. We were eating small chunks of some sort of dried meat. I hoped it was venison or boar, but I wasn't going to ask. If it was dried rat, well, it was assimilable protein. We ate what was available; the way the mists had ravaged the world meant that we couldn't be picky.

Then I recalled Alexei's words: the rogue band on our west ate human flesh. My stomach turned. We could not let the children fall into their hands.

Arthur's eyes glinted, but he didn't say anything about the rogue band. It was confirmation for me that the situation was as bad as Alexei had said. When Arthur went to the bushes to relieve himself, I looked for someone to interrogate. James was nearby examining a horse's hoof, muttering about how he wished Torsten were here. Theo lay on his back, unoccupied, so I hustled him off for a few words.

"They are wild. They will attack," Theo said. "They will kill everyone, keep a few women. And we have other big problem."

"Emma doesn't need to hear about problems right now," Arthur said, coming up behind me. "Let's just get her back safely."

"Arthur, you can't keep information from me!" I snapped.

"Look at you, so charming when you're frisky." He wrapped his arms around me, drawing my back into his chest, resting the underside of his chin on the top of my head. We fit together that way as if we'd been cut by a lathe to interlock.

But now I had other matters on my mind. "Have you put yourselves or the camp in danger by coming for me?" I demanded, trying to shrug him off. He was a big fella, not so easily pushed around.

"I'm cautious, you know that. We left a week ago at night, under a cloud cover, and we rode south to throw them off."

"I hope you fooled their watchers. Arthur, why don't you just send the mists in?"

"I've thought of it," Arthur admitted, scratching the black beard-shadow on his chin. "But recon shows them with women and children. I'm not willing to suffer those losses. Every life matters."

"So they're still amassing there, and there'll be a

confrontation," I murmured. "Hopefully not while all of you are out here getting me."

Theo squeezed my arm. "Do not worry. Torsten shoots good."

"Laurette is a fine marksman, and Will's an experienced sniper," Arthur said. "Claude's a good man. Even Bojana knows her way around a rifle."

"If she'll put Dragomir down long enough to pick up a gun," I muttered.

"No, she put baby on hip, like so, hold gun with other hand." Theo threw one hip out in an exaggerated S-curve and cocked the opposite hand, demonstrating. I giggled reluctantly. Of course that's what Bojana would do. She wouldn't put Dragomir down until he was taller than she.

"When did Laurette and Jeannie come from the women's camp?"

"Himself fetched them two weeks ago," Robert said. Beaming, he trudged toward us. "Sight for sore eyes is that Jeannie." His eyes drifted to where Jeannie stood, pouring water from a canteen over her neck and head. The glistening water made a beautiful sculpted bust of her high cheekbones and long neck, an ebony Nefertiti. Robert sighed.

"Did Caris and Ginny come?" I asked.

Arthur snuggled me deeper into his chest, as if to shield me from a blow. "Laurette felt it was too dangerous."

I felt a pang of disappointment, but immediately quashed it. "Of course. She's right. Their safety comes first."

"Jeannie's a welcome addition. She's a gifted fighter," Arthur said, admiringly. "She's as competent as any of my men. Laurette, too."

"Jeannie can shoot the scruff off a fly's arse from fifty meters." Robert gave a puckish smile. "I watched her shoot, when I was enjoying Tara's fine hospitality!"

"Hikaru and Kimiko are armed," Arthur continued. "So are Marco and the older boys and some new refugees; they

walk patrols. The refugee women you let in take turns on sta-
tionary watch." He was trying to reassure me that the camp
was safe in the men's absence. It was sweet of him.

"Laurette's been at camp for two weeks? I'm afraid to ask
what she's been up to." I threw up my hands in a gesture of
mock horror.

"The camp is shipshape," Robert said, shaking his head.

"She does like things organized rather precisely," Arthur
said, in a dry tone. "But she is an excellent herbalist, she keeps
the children in line, and many of her notions, however odd,
are useful."

"How does she keep the children in line?" I asked. "Is she
scaring them?"

"Yoga," Arthur said. "Their fear seems contained."

"She scares me," Theo admitted.

"Me, too," I told him.

"I think she likes Nwokocha, and he'll soften her up if
he gets his hands on her giblets," Robert said. He made an
extremely obscene gesture. Theo and I burst out laughing,
and even Arthur chuckled. Robert grinned. "So, have you
informed the prodigal Missy about the secret?"

"What secret?" I asked, eagerly.

"It'll keep," Arthur said.

"How can you guys keep a secret from me?" I sputtered. "I
was held captive by a psychotic Russian! You should show me
some sympathy and tell me right now!"

"I'll show you sympathy," Arthur said, in a tone that
was only slightly less suggestive than Robert's. Theo and I
blushed, though Robert laughed uproariously. Arthur kissed
the top of my head. "Drink more water, then mount up. We
ride through the night tonight. We sleep tomorrow."

AT MIDDAY ON the third day, Arthur sent Theo and Shinji
into camp directly. The rest of us looped around to return to
camp from the south, which took us a few more hours. It was

dinnertime when the rocky, verdant land opened up and the camp sprawled before us.

The sight of the green fields fuzzed over with purple lavender, the rectangular walls enclosing multicolored tents, and the empty horse corral made my heart exult. New shanties had grown up outside of the walls. Off toward the eastern ridge, a group of small people worked at the stream, washing clothes: my kids! I leaned forward on Rosie and jabbed her sides with my heels. She bolted. I did my inept octopus thing and held on tight. Arthur's laughter trailed after me.

Rosie reached the kids and, snorting with indignity, drew up short; I went sailing over her withers. But what were a few more bruises when I was suddenly at the bottom of a puppy huddle? Mandy, Newt, Shoshana and Felix threw themselves on top of me. We all laughed and squealed with joy. I scrambled to my feet, still plastered with kids. Hoshi stood apart, her hands clasped bashfully behind her back. I grabbed her, lifted her up, and kissed her for good measure. The kids all wanted to know if I was okay, if I had been hurt. I assured them that I was fine.

"You're awful skinny, Mommy," Mandy said, hiding her face behind her auburn hair. Then she broke down, wailing tears of terror and loss, her whole body heaving. I picked her up and pressed her fiercely into me, murmuring reassurances. Newt stood close to my elbow, rubbing her forehead into my arm. She left salty wet trails on my skin until I drew her in beside Mandy for a tighter embrace. Shoshana stroked Felix's head as I somehow managed to get an arm around them, too.

Eventually Mandy stopped quaking. She burrowed her mouth and nose into the juncture of my neck and shoulder, which, I thought, must smell like horse sweat combined with the salty yellow snot of a child. Mandy seemed comforted by it.

"Where's Marco?" I asked.

"He's a big man now, doing a patrol," Shoshana said. She

rolled her eyes a little to indicate how this assignment had puffed up Marco's ego.

Laurette appeared, grabbing for me. I bounced Mandy around on my hip so I could return the warm kisses Laurette planted on both my cheeks.

"Welcome home! You look like shit!" Laurette said happily. Mandy picked her head up and giggled, and soon we were all giggling.

"She looks good to me," Arthur, appearing out of nowhere, said breezily. He took Rosie's lead rope and gave me a wolfish look. "Why don't you all come in for dinner?"

"Arthur, aren't you going to show her?" Mandy asked, in a small quavering voice.

"Show me what?" I demanded.

"After dinner," Arthur promised.

"Now!" I shouted. The kids laughed. Mandy slid down and grabbed me by one hand, and Newt grabbed the other. They half-led, half-dragged me to the well. Just off one edge of the platform stood a small wooden hut. Shoshana threw open the door to the hut. Inside were two stalls, each with a spigot placed above head level.

"Showers?" I asked, with wonderment.

"Look, it works!" Shoshana ran inside and turned a lever. Water erupted from the spigot.

The children all looked at me to see what I would do. I was dumbfounded. Arthur pushed me inside, under the stream of water. I shrieked at the cold of the water, then I laughed with amazement. He joined me there, wrapping his arms around me and kissing me so enthusiastically that the kids squealed and Laurette whistled. "Ooh la la!" she said.

"You and your antiquated personal grooming issues," he said. "I thought this would make you happy."

I was wet and shivering despite Arthur's strong warm arms, but I was so happy in that moment that I didn't care.

AFTER DINNER, DESPITE Arthur's broad hints about meeting in our tent, I marched out to track down Marco, whom I hadn't yet seen. I found him walking along the north edge of camp. He wasn't alone. An entourage attended him, two women and three men and six children, all jabbering in Italian.

Marco's face lit up when he saw me.

"Emma!" he shouted. He raced over and leapt to hug me. "*Grazie dio!*"

"Look at you, carrying a weapon!" I laughed and patted the firearm at his belt. Marco's chest puffed up, and he stood a little straighter. I rumpled his hair, even though he was as tall as me now. When, over the past nine months, had that happened? Didn't he join us, between Orleans and Bourges, when he was a whole head shorter than me? I asked, "Did you grow while I was away?"

"Silly!" he said. He looped his arm through mine. "Emma, I'm so happy you're back. Come, you must meet my cousins. *Magari*, they are not really my cousins, but they come from my village. And one woman is sister to my mother's brother-in-law." He introduced me to the Italians, who had arrived in camp just after Arthur and the men had left a week ago. They were lean and weathered and sported various wounds, but their eyes were merry like Marco's. They formed a tight group around him, with Marco in the middle. It made him happy. And they were obviously happy to have survived and found a safe zone. They spoke little English, but their faces were eloquent.

"We can let the regular patrols do this, since the men are back," Marco said. So we all trooped back toward the tents.

I draped my arm around Marco's shoulders, which were muscular and strong. He was no longer the twiggy boy whose high spirits entertained the others. He was growing into a man. "Marco," I said. "I had a dream while I was at the Russian camp. Actually, two dreams."

His eyes grew serious. He threw a look back over his shoulder at his new-found cousins. They waved gaily. Marco said, "I have not told them...."

"That you can interpret dreams? It's something to be proud of."

He shrugged ruefully. "I am, *in fatto*, embarrassed."

"It's a gift, Marco. But no one has to know, unless you want them to."

"We know," he whispered. He waggled his dark brows at me, playful and secretive and mournful, all at once.

"We, you and me and the kids," I said. "We're a family. No one will say anything."

"It's true. Emma, I have to tell you something." He squeezed my arm. "I stay in tent with my cousins."

A pang, then ease. I kissed Marco's cheek. "I understand, Marco. It must feel wonderful to be with relatives."

"Yes, and we have talked together. We would like Felix to be with us. We will adopt him. If it is good with you." His merry dark eyes focused sharply. He was waiting to hear. He wasn't even breathing. He really loved the little French boy.

I loved Felix, too. I love them all. But, one by one, they were leaving. First Dragomir; then Caris and Genevra; now Marco and Felix. Of course, only Mandy was really mine. The others had just lent themselves to me. I couldn't help feeling proprietary, though, after all we'd been through together.

I said, quietly, "You've been a big brother to Felix. It will be good for him."

He kissed me, then, in his carefree, impulsive way. "Always you are so wonderful, Emma. Thank you. Now tell me, but softly, about this dream...."

Sotto voce, I told him about the wise, jolly Rastafarian in the field of lilies. I repeated his questions: "What took you so long?" and "What is time?"

After I'd finished, Marco drew up short. He said, incredulously, "You're leaving us?"

"What?" I exclaimed.

"You're going to Canada to see Mandy's papa? How is this so? The men only got the radio working for a little while and then it shorted, and they have to fix it!"

I grabbed his shoulders. "Marco, what are you saying?"

"But you must know! Theo and the others put together some mechanical thing." Marco gestured with his expressive hands, showing me how big it was. "They attach it to a radio and speak to Canada."

"What? No one told me!"

Marco shrugged. "Arthur, he would not worry you. They also talk to big ship in *il Mediterraneo*. The people have no food and must land. He would not think of helping them until you were back. Wait, Emma!"

But I was already running back to camp.

14

I SAW THE NEW TENT RIGHT AWAY, the one they'd put up to house their experiments. It stood by the gate on the short wall, the Praetorian gate. Other tents had been displaced for this one, which was a large, peaked yellow and white affair with a logo that said, incongruously, "Kodak." A many-pronged antenna contraption poked out of a hole in the top.

Evening was sloughing plum and lavender shadows into the alleys and squares of camp. People were slowing down, sitting in front of tents and shanties, chatting in a mélange of languages, lounging by the mess tent, forming a line in front of the new shower stalls. Directed by Laurette, the kids were washing and brushing their teeth and getting ready for bed. The usual ambient noises of a peaceful camp swelled up: people talking and bickering and laughing, dishes clanking and chairs banging, horses nickering, a cow lowing; and, somewhere, Vasily running a card game and Robert strumming a guitar and singing.

I trotted by a tent and heard muffled noises. I drew up short, worrying that someone was getting hurt. Then there was the unmistakable luscious rollick of a woman getting hers. Oh. I hurried past, but not before Torsten grunted loudly enough for me to identify him. Bojana emerged from the tent and passed behind me, her hair undone. I couldn't believe she'd left Dragomir's side, let alone put him down. It wasn't my business, but I wished them joy.

I drew up at the door to the new tent. Artificial white light flickered inside. It was much brighter than candles or flashlights, and I jumped.

"Emma!" Pyotr said, sounding exactly like Theo. He opened the tent flap and gestured for me to come inside. I tiptoed in. Will, Shinji, and Theo were in there, fiddling with equipment that was scattered everywhere. They all looked up and acknowledged me, then returned to the piles of wire and tubing, coils, spinning steel disks, metal rods, and glass tubes, along with assorted disemboweled electronics: old toasters, fans, vacuum tube televisions. A large metal cone rose in the center of the space. Weird, hairy strands of light flickered riotously out from its top. It had been a long time since I'd seen artificial light. The flashlights I'd used had long ago run out of batteries, and I'd never thought to scavenge those. But this bizarre light was different from anything I'd ever seen, and it amazed me.

"I could not wait to get her going again," Theo said, happily.

"She miss us," Pyotr agreed.

"*Hai*," Shinji uttered loudly, which was apparently some sort of joke, because the other men chortled as if on cue. Shinji's face was swept over with a big grin.

"How did you do this? Where did you find this stuff?" I wondered aloud.

"It's been here all along. Arthur was prepared, and we've been collecting," Will said. He grimaced. "I should say, Arthur had his men collecting, while little bugs were eating me alive from the inside."

"Marco says you got a radio working," I said.

"Only for a few hours," said Arthur's voice, making me jump. He shouldered aside the tent flap and stood beside me. He gave me a sidelong look. "Don't you have some duties to attend to?"

"I'm gone for a couple weeks and you guys build a power

source, hook it to a radio, and talk to Canada?"

"You were gone for three weeks, four days, and sixteen hours," Arthur said, his tone grim and uneven, like a car with a broken muffler. I gave him a look: he'd been counting? And what was time now? Only love was real. I put my hand on his arm and smiled at him. He slid his arm around my waist and drew me closer.

"We started talking about things as soon as I felt well enough," Will said. He sat on a small stool next to Shinji, and picked up a small rotor, a jar of oil, and some cloth. He began to oil the rotor. "We were experimenting before you left to return Laurette to the women's camp."

"We work well and quickly together," Shinji said. "What we know is complementary."

"More than complementary," Will said. He and Shinji exchanged an inscrutable look. Shinji nodded as if giving permission. Will went on, "Weirdest thing. When the four of us work together, it's like our minds join. Anything any of us knows is accessible to the rest of us. But only when we're physically together."

"Telepathy? Morphic resonance?" I wondered. "One of the gifts, like my healing abilities, that the mists gave in the wake of destruction?"

"The mists operate on the biomind, and that's not fully mapped out," Arthur said, in his professorial tone. "Who knows what the human mind is capable of, with the biomind activated? It's fascinating. Nwokocha is a brilliant observer and chronicler. I'll ask him to start a study."

"Some people see what come in future, like Nostradamus," Theo said. "Who need fortune teller or cards now?"

Shinji tipped his head to one side. "My wife hears things, like music, coming from trees and rocks. From the stars. From other objects sometimes."

"We are all different now, for better or worse," Arthur said.

"Pyotr now have photographic memory, remember every-thing in books," Theo said, proudly. "So we all see it, too!" Pyotr stood and took a bow, rolling his hand theatrically like a stage actor. Will applauded.

"Pyotr's memory has been a big help to our group mind," Will acknowledged. "Also, we had a lot to work with. In terms of physical parts and equipment to play with. Arthur was supplied from the beginning."

"We also scavenged from the École Centrale de Lyon," Arthur said, with an impeccable French accent. "The build-ings weren't intact, but the useful detritus amounted to more than fifty loads. We made several expeditions out to the ruins to collect things. I had a feeling we'd put the stuff to good use."

"I remember," Theo said. "My horse kick my nuts first day." He doubled over in pantomime, and squealed in a soprano voice. Shinji laughed.

"Holy crap, we have light," I said.

"We get oscillation good, light will be nice ball lightning, stable," Pyotr said.

"Let's go back to our tent and discuss it," Arthur said. He took my hand in his and lifted it to his mouth, kissed my palm. His eyes fizzed at me. He wanted some alone time.

But I had my own agenda. "I want to know what Canada said!" I cried. "You had contact with civilization for the first time in nine months. This is amazing! I want to hear!"

"The world is in a shambles, the mists have killed almost everyone, British Columbia and Alberta were left completely unscathed for no reason anyone understands," Arthur said. He moved about restlessly on the balls of his feet. "Everything we already knew was confirmed. Can we go now?"

But now James came into the tent and stood on my other side. "You found the happening spot in camp!" He flushed a little, and his face lit up with an expression I'd rarely seen during these long months: hope.

"We are cool people," Theo said.

"Definitely, you're the cool people!" I agreed. I was still dazzled by their achievement: communication with Canada! "Tell me about the radio conversation. Who from Canada did you speak to? What else was said? How many people do they have, and how civilized is it there? Can they come get us?"

"Why would we want that?" Arthur looked surprised. The men in the tent stared at me as if shocked by my question.

"Well, you know, Canada is safe...." My voice petered out under their curious eyes. They did not share my goal of reaching Canada, somehow, some way. Arthur had inspired his men with his vision of rebuilding. And now they'd experienced some success in powering the radio. They were on a different page from me.

I changed the subject. "What about this ship that needs our help?"

Arthur made a growling noise. "Let's make this brief, shall we?"

"We spoke first with a military electronics technician in Calgary who was monitoring frequencies for survivors. She ran and found their current head of government," James said.

"He was happy to speak with us; we were the first contact with Europe since December," Arthur said. "Except for the cruise ship in the Mediterranean and some family collective in Le Havre."

"How the cruise ship survived the mists at sea, I don't know," James said, shaking his head. "It's a miracle. More than four hundred people still alive. They've been in regular communication with Calgary."

"We'll come back for further discussion," Arthur said. He scooped me up and cradled me against his shoulder. "I want my woman."

"Arthur! Stop it!"

"I rode for her; I saved her; she's mine," Arthur responded. The other men were nodding.

"Put me down now!"

"Couple hours," Arthur said. "See you later."

"Couple hours?" I giggled. "Ten minutes, tops!"

"You'll pay for that, you betcha," Arthur said.

In the end, he was right. Then I was too tired to do anything except sleep.

EVEN BEFORE ARTHUR or the children were awake the next morning, I was up, standing in the Kodak tent. The air outside was cool and moist with dawn, and only the palest creamy rays slanted up over the horizon. Shinji was already there, fiddling with some wiring, taking notes in a spiral-bound notebook on his lap. His infant son lay on the floor beside him, wiggling happily and playing with his tiny toes. I went over and scooped up the baby, cooed at him for a few minutes, and then snuggled him in my lap.

"You must have been happy to talk to Canada," I said.

"Yes. And surprised. We powered the CB radio to see if we could find anything. Then we got a shooting skip and we were using twenty-seven point five five. Suddenly there was a voice. Theo almost fell over!" Shinji grinned, and I got the impression he found Theo humorous. I grinned back; Theo had a funny away about him sometimes.

"Will we be able to make contact again?" I asked. I laid the baby flat on my thighs and tickled his tummy, clapped his hands together, pat-a-cake, pat-a-cake. He gurgled with great charm and intelligence. I was happy to see that he was getting chubby. Tiny Hikaru would have to build her arm muscles to lug this beefy guy around.

"Yes. We need to modulate the power from the Tesla apparatus," Shinji said. "Will is working on that."

"And, um, when you spoke with them, did they ask who was here?"

Shinji tilted his head and stared at me, his eyes making rapid calculations. "Last night you asked if they would come get us. You have people in Canada?" I nodded. He frowned. "Arthur gave a list of everyone in camp. They are looking for relatives."

Theo and Pyotr came in carrying cups of tea. "Emma," Theo sang. "Cook looking for you. He have something special for you."

"I'll bet he does," I cooed, because I didn't want to disturb the baby in my lap.

"True word," Theo said.

"Is it edible?" I asked.

He shrugged. "Not poison," he said. He clasped his throat with one hand and made gasping noises, eliciting a laugh from Shinji.

I handed off the baby to Theo and went out, brimming with unanswered questions.

Could I find out about Haywood and Beth? Could I get a message through to them, let them know that Mandy and I had survived? Should I talk to Mandy about this possibility, or would it be intolerable for a five-year-old, to hear that she might, but might not, receive word from her father and sister? We had studiously avoided talking about them, by tacit, mutual consent. Could I break that unspoken agreement now, or was it too soon, given the vulnerability we shared? I was so deep in thought that I didn't see Arthur until he was right up on me, his hands on either side of my face.

"Hey, beautiful, you were gone when I woke up." He kissed me, my lips and then my forehead. He smelled like cedar and leather, fresh air and horses and pine needles—his personal scent which, of late, made me sway and melt into his chest. He brushed his lips across my ear. "I was looking for you."

"I have to hear more about contact with Canada." I nuzzled him.

"You know the gist of it," Arthur said. He stepped back and gave me a searching, quizzical look. "Now that we've retrieved you, we have to worry about the cruise ship. They're running out of food. They're afraid to disembark because of the rogue bands. They lost a landing party that went to shore a few months ago."

"Mommy, Mommy!" Mandy ran up, followed by Newt and Hoshi. Mandy threw her arms around me. Newt did the same, and Hoshi did her bashful thing, arms pretzeled behind her back, so I ruffled her hair. "Your baby brother is cute," I told her, and her broken-toothed smile appeared.

Laurette followed at a slower pace. She called, "Allo, Emma. Cook is looking for you."

"The question is, do I want him to find me?"

"Herself had better find Cook, or his mood might spoil and he might add something nasty to her morning feast!" Now Robert was coming towards us. He walked with his arm draped around Jeannie's slim, muscular shoulders. The kids clambered all over him, poking his pockets for candy, which he always seemed to have on his person. He laughed and teased and then passed out wrapped butterscotches and peppermints. He offered one to me, and I took it eagerly. The butterscotch dissolved on my tongue in a blissful rush of buttery sugar.

"You need strengthening," Laurette said, observing my face as I sucked the candy. "I make you some tonics, red raspberry and watercress." In front of us, the four girls were comparing sweets. Arthur said something at the same time about a quick breakfast, and I found myself trying to take part in three different conversations at once.

"Mister Sir," Robert said, holding one out for Arthur. Arthur shook his head, declining. Robert gulped a little. "Sir, Jeannie and me, we'd like to talk to you." He took Jeannie's hand, and she nodded encouragement. He turned back to Arthur with a resolute air.

"Go on," Arthur said.

"We'd like to get married," Robert declared. "We'd like to have you to perform the ceremony."

Everyone stopped talking. We all turned to stare. Robert drew himself up with military precision, while Jeannie lifted her chin.

"Married?" Arthur seemed mystified.

"Yes, sir," Robert said. "Jeannie and me, we don't want to be apart."

"We're in love," Jeannie said. "I will live here. I'm a good soldier—you said that yourself, I'm a good woman to have around."

"We're going to make a family," Robert said. He pulled Jeannie's hand to his mouth and kissed her knuckles. "We're going to be together for as long as a gracious God gives us. I want a dozen babbies!"

"We'll start with one," Jeannie clarified, with a fond look at her red-headed man.

"Well, uh, sure—I have no objection to that, um, you being together," Arthur said. A fine pink flush played on his cheeks. It was the first time I'd ever seen him look flustered, and it gave me a wicked pleasure.

"So you'll do it, then?" Robert asked.

"You'll marry us?" Jeannie looked tremulous and hopeful.

"Me?" Arthur said.

"You're the law now, and we don't have a priest in camp," Robert said. He and Jeannie gazed expectantly at Arthur. He nodded slowly.

"I'll officiate," he said. Laurette cheered, the kids clapped, and Robert and Jeannie smooched each other, then kissed all the rest of us. Jeannie was glowing, and Robert looked dewy and ready to cry. Torsten ambled over to greet me and inquire about the ruckus. Others came, too. We were a raucous group, congratulating and razzing Jeannie and Robert, planning a party for the whole camp. I looked up and found Arthur's eyes like gray torches on me, hungry and intense. I gave him our private smile.

That was when the trouble really began.

BREAKFAST CONSISTED OF an actual omelet *aux fine herbes* that Cook presented to me with exaggerated relish. I rolled my eyes and informed him that he was a diva of the first order. But it had been months since I'd eaten anything so delicious: steaming hot and fluffy, and seasoned with dill weed, parsley and salt. Maybe it was the best thing I'd ever tasted. I felt so grateful that I bussed him on one of his sweaty cheeks. He reciprocated by smacking me with a wooden spoon and snarling at me to quit insulting him, which Arthur, Laurette, and Mandy found exceedingly funny.

"We have two dozen chickens now," Laurette said. "A *grand-père* rode in on a bicycle with a cart full of chickens while you were away. I've never seen Cook so happy."

"Grand-père only has one arm," Mandy volunteered. "He had his shirt sleeve tied up in a ball. He did a good job, though, Mommy, pedaling with one arm and all those chickens."

"He's going to live a long time," Newt said. "He'll like the Portuguese lady." She smiled at me and then swallowed another bite of her scrambled eggs. Arthur narrowed his eyes at her; we didn't have a Portuguese lady in camp. Not yet, anyway. Arthur felt me watching him and raised his eyebrows. Uh-oh.

But it wasn't Newt's gift that had drawn Arthur's attention. It was me. Laurette wanted me to go with her, after breakfast, to imbibe her herbal tonics. But Arthur informed her with, some severity, that he wanted a word alone with me. She sniffed at him with injured dignity, but led the girls off.

Arthur and I trailed behind. Marco and Felix and their group entered the mess tent as we were about to leave, which gave me an opportunity to greet my boys and remind them to keep brushing their teeth.

"There's something in the tent, be right back," Arthur said cryptically. He strode off, leaving me in the mess tent, as James and Torsten strolled in. Torsten saw me and mimed vomiting, in a particularly grandiose and egregious way. He was poking fun at me for throwing up after the amputation, months ago. He held up his hand in the rough shape of the curved lamb castrator. He and James hooted with laughter, but I didn't deign to acknowledge them.

When Arthur returned, I was still admonishing Marco and Felix, this time about their studies.

"Come on," Arthur said, pulling me away. "You're in the same camp. There'll be plenty of opportunities to lecture them. Let them eat breakfast. I want to talk to you."

"Yes, let's have a restful talk," I said, with some mirth. He cut his eyes at me. I said, "I'm just saying, after last night, you know. I don't expect that you have any energy left."

"Let's go back to the tent. I'll show you some energy," he said, looking affronted. I laughed outright and waved away his suggestion. "I'm not the one who runs out of energy," he said. "Anyway, I have something for you." It was wrapped in a pillow case and clasped under his elbow.

"A Corvette?"

"Didn't know you wanted one," he rumbled. "But if you do—"

I had a flash of Arthur sending his men to scour the countryside, looking for an intact Corvette. Here, in what was once France, of all places. Sometimes my humor escaped the man. I said hastily, "Just kidding!"

He grinned with one side of his mouth. "About Robert and Jeannie."

I sighed. "It's so sweet of them. What an act of faith in a hopeless world."

"Why would you say that?" Arthur looked astonished. "We've got good people. We've recreated Tesla's technology—well, we've made a start. We've made a safe zone." He spread his hands, indicating the whole camp. "We have hope. We even have promise. Hell, we've got two dozen chickens, two cows, and almost a hundred horses! A family of refugees came in just before I left, and they had a suitcase full of seeds. Next spring, we'll clear the surrounding area and plant gardens. We're rebuilding, and we've only just begun. We'll create something better out of the ashes of the old world."

"I know you feel that way."

"So should you," he said firmly. "We have everything to look forward to. And, Emma, I want to look forward to it with you."

"Of course," I murmured. "That omelet was superb. Do you think Cook will ever make me another one, or was that a one-time deal, because I just came back from Alexei's camp?"

"Don't change the subject," Arthur said, his voice husky. He led me along the rocky stream, where we'd often walked before. "You do that every time. But not this time. I want to talk about us."

We'd reached the big rock where we often sat to talk. I climbed to the top and stretched out, looked up into a blue sky with no end. The blue was a little more deeply saturated than it had been, the air cooler. Fall was setting in. What was it, September something? October? I didn't keep track anymore. What was time? What took me so long?

"This is for you," Arthur said. He handed me the package.

"A pillow case!" I sang, still reclining. He nodded. I slid my hand inside the fabric, which had a lush, high-thread-count feel to it. Better save it; it would probably be another fifty years before we had the technology to recreate luxurious bed linens. If we were still here in fifty years.

Then my fingertips grazed wood. A bumpy painted surface; the unmistakable fine, patterned channels of craquelure. I sat up with a jerk. Slowly I pulled it out: a small wooden panel. It was no longer in a frame.

I was struck speechless.

"Do you like it?" Arthur asked. His tone was light and teasing. "One of Marco's friends gave it to me when I agreed to let them join the camp."

"It's a Fra Angelico *Annunciation*," I whispered. It was ravishingly beautiful and precious, and I thought I'd never see such a thing again. My throat closed up, and I felt dizzy. Arthur stretched out his arm behind my back so I could lean into him.

"So it's okay," he said, in a tone that only he could pull off, one that included both skepticism and certainty, all laced with humor. I nodded. I couldn't take my eyes off the small panel. I'd never read about it and didn't know it, although that meant nothing. The Renaissance artist, a Dominican monk who had been called Fra Giovanni during his lifetime, had painted many private devotional works, as well as the frescoes and altarpieces for which he was famous. But I knew Fra Angelico's hand almost as well as I knew my own. It was definitely his: simple, with clarity of form and an elegantly defined architectural space. He used the blues, golds, and reds of the Florentine marketplace, along with a brilliant lucidity of pink, vermilion and lilac.

If I could have wept, I would have, at the panel's beauty. But I no longer had any use for tears, no matter what.

"I don't have a ring. So this will have to be my promise to you. If it will suffice," Arthur said. "I've been thinking about this, about putting it off until later, but since Robert and Jeannie brought it up, I realized that I don't want to wait. Let's get married."

I tore my eyes from the panel. He was gazing at me with a peculiar expression on his handsome face. It took me a moment to place it: yearning. I was deeply moved. What had Vasily said? That Arthur availed himself of the women around him.

I still couldn't speak and shook my head No. Arthur said, "Come on. We'll get married when they do."

So, after all, it had come to this. I had avoided this moment for so long and it had finally caught me in its fangs. I spoke softly. "I can't marry you, Arthur."

"What do you mean? Why not?" He looked thunderstruck.
"I'm married."

"You're not wearing a ring!"

"I traded it for backpacks, the first week After," I said. A haggard gypsy woman, like the kind who used to beg for coins in Metro stations, had seemed eager to make the exchange: my ring for six schoolbook backpacks. I had immediately seen the utility and agreed, never regretted that choice for a moment.

But Arthur's roaring interrupted my reverie. "You have a husband? He must be dead. No man would have left you and Mandy alone!"

"My husband was in Edmonton visiting his mother when it all happened."

"Your husband is alive. Fuck!" Arthur jumped off the boulder and kicked a rock, which arced up and crashed into a tree trunk. Arthur picked up a rock and threw it, hard, so that it slammed into a boulder and actually struck a spark. He swiveled around and faced me. "Divorce him! I am the law here. I hereby grant you a divorce. You are completely and with finality divorced from your prior husband. I decree it so."

"It doesn't work that way, Arthur." My heart was getting heavier.

"Yes, it does. I'm the law; you heard Robert. He was right. The world has ended and begun again, and the old systems of governance are gone. Right now, I'm what there is. I didn't ask to be, but I've accepted the responsibility. I have the power to dissolve your marriage, and I do so, as of this moment!" Arthur stepped toward me. He was taut with high emotion.

"I can't do it this way, Arthur. I have to talk to him."

He tilted his head. The skin was stretched tight across the zygomatic structures of his symmetrical face, and his eyes were afire; but they were thoughtful, too. "That's fair. I don't like it, but it's honorable. We wait until Will gets the radio running again. Then we track down your husband, and you tell him." He put his hands on my shoulders. "You will marry me. You can't escape me. I know you too well. I know all your secrets, the secrets of your body, the secrets of your heart, the ones you think no one knows. I know them." He gripped me.

I cradled the panel into my chest. I didn't say it aloud, but I knew I would never end my marriage with Haywood over a radio. He was the father of my children. The memory of him and Beth had pulled me through the deepest, keenest despair I could ever have imagined Before: the despair of watching millions of people die, most of them in agony. I was alive now because of Haywood and Beth. Leaving Haywood was going to have to be done in person. Arthur and I weren't done with this discussion.

15

THERE WERE TOO MANY PEOPLE aboard the cruise ship for us not to go to their aid, and Arthur made preparations to rescue them. He sent Claude and Michio south to Toulon to try to make contact with the cruise ship, until Shinji and Will could get the radio working again.

"If we divide ourselves in half, both groups are prey," Arthur was saying. "I can call in the mists, if there's time when we're attacked on the road. But that won't help the camp." His arms, biceps bulging, were crossed in front of his chest as he stared down at the big map on the table where he held his strategy sessions. The table had been dragged to a clearing in front of the Kodak tent that housed the Tesla experiments, over by the Praetorian gate. That was now the center of camp.

"It's a hard ride to the shore," Vasily said. "It's going to be brutal."

"Not for our horses. They are in excellent shape," Torsten said.

"Most people in camp are in decent shape, too," James added. He stood next to me, fiddling with one of Torsten's tools that he had co-opted. Fine by me as long it wasn't the lamb castrator. James went on: "The latest few refugees are sick, but I can get them ambulatory. They'll be well enough to use weapons. I can see to that."

"Your last recon counted almost three hundred armed

men in the gang on the west. We ride out, they'll attack the camp," Jeannie said. She glanced briefly at me. "Surprised they didn't attack earlier, when we rode out to rescue her. They had the opportunity."

"They weren't ready," Arthur observed, quietly. "But they're getting ready. We've seen that."

"Ready for what?" Torsten asked. "For when we expose ourselves completely?" Arthur and Jeannie scowled and shrugged. Arthur shifted restlessly on his feet, and Jeannie placed her hand on the hilt of the knife stuck through her belt loop.

"So how do we do this?" James asked. "Do we bring everyone with us?"

"We can't abandon camp. Whatever we leave behind, unguarded, will be gone before we can return," Vasily argued. "What can we offer the cruise ship refugees if we lose our camp? Anyway, we need what we've accumulated. It's essential to our future. We must protect it."

"We leave a few trained soldiers, arm the women and children, pull in the perimeter, dig more fortifications in a hurry," Arthur mused. He cast a quick, slanted glance at me, his eyes full of calculation. I could read his mind. He was wondering how fast I could fire and reload, how accurate my aim was, how many men I could take out if I had to.

"Leaves us tight on the ride to the sea," Jeannie said. "We're ninety-five soldiers, max, counting me and the thirteen-year-old boys. The roguers can surprise us with an ambush on both flanks, north and south, kill us, then go back for the camp." Her cheerful Liverpool accent belied the deadliness of her words. "That's what I'd do."

"You have a devious and lethal mind," Vasily told her. "I'm beginning to see what Robert finds so appealing about you."

"Thanks, Vas. Me man says you're a cool hand with a piece." Jeannie grinned.

"I can't call in the mists to attack them if we're surprised.

I won't have the time or the concentration," Arthur drawled. "We also have to get back to camp with the passengers from the ship."

"Four hundred twenty seven men, women, and children, last we heard from Canada," James interjected. "Malnourished, weak people, most needing medical attention."

Arthur grimaced. "Can't count on them to help defensively."

"Pack up the camp and carry it," I said. "That's what the Russian camp did. Set up a new camp." They all turned to look at me. I wrapped my arms around my chest, mimicking Arthur's stance. "They put everything on pallets and carried it out. Everyone marched to a new place. It was a caravan."

"There'll be no turning back and no coming back," Arthur said. "That's a one-way trip to a new campsite."

"We'll all be building fortifications again," Vasily grumbled. "Digging, digging. Christ, we'll be out there again with chisel and mattock. My shoulders ached for weeks. I think the ancient Romans had it better than us."

"Emma help your shoulder," Theo told Vasily.

"She'll have to work full time on my decrepit carcass," Vasily said. But his blue eyes twinkled as he ran a hand through his unruly white hair.

"You're not so decrepit," Arthur growled. "Emma can keep her hands to herself."

"I'm happy to help anyone I can," I said, softly. Arthur gave me a skeptical look. He wasn't jealous of Vasily, was he? I shook my head at him.

James cleared his throat. "We need a bigger camp anyway. And this way, the sick passengers won't have to travel all the way back here."

"Definitely will draw the gang out. We'll make an irresistible target," Jeannie volunteered.

"Not pallets. Wagons," Torsten suggested. "We have strong horses; they can draw the wagons. I can train them."

"I build wagons," Theo offered.

"Two or three days to build wagons, a few more days to pack. We send some snipers to pick off some of their men in the meantime," Arthur said. "It'll be a blitz of work, but it will get us to the passengers in time to save most of them."

"I'll go with the snipers. I can pick off the watchers so they don't know what we're up to," Jeannie said. "Don't want them reporting back to their mates."

"Claude's a passable marksman. Will's an excellent sniper, though I hate to pull him off our Tesla power project," Arthur said.

"Wouldn't be for long," Vasily noted. "How many watchers have we counted?"

"Four, and if we time it properly, we do it while they're rotating watch, take out two at once." Arthur nodded. "Have to send a party to recon the shore and find a site to establish a good camp. Defensible, with fresh water."

"We'll lose the showers," I sighed. I was really grooving on being clean; it was such a precious luxury.

"We'll build new ones." Arthur smiled. He touched my cheek.

"Wouldn't mind running water in the hospital, when we set that up in the new site," James added. "I just want to put that out there."

"We're exposed during the whole march," Jeannie said. "But we hold back a small crew, keep them hidden, and flank the roguers when they attack. Mow them down from behind. Even the numbers."

"Brilliant," Arthur said. He gave her a nod of respect. "We should have some surprises in store for them."

"How long will it take us to reach the shore?" Torsten asked.

"It's about a hundred forty kilometers, so if we ride thirty-five kilometers a day, it'll take four days," Arthur said. "We'll have to push everyone."

"Now's when we need a Lear jet, or really anything with an experienced private pilot," I said, in a light-hearted voice. They all looked askance at me again, and Arthur's face took on a strange, sick cast. I didn't have a chance to inquire why, because Laurette approached. She waved me to her, gesturing at a mug she carried in her other hand. I knew what it was: her special prophylactic tea. Thistles, smartweed, and some-thing else. It had done the trick so far, and I was grateful for it. I snapped off a smart salute and went off. They didn't need me at the bull session.

"How is your menses?" Laurette asked in a low voice, as I took the mug. "You are still early in your cycle, *oui*?"

"Why would you need to know something as intimate as that?" Arthur demanded. Laurette and I wheeled around, startled. He moved so quietly for a big man. He stood in front of us with his hands curled into fists at his side.

"Emma endured an ordeal at the other camp, I have been bolstering her constitution," Laurette said.

"Emma's got a constitution like an ox. Remarkable, for a woman as slim as she is," Arthur said. His voice took on a grim and belligerent tone. "What's in the tea?"

"Arthur, it's not your concern, please," I started.

"It's a tonic, specifically to nourish women," Laurette answered, shushing me.

"It's to prevent conception," Arthur said. Some fierce emo-tion made him vibrate too rigidly, like an overtuned string on an instrument. "You don't want to have children with me."

"This isn't a world——" I started.

"After all your talk about how children are the goodness of life, and your happiness at the birth in Alexei's camp, why don't you want to have children with me?" he asked. He made a gesture of dismissal. "Don't pretend it's about the state of the world. I won't buy it."

"It's not that I don't want...."

"Is it because you want to go to Canada to be with your

husband?" Arthur cut me off. "Is that why you keep mention-
ing airplanes? Because you want to leave me and be with him?"

"Arthur!" I said. "It's not about leaving you. Canada is
safe...."

"You're safe here. I keep the mists away. I rescued you
from the Russians. You have showers. Food is plentiful."

"Haywood and I have been married for nine years—"

"So? What is time?" he demanded. "A convenience. A
continuum, and one that's been irreparably shattered in two:
Before, and After. We've been together for five months now,
After. That's what matters."

"Haywood—"

"What does he have that I don't? What's so special about
him?"

I stumbled backwards, deflated. "I don't think that way.
There's no comparison. Please, it's not like that. Arthur."

Arthur took a step toward me. "You don't have to be married to him. It's a new world, a new order, with new laws.
Marry me. Marry me today."

"I'm not going to marry you until I've ended things with
Haywood," I cried. I was appalled and adrift, terrified and
anguished, all at once. Didn't Arthur understand what he was
asking of me? "That's not right!"

"But it was right for you to give yourself to me in the first
place?" he yelled. Laurette stepped back hastily. The people
standing at the table seemed to shrink into themselves. I saw
Vasily drop his face into his hands.

"I didn't have a choice," I said, closing my eyes. "It wasn't
just about me."

"There are always choices. You were doing a splendid job
with your little group."

"They needed more than I could give them."

"*I* need more than you're giving."

"I've given you everything!"

"Liar," he said. "You're always holding back, always

touching inside yourself to things that aren't here. It keeps you from being with me." His cheeks were flushed with high color. "The radio will be working again in the next few days. You will end things with your former husband then!"

I need the things I touch into. Why doesn't he understand that? Despairing, I stepped backward. "He is the father of my children—"

"I want to be the father of your children," Arthur said. "I've had enough of you closing yourself to me. Stop drinking that shit that keeps you from having my baby!"

I took a deep breath. "I have to speak to Haywood in person. To tell him I've met someone else. I owe him that."

Arthur drew himself up. The look he gave me was one of fury and contempt and something else—sadness, I thought. "In person. Really, Emma? Because we won't have transportation to Canada for *years*."

"Maybe it'll be sooner," I said, a little lamely. "They might have planes that work, a pilot who is willing to risk a flight...."

"What is it with you and your fixation with private pilots? No one in their right mind would risk flying across the Atlantic right now!"

"Eventually there'll be transport. Things can go on as they are until then...."

"I won't wait ten years for you," he said. "This ends now. It's him, or it's me. Make a decision."

"Stop bullying me! You're here and he's there!"

"Exactly. So what's it going to be? Are you going to cling to a past that's gone in hopes of a future that may never come, or are you going to be here, now, with me?"

"It's not that simple!" I cried, bereft. "This isn't fair!" Arthur's lids fell down over his gray eyes. For a moment, something hurt and vulnerable and disbelieving swept over his face. Then he shook his head and walked off.

A little while later I found my clothes and backpack in the children's tent, along with the Fra Angelico panel.

THE CAMP ERUPTED into furious activity like never before. Jeannie and Will walked out with rifles slung over their shoulders and cans of food stuck in pouches at their waists. They were, oddly, a perfectly matched pair: the tall, slim black woman and the narrow, fine-boned Brit who leaned on his cane. They talked wind speeds and sights, and haggled over camouflage and infiltration techniques. Will said good-bye to Laurette with a sweet smile and a bouquet of daisies, but she just shrugged at him. James was glad to have Laurette to himself, but she seemed more interested in Nwokocha. It was going to be interesting to watch this quadrangle play out, since Laurette now seemed to consider herself an established member of our group. I didn't think she would return to the women's camp any time soon, and I also didn't think that had anything to do with our camp moving location.

Vasily and Shinji rode south to find us a new home. I overheard Arthur telling them to look for a good spot, and that he'd take care of the mists when we arrived. He knew how to create a safe zone. It seemed to me that he'd grown even more confident since that day in the Gorge. I wondered if he ever thought about how we'd made love on the ledge. He now would not speak to me or look at me.

Torsten and the ever-resourceful Theo and Pyotr went to work teaching the other men how to build crude but tough wagons out of wood, metal, tents, tables, cots, and any other detritus that had been found, or tree limbs that could be cut. The children, other women, and I went to work organizing and packing. Our camp was not mobile; Arthur had never planned for it to move. There was a lot of stuff, and that meant a lot of work disassembling. We didn't sleep much, working far into the night by the light of torches because Theo and Pyotr wouldn't run the Tesla apparatus without Shinji and Will. We all were drilled in weaponry, though we didn't practice shooting. Arthur didn't want to waste bullets; we had a limited supply. He showed us how to throw knives and the spears that the thirteen-year-olds were making.

We were waiting for Jeannie and Will to return to camp when James and Newt came to get me. James was holding her hand. Her eyes were big and glossy with prophecy. I recognized the look, which came into her more and more often lately, and left her with fewer and fewer rational words. What would I do when Newt could no longer come out of her trances? I touched her cheek gently, willing her back into the here and now.

"Em, I think you'd better come with us," James said, in a low voice. I was busy nailing together a box out of wooden slats salvaged from an imploded building, but I kicked aside the hammer and went with them, motioning to Bojana that I was leaving. Mandy watched me go, and I blew a kiss at her.

We went outside the thick walls of the camp. I realized that I'd miss those walls, which had made me feel safe for the first time since Before.

"What's going on?" I asked. James held his finger to his lips. We passed Arthur and a group of men putting together a wagon, discussing the issue of axles. Arthur didn't look at me, but I knew that he knew I was there. His cheeks flushed and his spine stiffened. I could feel the tension in his body as if it were in mine.

We hiked up the same northern path that I'd taken to find Marco on patrol, when I'd first returned from the Russian camp. James and Newt kept silent until we were high up on the ridge, looking out over a sunny expanse of rolling lavender fields and thickly-leaved trees, scattered rocks and crumbled houses.

"They're coming from there," James said. Newt pointed.

"Who?" I asked.

"Your Russian friends," James answered. Newt smiled dreamily.

"Crap." I wiped my hands over my face.

"The question is, why?" James asked. "Newt says they aren't here to attack."

"They want me back at their camp?" I wondered.

"No. Yes, but they want to help us." Newt spoke for the first time. "The big yellow-haired man, he is looking and looking for you. He looks into me to see you. I feel him in my mind."

James and I exchanged a look, and both of us put our arms around Newt. After a few beats, James said, grimly, "I find it hard to believe that that Russian...."

"Alexei," I supplied.

"That he would want to help us, after what you've said about him. He's a dangerous sociopath."

"They are coming to help," Newt insisted.

"Will Arthur listen to them, or will he just order them shot on approach?" James asked. "He wanted to kill them when we found you. What will he do when they ride up? He won't give them a moment to explain their intentions."

"Crap, crap, crap." I thought for a moment. "I'll get a horse, ride out and meet them."

"Arthur might kill you for that—and not in the good way that leaves you screaming in his tent," James drawled. Newt giggled and covered her mouth with her hand.

"He's angry anyway; what the hell," I said, crossly. We walked back the way we'd come. The silk slipped out of Newt's eyes and she held my hand and skipped and sang like any other little girl.

When we reached camp, I kissed her and told her to find Mandy and help her pack. James squeezed my shoulder and went back inside the walls to the hospital tent. I went quietly to the corral and saddled a horse. These days I could place a pad and cinch a girth almost as expertly as Arthur himself, though I was still a tentative rider.

I mounted, and rode out quietly in the direction which Newt had indicated.

I HID, RIDING through the trees, slapped by low branches and scratched by the underbrush. The air was cooling and scented with pine and lavender and thyme. Small animals rustled and birds sang.

I heard the riders before I saw them. I let Rosie pick her way out to the road. We came out onto a group of riders, some thirty strong, a football field's distance away. Alexei spied me and raced toward me, his big raucous laugh ringing out. He called, "We got her! We go home now, boys!"

"You're not here to take me," I said, as he reined in before me.

"I will take you back. You will ask me to!"

"Not going to happen."

"I have seen it. In my mind, and through eyes of your little dreamer there in camp. I am eager to meet her in person. I know her little mind."

I shook my head. I was not going to discuss Newt with him. That could not be safe for her. I would have to warn the others to keep her apart from Alexei when we got back to camp.

"How is everyone at your camp, Alexei? How's Mikhail?"

At the mention of his son's name, Alexei's face transfigured. Briefly, it shone with the same radiance that always surrounded Mikhail. Then the old skewed expression of wariness returned to Alexei's rough-hewn features. "Mikhail is good. Strong. Healthy. He send love and good wishes. Marina, too. So too your Thai whore."

"Give them my love when you go back," I said.

"You will come with me and give it to them yourself," he said, with implacable certainty. Then Dmitri reached us, his big smile pulled askew by his thick scar. He shouted words of greeting and hugged me, leaning across the withers of our horses. I recognized some of the other men, who laughed and pounded me on my back and shoulders. This reunion was going to leave me bruised. Didn't they all, now?

"We are here to help you fight," Dmitri said. "Alexei says there is a battle. We must help you." I twisted around in my saddle and stared at Alexei. He winked at me. But his blue eyes were full of clouds and anger. Why had he come? Newt said he wanted to help. But there was more to this than my beloved little seer could foretell.

ARTHUR AND A group of men galloped toward us at a dead heat. It didn't surprise me that Arthur had sensed my absense. He could kick me out of his tent, but he couldn't break the connection between us. I knew that because I couldn't, either. I'd tried, during these last days in the children's tent. I thought about Haywood with every fiber of my being, trying to feel him and the calm familiarity of our bond. It had been futile. My marriage felt as cold and absent as the old world from Before.

"Emma, ride out behind me!" Arthur commanded. He aimed his gun at Alexei's head. Alexei dropped his reins and lifted his hands: peace. None of Alexei's men raised their weapons, even though Arthur's men all held cocked guns. Everyone took a breath and held it. I rode out in front of Alexei, interposing myself between the two. Arthur's mouth tightened. His hand didn't drop.

"Arthur, they're here to help."

"We don't need their help."

"Yes, we do. There's a battle coming. Why don't you listen to what they have to say?" I looked Arthur straight in the eye. Then I smiled, a small, wry smile that he would recognize from the many quiet conversations we'd shared by candlelight in his tent. He paled, his hand trembling almost imperceptibly. No one but I would have been able to see it.

For a moment, time froze. Then, fluidly, he holstered his gun.

"Speak, Alexei," Arthur said. He looked at Alexei, not at me.

"Arthur, that how you greet old friend?" Alexei called, in reproving tones. He kicked his horse and moved around me and Rosie. "We know each other long time now, no embrace for old friend?" Alexei threw a grin back over his shoulder at me. "After what I did to get you what you needed. I move heaven and earth for you."

"It didn't help," Arthur murmured. He kicked his horse forward. Alexei followed him, and soon they were out of earshot.

"I'm curious to see your camp," Dmitri said, drawing his horse up alongside mine. "I will meet the animal doctor who used a castrating knife to amputate a foot?"

"He's your kind of fella, Dmitri," I said. "He'll be happy to meet you."

16

THE CAMP FELL STILL WHEN WE RODE in to the corral. Everyone stopped what they were doing and swarmed to look over the walls at the strange group of riders. I waited, thinking to join the conversation between Arthur and Alexei, but Arthur waved me on. His eyes were coal-black with anger. I went back to packing. That night, Alexei and his men joined us in the mess tent.

"Arthur give us tents," Alexei said, from a few inches behind me. I jumped, not expecting him. Mandy was at my elbow, and she started, too.

"I didn't know we had any left," I said. I tried to step away from him, but Alexei kept the distance between us narrow.

"He move people around." Alexei shrugged. "We get nice tents, near his."

"So he can keep a gun on you all night," I said wryly. This made Alexei laugh. On the other side of the mess tent, Arthur shot us a stony look.

"Where is little dreamer girl?" Alexei asked. He looked around the tent. But Newt wasn't here. I had asked James to keep her in the hospital tent. I intended to keep Alexei and Newt separate.

"Mommy, is this the Russian man who took you away?" Mandy asked, in her fine, husky voice. She glared at Alexei.

"Your mommy come back," Alexei said. He stared back at Mandy. "You are pretty. I have beautiful son."

"Mommy told me. His name is Mikhail," Mandy said, with a matter-of-fact air. "But you should not have taken Mommy away. That wasn't nice."

Alexei bent down and whispered something in her ear. I couldn't hear what it was, but her face lit up. He nodded solemnly at her, then strolled ahead of us in the line for dinner.

"What'd he say?" I asked Mandy.

"He said that next time, he'll take me and you so we can meet Daddy!" Mandy looked thrilled. I felt troubled. Alexei tossed a knowing look back over his shoulder at me. I felt Arthur's stare burning my back, and I just shook my head at Alexei. What was his game? Why would he mention her father to Mandy? What was he really up to here?

THE NEXT DAY, Jeannie and Will walked back into camp. They were laden with clothes and weapons they'd stripped off the dead watchers. And they had something else: walkie-talkies. Arthur picked one up, turned it on. It hissed and squawked. He raised an eyebrow and turned it back off, threw it down contemptuously. Then he picked it back up and assigned Claude to monitor the walkie-talkies, keep track of the rogue bands' communications. The Russian men watched with interest, from a distance. Arthur had put them to work building wagons and making weapons, the same as everyone else.

Will didn't take time to eat, but went straight back into the Kodak tent. I asked Laurette to take him a plate of food because I knew he'd eat if she insisted.

"Why can't he get his own food? I look like a maid to you?" Laurette asked tartly, arms akimbo.

"You look like hot piece of French pie," Alexei said. He had come up to stand beside me, and he looked Laurette up and down approvingly. She sniffed at him and flounced off. But she cut her eyes at him, so I thought she liked his attention. Despite his madness, Alexei had a lot of male presence.

"What do you want, Alexei?" I asked.

"Where did William go?" Alexei asked. "What is that tent?"

"They're doing the Tesla experiments in there. How do you know Will?"

"He was Arthur's man when they do experiments Before," Alexei said. "I cannot believe Arthur still does experiments. Some balls on that man."

"They succeeded, once. They got the radio working. That's how we know about the cruise ship. The people we're going to save."

"I know about cruise ship," Alexei grinned. "I do experiments at my camp. We have many smart people. But I do not yet need Tesla. I find family with generator working. We talk to Canada, too."

"You spoke to Canada? Does Arthur know this?" I cried.

"Does Arthur need to know?" Alexei laughed. His blue eyes fuzzed over with madness. An expression of vengeance hardened his face. It turned my innards to ice.

"Are you planning to hurt him, Alexei?"

"Yes. I will hurt him. I will hurt him like he hurt me...." Alexei's eyes liquesced like a tide eddying out. He went to some place far, far away. Then his gaze solidified and snapped back like a rubber band, just as fast, just as painful. He laid his big hands on my shoulders and stroked my neck and back. "You are too tense, Emma. You must not feel such stress. It will kill you. No worry, I do not injure your man. I fight for him, fight good. Maybe, with our numbers add to yours, we will win, and the rogue militia will not kill us and eat us. I hope so. I do not want to be eaten. I have little surprise in store for those cannibal bastards. They will be sorry."

"Let go of me, Alexei," I whispered.

He put his mouth beside my ear. "Why do you worry about Arthur? He does not even let you in his tent. If you were my woman, I would not let you out of my tent!"

"I will never be your woman, Alexei."

"No, because you belong to another man. To Haywood Anderson," Alexei enunciated the name very slowly, very carefully. The chill in my gut turned to ice. How did he know about my husband? I'd never once mentioned Haywood's name to him. I'd never uttered Haywood's last name to anyone, since Before. Alexei patted my cheek and strolled off, whistling a lively Russian tune.

He must have felt me watching because he performed a few acrobatic Cossack dance moves, leaping, whirling, and squatting with his arms crossed in front of his chest.

VASILY AND SHINJI rode back as we finished packing. They'd barely bothered to sleep; they'd found a likely site and then turned right around and come back. Shinji waved once and disappeared into the Kodak tent. Theo and Pyotr went running in after him, leaving the last of the wagon-building to the other men and the Russians. The telepathic mind linkage that Will, Shinji, Theo, and Pyotr enjoyed was re-established.

Two days later, the radio came back online. Theo's shouting pierced the entire camp. I dropped the crate of books and papers I was shuffling together at a staging area and ran to see. My girls followed me. We tripped into the tent, where Shinji was scribbling furiously into his notebook and Will was speaking into the shiny black hand-piece of the CB radio.

"Got 'em!" Theo was singing and gyrating around the tent, stumbling over the mechanical innards scattered on the floor. He grabbed me and twirled me, dipped me in a waltz as I giggled. Arthur and Vasily burst into the tent. Arthur's eyes narrowed to thin gray lines when he saw me in Theo's arms, but Arthur didn't acknowledge me. He brushed past me en route to the radio, and I caught his personal scent of wind and cedar, horses and leather, just as I had smelled it on my breasts and belly a hundred times over the last months. It struck me to the core.

Arthur took the transceiver. "This is Arthur. I am in command of a camp located in the area that was formerly southeastern France, near where Valensole stood."

"Glad to hear you again!" burst a scratchy voice from the radio. "We spoke to a Russian group, asked them to help you while we waited for you to make contact. The passengers on the cruise ship are desperate."

"You spoke to Alexei?" Arthur asked, his voice brusque.

"They're a friendly group. Came by a generator-powered radio in Le Havre," the voice said. "Did they arrive at your camp?"

"Yes," Arthur said, biting off the word. There was silence on the other end. The tent door lifted, and Alexei and Dmitri peeked in. Arthur looked coolly across the tent at them. "Alexei and his men arrived. They didn't mention that they'd spoken to you." His face tightened. Alexei shrugged.

"As long as they'll help you," the voice said. "We hear it's bad there, mass insanity and vicious attacks. The passengers are terrified to leave their ship, but they can't stay aboard much longer. Their food is gone. They're sick and starving."

"We finish packing today, we leave tonight to get them," Arthur said. "We'll ride hard. Tell them four more days. Be ready on the morning of the fifth. They should be at the port of Toulon. We'll find them and escort them to safety."

"Today?" Mandy yelled. "Mommy, did you hear?" Arthur waved for me and the kids to leave. I ushered them out of the tent. I was glad to get them away from the tension that was brewing between Arthur and Alexei. Arthur did not like to be misled. He did not like Alexei, and that had as much to do with their history as with me.

As we passed Alexei, the big Russian reached down to grip Newt. Her face lit up, recognition and delight and the slow unraveling of mist-catalyzed prophecy. His face mirrored hers. They osmosed closer. But I grabbed her away, and then hustled my group to the other side of camp. There was some sort of connection between Newt and Alexei, but it could not benefit my little Newt. I would not allow it.

"Mommy, they're talking to Canada!" Mandy said. She wove her arms around my waist. "Do you think they're talking to Daddy? Do you think we'll ever talk to him? Is it going to be just like Alexei said, and we'll go back to Daddy?"

"Someday, Mandy love," I promised.

I didn't realize how soon someday was.

THE LAST THING packed was the Kodak tent. Pyotr and Will had conniption fits, supervising. Theo told jokes. Shinji became a Samurai, emotionless and intent and gracefully self-contained. All the Russian men stood in a tight group nearby, watching. Arthur had given Alexei a tongue-lashing that everyone in camp had heard. In response, Alexei had grinned and told jokes. I thought his impudence would drive Arthur to murder. But we needed the Russians if we were to survive the journey to Toulon and rescue the cruise ship passengers. Arthur's hand rested on his knife but he never drew it.

I was on hand to help, both in packing and in calming everyone. When the tent was mostly empty, I looked around and spied Shinji's notebook on the floor under a gutted CD player. I tucked it into my backpack. Then the men were yelling at me to get out so they could strike the tent. Within the hour, in twilight, we were on the move: all one hundred ninety-seven of us from our camp, plus thirty-two Russians. When the kids and I had joined the camp, it was less than half this size, and I was the only woman.

Flashlights, oil lamps, and a full moon lit our way. Against my better judgment, I drove a small wagon. Torsten had given me lessons in holding the reins and pronounced me "good enough," so I was in charge of a wobbly, jury-rigged thing attached to Rosie. The wagon itself was made of a trunk affixed to an upended kitchen table, and the mismatched wheels had been taken off of bicycles. It was a squeaky contraption, but Theo swore it would hold together and carry its load. Laurette had made quite a fuss about driving a wagon herself, and she insisted that it be a big one. I saw her scanning mine to make sure hers was bigger.

Torsten had a large cart drawn by two horses, and he handled the reins so expertly that I insisted that Mandy, Newt, and Shoshana ride with him. That was where they'd be safest. Bojana and Dragomir sat with them, and they were a merry crew. Arthur drove a heavy wagon pulled by his leggy roan and the piebald he'd ridden while the roan was at Alexei's camp. Arthur drove his horses fast, and passed me at a good clip. He looked me over in my seat as he drove past, but he didn't make eye contact. And he didn't speak.

Several people were on bicycles, including the elderly, one-armed man who had brought the chickens. The cart attached to his bicycle was full of metal bird cages holding the squawking fowl. Half the cages looked like they had been designed to hold parakeets, not egg-laying hens. The hens cackled at the indignity. It was remarkable to watch Grand-père balance himself, the bike, the cart, and the chickens on the grassy, uneven ground. He even had a flashlight tied to his handlebars.

Robert rode a horse and herded two cows, a goat, and three sheep ahead of him, which left me wondering when we'd acquired the extra animals. A working dog would have been a big help. A dog would also be an amiable camp mascot. I'd seen few dogs since the first month After; they seemed to have been slaughtered wholesale by the mists, though probably many had been eaten when survivors got desperate during the cold winter. Claude, Will, Shinji, the Russians, and two dozen others rode on horseback in a rough circle around the unruly caravan. They kept their guns ready. I didn't see Jeannie, and I guessed that she rode in secret behind us, leading a group to defend us from behind if we were attacked.

We rode without stopping through the first night, and

all the next day. We didn't worry about noise because we couldn't. The makeshift wagons in the caravan were loud with thumping and rolling. Horses whinnied and stamped, kids quarreled, Robert led us in songs. The Russians sang folk songs in such tight harmony that the men sounded like a professional chorus. When songs fell away, jokes were told and anecdotes were spun. Vasily told an interminable shaggy-dog story about crawling through the Paris sewers with a group of undergraduates from Cambridge, and I was sure it was at least half fictional. I mean, did he expect us to believe in mole men living underneath the City of Lights?

On the second and third days, the skies darkened and thundered. Deluges alternated with sprinkles. Fall was setting in. Vasily brought me a large men's trench coat and hat. The kids carried rain gear in their backpacks; they shrugged it on and scrambled under tarps. We adults covered our loads with canvas and plastic trash bags, coats and unfolded nylon tents—anything that would keep the water out. It was wet, miserable going, a slog through muddy red hills littered with boulders, but none of us complained. We were alive. We were together. We had food, and Arthur kept the mists away. I was sure we were all looking forward to a new home. Cook insisted that we stop for a lunch of hot soup under a tent on both days, but some of the children and several men developed coughs anyway. Laurette concocted a foul-tasting brew and made everyone drink it. She was popular with the Russian men and spent a lot of time with them.

The rain tapered off to sunshine in the afternoon of the fourth day. We stopped under some trees where the ground was less soaked. Everyone climbed down and shucked off wet outer garments, hanging them in low branches to drip dry. I had a brief flash of the memory trees in the women's camp, with their ornaments of artifacts from the world that had passed. Robert and Torsten and Dmitri took care of the horses. Cook and his aides got two big campfires going.

I was clustered in with Mandy, Newt, Shoshana, Marco, Felix, Marco's Italian cousins, and Laurette when a sudden gust of air wafted the scent of lilacs and sulfur. A big mist like a giant white orb rolled toward us. The kids screamed and clung to me. The Russians stood together, shoulder to shoulder, like a line of silent sculptures. Everyone would get to see Arthur in action.

With complete aplomb, Arthur stepped directly into the mist's path. He held up his hands, palms out; the huge pulsing, scintillating sphere paused in its tracks. He flung out his hands, and the mist scattered into billions of defanged droplets, then vanished completely.

There was a moment of silence. Then the entire group erupted into celebratory cheers and applause, with many shouts of "Bravo, Arthur!" Even the Russians whistled and stamped—all except for Alexei. He just watched.

At first, Arthur looked surprised by the ovation. Then a pleased expression came over his face, softening the perfect symmetry that lately had looked so strained. His gray eyes sought me out. I smiled at him. But he stiffened and turned away.

COOK SENT CLAUDE and Will with some Russians to hunt game, and they returned with two dozen pheasants and partridges, six rabbits, and two wild boars. Cook slathered the pheasants and rabbits with olive oil and rosemary the kids had picked. He then roasted them over fires. He had his aides butcher the boars, and he roasted the back legs, fried some steak-looking fillets from under the spine, and bubbled the shoulders in a stew pot with red wine and canned broth. As an accompaniment, we had leeks sautéed until they were delectably soft but still full of flavor. The rich, savory smell had us all salivating, and made the kids a little cranky with hunger. Surreptitiously, I scrounged a tin of biscuits for them. If

Cook had seen me, he would have beaten me with his wooden spoon, worse than Alexei had.

The sun kept slanting down in the west, the air thickening and cooling and filling with hazy violet light. The land smelled of rosemary, pine, lavender, and thyme. We all drifted toward the fires. Robert came up and laid his hand on my shoulder.

"We'll ask him to do it now," Robert said. "Right now." He had a starry look in his eyes. It took me a moment to understand. Then I grabbed him and hugged him.

"You're going to get married now?" I asked, with excitement, but in a low voice.

"Why not? That's me wedding feast if ever I smelled it," Jeannie said, joining us. "We may all get killed tomorrow, and I won't meet Saint Peter 'til I've been a bride!"

"We're going to make it," I said, as I hugged her. "I thought you guys were hanging back, in reserve. I didn't know your team would be joining us."

"Caught scent of that meat and had to," she said. "Best thing I've smelled in months!" She paused, dropped her voice to a whisper. "I think you should throw off the old man in Canada and settle with Arthur," she whispered. "What's the past mean when there's love here, now? Why take so long?" Her deep, velvety eyes perused mine. I couldn't answer, and she smiled and took Robert's hand. They walked away as I tried to swallow the lump in my throat.

I watched them talk to Arthur. He paced back and forth, his hands on his hips. He tilted his head, Jeannie and Robert said a few more things I couldn't hear, and finally he nodded. I ran off to round up the kids and everyone else.

In short order, we were all gathered by the fires. I sat near the front with Mandy and Newt in my lap and Shoshana leaning on my arm. Marco and Felix and their crew sat nearby. Laurette, with James on one side and Will on the other, sat in front of us, and Bojana, Dragomir, and Torsten were right behind us. The Russians had clumped together on one side. In front of all of us stood Arthur, with Jeannie and Robert to his right and Vasily to his left. When a cheerful, expectant silence came over the group, Arthur nodded at Vasily. Vasily sang, *a cappella*, "All Things Bright and Beautiful." The sweet hymn left us reverent, full of the joyful sacredness of the moment.

Arthur let a few moments of quiet stretch out before he spoke.

"Ten months ago, the world ended. All I wanted to do was live, and keep my friends alive." He squeezed Vasily's shoulder and nodded at Will. "As the days wore on, it became clear that I'd be able to do that. Then Vasily and Will found a couple of brothers with a sweet stockpile of weapons and a ready supply of jokes, and Theo and Pyotr joined us." Arthur paused because various members of the convocation had to throw out some *bons mots* at Theo and Pyotr's expense. When the teasing died down, Arthur continued. "Theo almost got shot when a scrappy red-headed Irish kid found him digging through a hidden cache of supermarket stock."

"Who are you calling scrappy?" Robert said, with mock indignation, and everyone hooted. "Those were *my* bloody supplies!"

"He shoot me, his aim is bad. He hit tree," Theo called, eliciting more laughter.

"Next time, I won't miss," Robert promised, which earned him a slap and a reproachful look from Jeannie.

"If Robert had managed the shot, and I'm not saying he's not capable," Arthur said, pausing for more laughter, "it would have been copacetic. We picked up a dermatologist around the same time. A doctor who could do a lot more than diagnose rashes."

"Not picked me up, saved me from the mists!" James called. Everyone nodded. So did Arthur. The Russians watched and listened.

I saw that Alexei was wending his way through people, moving toward me. He squatted down beside me. Newt twisted around in my lap. She and Alexei stared at each other. She reached out her hand to hold his. It made me uneasy, but I didn't know what I could do without making a commotion.

Arthur was saying, "It went like that, a guy here, a few men there. We came across a standing stable and acquired our first dozen horses. We found a defensible location and built a camp. We rode out on missions to acquire food, clothing, items of use. Life settled into something. It was barbaric and dangerous, but we had a sense of its rhythm. Then, one day, we rode into a village with half the buildings still standing." Arthur's eyes swept through the crowd to hold mine. "There we found a blonde woman and the sweetest, most resourceful bunch of children I've ever encountered." He paused.

"They are sweet, but Marco cheat at football," called Theo, making everyone laugh. Marco made a wet razzing sound with his tongue.

"Yeah, I'm sure of that," Arthur said. "The woman followed me into a house, and she said, 'I'm here, now, so what do you have to lose?' It convinced me. It shouldn't have. Because although I didn't know it then, I had everything to lose: my heart."

A deep silence descended on the crowd. I wanted to tear my eyes away, but couldn't. I could barely breathe. Beside me, Alexei was nodding with satisfaction. Arthur's voice was deep and soft. "My life, that I'd worried about so much, meant nothing, in comparison.

"It wasn't long before I realized that I was in too deep. This blonde, with her healing hands and her wise-acre mouth, who wanted everyone clean and nice-smelling, had gotten inside me in a way I couldn't have imagined, Before. She's the first thing I look for in the morning, the last thing at night. There are a thousand moments during the day when I want to talk to

her and touch her and watch her eyes light up. I can't wait to
have a conversation with her, just to find out what's going on
inside her. The time I have alone with her has made this time
After worth living. It's made me alive in a new way. I can't
ever be grateful for the Apocalypse because of all the suffering and death and destruction, but in its wake, it brought me
an incredible gift: her. I am grateful for her."

Laurette turned all the way around to look at me, her eyes
filled with tears. Other people craned around to look, too.
Arthur took a deep breath. "So when Jeannie and Robert came
to me and said they were in love and wanted to get married,
that they wanted to make a sacred and permanent commitment to each other, I was moved, and a little jealous. Mostly,
I was impressed. This obliterated world that we've inherited,
it's a bigger challenge than human beings have experienced in
millennia. The mists are still around, still ravaging, still killing. Most of the world's billions are dead. Of those who are
left, many have gone mad. Some have formed lethal gangs.
Food and the basic necessities of life are at a premium. Any
day could be our last.

"It's not easy to make a commitment under these circumstances. It takes courage and faith. Those qualities are in short
supply, and for good reason. We've all lost too much, suffered
too much, witnessed too much." Arthur's face wore a look of
intense suffering. "Which makes it even more incredible that
Jeannie and Robert want to be married. We, as a community,
we must support them." He put a hand on each of their shoulders. "They have my blessing. Do you two have vows you'd
like to say to each other?"

They nodded. Jeannie went first, and started crying when
she said she'd loved Robert from the first moment that she'd
knocked him out with her gun. Then it was Robert's turn. By
the time he promised to love her and be one with her forever,
no matter how much the Apocalypse had destroyed the world,

everyone was tearful. Even the Russians. Everyone except for
me, that is. I had no use for tears. Even in a moment of such
profound joy as this.

Then I noticed someone else with dry eyes: Alexei. His
face was filled with intense concentration. His hands and
Newt's were completely interlocked.

Arthur asked of them the traditional vows: "Do you,
Jeannie, take Robert to have and to hold from this day forward, for better or worse, for richer, for poorer, in sickness
and in health, to love and to cherish, from this day forward
until death do you part?" Jeannie said yes. Then Robert said
yes to his vow. And Arthur pronounced them husband and
wife.

Jeannie laid her hands on either side of Robert's face, and
they kissed while everyone yelled and cheered. Vasily tried
to sing again, but the whole camp leapt, yelling, to its collective feet to kiss Jeannie and hug Robert. Vasily's rich voice
was completely drowned out by the clamor of buoyant good
wishes. Cook chose this moment to pass out plates of food.
Suddenly we were a party, dining on a feast of succulent meats
and sweet, soft leeks. Vasily badgered and bullied Cook until
a few bottles of red wine appeared, and Dmitri brandished a
bottle of vodka. Vasily passed the liquor around for everyone
to quaff. Alexei went over to drink with his men.

I made sure the kids got food, then I ate. When I was done,
I went to join the rowdy, happy circle that still surrounded
Robert and Jeannie, whom I hadn't yet congratulated. People
were chewing and taking chugs of wine and crowding the
newlyweds, all the while hollering off-color suggestions for
their wedding night. I intended to shoulder my way in to
embrace them.

Something plucked at me. I swiveled on my heels and found
Arthur gazing at me. He stood about ten meters away, arms at
his sides. His beautiful face was a study in total vulnerability.

He had no defenses. He wanted me, and it was naked on his face.

I couldn't resist; I was magnetically pulled toward him. As I gazed back at him, I felt totally, exquisitely exposed. I was stripped of everything except the tenderness between us. I couldn't wait to be in Arthur's arms, where I belonged. Maybe I had always belonged there, even before I'd met him.

I couldn't fight it anymore. I didn't want to.

What had taken me so long?

Someone grabbed my hand. Newt.

I always wonder, what would have happened if I had ignored her? If I had surrendered utterly, and gone to Arthur in that moment? If I had held him and let him hold me? Would we be together now?

Would we still be alive? Would anyone from the camp still be alive, if I had shaken off Newt and crossed those last few steps to Arthur?

But this was Newt, Newt who had lost her memory, Newt whom I'd named, Newt who had some unholy connection to mad Alexei, Newt who was like my own daughter. I couldn't shake her off, even at the crux of my life. I turned to her.

"Emma! I hope they'll still be alive tomorrow," she said. Her hazel eyes were bleak. "They look so happy right now."

This was serious. I turned back toward Arthur, to gesture to him that I had to speak to Newt, that I would come to him in a moment. But Arthur was gone.

I felt bereft, frustrated, irritated, hurt, confused, lost. But what use were those feelings, or any of my feelings, when a child needed me? That question had been my mantra since the Day. Arthur claimed that time was now bifurcated into Before and After. But I lived with the Day replaying inside me endlessly. "What is time?" the Rastafarian in my dream had asked. The answer: time was what tormented me.

"Emma!" Newt said.

I pushed aside my despair. I knelt and gripped Newt's shoulders. "What do you mean, alive tomorrow?"

"They're coming," she said. "They're coming. Two on a horse."

"Who's coming? What does that mean, two on a horse?" I pushed a lock of Newt's stringy hair behind her ear. But Newt's face relaxed and her eyes went vacant. Her hands dropped limply to her sides. She was a husk, empty of the consciousness that made her who she was. "Newt! What do you mean, two on a horse?"

"She cannot hear you." Alexei stepped up, laid his hand on her head.

"Do you know what she saw?"

"Woman ride in front, to take bullet," Alexei said. "Child in front, if child is tall and soldier is short. Protect soldier." Alexei stroked Newt's head. "Nasty gang comes. They come before morning. They listen to Arthur on radio and they know Arthur's plan."

"Why does she go away like that?" I cried. "Do you know, Alexei?"

"Why not ask Arthur?" he said. "He know everything. He know much more than he tell you."

"Right now I have to tell him that the rogue gang is coming!"

I raced to find Arthur. He stood with Vasily and some others. He saw me approaching and turned his face away, crossed his arms in front of his solar plexus. Vasily gave him a sympathetic glance.

But this wasn't about Arthur and me. This was about the camp's safety.

"Arthur, they're coming. The rogue band from the west of our old camp," I said.

He straightened. "Coming now?"

"They'll be here by morning," I said. "They eavesdropped on our conversations with Canada. They know we're making

contact with the cruise ship tomorrow." Arthur barked commands, and the men around him jumped. The Russian men
saddled their horses so fast it was if they'd never dismounted.
The wedding feast was over.

I touched Arthur's shoulder. He cast a wrathful glance at
me and threw my hand off his body, as if my hand were boiling with poison. Of course, he was hurt that I hadn't gone to
him. But why wouldn't he understand?

I swallowed. "Arthur, they're using women and children
as shields." His face darkened with contempt. I said, "One last
thing. They're cannibals. If they succeed, they won't just kill
us. They'll eat us."

17

THE ROGUE BAND ATTACKED AT dawn. By then we had hidden the children in the top limbs of the tallest trees we could find and sent out a group to hide, a group which included half the Russians. The plan was for them to flank the attackers. Jeannie and Robert led them; that was their honeymoon, I guess. The rest of us clambered onto our wagons, waiting and dozing, alternately bored and terrified, pretending we didn't know what was coming next while concealing firearms with their safeties off.

The first salmon-colored rays of light seeped in over the rolling green hills, and with them came a whooping, blood-curdling ululation. Hundreds of horses galloped toward us from the west; a few dozen motorcycles roared alongside them. Red capes flew back into the wind like war pennants. The riders were firing bullets and arrows and throwing spears without even slowing down. The air was thick with machine gun rattles and wooden projectiles. It took a few moments before I could see that Newt and Alexei were right: each rogue soldier rode with a woman in front to absorb the return fire.

The next period of time, however long it lasted, was a haze of brutality and confusion, blood and the acrid smell of munitions, groaning and swearing and screaming. Time sped up and slowed down at once. Horses thundered in, kicking up red dust. Screams erupted, bullets flew everywhere, clots of blood and scarlet chunks of flesh and shell casings rained on the ground. It was a deadly maelstrom of lethal confusion. I was crouched down behind the trunk that had been my wagon seat, firing carefully with a Kahr pistol. I had always found it reliable. It did not let me down now.

Several horses dropped. I saw Theo, a few meters from me, take a bullet in his side. He fell, spewing blood in all directions, and would have taken another, but I centered my gun on the forehead of the rogue soldier aiming at him— the cannibal had thrown his head back, leaving a few inches between himself and the woman seated ahead on the horse's withers—and I took him out.

His horse was a thick-necked white Arabian which raced past as the man's body slammed to the ground beside me. I stripped him of his machine gun, which I did not know how to use. He moaned a little, and I saw that I'd only creased him in the neck. A nice shot, but not the one I wanted. The next one, at point-blank range, did the trick.

Then I slid the machine gun strap over my shoulder, got on my belly, and wiggled out toward Theo. I was not about to leave Theo exposed.

"Emma, hell you doing, get cover," Theo rasped, when I reached him. I didn't have time to answer, because four iron-clad hooves pounded toward us. Being trampled by a horse would be just as lethal as taking a bullet. I rolled over onto my back and fired almost straight up. The bullet went through the woman's shoulder and into the rider behind her. They both fell from the horse and rolled toward us. I was sorry for her, but hopeful she'd survive her wound. We could tend to her later. I popped another bullet into the rider's chest. He grunted and jerked.

"Theo, I don't know how to use this," I said. I laid the machine gun in his crimson hands and wound my arm around his thick chest, under his armpits. I tried to drag him, but I couldn't.

Alexei ran out toward us, firing indiscriminately in a circle—I hoped he didn't hit any of ours. He hooked his left hand under Theo's shoulder, still firing. Alexei jerked his head at me, so I took Theo by the other shoulder. We heaved him back toward my position.

Then Bojana screamed, and I let Alexei take Theo. I ran toward Bojana, who wasn't hurt, but who was pointing at Vasily. He had an arrow in his calf and lay half out from, half under a horse. Somehow, I pulled him up and pushed him toward Bojana.

What had Arthur said, that I had a constitution like an ox? I was glad to prove him right. He must have heard my thoughts because he appeared beside me just as two riders converged on me. I would have died choosing which one to shoot. Arthur had a rifle in one hand and a pistol in the other, and he got them both, then turned with balletic grace to shoot another soldier whom I hadn't even seen. Three men dropped to the ground and the women, unscathed, passed by on whinnying horses. That's when I noticed that the women were bound and gagged.

"Take cover," Arthur snarled. Then he was gone.

The most concentrated part of the battle was taking place a hundred meters south of me, by the biggest wagons. I slogged on my belly back toward Theo and Alexei. Alexei pushed Theo underneath my wagon, and I scrambled in beside him.

"Emma, stay alive," Alexei said, tersely. He ran off. I heard Rosie whimper. She'd taken an arrow in her front left leg and lay on the ground nearby.

"I good," Theo said. He rolled to his belly, shedding puddles of blood, and fired the machine gun. "Sorry, horsie," he said. A big black gelding dropped alongside us. I got the rider in the throat. While he writhed, dying, I crawled out and untied the woman sitting in front of him, whose leg was now wedged under the horse. She was dark-haired but fair, with the handsome, strong features I associated with Roman women. I helped her take out her gag and then gave her a hand as she shimmied out from under the moaning horse. She didn't wait to be invited, but threw herself under my wagon, alongside me and Theo. I handed her my extra gun. She grinned wolfishly. The next moment I was glad I'd done that, because she fired at a cannibal, down on his back, with a bullet in the thigh. His rifle was aimed at my head and I'd never even seen him.

The second wave followed immediately after the first. There were more soldiers. Where were they coming from? The three of us lay under my wagon. I was pressed against Theo, with the Roman woman lying almost on top of us, her feet in our faces as she faced the opposite direction. We took heavy fire, but it was just then that our sharpshooters took aim. Claude and Will were hidden in trees near us, and their shots suddenly got focused. At least ten men dropped out of their saddles. Theo and I and the Roman shot them in the heads, making sure they were dead. Red-cloaked riders howled as they rode through our wagons, but Jeannie's group rode after them and decimated them.

There was a moment's breath, during which Alexei knelt by the wagon. "So, Emma, you are good?" he asked. He winked at me.

"I'm okay," I said. "Not hit."

He looked pleased. "It will get worse. But don't worry, I have surprise. Good surprise. Arthur will be pleased."

"What surprise, Alexei?" I cried.

"Sister Marina is better fighter than you, almost good as me," he said. I wanted to ask him what he meant, but the moment's quiet was shattered, and Alexei ran off again.

The melee intensified: a third wave of stampeding, screaming riders followed. It was horrific. In the first few seconds, Pyotr took a bullet to his gut. Bojana and one of the Turkish women got hit. Torsten ran toward me and Theo, pointing his gun at a pair of riders behind us. Torsten got them, but he grabbed a bullet with his thigh. He went down on one leg, swearing in a language I didn't even know was a language. I swore, too, and wiggled back out on my belly. How the hell was I going to get Torsten to cover? He was a big man, lean now like all of us, but as tall as Arthur. Torsten had me by eight inches and fifty pounds.

He fired over my head and took an arrow in his other thigh. He slumped down onto his back, still firing. A rider rolled off next to us, pistol smoking. I put a bullet in his brain. Then I was out, out of bullets, out of cartridges for reloading. I tried to hook my arm around Torsten the way Alexei had done with Theo, so I could drag Torsten to safety. The Roman woman crawled rapidly on her hands and knees to help me. Torsten laughed.

"I am out," he called, still laughing. He seemed to find the situation funny. "You two cannot move me. I am large," he exclaimed, his singsong voice booming in my ear.

"I'm out, too, and we sure as hell are going to move you," I said, not laughing.

That was when I heard Claude grunt. He was down, not far from us, having fallen from a tree in an awkward pretzel of limbs and gore. I couldn't study his injuries because four horses cantered straight at us. The woman perched in front of the lead rider had been shot a dozen times; she was clearly dead, held up only by her bonds and the bouncing of the horse. The rider lined up his sights at my head. My mind flashed to Mandy, and to Arthur. I was sorry to leave them.

That was when the miracle happened: another group rode in, yelling something I could not understand. The rider aiming to blow off my head thudded out of his saddle and rolled to within a few inches of me.

The rogue soldier's eyes were wide open, blue and deeply inset and full of insane hate. He had a pale, even face framed by a tangle of brown hair, and he wore a red band over his forehead. He pulled a small gleaming pistol from his belt and pointed it at me. He grinned. I saw that his teeth had been filed into sharp triangular fangs. There was a kind of sickening inevitability about the moment.

Then something hard was in my hand: Torsten's lamb castrator. I jammed it into the rider's throat. Torsten laughed again, then eased into silence. The Roman woman and I lugged him, unconscious, toward the wagon as best we could. It was slow going but the bullets whizzing near our ears sped us up. Finally, we were close enough that Theo extended his arms and helped pull Torsten in.

That was when I finally had a chance to look. The new group was all women, led by Tara—and Marina. Marina held a machine gun and fired with the same cool as her brother, who ran up beside her and vaulted onto the back of her horse, firing the whole while.

The shooting after that was measured and effective. The group from the women's camp, which was only forty kilometers from the battlefield, wreaked havoc on the remaining rogue soldiers. At the same time, our people rallied. Theo grabbed a gun from a fallen soldier and fired it with quick, rapid strikes. Nwokocha, who lay on the ground near Claude, roused himself and scrabbled backwards to prop himself up against a tree, firing with perfect accuracy despite the hole in his arm. From under the wagon, I saw Arthur on his belly. He was spattered with blood, but he had two working guns and was pumping bullets out of them with cool precision. Jeannie, who'd fallen off her horse, coughed blood and crawled to take an Uzi from a dead guy, and used it against his buddies. Shinji rode through, firing directly into the heart of the last cluster of the rogue riders, taking down at least seven before his horse fell over on its side.

Suddenly there was a cessation of gunfire: silence.

"Theo, you have a knife?" I asked. Theo giggled, a sick, wet sound, and pulled a long, slim blade from a sheath at his thigh. I crawled out from under the wagon and went from man to man, slitting the throats of the rogue riders who were down but not dead. They had to be dispatched because the ones who were still alive were trying to get their guns, trying to throw knives. I bent over a big guy who looked Spanish. I raised my hand, but Laurette grabbed my wrist.

"My turn," she sang. She slammed a wicked-looking blade of her own into his throat. She gave me a beatific smile. "I kill at least seven, you?"

"If you got seven, I got eight," I said.

"I got nine," she returned. We hugged and moved on to the other fallen riders.

It wasn't long before Arthur stood in the center of the field, barking orders, calling people to account for themselves, reminding us that we had to get to Toulon to help the passengers of the cruise ship. We had to regroup, bandage on the fly, and press on to prevent more deaths; every living sane person was precious. Besides, there might be more gangs, or the remnants of this one, waiting to attack.

Robert, Laurette, Kimiko, and I were unscathed. James was unhurt and covered in other people's blood. He, Laurette, and I went to work triaging. Two of Tara's women who were trained nurses joined us. Claude was dead. The Turkish woman whose foot we'd amputated was dead, too. Torsten, Theo, Nwokocha, Jeannie, Bojana, Hikaru, Vasily, and Arthur, along with dozens of others, including the Grand-père of the chickens, were injured. Shinji was bruised from his horse falling on him, but otherwise whole. Pyotr was in a bad way.

Torsten was the worst off. He'd lost a lot of blood, having been nicked in an artery in his thigh. He hovered near death. I held my hands over him, letting the healing current shut off the geyser of blood, while James stitched him up. There was no I.V., no blood to transfuse, and no medication. Laurette brought over vinegar and a jar of one of her herbal infusions, for bathing both the wounds and James' hands between casualties.

"Let's stop the bleeding first," James said, grimly. When he'd sewn several crude stitches into Torsten, he asked one of Tara's women to exert pressure on the wounds and keep watch. We moved on to Pyotr. Then to Nwokocha, who was suffering from a hole through the meat of his upper arm. James instructed Laurette to make a fire and heat up her knife to cauterize Nwokocha's wound. He didn't pause, but moved to Theo. We went from person to person like that, treating them together. I pumped in the feathery healing current to stop the blood flow, and James cut, extracted, stitched, and bandaged the flesh. He had some of Torsten's tools, a forceps and retractor, to help him. Laurette got to do the cauterizing behind us. Her face was a mask of efficiency, but I was pretty sure she was nauseous from the smell of burning flesh. I was. But with any luck, she'd vomit and I wouldn't, and I could tease her forever.

Tara's women chased and dispatched the last few rogue soldiers. Then they rode back to help with the fallen. Tara's two nurses helped stanch bleeding, dress wounds, and get people back on their feet. Others tended to the captives who'd been used as shields. They were grateful to be untied. The green field was slick with blood and the air was choked with the smell of cordite, but the mood lifted as we realized that most of us were alive. We'd come through it pretty well.

In fact, after we'd tended to the worst injuries, a definite feeling of lightness came over the group. Theo cracked a lame joke, which prompted Vasily to do the same. Two of the captive women started singing, softly at first and then with more energy. It was some soul-stirring anthem in Italian. One of the nurses knew it and joined in, and soon others were singing it, too. Torsten woke and cuddled with Bojana, who'd been creased along her rib cage by a bullet but was otherwise remarkably well.

Finally James and I reached Arthur. He had caught a bullet in his left hip and another in his right bicep. He leaned back against his wagon, wiping blood off himself with his shirt, eying the damage to his body. James rinsed the two areas with rubbing alcohol and dug in with his scalpel. I saw Arthur's eyelids droop and his lips whiten as they pressed together. My heart wrenched in my chest, and I laid my hands on his bare shoulder, hoping to ease his pain.

Arthur's lids fluttered open. He grabbed my hand, his thumb over the center of my palm, and he looked at me. That was it—he just looked at me. His gray eyes played over my face. I directed the healing current to flow out my other hand, the one that still rested on his warm shoulder. Arthur uttered not a sound as James worked, though it must have been excruciating. James murmured about Arthur's good luck and superficial wounds. I barely heard it because all I could take in was Arthur's blazing eyes as they moved over me. I could not read his expression, nor could I look away.

"We're done here. Let's move on, Emma," James said. I lifted my hand from Arthur and stepped away to follow James.

Arthur wouldn't release my other hand. He kept me there in front of him.

It was the last time we touched.

"Emma, I need you!" James yelled. I tipped my head apologetically. Arthur threw my hand away, scornful and full of rejection, like last night. I exclaimed, hurt, but he turned his back to me. Slowly I followed James. I peeked back over my shoulder, saw Tara move in to speak with Arthur, laying her hand on his bare chest.

"We found William in a tree, alive," I heard Tara telling Arthur.

A babble of languages rose up, conversation and song and high spirited joshing. People had started to repack the wagons since we still had to get to Toulon for the cruise ship, whose passengers were in such dire straits. Other people were going to work on the horses. There were now several hundred rid-erless beasts standing around, grazing or swishing their tails uncertainly. At least a hundred lay on the ground. Many were grievously injured and writhing in pain; they would have to be put down. Other horses could be patched up. One of Tara's nurses, inspecting Rosie, called out, "This one can be saved." Rosie's arrow was extracted from the meat of her foreleg. It made me happy to see the nurse bandage Rosie, whose heart was always bigger than her abilities.

James came to a man with a bullet in his groin. He was one of the Italian men from Marco's family.

Marco. We'd left him in the tree, guarding the other chil-dren. My heart almost leapt out of my chest. Were the chil-dren safe? Had they been found by the rogue band during the battle? Was Mandy all right?

"James, I have to get the kids," I said, urgently. It didn't matter how many wounded people needed me. The children needed me more. James nodded without looking. I ran off, clambered onto a horse, and rode to get the children.

THEY WERE TWO kilometers away, high up in two large and very old oak trees with a 360-degree view of the green hills, the forests, the river, and the gorge to the north. They saw me trotting toward them and climbed down from branch to branch, dropping and swinging like monkeys. Mandy, Newt, Marco, Felix, Shoshana, Dragomir, Hoshi with her baby brother in the carrier on her chest, Kei, Kimi the toddler, the Swiss boy, the two-thirteen-year old boys from the women's camp, Marco's six young Italian cousins, and a couple of other refugee children. All of them were unharmed. Twenty-six small people, each one immeasurably precious and valuable. The future of the human race, if we had a future. Arthur claimed we did; I wasn't so sure.

"Is it over? Did we win?" Mandy asked, throwing herself

at me when I dismounted. I whooped and lifted her up to kiss her sweet face.

"Of course we won, Mandy. We were always going to," Newt said, in her arch way. "Some things you can't change, even if you try. Even if you really, really want to. They have to happen. Time is already set around them."

Shoshana bounced up and down, then pulled my head close to hers. "Emma, Newt says that a woman related to me is on the ship, and I'll see her," she whispered into my ear. "Isn't that exciting?"

"So wonderful, Shoshana," I responded. I smoothed her thick black hair back off her face, happy and grateful that another one of my charges would be reunited with someone close to them, and also a little sad to lose one more.

Shoshana's eyes shone. "It must be Ema's cousin, who was in the army and was taking a vacation with her boyfriend!"

Newt was still talking. Marco stuck his elbow in my side. "She won't be quiet," he said, grinning. "She's been talking and talking for the last hour! She keeps talking about the women that the Russian sent."

"He showed me in my mind," Newt said. "They all left their camp together, and then he sent his sister to the women's camp. I wonder if she saw Ginny and Caris." She was speaking so fast and so breathlessly that I hugged her. She kept going even with my arms around her. The blue streak she was talking came out of some unnamed anxiety.

But I was too busy to pursue it, too busy hugging all the kids and inquiring about their hours in the trees. They wanted to know what had happened. I had to explain that the battle was hard fought and many people were hurt, but we'd emerged victorious. Now we would finish our journey to Toulon to rescue the dying cruise ship passengers. I gave Shoshana the horse's lead and took the baby from Hoshi. We ambled back toward the wagons, jovial and conversational.

The kids pressed me with questions: who was hurt, how

many soldiers there were, what it was like. I gave them an abbreviated version of events. They were children, after all. Newt already knew about Tara's women joining us at the crucial moment.

"He's very smart, Alexei," Newt said, still babbling. "He showed me his plans in my head when I was worried."

"Look at the big blue butterfly!" Mandy called, pointing. It fluttered away, toward the rising crest of a hill. Mandy laughed and gave chase. In the distance, a horse raced toward us, and a feeling of foreboding, like a ghost rider, rose up within me. My gut twanged. I hurried to unbuckle the baby carrier. My hands shook.

"Mandy, come back!" I called, anxiously. She had dropped out of sight, running down the other side of the hill. I couldn't hear her, and she probably couldn't hear me. "Mandy!" I screamed. "Come now!"

"I'll get her," Marco yelled. All I saw was the muddy soles of his sneakers as he flew toward the hill. But Newt had beat him to it. She was almost there. I finally got the baby off my chest. I handed him off. Dread growing in the pit of my belly, I raced after Mandy, Newt, and Marco.

I was coming up over the hill when the screaming started. That's when the scent assailed me: sulfur and lilacs. Down at the base of the hill, tearing itself out of a cleft in a rock outcropping, a truck-sized, vaguely cubic mist hovered, white and sparkly, only inches down the incline from Mandy. She wasn't moving; she was rooted to her spot with fear. I could see her terrified, quivering back as she screamed.

"Mandy, Mandy, come back here!" I cried, but she was out of her mind with terror, and screaming too loudly to hear.

That's when Newt reached her, grabbed her, and bodily tossed Mandy up the hill, away from the mists. And in doing that, Newt lost her balance. Her arms windmilled. She teetered on her heels. Then she fell backward into the mist. Marco caught Mandy, pressed her into his shoulder, and bolted back up the hill toward me.

"Get the kids away!" I yelled. He nodded, didn't slow down, kept running with Mandy toward the others. I didn't have to watch to know he'd hustle them out of this area, back to the wagons and Arthur and safety.

I watched Newt as my heart shattered. She fell to her knees inside the mist. It wasn't a thick one, so she hadn't been instantly dissolved into water and sand. It was one of the less viscous mists. It was still going to kill her, just slowly. It dissolved pieces of her hair and popped one of her eyeballs. She had been holding her breath, but now she screamed in pain. Two horses cantered to the hill: Shoshana was on my horse. Alexei rode the other. But it was too late. Newt had taken in a shuddering breath. Besides, the pounding of two horses' hooves wasn't enough to influence the mists. Newt now had a face, and lungs, full of blood and mist.

"Emma," Shoshana said. I looked up at her. Her face was solemn and swollen with tears. She said, "Do it." She pulled the reins to turn the horse, and rode away. She couldn't watch. She was right not to. Alexei dismounted and walked toward me. His big shaggy head swung from side to side, like a German shepherd's.

I walked down as close to the pulsating white cube as I dared. I pulled out my gun. It was empty. Only Theo's knife was left. I'd secured it around my waist with a leather belt stripped off a fallen rogue soldier. Newt coughed blood and moaned and shrieked. One of her hands had been partially disintegrated down to her knuckles. She was hunched into herself, her back like a carapace, protecting her vulnerable parts. I couldn't get the knife into her, with her all curled up into herself like that.

I had to get her attention, but I couldn't speak. I held the knife out. Alexei called, "Little Dreamer!" She looked up, exposing her throat. I threw the knife, hard but carefully, as Arthur had shown us all how to do. A perfect hit.

ALEXEI DRAGGED ME back up the hill when I collapsed. We sat on the crest, watching the pulsing cube, which was slowly condensing in upon itself. In a little while, the mist would suck itself up and sluice back into the rocks. Newt would be gone, dissolved. Only a handful of sand would be left of my sweet little seer, who had walked alongside me these last ten months, trusting me to take care of her, to protect her.

"Newt, oh, Newt," I said. "Why?" I rocked back and forth, barely able to breathe because of the pain in my ribs and chest. I could only think of Arthur. I was going to go to him. I was going to ask him to hold me. I was going to give myself to him the way he wanted. I ached for that, fiercely. To hell with Haywood. Who knew when or if I would ever see him again? I loved Arthur. What had taken me so long?

"Why? Because Arthur go too far," Alexei said. "Poor little dreamer girl. Her mind was sweet like nectar of flower. I will miss her. So much Arthur take from us."

"I know you hate Arthur, but what does he have to do with this?" My voice scratched painfully through my raw throat.

Alexei stared at me. His blue eyes were stark and clear. "He never tell you. Of course, he is ashamed."

"Told me what? Stop playing coy and just say it!"

Alexei looked at me for a moment before speaking. His voice was solemn. "Arthur invent the mists," he said. "They were his project. He try to create new kind of weapon to distract minds of soldiers and destroy munitions, weapons, and militia buildings without killing people. New kind of war: no casualties. Mists give victory through psychological defeat. Mists dissolve bullets and missiles and tanks." He paused. "But Arthur mess up."

"What? What are you talking about?" I cried. "Don't be ridiculous! Arthur did not invent the mists! No one invented them. They're a, a—a bizarre natural phenomenon!"

"No, Emma."

"That's what all the scientists said!"

"Scientists are liars. Government are liars. Arthur is liar—and murderer."

"Alexei, you are insane. You are insane with hate. Arthur did not do this to the world!"

"Arthur reach too far. His ambition destroy world. He want to save it, but it all go to hell. He crush the world under big white stone of death by mists."

"No! Stop it! Stop what you are saying!"

"When he know his mistake, he come to me. He ask me for nuclear device. A bomb. He will destroy his lab to destroy mists. It is irony, no?" Alexei laughed. "Arthur the do-gooder fulfill dreams of terrorists: detonate nuclear device in central England, outside London. People he want to defeat, he carry out their objectives. Many people would die. But not as many people as in his Apocalypse, no? Hundred thousands, compared to billions. He make correct choice. But mists chose different."

"Shut up!" I leapt to my feet.

"He do not know how else to destroy mists, when he see they have will of their own. He want to make sure no one resurrect his experiments. So he plan to bomb his own facility."

"This is not possible!"

"I got him nuclear bomb, oh yes. I am Alexei; I can get anything. But he is too late." Alexei laughed again. "He is too late. Mists escaped containment. They fly out. For few months, there is silence. Then they come out, in Antarctica, other places. People are killed. My wife, Mikhail's mother. Everyone else."

He was still speaking, but I fled.

I PASSED THE kids near the camp. They were sobbing and keening for Newt. They clung to me, though I was stunned and frozen and could barely breathe. We got to the wagons, where people sang and laughed and bustled as they repacked and re-harnessed horses. Cook was spattered with blood and sported a bandage over one arm, but he was passing out food. Wounded people were laid on top of packs in the wagons. The dead were stripped of their gear and clothing and then piled off to one side, atop piles of kindling. There would be funeral pyres to light our departure.

Laurette rushed over. "What has happened?" she demanded breathlessly. Her sharp eyes scanned the children. "Where is Newt?" I shook my head. She covered her face with her hands. Then she fell to her knees to clasp as many kids as she could to her bosom. At least a dozen of them tumbled into her slim arms. Some part of my traumatized mind registered this: Laurette was always surprising me. The rest of me was in shock.

"Where's Arthur?" I asked, numbly.

"He's making rounds with Tara and Vasily and Dmitri to rebuild wagons and check our supplies. He wants to leave as soon as possible and...."

I sprinted away. I had to speak with Arthur.

A few hundred meters away, beside the wagon with the Tesla equipment and the now-folded Kodak tent, I found him. He wasn't alone. He stood beside Tara, and Vasily sat on the ground next to him. Arthur's bare back faced me. Dark smears of dried blood over his ribs and kidneys showed where he'd bled from the bullets. I ran to him, grabbed his arm, and jerked it so he'd face me.

"Tell me about the mists and the biomind and a weapon to dissolve metal, Arthur," I said. My voice shook. "Tell me about the way the mists eat iron, cobalt, nickel, copper, and zinc. Tell me how you know so much. Tell me!"

"I've told you...."

"Liar!"

Arthur paled all the way into his lips. "The mists attack the biomind."

"*And?*"

Arthur turned and walked away. I followed him. He

swiveled around, smartly, as if executing a military drill. His affect changed. He became the brilliant military professor, full of haughty cerebral words and formulistic phrases to hide the painful truth of death and destruction. He was not the man who held me and loved me all night. He was a stranger of arrogant and brutal mien. He said, "The biomind is the individual's heightened perceptual system. It's the receiver and the tuner for the Morphic fields, which operate via Morphic resonance. The biomind's state of receptivity is the measure of psi quotient in the individual. The biomind can be influenced to inhibit or allow greater attunement to Morphic resonance, which can render an individual susceptible to psychological control. It also increases psi quotient, enhancing psychic abilities. I designed the experiments and used the data about biomind and Morphic fields to create anti-personnel, anti-weapon ordnance." His eyes were like lit coals in his blanched face.

"Talk like a real person," I said. I felt broken inside.

"I created a weapon to control the minds of enemy soldiers and to disintegrate the instruments of war. It was supposed to eradicate war."

Vasily had come to stand beside Arthur. Vasily curled his arms around his middle and said, softly, "Arthur. No. You don't have to do this."

Arthur said, "It was supposed to bring peace."

"Billions have died," I said.

"I was trying to end war forever," Arthur said, in an anguished voice. "I was trying to save people. To end the threat of nuclear war. To save the world. My intention was pure. I thought I could give humanity its greatest gift ever: lasting peace. You must understand, Emma."

"It was a worthy goal! The highest, most important goal ever!" Vasily burst out. But he was gripping himself tighter and tighter around his stomach, stanching an imaginary wound. Tara shook with tears, her lovely face crumpled and gray.

"Newt is dead," I said softly. I turned around, numb. I walked back to the wagons, not breathing. I don't remember the walk and don't know what route I took.

I found myself at my wagon. Alexei was there, holding Mandy with one hand and my backpack with the other.

"Emma, when we talk to Canada, I ask for your husband. I speak to Haywood Anderson," Alexei said. "He say he is pilot. He say he fly plane to Le Havre. Come, I take you to him."

At last, someone had given voice to the thing I'd secretly hoped for, but been afraid to speak aloud all this time: that Haywood, who was a pilot, would come to rescue Mandy and me. Haywood was a private pilot with extensive flight experience, including a decade with the civil air patrol. He was a lawyer by profession, but had almost as much training as any commercial pilot. I dug in the wagon for the Fra Angelico panel, stared at it, and then left it there.

I nodded at Alexei. He handed me my backpack, then set Mandy up on his horse and mounted behind her. I pulled a Walther ppk out of a corpse's hand, dug past his red cloak to take the extra cartridges off his belt. I adjusted the stirrups on a horse that grazed nearby, climbed up, gathered the reins.

We rode out. Theo called my name a few times and Laurette chased us, hollering, "Emma, please wait!"

But I was done here.

18

TIME AND SPACE WERE A SOFT BLUR, warping past me like threads on a loom, tangling around a peacock feather's eye. Alexei and Mandy and I rode out to the North. I could barely breath, and I barely noticed what was around us.

Some hours elapsed. Twenty kilometers later, we discovered a camp. Alexei reined in his horse. Silently, he pointed out where dirt walls had been dug. Just beyond the walls, crude shanties and tattered tents stood. The ground was littered with human femurs and skulls. Partially eaten female arms lay alongside piles of horse manure.

"Alexei, hang back!" I shouted. I didn't want Mandy to see. I kicked my horse and rode ahead recklessly, daring a rogue bullet to find me. I saw an old campfire with a spit, off which hung a human rib cage. Mutilated women were staked to trees; they'd had arms or legs hacked off and then crude belts cinched on to stop the blood flow. They were being eaten piecemeal, and kept alive through the process.

Rogue headquarters. But what did I care? I rode straight in through the dirt embankment. A man raised his gun, but he moved slowly, as if underwater, and I shot him, as well as the guy next to him. Behind them were several dozen women and about a hundred children, most of them bound and gagged. About twenty women were loose. As soon as I fired, they leapt on several other men who were drawing weapons.

"The rogue army is dead," I said. Utter silence. Then one woman cheered. A number of voices rose up, repeating what I'd said in other languages. The men were stripped and tied together while the women went about freeing other women and children. In a few minutes, the freed prisoners leapt on the men. Handfuls of bloody tissue floated up like confetti. I stayed on my horse and leaned down to grab the arm of a brown-haired woman who was placidly gathering the dead men's guns.

"Go south," I said. "There's a group heading to Toulon, Arthur's group. You'll be safe with them. You'll be happy with them. They want to create something better."

"Happy? You are crazy with the mists?" She laughed. "What is happy now?" She had a point, and I shrugged. I didn't expect to ever be happy again.

"You and the children will be safe with them," I promised. She handed me one of her guns, returned to her work. I rode back out to Alexei and Mandy, tossed Alexei the gun. I'd been gone not even thirty minutes. But what did time matter now?

"We have eight hundred kilometers to reach Le Havre," Alexei said. He cantered ahead, sheltering Mandy in his arms. I followed.

MANDY, ALEXEI, AND I rode nearly forty kilometers a day. We stopped to forage one day near where Moulins once stood, and Mandy and Alexei walked out into the Allier river to wash themselves and the horses. I walked down the river to the other side of the base of a stone bridge to relieve myself. When I was done, I sat on a rock and rested my head on my arms. The last several months played in my head like a movie, with the same clips running over and over: Arthur and his men saving Mandy from the mists; Arthur dissolving the mists at the Verdon Gorge, and then making love to me on the ledge; Arthur yelling at me to keep my heels down when I rode; Arthur giving me the Fra Angelico painting; Newt dying. Arthur morphing into a harsh military professor as he tried to explain the inexplicable.

The splashing and laughing from upstream fell into sudden silence. I picked up my head. Not a sound. This wasn't good. Mandy and Alexei were a boisterous duo. Mandy was eager to see her father, and Alexei, for his own reasons, rejoiced in bringing us to Haywood. I rose quietly, and then cursed when I realized I didn't have a gun or knife. I wasn't even wearing shoes. I'd taken them off to cool my feet in the water—the last few days had been hot.

I tiptoed through the bushes along the riverbank and then squatted behind a tree. Peering around the bole, I saw Mandy and Alexei standing in the river. Five ragged men with the red capes of the rogue band stood at the riverbank, training guns on them. Mandy reached out and clasped Alexei's hand.

I sank down onto my knees onto pebbly, muddy earth. Had we come this far only to have it end like this? Should I just run out and let the men shoot me, along with Mandy and Alexei? Would they eat us after shooting us?

No. I could not give up without trying. There had to be something I could do. Throw rocks, create a diversion? Alexei had a gun at his waist, but could the wily Russian shoot all five men fast enough, before they shot him and Mandy?

What would Arthur have done? But I shuddered as I remembered his cold, intellectual speech about the biomind. I hated him.

The biomind. Those men shared in it, and we had all been affected by the mists. The mists preyed on the biomind. The mists had been developed as a weapon to soften the biomind, to open up soldiers to psychological influence. I wished I could psychologically influence them.

Maybe I could. I had a gift: the healing current that flowed through me. Maybe I could use the healing current to affect these men. Maybe I could influence them to walk away from my daughter and Alexei.

A gun clicked as it was cocked. Now was the moment, else

Mandy would die. I took a deep breath and forced myself to drop into the state of concentration that had been present to heal Pyotr and Mikhail. I was practiced at it now, so it swept over me instantaneously. Then I was open and expanded, and I could feel the five rogue men as five separate strains of music, each with its own individual wild cadence and unbridled melody. I stepped out from my hiding place and walked around behind them. They slowly turned, with the disjointed motions of robots.

"Mommy?" whispered Mandy. I didn't answer. I couldn't. Because I had caught up the minds of the five men inside myself. It was like gathering five threads of yarn into my hand. They stared at me and their eyes emptied into me. They stood as still and melting as ice sculptures, with their forms dissolving into the current that flowed through me into them and back into me. I knew what I had to do: I had to go down the rabbit hole, down into the well of terror and loss inside myself, and take them with me. I had to surrender to the madness.

It didn't take me long at all.

Alexei's people in Le Havre were looking for us. The town was in a shambles, what was left of it, but there were people about. At first they just looked like the whirling colorful spots on a kaleidoscope screen. Then they resolved into figures. I was riding a horse. We had ridden just a little ways along the Seine into the debris when Kulap, on a bicycle, called out. She had cut her black hair and wore a big coat so that she looked like a boy, until her radiant face turned toward me. She practically leapt up on top of my horse to hug me. She was demure with Alexei and lavished smiling praise on Mandy.

"There is a plane just flew in this morning," she said. Her words addressed Alexei, but her shining black eyes were on mine.

"A plane," I said, numbly. The first words I had spoken in days. The first words I had understood in days.

"Mommy, are you okay now?" Mandy asked anxiously.

Alexei leaned over to touch my cheek.

"Brave Emma, you come back to us?" he asked.

"What happened to the men?" I asked. "The men at the river?"

"They sat down on the ground and cried. Alexei shot them," Mandy said. Her voice was unconcerned.

"Come, we take you to your husband," Alexei said. "You go away with him. Never come back."

We dismounted, and I was surprised to find my legs and feet beneath me, whole and working. We walked our horses along a strip of what was once highway in the *ville haute*. Mikhail, Ludmilla, and others converged on us, having heard, in the invisible yet instantaneous communication that characterized camps, that we were here.

Mikhail was as loving with me as he was with his father. His light brought me back a little more. He took Mandy's hand and spoke to her with great affection. She responded with equal animation, although, as far as I could tell, her words were in English while his were in Russian. It was difficult for me to interpret anything. Something gauzy had blanked out my brain and dissolved all rational thought, and I could still feel the gauze. From the scene at the bridge over the Allier River until this very moment, I had seen only faces, like Messerschmidt heads, floating in the air around me: Genevra, Caris, the old German who taught me to use an Ortgies, Claude, Newt. Arthur. I felt fragile and raw, unsure of my body and my speech. The others seemed to sense it, and they hugged me repeatedly. Even Alexei.

A Piper Warrior sat on a stretch of asphalt. A lean man crawled around on his hands and knees, performing maintenance. I have watched him do it before, I thought. Not on this particular plane, but on others. I have flown with him many times, I somehow knew. Alexei shouted and the man scrambled out. He saw me. His face lit up and he bolted toward me.

Haywood grabbed me into his chest, embracing me.

He stepped back and stared. His auburn hair was long and ragged, longer than the last time I saw him, almost eleven months ago. His face was far more lined, and it was covered with stubble in shades of gray, black, and red. He was only seven years older than me, but he looked twenty years older than the last time we were together. His eyes were damp. He spun around and swept Mandy up. Mandy wept and yelled, "Daddy!" I caught sight of Alexei, who wore an expression of great satisfaction.

"Father should be with child," Alexei whispered, his mouth next to my ear. "And Arthur must be alone."

A FEW HOURS later, Haywood refueled the plane out of portable fuel tanks that were inside the cabin where two passenger seats should have been.

"Desperate times, desperate measures," Haywood said, shrugging. He talked non-stop, telling me about Beth, about what it was like in Edmonton when the rest of the world was ending. They were running out of food and manufactured goods, just as we were in ravaged Europe. They had limited resources for power. I thought that Shinji's notebook about the Tesla experiments would be appreciated. It was still in my backpack.

"Is this little plane going to make it to Canada?" I asked. "It's a fuel tank strapped to an engine."

"Ouch, Em," Haywood said, but with a grin. "I don't have a death wish. Everyone thought I did, when I said I was going to get you. They tried to talk me out of it. But there was no way I would leave you and Mandy out here alone, once Alexei told me he could bring you here." He paused, his face grave. "I thought you were dead."

"I knew I'd see you again," I said.

Haywood reached out to smooth my hair back off my cheek. "We'll stop in Newfoundland on the way back. Gander's intact. No one's there, but I can get us some fuel. Lucky we have a few satellites still working and we knew Gander was okay, that's how I dared to make this crazy trip. And we have an unusual streak of sweet weather all the way back, which is why I'm taking off as soon as she's ready." He paused again, grinning. "Plus, I think your friend Alexei can't wait to get rid of us."

"He wanted me to be with you," I said. I didn't tell Haywood that Alexei was exacting revenge on the man who created the mists, that he was taking from that anguished man the one person he prized most: me. It was enough that I knew, and that Alexei knew that I knew.

An hour later, we were buckled into the two remaining passenger seats, ready to take off. I reached over and brushed Mandy's auburn hair out of her eyes. She was smiling; it's a grand adventure, she's with her dad and her mom, going to see her sister. The engine purred, and then whined into life.

"Look, a butterfly!" Mandy pointed. Slowly, across the window, winged a large orange butterfly with black spots.

"Arthur!" I cried. There was almost no room to maneuver—I unbuckled and pressed against the window just as the plane's engine sped up and roared. The plane was taxiing down the strip of highway faster, more purposefully. I saw him: sitting tall and straight on the leggy roan, his black hair, the silhouette of his broad shoulders. He was watching the plane take off. Alexei stood behind him, his rifle trained on Arthur.

"Arthur!" I said again. His eyes were turned toward us. I could feel him. Then we were airborne.

Haywood turned the plane in a slow arc toward the north and east. I watched until I couldn't see Arthur anymore. Then I huddled into my seat. I couldn't speak, because I was weeping.

I was also praying, feeling sure that the divine Source who brought me to Arthur in the first place would somehow bring me back to him.

ACKNOWLEDGEMENTS

I MUST THANK Lori Handelman, whose wonderful editing skills helped shape this novel.

I always thank Gerda Swearengen for her loving support and wisdom.

Stuart Gartner has been a source of humor and sage advice, and I am grateful. 1-800-STU-KNOWS-BEST.

I am grateful to Lane Shefter Bishop for her ongoing support and encouragement, especially regarding **IMMORTAL**.

I would like to thank Mary T. Browne for her warm support, good advice, and excellent quote. I am also very grateful to Komilla Sutton for her support and belief in me. Dr. Daniel Booth Cohen has been of profound help and encouragement.

Victoria Wells Arms has cheered and edited this manuscript from the beginning: thank you! You have beautiful children!

Rachel Leheny is the best drinking buddy in the whole world, and one of the smartest people.

I am grateful to Kirstin Peterson for her copy-editing.

Many thanks to Kate Gleason for her early, intelligent reads.

To Joe Mills, Maria, and everyone at Black Sheep Design in the UK: Thank you! Joe, you are a genius!

Many thanks to Fauzia Burke, Heather Belfer and Leyane Jerejian at FSB Associates for their terrific work.

I am most grateful to everyone at Telemachus Press for their outstanding work and help.

Many thanks to Adrienne Rosado.

I send love and gratitude to: Caitlin Alexander, Dani Antman, Thomas Ayers, Barbara and Stephen Baldwin, Ali Baldwin, Matthew Baldwin and Dana Harlan, Timothy Baldwin and Megan Adams, Lori Belilove and John Link, Paul Brodeur, Michelle Czernin von Chudenitz, James Cooper, Kristin Gamble and Charlie Flood, Tommaso Gobbi, Elizabeth Haase and Andrew Meyers, Debra Jaliman, Alain Kattnig, Sue Perillo, Stephanie Kip Rostan, Geoffrey Knauth, Marcia and Howard Levy, Jennifer Weis Monsky, John Morehouse and the Salmagundi Club, Frederick Morton, Margery Newman, Sarah Novotny, Rusty Shelton, Don Steelman, Mark Swearengen, Peter Thall.

A special thank you to Steven Beer, who always rocks.

I am grateful to my four daughters for their constant inspiration: Julia Howard, Jessica Hendel, Naomi Hendel, and Madeleine Howard. You are the reason for everything; you are all wonderfully imperfect, and so lovable.

Finally, to Sabin Howard, thank you most of all.

TRACI L. SLATTON is a graduate of Yale and Columbia. She lives in Manhattan, and her love for Renaissance Italy inspired her historical novel *Immortal* (BantamDell). Also the author of novels *The Botticelli Affair*, *Fallen*, *Cold Light*, *Far Shore*, and *The Love of My (Other) Life*, Slatton has published *The Art of Life*, a photo essay about figurative sculpture; *Dancing in the Tabernacle*, a book of poetry; and *Piercing Time & Space*, a non-fiction title on science and spirituality.

www.ingramcontent.com/pod-product-compliance
Lightning Source LLC
Chambersburg PA
CBHW071232250626
47163CB00001B/146